Sensation and Sublimation in Charles Dickens

Sensation and Sublimation in Charles Dickens

John Gordon

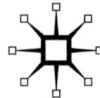

SENSATION AND SUBLIMATION IN CHARLES DICKENS
Copyright © John Gordon, 2011.

All rights reserved.

First published in 2011 by
PALGRAVE MACMILLAN®
in the United States—a division of St. Martin's Press LLC,
175 Fifth Avenue, New York, NY 10010.

Where this book is distributed in the UK, Europe and the rest of the world, this is by Palgrave Macmillan, a division of Macmillan Publishers Limited, registered in England, company number 785998, of Houndmills, Basingstoke, Hampshire RG21 6XS.

Palgrave Macmillan is the global academic imprint of the above companies and has companies and representatives throughout the world.

Palgrave® and Macmillan® are registered trademarks in the United States, the United Kingdom, Europe and other countries.

ISBN: 978–0–230–11088–5

Library of Congress Cataloging-in-Publication Data

Gordon, John, 1945–
    Sensation and sublimation in Charles Dickens / John Gordon.
        p. cm.
    ISBN 978–0–230–11088–5 (hardback)
    1. Dickens, Charles, 1812–1870—Criticism and interpretation. 2. Senses and sensation in literature. 3. Sublimation (Psychology) in literature. I. Title.

PR4592.S43G67 2011
823'.8—dc22   2010043431

A catalogue record of the book is available from the British Library.

Design by Newgen Imaging Systems (P) Ltd., Chennai, India.

First edition: July 2011

10 9 8 7 6 5 4 3 2 1

Printed in the United States of America.

One more for the Rose

Contents

List of Illustrations	ix
Introduction	1
1 "What Right Have They to Butcher Me?"	7
2 "Thankee, Mum," Said Toodle, "Since You *Are* Suppressing"	51
3 "In a Thick Crowd of Sounds, But Still Intelligibly Enough to Be Understood"	113
4 Is Esther Pretty? and Nine Other Questions About *Bleak House*	155
Afterword: Having It Both Ways	189
Notes	195
Index	217

Illustrations

1	"Miss Tox Introduces 'The Party'"	53
2	"The Railway Dragon"	67
3	Detail from *Dombey and Son* frontispiece	68
4	"The Shadow in the Little Parlour"	74
5	"Abstraction and Recognition"	94
6	"Coming Home from Church"	104
7	"Lady Dedlock in the Wood"	120

Introduction

The Pickwick Papers is, for most of its length, a sunny book occasionally interrupted with what are in general gloomy tales of madness and melancholy. At about the two-thirds point, a comical imbroglio winds up putting Mr. Pickwick in prison. He is then made to confront some dark realities of contemporary life that those tales, blunted as they were by their relative familiarity and buffered by the high spirits around them, had not made him see. His memorable summation, in four words: "Can such things be?" It is as if all earlier intimations, miffed at not being attended to, had decided to make a fist and hit him in the face.

Perhaps since John Forster's biography, and certainly since Edmund Wilson's essay "The Two Scrooges," informed readers of Dickens have usually understood that there is something going on down there, underneath, subnarrative-wise—that indeed the futility of ignoring or suppressing it is one of Dickens's main themes. "Suppressing" is, as used here, mainly a Freudian trope—and without doubt, Freud's preeminence in the first half of the last century had much to do with Dickens's concurrent rise in critical assessment. What was being suppressed? That was the question. Among the answers: beneath the near-photographic chronicling of London's streets, a compulsive night walker who could not bear to enter certain neighborhoods associated with the humiliations of his youth; beneath the beloved font of domestic fireside entertainment, a broken marriage, a young actress on the side, a double life of dodges, denials, and—perhaps the worst of Dickensian sins—hypocrisy; beneath the love affair with his audience a craving that probably hastened the end of what was always, by any standard, an overstretched life. Jovial and driven, Mr. Christmas to the public but, to Ralph Waldo Emerson when they met in Boston, a man so "harnessed" to his talents that he had not "a thread of nature left." Another American, Annie

Fields, remarked simply that it was "wonderful, the flow of spirits" Dickens had, considering that he was clearly "a sad man."

What was going on in there? The following is a consideration of three novels, *Oliver Twist, Dombey and Son,* and *Bleak House,* each of which, I believe, shows Dickens asking such questions about his work—about, in Fred Kaplan's words, the "hidden springs" of his fiction. Just where was this stuff coming from, and by what processes was it making its way onto the page? I have chosen these three books, in part, because I think they allow me to avoid some of the more-traveled pathways already laid down by critical inquiries into this large question. Biographical analysis—blacking factory and so forth—will in general be given short shrift. Michael C. Cotzin, Harry Stone, and others have admirably demonstrated the importance of the fairy tales and other popular entertainments absorbed by Dickens in his early years; no need to duplicate their work. Freudian issues will certainly crop up, but when it comes to, for instance, dream analysis, my focus will be on what Dickens and his contemporaries, rather than later theorists, had to say on the subject.

Being about presences and processes obscured, this book will of force dwell on mystifications. As a teacher of literature I regularly tell my students that it is better to begin their projects with questions to which they do not know the answers than otherwise, and I have here tried to follow my own advice. In fact, the germ of this study may be said to have been a shock of nonrecognition and the questions that arose from it. In graduate school I took a seminar with Professor Harry Levin on Dickens's novels, most of which I had already read at some time or other. The major exception was *Oliver Twist.* I knew it by reputation as an early, apprentice work with some Hollywood-friendly characters, one of whom, the villainous Jew Fagin, bothered some people in much the same way as did Shylock. That seemed, I thought, like a nonissue. Dickens's works abounded in villains; so what if one of them happened to be Jewish?

Anyway, *Oliver Twist* was required reading, and I duly read it. What I experienced was not the book I expected, or anything for which the other novels had prepared me. Like Mr. Pickwick, I wondered how such things could be. How *could* he have written *this*? "This" was, as I thought and think, the obvious mix of sadism and pedophilia going on between Fagin and his boys, complemented by the masochism binding the prostitute Nancy to her brutish pimp, in both cases leading to frenzied scenes the gist of which was that sexual desire is always a form of either hatred or self-hatred. It was the shit—"filth" and "offal" were some of the transparent code words—to a degree far surpassing the vaunted "dust" of

Our Mutual Friend. Oliver Twist invited you to imagine people eating it, swimming in it, excreting it, like pigeons, from heights, and, in the case of Fagin, going through his own deposits of it to pick out swallowed coins. It was, more creepily on display than anywhere else perhaps excepting *Barnaby Rudge,* Dickens's morbid obsession with capital punishment, especially hanging. It was the crowds bellowing for scapegoat blood, with the author apparently on their side. And at the center of it all—child molester and child queller, eater of "offal," the gallows' best friend and prize trophy and the mob's prize blood offering, was "the Jew, the Jew!" In fact, the crazy repetition of that phrase, "the Jew," was by itself enough to set *Oliver Twist* apart. Although Dickens's work does indeed abound in villains who come to bad ends, one does not finish *The Old Curiosity Shop* or *Little Dorrit* with "the Dwarf! The Dwarf!" or "the Frenchman! The Frenchman!" ringing in the ears.

Boy, I remember thinking at the time, something really got out of the box here. Years later, the first chapter of this book is an effort to understand what. Briefly, my thesis is that *Oliver Twist* shows one of history's great tale-tellers discovering the power his gift conveys while in the process of, and as a result of, succumbing to one of his culture's master narratives, the blood libel. How does someone who is not an anti-Semite—someone who in fact spent much of his life opposing the kind of intolerance of which anti-Semitism is a very large example—write English literature's most virulent work of serious anti-Semitic literature? (At least Shylock gets his day in court.) That was the question, back in the day. Further reading since has, regrettably, taught me to qualify the earlier assumption about Dickens's humane impulses—he could, in the fashion of the time, be a casual anti-Semite, among other things—but not nearly enough to make that question go away. So what happened? My answer is Frankensteinian: he began by having a story; then the story had him. At the end he was, at last, able to reflect on the quite appalling thing he had done.

For *Dombey and Son* the question is, how to explain the extraordinary advance in rhetorical mastery over that of anything Dickens had written before? My answer is that in this novel Dickens is and knows himself to be tapping into the resources of language to an extent comparable to his discovery of tale-telling in *Oliver Twist,* and that as in the earlier novel he is periodically driven to reflect on the implications of the power he now finds to be his. Before the twentieth century, nothing I know of in prose fiction equals the scene (chapter XXX) in which Mr. Dombey polysemically ponders his own image in the clouded reflection of a mahogany table. What makes such passages possible—and there are many in *Dombey and Son*—is that the author's macroscopic project of social excavation has as counterpart the microscopic exercise of linguistic excavation. One might normally here talk of the "overtones" of language, were it not that in *Dombey and Son* the stress is very much on powers, including the powers of language, seeping or erupting from underneath. Undertones, not overtones—etymologies and folketymologies; intricate half-realized networks of puns, double entendres, and what Garrett Stewart has identified as syllepses; names hinting at a hidden language of which they may be the outcrops. The vertically repressed—sexuality, ambition, truth—erupts upward like a geyser and then spreads outward, horizontally, like a flood. The medium of that dispersion is language, and the author's job is accordingly to make you sense that fact, to charge enough words and phrases with undertones problematically on the verge of fusing with other words and phrases into deeper significances—so that, like many a character in the book, you can never be sure of your ground, never be sure of how far down, or far afield, you should go.

That last sentence could also be applied to *Bleak House,* which I think represents yet a further development in verbal proficiency. The major difference is that the underneath being excavated is underneath language too. Dream logic, implicitly preverbal—not polysemic but infrasemic—is in charge. When Dombey evokes his life history out of the shadowy reflections in a tabletop, the logic at work functions mainly by way of words and their associations echoing other words and their associations. Various such influences make him think of the tabletop as a "dead sea," which makes him think of the Dead Sea, which makes him think of the Dead Sea fruit that according to biblical and literary tradition turns to ashes in the mouth, which makes him think of his life as having turned to ashes, and so on. In *Bleak House,* comparable visions arrive by a different path. Esther, blind and near death, dreams of a "flaming necklace" in a black sky. Neither "necklace" nor any of the other salient words of this scene are identifiable features of her verbal repertoire. (Or of the narrator's, either.) On the contrary: as I will be arguing in my *Bleak House* chapter, the necklace is Esther's vision of what cannot be faced, therefore cannot be put into words. The language describing it is at two removes. Coming between it and the unfaceable is a visual image that we are invited to interpret as a conjunction of Esther's buried fears and her present feelings, emphatically including physical feelings. The "beads" on the necklace probably come from the beadlike pustules she fears may result from the unnamed condition—smallpox—which she knows she has, the circular "necklace" from the circular ring of the unwanted marriage the disfigurement caused by those beads will force on her. The background is black because of what black skies, whatever they may be called, usually signify.

It is also black because Esther is blind at the time. This is the "sensation" part of my title. The psychology to which Dickens subscribed saw the mind's actions, however extreme, as being primarily somatic in origin. Madmen hallucinated because their brains were overblooded. When we dream of being cold and half-naked in a public place, it is probably because our sleeping selves have kicked off the blankets. So with Esther. The background is black because, again, she is blind; the bright circle appears as the first sign that her sight is returning; it is "flaming" because the fever that accompanies smallpox is reaching the crisis point; it hurts her eyes because when one has gone as long as she has in total darkness, any light will. Perhaps half a dozen times elsewhere in the novel, some liminal or visionary experience is facilitated in part by the rapid dilation or contraction of the subject's pupils. I will be tracking this theme, of how one kind of "sensational" (hearing, sight, and so on) translates into another kind (theatrically visionary manifestations of altered mental states), asking, for instance, why Oliver should experience his most disturbing apprehensions of Fagin's true nature when half-asleep.

This book's methodology is the one mentioned already: to go with what I don't yet get. It has led me down some curious ways, and, I hope, turned up some items of interest. Among other things, the investigations herein will lead to such questions as this: When did pigeon racing first take hold in England? When was the first photograph taken of a solar eclipse? How many headlights were typically featured on a Victorian locomotive, and how were they placed? Could a traveler in Dickens's day make a channel crossing from Boston, Lincolnshire? What is the difference between a phaeton and a barouche?

Readers familiar with the body of James Joyce criticism will recognize these as being the sort of questions that hard-core types in that field like to ask, and they will be right. Most of my previous work has been on Joyce. To me, the transition from Joyce to Dickens seems natural. I can think of no two writers in English with more in common. To begin with, I believe Joyce to have been, literally, a sensational writer in much the same vein as Dickens. Joyce also attends to the dilations and contractions of the pupils of his characters and stages his dramatic effects accordingly. That aside, the similarities between the two are striking. Both had the same larger-than-life father, as a result of whose improvidence both were plunged, at almost the same age (around twelve), from relative affluence into borderline poverty. At least partly as a result, both were restless, driven men whose lives were probably shortened (at the same age, fifty-eight) from an inability to let go. Part of the reason was that they shared the same phenotype: middle height, always thin though never abstemious, nervously alert and hyperkinetic—as Shelley would say, swords bound to outlast their sheaths. Both were outsiders looking in (and back); both, perhaps in reaction, mastered and rearranged the facts of their respective cities, London and Dublin, to the point of expropriation. Neither ever wrote the same book twice. In their later works in particular, both can seem torn between centripetal and centrifugal impulses: they want to make everything cohere and they want to incorporate tracts of material so dissimilar that coherence would seem to be out of the question. (As Joyce certainly knew and Dickens probably didn't, they were both thus testing the limits of Aristotle's aesthetic prescription of unity in multeity.) Hugh Kenner once remarked of Joyce that he may have been the hardest-working writer ever; maybe so, but if not the award might well go to Dickens. Both had wonderful memories, although here Joyce had the edge. In particular, both seem to have been spared the veil of forgetting which cuts most of us off from memories of our earliest years: see, especially, the first third of *David Copperfield,* then the first chapter of *A Portrait of the Artist as a Young Man.* Both were virtuosos of English prose, whose achievements in that medium had, I believe, more in common than has been recognized. Ironically, considering their reputations, the main difference between them, apart from the contrasts inherent in the different islands from which they came, may be that Joyce was the better family man.

Finally. Maybe this is a first. I want to thank Google Books for making the ridiculously obscure fact-searching component of this book possible, or at least sometimes possible. Google Books is the best bit of news since the *Oxford English Dictionary.* In the same ballpark, I am grateful to members of the Victoria, Dickens-L, and *Ulysses*-for-Experts e-mail lists for helping me track items down. Much of this book was written on sabbatical from Connecticut College, for which I give my thanks. It was in part subsidized by a grant named after the late Nancy Rash, a splendid scholar and teacher whom I remember fondly. The Connecticut College librarians have been helpful and generous. I have already mentioned Harry Levin, a lovely man. I close by remembering Edwin Barrett, another lovely man. He taught me to pay attention to what Dickens was saying. "Last but not least" doesn't cut it here. In the end, this much, anyway, is clear to me: no Ed, no book.

CHAPTER 1

"What Right Have They to Butcher Me?"

I.

It is a good question.¹ Based solely on the king's-evidence testimony of an obvious liar, Fagin is charged as accessory to the murder of Nancy, a prostitute. Within little more than a week after the murder, he is taken, tried, convicted, and executed.

That is not normally how the law functions in *Oliver Twist*. Beadle or Bow Street, magistrate or constable, all the officials on show are buffoons. Supervisory "boards" are clueless. Entire streets are given over to the open fencing of stolen goods. Thieves' dens dot the map. Prostitutes, including child prostitutes,² are widely on show. Dead or alive, murdered or self-murdered, floating in the Thames or padding the hoof, they are part of the scene, and everyone knows it. One might think that the authorities, who have pulled out all stops to nail this one old man, had better things to do.

No wonder Fagin, sitting in the condemned cell, is incredulous at the unwonted spasm of whirlwind justice. Then it gets even curiouser. Enter, of all people, Oliver Twist, brought by his guardian Mr. Brownlow for the purpose of taunting Fagin on the vigil of his death.

That is not, to be sure, according to Brownlow, who says he wants to teach Oliver a lesson about the wages of sin (362).³ But, please: there is zero chance that the goody-goody Oliver will follow Fagin's course. Doubtless Brownlow, in his characteristically oblivious way, believes what he says, but to Fagin it can only come across as the last straw. Of all the death cells in all the prisons in all the world, the kid walks into his. No wonder he reacts with a series of screams "that penetrated even those massive walls" (364).

The insult is all the more pointed given what he has by now come to realize about his uninvited guest, that "he has been the—the—somehow the cause of all this" (363). Fagin is raving, but Dickens's ravers tend to tell the truth, and nowhere more so than in *Oliver Twist*. What, at this time of all times, is Oliver doing here? He has been bad news every time he entered Fagin's life. Now this. You would think that he would at least have the decency to stay away. For one thing, he has, indeed, in a circuitously plotwise way, been a cause of Fagin's plight: Nancy was killed as a consequence of a chain of events that began with her expression of solicitude for Oliver.[4] At the moment, however, Fagin is not up to figuring that out. "*Somehow* the cause of all this:" these are the words of a man who knows something for sure but does not know how he knows.

There are a number of these moments in *Oliver Twist*, of people in states of disorientation sensing something deeply true but dimly graspable. They constitute the novel's main version of the subconscious. Oliver himself experiences most of them, so much so that we may want to speculate that Fagin's *éclaircissement* is due not just to Oliver's presence but also to his influence. (Others in the book—Brownlow, Nancy, Rose Maylie—have sometimes seemed to see glimpse some hidden truth, courtesy of Oliver's mediumship.) That these moments are always fundamentally true is one of the book's house rules.

What, then, is the "all this" of which Oliver is the "cause"? By itself, "this" is surely the fact that Fagin is about to be hanged. He has a point: had the two never met, he would not be where he is, at least not now. But the same could be said of Brownlow, among others, and it is not Brownlow whose appearance cuts Fagin to the heart. Oliver is not just a contributory part of Fagin's situation. He is Fagin's nemesis. He is the one whom Fagin gathered into his web and set apart as worth more than all the others together, the one whose two escapes both rendered him hysterical. He is also the one whom Fagin seemed most bent on having killed, preferably by way of the gallows, thus adding the acid of irony to their last encounter: you, not me. He is the agent that Fagin willed throughout. "This" may be the terrifying here and now, but "all this" is that plus what led up to it, the "cause" of which has been Fagin's special relation with Oliver.

As many have surmised, pedophilia is part of it. Oliver is twelve, a pretty boy at the prepubescent moment that Socrates relished. He is pure in a book where sex is vile, a forever-swooning virgin ripe for defilement, and Fagin is the arch-defiler. Borrowing an old bit from Swift,[5] Dickens hints at this state of affairs by introducing Oliver in Fagin's lair to "Master Bates" and then having Bates walk around with his hands in his pockets. We get the joke; Oliver doesn't. That is because he is innocent and we are not. If the feral, thirtyish, alcoholic, drab-drubbing pimp Bill Sikes embodies the post-grad stage of Fagin's tuition, Oliver is the sub-freshman. Headmaster Fagin's calling is to turn the latter into the former.

As the slow-learning Sikes finds out later than he should have, commencement is solemnized at the end of a rope. Was Dickens familiar with underground tradition linking hanging and sex—autoerotic asphyxiation, erections triggered by the snap of the neck, all that—in circulation since Sade at least? The fact of Fagin argues the affirmative. Fagin likes boys, but he loves the noose. More, he loves to bring the two together. In many ways, he forecasts Dennis, the hangman of *Barnaby Rudge,* a voluptuary of the rope for whom to behold a fair young neck is to long to stretch it, who surveys a mob of rioters likely to end up in the condemned wards of Newgate like "a farmer ruminating among his crops, and enjoying by anticipation the bountiful gifts of Providence,"[6] and who winds up, in a sequence as ghastly as the one that elicits Fagin's screams, being turned off from his own proprietary scaffold. "It comes home to the Hangman," reads one of Dickens's running titles for this sequence. It comes home like this, from the babbling Dennis, frightened to a degree far surpassing that of the other condemned man sharing his cell: 'You don't know what it is. I do" (*BR* 585). Fagin also has his crops a-ripening—the young Phil Barker, for instance, part of a company whose "time," he says, has not yet come, but will, which company should therefore "lead merry lives *while they last*—Ha! ha! ha!" (165). As with Dennis, one reason that, when his time comes, Fagin is more terrified than anyone else ("even" his death cell guards, "used to such sights, [recoil] from him in horror" (361)) is that his life has been so involved in it. He, too, knows what it is. He has witnessed any number of hangings, for reasons of both business and pleasure. Especially the latter.

Along with Fagin, the discourse of *Oliver Twist* hovers obsessively around two dread realities. Hanging is one. At its calmest, the novel incorporates a critique of capital punishment of which John Stuart Mill might have approved. First, Fagin and his charges favor public hangings as a prime place to go a-pick-pocketing. So much for the deterrence argument.[7] Second, Oliver, we are told several times under credible circumstances, is bound to be hanged. That is, the death penalty may irreversibly cut off the innocent. Third, "The tinker busied himself in endeavoring to restore Oliver, lest he should die before he could be hanged" (186). Then as now, we are reminded, the barbaric absurdity of assuring that the condemned stay alive and well and fit to be killed is part of the routine. Those two death-cell watchers are there to see that Fagin will not, as the saying goes, cheat the hangman.

The fourth, and major, indictment is a matter not of argument but of exhibition. It is that capital punishment is essentially Faginesque. In public debate, Dickens's primary objection was less to hanging itself than to public hangings, because they depraved the spectators. Fagin is, among other things, an embodiment of a hanging-day mob, the end product of a morbidly voyeuristic instinct too often satisfied. His rendezvous with the rope has been earned, as fated as Ahab's with the whale.

This is the reason that, well before the consummation, his person attracts variations on the theme like filings to a magnet. Those excursions of his to Newgate, to begin with. The three hanged bodies in the picture that Cruikshank puts over his hearth. The flocks of handkerchiefs dangling everywhere around his digs, and the handkerchiefs tied premonitorily around his own neck and that of Sikes[8]—who, playing hangman, likes to jerk at his (77). (Even Sikes's dog, ever threatening to go for the throat, seems to share the company's *idée fixe*.) His "knotted" club (102); the 'hard knot" knit by his eyebrows (101); the constant talk of throats and necks, scragging and stretching; the constant repetition in his company of the very words "hang," "hangs," and "hanging"—"hanging" a key on Nancy's finger, "Toby Crackit has been hanging about the place" (80, 123), and so on. "What a fine thing capital punishment is," Fagin says (92), and he means it.

Fagin and the hangman are a set. One reason for his genuine outrage near the end is that he feels rooked. To repeat his question, with my italics, "What right have they to butcher *me?*" Imagine an *Animal Farm* sequel featuring a real butcher who says this while being dragged, by his own livestock, to his own shambles, and you can see something of Fagin's point of view. There was this deal. The blood he fed into the system would take the place of his own. Behind that was his, for want of a better word, faith that in keeping the hangman supplied with fodder he was propitiating death itself.

In a less lurid vein, this attitude reflects the natural inclination of the elderly to extend their time on earth. The "white-haired grandfather" who insists that a recently deceased contemporary might have had many more years "if he had taken care, if he had taken care," (325) is, in this sense, being Fagin's folksy counterpart. For Fagin, however, the issue is not relative but absolute, not of long life versus short but of immortality versus an eternity of nothing. Death is not an unpleasant eventuality to be put off as long as possible. It is something both ever-present and unthinkable, something he keeps at bay by embracing. His flirtation with the gallows epitomizes precisely the "attraction of repulsion" that Dickens found at work in public executions.[9]

For most of the book's length, the strategy would seem to be working. Fagin is, literally, a wandering Jew (he constantly shifts from locale to locale; his mind in the death cell is "wandering" [363]) whose portrait likely owes something to the Wandering Jew mentioned in *Great Expectations*—Ahaseurus, spurner of Christ, typically depicted as a bearded old man, sentenced to immortality until the Day of Judgment. In a novel where life and afterlife sometimes verge on intersection, such a fate can seem attainable, and not just for Fagin. Although occupying different modules of the novel, the workhouse crones who hover over the expiring form of Oliver's mother's old attendant have two things in common with him: they feed off the dying, and we cannot begin to guess their ages. They could all be 200 or 2,000 years old, or whatever. Together, they and Fagin are of the company of Lilith and Cain, the devil and his dams, Dracula and his brides.[10] Indeed, like Dracula, whose coat spills out "a bundle of banknotes and a stream of gold"[11] when slashed, Fagin walks around in a coat lined with valuables. (He also swallows coins to keep them hidden. If you prick him, does he not bleed? Actually, probably not.) He is a living skeleton, and yet why is his beard not grey, and why is his vitality undiminished? Like the witches of folklore, Fagin keeps himself going through periodic immolations of the young and innocent. When fate sends him the ever-young and purely innocent Oliver, he cannot resist. It is too much. That is the beginning of why Oliver can go on to become "somehow the cause of all this."

Again, Fagin is closest to the fact of capital punishment, what I have called one of the novel's two dread realities. The other is infanticide, by which I mean not the occasional killing of a child, but a policy of killing children because they *are* children. Oliver Twist is born into a system the main business of which is killing kids, and although the Poor Law's regulations are certainly part of that system, its reach extends well beyond workhouse walls. Eventually, it will extend to Fagin, in the process bringing the novel's two dark sources of denial as close as they can get to one point of focus.

II.

Before that comes most of volume I.[12] The facetiousness with which Dickens introduces the child-stifling apparatus on show in the opening chapters is probably indebted to "A Modest Proposal";[13] for instance when the undertaker Mr. Sowerberry, pleased at a sudden rise in the baby-burying business but at the same time concerned that the necessary outlay for coffin timber will cut into profits, is gladdened by reflecting on how much less of that commodity will be required to box the starved-down little bodies being turned out by the parish. But for the jokiness, such passages could bring us uneasily within range of the last century's newsreels of gold fillings in piles and pillows stuffed with human hair. Oliver's first prospective employer, Mr. Gamfield, picks out the smallest boys he can find, sticks them up chimneys, and roasts them alive. Ho ho. Had Oliver been sent to sea instead, it would have been in the expectation that "the skipper would flog him to death" (19). Coach passengers on the road to London seem intent on running him to death; the worthy citizens of the towns along the way would be happy to see him starve. The nurse attending his birth has had thirteen children and lost eleven of them, so far. One of his guardians, the unsexed Mrs. Mann, from whose tough bosom no milk doth flow, runs a "baby farm" whose harvest, like that of Dennis, that "farmer ruminating among his crops," is the corpses of those entrusted to her care. If there is a standing body of water near her home, count on its bottom being strewn with little skeletons.

In volume I, all this is conveyed with a Bozian vivacity, which, like Swift's equivalent, is setting us up. When the facetious Dickens of the early chapters tells us, jocosely- parenthetically, that Mrs. Mann's establishment runs a mortality rate of about 85 percent (8), we may be inclined to think he is kidding. He is not. At the time he was writing, that was a perfectly realistic number. It is my belief that the buried, shaming, atavistic, age-old, collective-conscious fact of infanticide, of babies abandoned on mountain sides, sacrificed to stone gods, left in ditches and dumps, deliberately strangled with umbilical cords, stifled with pillows, beheaded, beaten to death by mothers or midwives, sacked up and drowned, suffocated with bunched-up bedsheets or "overlain" by mother or nurse, or otherwise dispatched by having their fontanels pierced with knitting needles, or by being doped to death with laudanum or (most popular) by being dropped into drains or privies—that this prehistorical and historical and contemporary fact of life is the underground reality whose eventual emergence contributes most to driving the novel and changing its tone. That such things had always gone on is something *Oliver Twist* knows in its bones. That it is still going on is something it challenges us to try to face, by degrees.[14]

This is, at least partly, because, at the time, it seemed to be coming back. For whatever reasons(the new Poor Law was partly to blame) infanticide appears to have spiked in the years leading up to *Oliver Twist,* after about a century of gradual decline. As often, Dickens was being topical.[15] The year 1837, when he began on *Oliver Twist,* saw the first publication of what Lionel Rose calls an "annual holocaust of infants"[16]—the regular government report on the previous year's confirmed cases of infanticide. By 1845 Benjamin Disraeli could write that infanticide was as common in England as "on the banks of the Ganges." (Just twenty-one years earlier, an authority on the subject had cited reports of child quelling in India and other eastern lands as the kind of thing that almost never occurred in England.[17]) In one way, at least, England could even be said to have surpassed all tales of Asiatic barbarity. A popular innovation of the period was the formation of "death clubs" and "burial clubs," private insurance consortiums whose members would collect payments for infant deaths in the family. Suspicions soon arose that many of these infants had been murdered, in some cases conceived to be murdered, for the money.[18]

That Dickens was au courant on these matters is certain. *Oliver Twist*'s Mr. Brownlow, it is widely agreed, was based on the real John Brownlow, secretary to the London Foundling Hospital—or, to give it its full name, the Hospital for the Maintenance and Education of Exposed and Deserted Young Children. Brownlow was an expert on and crusader against child abuse and child murder in the England of his time. Dickens's Brownlow rescues Oliver from Fagin's band of urban child-killers and fends off their rural counterparts. He is in this novel because he is needed, because without such a figure Oliver and every other child we see would probably be consumed by one baby butcher or another.

The eighteenth-century founder of Brownlow's hospital, Thomas Coram, had been moved to his good work by the repeated experience of encountering babies abandoned in ditches. His experience was not unique. At the time, the baby in the ditch was a familiar, widely recognized image. Hogarth twice featured it in his advertisements for Coram's hospital.[19] Dickens, who revered Hogarth, was likely familiar with these illustrations, and certainly familiar with the history behind them.

In an excellent essay, Catherine Robson makes the case that Oliver's edge-of-death, mid-novel crawl from the ditch in which he is left by

Fagin's gang to the Maylie doorstep draws on a classic foundling narrative. This drawn-out escape,[20] implicitly recalling how many other children out there have not made it out of wherever they were dumped, inaugurates volume II. The narrative strand it begins, that of Oliver's adoption by the Maylie household, puts paid to the previous volume's jokiness. Usually the section likeliest to be abridged or skipped, volume II is the novel's sweet heart—lovers and lovers' vows, kindly old ladies and wise old gentleman, church going and summer cottage, rose and honeysuckle. With its introduction of genuine religion and authentic goodness, along with the death of a child and near-death of a saintly young woman—both of which events, we are made to understand, are, this time around anyway, undismissably serious matters—volume II, if the reader will go along with the change in temper it demands, can only make the facetiousness of the opening chapters seem to belong among those childish things the adult must come to put away. After that, volume III will emerge as an answer, even reproach, to the tone of the opening. The Artful Dodger, everyone's comical favorite, is packed up with his store of japes and pushed off stage. Nancy, blowsy at the beginning, has, by the late chapter in which Sikes kills her, wasted away to suitably poignant dimensions. (Cruikshank, who keeps her zaftig throughout, evidently didn't get the message.) Mr. and Mrs. Bumble are still funny (hilarious, actually), but the *lex talionis* judgment assigned them in the last chapter is not: they have gone from a Disneyfied Punch and Judy back to the original, in which the baby gets eaten and Jack Ketch has the final word. The lightsome Master Bates is scared straight when Sikes jerks dead right before his eyes. The narrative will by then have dropped the "Master Bates" wheeze, as it will have stopped calling Fagin a "merry old gentleman."

And, little Dick finally dies. He was about to die early on in the book, but as an alternate Oliver, the Oliver unprotected by the grace of his creator from the world's infanticidal cravings, that would have struck too grim a note then, if only because he had a name and a voice and an established air of pathos setting him apart from the blighted young perishers being snuffed out around him. Save his quietus for the end, for that different book when the hideous extinctions of Nancy and Sikes and Fagin have shifted the subject of death well out of the range of persiflage, and Dickens has stopped sillily blaming "philosophers" and their fellow boobies for all that's wrong and settled on something far darker.

We are, for one thing, thereby reminded of how blood-soaked, behind their jollity, those chapters truly were, of how extraordinary it was that Oliver survived to escape, then survived to return and learn of Dick's death. Where Oliver comes from, Dick's story is the norm. In London, Fagin's nest of gallows birds is the norm. It is remarkable that he survives either; doubly incredible that he survives both.

These incredibilities are there, I think, not in spite of their incompatibility with the corpse-strewn reality of much of the rest of the book but in collaboration with it. They emphasize how amazing a trick it must be for any child to survive, these days. Certainly, Dickens shows no sign of being embarrassed by the accumulating implausibility. Far from downplaying the hairbreadth scrapes through which Oliver manages to make it from first page to last, the novel multiplies them well beyond anything its story demands. It was amazing that Oliver's mother, "'against difficulties and pain that would have killed any other...woman weeks before'" (41), lived long enough to give him birth, and almost as amazing, "the balance" of chance being "decidedly" against it (1), that he survived the delivery. A literal casting of lots results in his famous request for "more" and thus his exile from the workhouse that would otherwise have starved or broken him. A pair of spectacles momentarily misplaced by an addled old bureaucrat saves him from being assigned to Gamfield the child roaster. A kindly turnpike man and "benevolent old lady" are all that prevent his dying on the road to London (45). Once there, his career slithers between near-misses and just-rights. One could identify, I'd bet, twenty points at which, had Oliver's angel chosen door A instead of B, his story would have been over.

That applies to his soul as well as his self. Had he, once taken in by Rose and put to bed, been actually rather than seemingly conscious while Mr. Losberne was, on his behalf, deflecting the police with a pack of lies, he would have had to choose between complying in a fraud and betraying a benefactor. Instead, "he managed to sit up in bed for a minute or so; and looked at the strangers without at all understanding what was going forward; in fact, without seeming to recollect where he was, or what had been passing" (203). Under the circumstances, a perfect witness.

Oliver is charmed. Others abide our question. They die in droves, compromise themselves (Mr. Losberne is an honest man, but lies when he has to), stumble and fall. Enwrapped in innocence, selective ignorance, and a knack for losing consciousness when keeping it might force him to make morally awkward choices,[21] Oliver threads through physical and spiritual perils like a sea snake through eelgrass. In fact, that is probably one reason for his last name. If anything, he gets purer—refined, as it were—as he goes along. Early on, he was guileful enough to "make a feint of feeling great regret" when parting from Bumble (8) and to put on a mournful look when begging from strangers (45). On first meeting the Artful Dodger, he even "secretly resolved" to ditch him and to play up to Fagin, if that looked to be the smart move (48). After volume II's stay at Chertsey has tempered him with a near-death ordeal and sanctified him with the influence of Rose Maylie and her mother, it is impossible to imagine him doing any such thing, let alone "secretly." The untouchability is now sealed in. He has become the artless dodger.

It is therefore fitting that the two salient physical facts about him should be that he has an angelic (meaning childlike) face and a diminutive body. The latter guarantees the former, and both together preserve him. The good people—his kind—are naturally inclined to give him a break because of his looks; his looks stay untainted because of his knack for twisting, untouched, through the world's hazards and away from its contaminants. He preserves the register of his original innocence by virtue of a unique ability to disappear, mainly by squeezing through, in and out of, apertures. At the beginning, Oliver's low birth weight probably helped account for his being carried to term and born alive—his first, so to speak, tight squeeze. The famishing world into which he came would probably have killed off a heftier version, not just half to death but all the way. He would not have wound up with the Maylies were he not the only one small enough to get through their "little lattice window." (Another tight squeeze; Doctor Losberne: "That's the little window that he got in at, eh? Well, I couldn't have believed it" [189[.) At such times, Bumble and company's starving-down regimen can seem to have been providential.

J. Hillis Miller comes close to recognizing this distinctive feature of Oliver's progress when he notes the novel's "imaginative complex of claustrophobia," its succession of coal cellars, coffins, cells, locked rooms,[22] and so on, but does not go on remark their necessary plotwise corollary—the chinks, keyholes, trapdoors, crevices, hidden windows, and so forth that riddle these enclosures and make up the colanderlike surfaces that Oliver seems uniquely able to negotiate. It is a world of walls, right enough, but the walls have a way of having holes, leading by conduits to secret openings in other walls. (The cat's-cradle plotline grows out this feature.) This is the landscape Oliver must come to work through, and does. To me, anyway, the novel is often most disturbing in the *Matrix*-like moments when Oliver learns this, learns that London overlays a network that can reclaim him no matter how broad the daylight—when, for instance, Nancy snatches him back to Fagin from out of a crowded street, or when she pulls him from a house door to a cab, its curtains closed, its anonymous, bought, headlong driver requiring no directions, to another house, the door of which is opened and shut on them before he can think to cry for help. In both cases, the scene of the crime is a public thoroughfare of the world's most populous city, and in both cases it may as well have been the sewer system.

Oliver's escape-artist qualities take him, safely in the end, through and out of the entanglements of his captivity. Were he evil, it would be obligatory that any character so small and compressible be compared to a rat. Fagin, of course, is often. Getting out of traps is his specialty, too. That is one thing the two have in common. "Twist" would have served Fagin admirably as an underworld nickname. After all, perhaps because of the hangman's distinctively twisty rope,[23] the word "twist" at the time was street language for "hang."[24] In *Oliver Twist* it is applied directly to Fagin once, in the condemned cell, where "his beard is twisted into knots," "knots" being another unwelcome word (361), all too pertinent at the moment.

There are other similarities. Also like Oliver, Fagin is the beneficiary of what, until it runs out, seems an inordinate amount of good luck. His world likes him. When he goes for a walk, the wind is at his back (168). People show up at just the right times for his purposes. He might, with some justice, protest that unlike Oliver he makes his own luck, that the doors that open to him do so by prearrangement, that the maze he maneuvers so expertly was laid down by him and his. In either case, by hook and crook, he has managed to grow ancient in a mazy, murderous, board-game world whose track runs between child stiflers and neck breakers, baby farms and gibbets. He and Oliver make it, respectively, almost through and through. Only one of them can survive, and it is a close call. They are, in their way, a match. The point of the match for Fagin is to keep Oliver trapped in some sunless room long enough for its influence to pervert him. (Up until the Chertsey chapters, we are sometimes encouraged to imagine that, given enough time, this plan might succeed.) The point for Oliver is not to let that happen. Oliver wins, and the upshot is that in their last encounter the two wind up facing one another in a stone box, which Oliver is allowed to leave and Fagin is not. The rookie, out of nowhere, has trounced the champ at his own game. It was supposed to be the other way around.

III.

I have said that Oliver owes his escapes in part to his angelic looks. Those looks are not fortuitous. They are a fair index to his unjaded inner self. The good people instinctively recognize his appearance as signaling a pure soul within, and they are right. The bad people, lost innocence envying the unfallen, recognize it too, and just as instinctively try to pervert it. In an overtly pornographic novel, Oliver would be the unsullied virgin against an army of would-be debauchers: Clarissa, for instance, versus Lovelace and company. The corrupt are drawn to Oliver both because of his face and out of a combination of nostalgia and *Schadenfreudian* envy of what lies beneath. The undertaker Mr. Sowerberry looks at the poignant "expression of melancholy" (29) natural to Oliver and shrewdly thinks to exploit it to tear-jerking, money-cadging effect at children's funerals. Fagin operates in part from the same calculation: Oliver, he says, is worth twenty of the ordinary, street-hardened candidates for juvenile crime because, unlike his, "their looks convict 'em" (126). He is the one child who still looks like a child.

That is, outer faithfully mirrors inner. (At her first appearance, Nancy looks dissipated because she *is* dissipated; by the time of her martyrdom, she has, *pace* Cruikshank, shed enough pounds for her new role.) The novel's rationale for this convention is first, Rousseauvian-Wordsworthian, and, second, what might anachronistically be called Dorian Greyian. First, man—Noah Claypole perhaps excepted—is born innocent and beautiful, and everywhere, especially in the city, he is ugly. Second, his later ugliness has been earned, as the externally registered index of evil influences or evil behavior or both. Though at odds, certainly, with medical opinion in his time and ever since, Mr. Brownlow is nonetheless spot-on, in this book, when he traces the Monks's epilepsy to bad living (336). Indeed, we may be meant to take Monks's freakishly deep-sunk eyes as the self-inflicted result of a history of aggrieved brooding (314), a variation on the old folk-wisdom injunction against crossing one's eyes. Like the minute hand of a clock, such processes can border on being detectable in real time, for instance, with the depraved women in whom "the last lingering tinge of their early freshness [was] almost fading as you looked" (164).

Outer signifies inner because the former has molded the latter. The abandoned women have had their womanhood "beaten out" of them; Sikes murders Nancy by repeatedly beating her upturned face; both Bumble and Fagin thrash their charges into submission. The resulting (in multiple senses) impressions show in the form of scars, dints, cavities (the nose of one criminal has been "almost beaten in" [339])—or to use a word adopted by the novel itself, "pock-marked" exteriors (119). The ubiquitous porosity noted earlier—all those pits and punctures—extends to surfaces of the personnel. That "pock-marked" face belongs to Tom Chitling, who matches it with his suit, riddled with "burnt holes" (119)—an extreme example of the sartorial perforations elsewhere on display among the book's down-and-outs. Later, Sikes will similarly ventilate his own clothes by scissoring out the spots left from Nancy's bloodstains, fatally overlooking one bloodstain on his hat—the one that will later catch the attention of a roving salesman whose patter on the subject sends him round the bend—doubtless because he always wears that hat perched on the back of his head. (A miniature allegory, there, of too much self-centeredness.)

Sikes's obliviousness to the possibility of such reciprocity is typical of his crowd. Chitling's doubly pocked appearance in Fagin's den should remind us that the main business of the place is the picking of pockets, which are, speaking literally (and etymologically) in a way the book endorses, pockings—holes—in suits. Pockets in suits are what make the gentlemen victims wearing such suits vulnerable to the depredations of Fagin's crew (its commonest prize is a "pocket-handkerchief") but the practice has an unpleasant way, as with Sikes, of biting back. Both Fagin and Monks gnaw at themselves, and the company as a whole is not averse to pecking at their own if no one else is available: when he enters their den, Oliver, like some grub stuck on an anthill, is liable to be covered in a swarm of pocket riflers (51, 100). Fagin considers this a law, the law, of nature: you "need be always emptying a till, or a pocket, or a woman's reticule." (289).

As usual, he has a point, which, as usual, goes further than he realizes. For one thing, as a practical matter you cannot go seriously pickpocketing without first making your own outfit as pocketed as possible, so as to stow the takings. Charlie Bates sets to work with pockets "so surprisingly capacious, that they seemed to undermine his whole suit of clothes in every direction" (57). "Undermine": once again, reciprocity seems built into this business of breaking and emptying, a fact Fagin ought to have pondered as those being hanged before his eyes suddenly had their insides punctured like bladders, suddenly changed "from strong and vigorous men to dangling heaps of clothes" (360).

Human and otherwise, the nature Fagin descries, *pace* Shakespeare's Ulysses, is less universal wolf than universal rat, gnawing and nibbling rather than ravening itself up. Boats are leaking, iron is rusting, the urban atmosphere is acidic, and houses accordingly—in one exemplary neighborhood with "old worm-eaten ship-timber" precariously supported on piles "weakened and rotted" by the "rat, the worm, and the action of the damp" (249)—rot from both sides. The above-noted penetrability of surfaces—keyholes and so on, with the gallows trapdoor the ultimate example—often contributes to plot twists and turning points. Outside, wind, wet, and cold freeze and pierce, blow "through" all those leaky clothes into and through the bodies underneath, real and anthropomorphic. (When Fagin remarks that the weather "'seems to go right through one,'" Sikes answers, "'It must be a piercer if it finds its way through your heart'" [121].[25]) A fever is not, in the standard diagnosis of the time, a fire within, but instead like a "subtle acid that gnaws into the very heart of hardest iron" (67).

Body politic and social body follow suit. For both, assaultive impingements work inward from without, surface to center. Oliver's first experience with the law is in the court of Chief Magistrate Mr. Fang, who proceeds to live up to his ratlike name. His first experience with the London public is to be torn at by a mob, a mob of the same order that will later tear at Fagin. The region beyond England's coasts consists of sea (homicidal captains) (19); shipwreck (46); whoever or whatever beat in the nose of a returned transport (339); the continent whose fevers (Rome) and vices (Paris) killed off Oliver's father, Oliver's father's servant (334), and Monks's mother (333, 352); and the New World, where slaves are flogged and where Monks rots and dies (259, 365).

Refuge is accordingly within, and, given the pumice-and-swiss-cheese consistency of apparently every exterior, as far within as possible. Charlie Bates, the one member of Fagin's gang not to be lost irreparably, finds happiness as a grazier in the inland, landlocked county of Northamptonshire. Oliver's own salvation comes from a similar withdrawal from his island's treacherous shores and ports, to an "inland village," "some distance in the country"[26]—the sweet heart introduced, not incidentally, into the second, middle, volume of the book, at the farthest remove from both the workhouse of the opening pages (site of Agnes's wretched death) and gallows of the last (site of Fagin's wretched death). Here "peace and quietude" can "sink into the minds" of the most hardened (210), and the "delicate" "hues" of nature can consequently be perceived, and therefore absorbed, by heartlanders whose "clearer vision" is free of the "jaundiced" humors and "jaded" reflexes incurred by those on the outworks (226).

That can happen there because the heart, core and "cor," is inmost, therefore farthest removed from surface depredations, therefore the last to develop callous or scar tissue. Soft core can respond to soft core. Whereas gravesites elsewhere are set with stones, in the Maylie's village there has been no need for such protective petrifaction; instead, the graves are "covered with fresh turf and moss" (210). The sensibilities in their vicinity, like the "thirsty ground," (213) are likewise spongy, permeable because never harshly penetrated. It is during the three months spent here, for instance, that Oliver, quite incredibly, acquires most of his learning—soaks it up, as we would say today. At heart's heart is Rose Maylie, invariably spoken of as soft, delicate, emollient—a rose of May, in short, whose rosewater tears twice live up to their pharmaceutical power, widely advertised in Dickens's day, to soothe and soften the skin on which they fall (191, 232). (Fulfill, and in one case, surpass: the tears that drop on Oliver's forehead awaken "some pleasant dream" from within (191).[27]

In fact, Rose, true to her name, is one character who, if anything, might be called too soft, too prone to blasting or withering. A creature of nature at its tenderest, she is in peril of illustrating a lesson that nature can teach in another, less Maylike season:

> The snow lay on the ground, frozen into a hard thick crust, so that only the heaps that had drifted into by-ways and corners were affected by the sharp wind that howled abroad: which, as if expending increased fury on such prey as it found, caught it savagely up in clouds, and, whirling in into a thousand misty eddies, scattered it in air (145–46).

As Grimwig might attest, to lack crust in *Oliver Twist* is to be subject to the world's "fury." Rose, "so slight and exquisite" that "earth," even "the gross air of the world" (128) seems "not her element" (187), is repeatedly represented as verging on the heaven of the angels, of being whirled into their "misty eddies," "scattered" in their finer air. Even Brownlow diplomatically suggests that she could do with more "firmness" (338); she herself admits that she couldn't "harden" her heart if she tried (356). She seems to be forever fainting or on the verge of fainting. She speaks in whispers and glides noiselessly along the ground. Her near-fatal illness is apparently brought on by an unusually long walk on an unusually warm day, a walk that merely fatigues her older but tougher stepmother (213).

So it is not surprising that she should be in perennial need of rescuing. Three times in her seventeen years, her life has been saved. First, Mrs. Maylie, her second mother, has rescued her from what in this book amounts to the death sentence of orphanhood. Second, Harry Maylie, who by the novel's logic is exactly the man she needs—on the one hand literally a "man on horseback" (344) forever galloping to the rescue; on the other, as cousin, childhood sweetheart, and, eventually, clergyman, a familiar enough figure to avoid any shocks to the system—saves her from a self-abnegation verging on the self-destructive.

And then there is Oliver. He, too, saves her life. When Rose's fever reaches its crisis, at the moment when her physician says that "it would be little short of a miracle if she recovered" (218), Oliver goes for a walk. The day before he had spontaneously assured Mrs. Maylie that he was "quite certain" that "Heaven" would not allow Rose to die (215). Now, he walks to the churchyard, sits among its "green mounds" (those mossy gravesites characteristic of the region; clearly their green presence helps him to the insight that follows), weeps, looks around, and for the length of one paragraph, takes leave of his anxiety, drifts into reverie, and thinks:

> There was so much of brightness and mirth in the sunny landscape... [that] the thought instinctively occurred to him that this was not a time for death, that Rose could surely never die when humbler things were all so glad and gay... He almost thought that shrouds were for the old and shrunken, and never wrapped the young and graceful form within their ghastly folds (219).

"Instinctively:" instinct is that which one knows in one's heart of hearts, and in this book of inward validations cannot be wrong—at least not in this sequestered place, as experienced by one who has just been told by the wise Mrs. Maylie, "You think like a child" (215).

Yes, of course he does. Here, where the language is at its most Wordsworthian, where Oliver is absorbing health-giving Bible (always, for Dickens, New Testament) lessons, and learning, assuredly, that the way to heaven is the way of "little children," that is the innermost, heart-most way to think. It is here that, in a book often on the brink of the uncanny, ideas of precognition, including infantile, even prenatal precognition, have the greatest authority, and "there lingers, in the least reflective mind, a vague and half-formed consciousness of having held such feelings long before, in some remote and distant time" (210). In such a place, Oliver's intuition cannot be wrong. His instinctive sense that Rose will live comes from a clairvoyant core. He knows this, and in knowing he effects it—works, in the physician's word, "a miracle." After his spell in the churchyard he walks home, thinking of Rose. Ever the quiverer (like Rose, he is given to frequent faintings)... he trembles

(218) (like Rose, again, who is "trembling between earth and heaven" [231]) at the news that the patient has reached the critical point. He and Mrs. Maylie fast and watch. They observe the equivocal spectacle of the setting sun's "brilliant [this word, again] hues." Then their "quick ears" pick up the faint sound of "an approaching footstep"—the physician, coming to tell them that Rose has turned the corner.

Again, Oliver has participated in this, simultaneously as seer and agent, at a time and place where the two capacities can interact. "If fervent prayers, gushing from hearts overcharged with gratitude, be heard in heaven—and if they be not, what prayers are!—the blessings which the orphan child called down upon them, sunk into their souls, diffusing peace and happiness" (205). Dickens means that. Oliver has his prayers answered, because under the influence of the Maylies he is attuned to, trembles in touch with, the fellow feeling of his fellow orphan.

He is, that is, being sympathetic, in a specific way. Sympathy in *Oliver Twist* requires two things. First, that fine-grained sensitivity (to the gradations of "hues," for example) bordering on or crossing over into clairvoyance, which the inland Oliver supremely possesses. It is, conventionally enough, especially active in semiconscious states. Oliver's "instinctively" felt conviction that Rose will recover arises during his churchyard revery. It is a product of the intersection of his own cleansed, softened, sensitized self with the environment, the same kind of intersection that in the next chapter (the logic is probably dialectical) will bring to him, half-asleep and still snug within the Maylie nest, his vision of Fagin and Monks at his window (228–29). This latter scene is *Oliver Twist* at its uncanniest: the visitors are seen by no one else and leave no footprints in the grass, and the later explanation of how they came to be there is perhaps the most far-fetched thing in the book. Still, as with Rose's recovery, the experience is, probably, fundamentally sensory, or perhaps super-sensory, as opposed to out-and-out magical. People in Oliver's state, the author assures us in italics, can indeed behold "visionary scenes" produced by "*the mere silent presence*" of figures shut out from their sight (228; italics in original). Oliver's vision extends from the same refined faculties that allowed him, with his "quick ears," to pick up Rose's physician's footstep, and, just before that, sitting in the churchyard, to tune into (the auditory equivalent, here, of "hues") the "blithesome music" of the "summer birds" (219).

At its sharpest, this first condition of sympathy can extend into the Romantic trope of sympathetic vibration. Taken to this limit, it engages with the novel's second condition for true sympathy, that the parties involved connect via something from the past—orphanhood, for example—usually the buried past. On this level, sympathy is memory.[28] The principle is established early on. "Little" Dick is "little Oliver's" only friend, the one resident of his hometown Oliver is eager to see again because both are diminutive starvelings who grew up in the same workhouse. The "benevolent old lady" whose alms save the footsore Oliver from dying on the king's highway is thinking of "a shipwrecked grandson wandering barefoot in some distant part of the earth" (45–46). Mrs. Bedwin and Mrs. Maylie, protectresses of Oliver and Rose, respectively, have both lost children: the former testifies that when she thinks of Oliver she sees him and her own "side by side" (280). Nancy switches loyalties in the moment when Sikes's dog, attacking Oliver, reminds her of how she herself was treated at his age. For his part, Mr. Brownlow instinctively becomes Oliver's patron by way of an affective memory of Proustian proportions,[29] "a glimpse of some old friend flashing on one in a vivid dream" (335).

Sympathy's vectors, that is, are inward and backward, toward the heart and the past. At their most profound, they can, as with Rose's remote-control resurrection, transgress the middle region "trembling between earth and heaven," akin if not identical to what Mr. Brownlow thinks of as the "dusky curtain" between present and remote past (61). In Brownlow's case it seems, indeed, as if the shock of spotting the eerily familiar Oliver does incite a second-stage regression reaching beyond a further dark curtain dividing this world from the previous (or next). The rearward momentum of Brownlow's sudden apprehension of years gone by carries him across that divide: he imagines/remembers, in reverse-chronological order, young friends now old, then young friends now dead, then long-dead friends resurrected through the intercession of his mind, then, finally, "the beaming of the soul through its mask of clay, and whispering of beauty beyond the tomb" (62). This momentum, from past world to other world, is one of the book's recurrent rhythms. Little Dick, Oliver's dying double, sees angels in his last sleep; the stricken Rose *is* an angel, tenuously attached to the coarser earth; a token from her helps Nancy, at the moment of death, to lift "up her folded hands as high towards Heaven" (322–21).

Such scenes certainly bring out the florid in Dickens, but there is method to the melodrama, and a rationale behind it. A character's proximity to what lies beyond the veil is directly proportional to the capacity to fellow-feel with someone else, above all with Oliver. When you look at Oliver for the first time, you either do or do not see through him and into his heart, either do or do not realize that he is, exceptionally if not uniquely (Rose, another small and fragile being, also qualifies, probably), unencumbered by the usual abraded carapace of defenses, that in becoming attuned to him you are re-becoming attuned to the softly receptive center of yourself, itself once attuned, in your past, to an extra-earthly source that the years since have worked to coarsen. You become like him, in the middle of the book, on waking up for the first time under a loving mother's influence, from "a dream of love and affection he had never known," one calling up "remembrances of scenes that never were, in this life" and reviving "some brief memory of a happier existence, long gone by" (191).

As such passages attest, *Oliver Twist* is Dickens's most religious novel. It is the only one, for instance, in which a clergyman gets to play the romantic lead. Those Wordsworthian sentiments evoked under inland influences in effect amount to scripture, intermittently secularized. That by the treatment of one tiny, ragged outcast someone may reveal the true measure of one's moral worth would not have come as news to any contemporary church-goer accustomed to hearing that "inasmuch as ye have done it unto one of the least of these my brethren, ye have done it unto me" (Mt 25:40). That inner blessedness might reside in one melancholy waif, condemned from infancy to hang, ought not to have shocked a congregation taught every Christmas that the prophesied coming of their savior as one "acquainted with grief" and "esteem[ed]...smitten, stricken of God, and afflicted" (Is 53:3–4) had been fulfilled in the arrival of the baby Jesus. The conditions of Oliver's birth, the odds against his survival, the swarms of officials out to kill him—these might well have reminded them of the manger and Herod's soldiers. When they reached the last paragraph of the novel, beginning, "Within the altar of the old village church there stands a white marble tablet, which bears as yet one word—Agnes!", some astute readers might have remembered how in the first chapter the attending nurse had addressed the as-yet-unnamed Agnes, Oliver's mother, as "a dear young lamb" (368, 2)—and, as Susan Meyer suggests, might then have gone on to remember that John the Baptist called Jesus the *"Agnus Dei,"* the Lamb of God.[30] (Given that the nurse in question probably does not know Agnes's name and certainly does not know Latin, this may qualify as the novel's first case of supernatural psychic sympathies.) Whether or not "Agnes" rang a bell with them, English readers raised as Christians would know that a little child was to lead them. From Matthew 18:6, they would know as well that their Lord had suffered the little children to come to him, enjoined his followers to become like them, and, with shockingly uncharacteristic ferocity, had proclaimed that, for anyone offending against them, "it were better for him that a millstone were hanged about his neck, and that he were drowned in the depth of the sea." Matthew 18:6 was Dickens's favorite verse.

IV.

The point here is not just that Oliver is redundantly Christlike. So, in a manner of speaking, are a number of other Dickens children. Oliver is something else again: Christ re-presented. The connection is of a higher order, the match closer, than any obtaining with Little Nell or Tiny Tim. The name, to begin with, may, as often, be a clue: "Oliver" recalling the olive branch of peace and the Mount of Olives (that is, "Olivet"), "Twist" a prophecy of hanging (Jesus in folklore and verse is often presented as "hanging" from the "tree" of Calvary) and perhaps—maybe a stretch, this—the crown of thorns, which according to Dickens's *The Life of Our Lord* was "plaited," that is twisted, around Jesus' brow.[31] In short, the tortured peace-bringer.

Dickens's names can be slippery, and I would not wish to put too much weight on the readings just suggested. In fact, one striking fact about Oliver's naming is its uncertainty, a feature that, as it happens, he would, in Dickens's view of the matter, have shared with Jesus. Roland F. Anderson points out[32] that when the book's last paragraph prophecies the time when our hero's name will appear above "Agnes" on the church's tablet, one thing it is not doing is telling us what that name would be. That is because it cannot. There would be at least four plausible candidates. If Oliver were to go about his father's business, whose business would it be? And according to Dickens, who did not believe in the divinity of Christ, much less the virgin birth, the same would apply to Jesus. Dickens's Jesus could not have known who his father was.

As they do elsewhere in Dickens, notably *Bleak House,* the alternatives raised by illegitimacy come together in a portrait, one that belongs in the fairyland of magic mirrors and statues brought to life. It is the painting in Mr. Brownlow's parlor, according to Monks "an idle daub" of a dead man who was one half of a "maudlin pair" (336)—"maudlin," as Monks probably and Dickens surely knew, implicating Oliver's Magdalen of a mother. Well, fie on Monks. This is a novel in which one Magdalen dies to save Oliver's life and goes to heaven in consequence, and another, at least as designated by Monks, cherishes and (from tablet, painting, and heaven) beams down on the issue of a sin neither she nor her creator could wish away. By the last paragraph and corresponding illustration, with the "porochial" authorities banished to outer darkness while sunlight becomes churchlight embracing "Agnes" and Oliver, Alpha and Omega, both Maries, the Magdalen and she of Nazareth have achieved their conjoint place in the company of their son and savior. The "daub" derided by Monks has presaged this consummation. Actually, it has helped facilitate it. It is a painting by Oliver's father of Oliver's mother, an artistic conception made around the time of the sexual conception of their child. So far as we know it is an amateur's only effort, a single loving gesture—all to the good, in this tale of innocents prevailing over worldlings. Whatever it may lack in technique is more than compensated for by its spirit. It is the "living copy" of Oliver, bearing what the early editions of the novel describe as a "perfectly unearthly" likeness to him.[33] When Oliver fixes his sorrowful eyes on its sorrowful eyes, they reciprocate—"as if," he says, "it was alive and wanted to speak to me, but couldn't" (71). The inference is clear. A few pages earlier, Brownlow's Oliver-induced involuntary memory of youth had evoked visions of "the beaming of the soul through its mask of clay" (51); this is the beaming of Oliver's mother through a mask, or screen, of canvas and paint. It is a living spirit, looking down on the child it recognizes. Understanding this helps to resolve an apparent anomaly— that in instinctively responding to a likeness of the mother who died at his birth, Oliver seems to be sensing the identity of someone he either never saw or barely glimpsed under what, to say the least, were distracting circumstances.

    Let us entertain the possibility that this conceit is not just a matter of magic-show mumbo-jumbo, that it at least has a logic behind it. To begin with, Kerry McSweeney is, I think, correct to take it as an extreme instance of the novel's investment in the "lasting power of early memories," in this case of a "memory trace" implanted when Agnes called out for her baby, kissed it, and died.[34] The mother's portrait can recognize Oliver because (and only because, I'd suggest) its original glimpsed him: once again, supremely heightened sensation is coextensive with visionary powers. That the memory was forged in an eyeblink does not make it less plausible; on the contrary. Here and elsewhere—as when Brownlow recalls having seen, in his glimpse of Oliver, a "glimpse of" his "old friend," Oliver's father (335)—Dickens endorses the primacy of immediate, unmediated perception. Consistent with similar such occurrences in the novel, virginal experience prevails over jaded, as instinct over experience. Brownlow, for instance, loses his moment of clarity through dwelling on it, crowding it out amidst the "vast amphitheatre of faces" his act of willed remembrance calls up (61). But Agnes, who twelve years ago glimpsed her child and forthwith died, suffered no such dissipation. She died at the moment her son's new face was imprinted on her eyes, leaving the spiritual equivalent of a bright light's afterimage to be shelled in, shut and preserved behind her sealed lids. In Brownlow's parlor that light is rekindled by that son's presence. So, too, reciprocally, from Oliver, returning the gaze. His response to the picture is in the nature of a reunion after long absence, reopening a circuit that was there all along.

That the mother should be recognizing the image of her minute-old newborn in the person of a fully dressed twelve-year-old is, certainly, another apparent anomaly also requiring some explaining. The logic is not new, although the application may be: as in Shakespeare's "Sonnet Three," the principle at work is simultaneously genealogical and mnemonic. Agnes recognizes Oliver by way of her blood as well as her eyes. Her portrait is both mirror to the orphaned present and window opening on family past. Once again, Brownlow's first, unmediated sight of Oliver is instructive, setting out some ground rules for the more complicated business to follow: it was "like a glimpse of some old friend flashing on one in a vivid dream" (335). It was a fleeting memory of the dearest friend of his youth, Oliver's father, called up by the son's filial resemblance, but as we have seen it was soon dispersed, even while Brownlow was in Oliver's company. Yet, later when Brownlow sees Oliver sitting in front of the mother's likeness, he is thunderstruck by the "perfectly unearthly" resemblance. Why the discrepancy in reactions? To some extent, probably, because a painted image is psychologically more salient than its mental equivalent. But there is something else going on. Oliver's father was not only Brownlow's best friend but also the brother of the woman Brownlow loved. When she died, the "strong attachment" between the two men took "root in the earth that covered one most dear to both" (334). What is more, the brother "had the sister's soul and person" (333). Thanks to Oliver's positioning before the portrait and the sudden synchronization it effects, Brownlow is simultaneously able to see through Oliver, through the image of a woman he never met, through the memory of her lover his friend, into its blending with the memory of his own one love. The experience sustains the hunch that earlier came and went. Thus does the young man before him engineer a flashback to the young man Brownlow was at the decisive interval of his life, the buried memories of which, until Oliver arrived, have driven him into the forgetful "abstraction" that is his distinguishing feature (58). (That habitual abstraction, the book makes clear, arose out of a wish to shut those memories out, behind the "dusky curtain" of his habitual obliviousness.) Once its secret is breached, the portrait is more powerful than any single memory because it is a (in a word) fuller (in another word) composition. Characters in this novel are sometimes described as "composing" their scattered thoughts before sleeping—which in this book is always dreaming, which in turn is always consciousness meaningfully condensed. Outdoors, a glimpse of Oliver had elicited from Brownlow a crowd of memories, jostling for attention before he dropped his inner curtain on them. Indoors, the portrait acts as a double lens to compose the acutest of those memories into one three-dimensional mirror/window. The scattered persons come together in one. It can do that in part because of the genuine genealogical affinity—the natural tendency to look like one another—between many of them. But as Goldie Morgentaler astutely says, the genealogical conceit is carried to another level, to what she calls the painting's "procreative symbolism."[35] Oliver's father struck off the painting while in the full flush of what since the time of the troubadours has been understood as the all-consuming state of forbidden passion. It was an intense act of love. That is why the painting is so perfect a replica of the subject: his enamored soul was filled with her image, to reproduce which was his whole amateur's (from *"amare,"* to love) purpose. (The same was true, we may be sure, of the act of Oliver's conception.) It is also why, prompted by the portrait, Brownlow vividly recognizes Oliver's identity with the woman he never knew rather than with the man whose image rests in his heart—the painting, not the painter.

And yet the painter is present too. He made the painting magic. How else, after all, could it simultaneously be the living image of a newborn, of that newborn's later twelve-year old self, and of the nineteen-year-old mother who gave them birth? How but in the mind—the spirit—of its only begetter? If the mother's image comes to life in Oliver's presence, so does the father's spirit behind it. (For Brownlow, so does the "soul and person" of that father's sister.) That is one reason Brownlow sees the connection so much more forcefully than before—from the combined power of replica (mother) and replica's generative spirit. The portrait is not just fuller, composed of more congruently matching persons, than any ordinary mental image. It is also deeper.

In her discussion of what she calls the "mysterious workings" through which Oliver and portrait match, Morgentaler applies the word "transcendent" to this artifice-engendered union of the parents.[36] *D'accord.* Professed—more or less—Unitarian though he was, Dickens went through spells of what seems at least to have been intense nostalgia for the transcendent mysteries of the old church, and at such times otherworldly images of women were likely to play a central part.[37] Probably the best-known instance is his dream-vision in Genoa of Mary Hogarth, the beloved sister-in-law who had died in his arms at the age of seventeen. Appearing to him wearing "blue drapery, as the Madonna might in a picture of Raphael," Mary answered Dickens's question, "What is the true religion?... perhaps the Roman Catholic is the best?" with the words, "For *you*, it is the best." Ever the self-analyst, Dickens speculated on how local associations might have contributed to this apparitional exchange: there was an altar in his bedroom, church bells had been ringing; the woman did, after all, bear the name of "Mary"; Genoa was, after all, a Catholic city. Most intriguingly, in light of the effects induced by the *Oliver Twist* painting: "I had observed within myself, before going to bed, that there was a mark in the wall, above the sanctuary, where a religious picture used to be; and I had wondered within myself what the subject might have been, and what the face was like."[38] Clearly, he thinks this "wondering" may have aroused and channeled his imagination into his Raphaelesque visitor, as the portrait in Brownlow's parlor comes to life only under Oliver's gaze. About two months later, in the same city, he was to begin his "Mesmeric" cures of Madame de la Rue, believed to work by concentration of his eyes, his "visual ray,"[39] on his subject.

The Mary Hogarth dream, I suggest, shows that at the time his mind was already running on matters Mesmeric as well as Mariolatric. It combined two strains of mysticism, Dickens's faith in his ability to restore some distant person's well-being through influences telepathically directed, and the (somewhat more qualified) faith in his ability to learn about God from a saint.

Mary Hogarth had died during the writing of *Oliver Twist,* and it is generally accepted that the seventeen-year-old Rose Maylie's near-death owes much to that event. The difference is that Oliver brings the young woman back to life through that instinctive power of his to work such a "miracle." Aside from himself (and even he, after all, had failed in this one crucial test of his power) the other figure in Dickens's writings given to such feats is Jesus. Here are two examples from *The Life of Our Lord*:

> There was a Centurion too, or officer over the Soldiers, who came to him, and said, "Lord! My servant lies at home in my house, very ill." Jesus Christ made answer, "I will come and cure him." But the Centurion said "Lord! I am not worthy that Thou shouldst come to my house. Say the word only, and I know he will be cured." Then Jesus Christ, glad that the Centurion believed in him so truly said "Be it so!" And the servant became well, from that moment.

But of all the people who came to him, none were so full of grief and distress, as one man who was a Ruler or Magistrate over many people, and he wrung his hands, and cried, and said "Oh Lord, my daughter—my beautiful, good, innocent little girl, is dead! Oh come to her, come to her, and lay Thy blessed hand upon her, and I know she will revive, and come to life again, and make me and her mother happy. Oh Lord we love her so, we love her so! And she is dead!"

Jesus Christ went out with him, and so did his disciples and went to his house, where the friends and neighbours were crying in the room where the poor dead little girl lay, and where there was soft music playing; as there used to be, in those days, when people died. Jesus Christ, looking on her, sorrowfully, said—to comfort her poor parents—"She is not dead. She is asleep." Then he commanded the room to be cleared of the people that were in it, and going to the dead child, took her by the hand, and she rose up, quite well, as if she had only been asleep.[40]

Unitarian or not, in this work at least Dickens sometimes appears conflicted about the issue of Jesus' divinity. The earthly Jesus seems to predominate when, for instance, Dickens says that God loves Jesus "*as is own son*"[41] or "that Joseph and Mary, and *her* Son Jesus Christ" "are *commonly* called The Holy Family."[42] (My italics.) At other points, he seems to be leaning the other way. In the account of Jesus' baptism in the Jordan River, he has God speaking from on high to proclaim, "This is my beloved Son, in whom I am well pleased!"[43] Perhaps we are to suppose that God was carried away by the occasion; perhaps the words were so well known that Dickens felt obligated to honor them; perhaps sonship is to be understood as being in nature more homoiousian than homoousian. Taken as a whole *The Life of Our Lord* is elusive on the subject. The same is true for *Oliver Twist,* similarly equivocal on Oliver's standing in relation to this world and the next.

In part, this is due to the curious ways in which it works to narrow the gap between the two. With the bar for getting across into heaven lowered and the bar-clearing capacity of certain spirits on earth correspondingly raised, the chances of one realm converging with the other are increased. For instance, again: "If fervent prayers, gushing from hearts overcharged with gratitude, be heard in heaven—and if they be not, what prayers are!..." (205). Starting as a conditional but talking itself into affirmation, this proclamation typifies Dickens's see-sawing stance on matters spiritual in *Oliver Twist*—and, for that matter, in *The Life of Our Lord* as well, where Jesus' miraculous healings can seem awfully close to the telepathic, edge-of-death resurrections that Dickens, at least at times, believed could be pulled off by certain rare earthly spirits in certain rare earthly circumstances—such as himself, entranced and entrancing, and such as Oliver, in that churchyard. Under these relaxed rules, it becomes possible, upward-verging meeting downward-merging, that a mortal as pure as Oliver might, at his sublimest, replicate the miracles of a divine spirit as human as Jesus at his earthiest. That, I think, is the rationale according to which Rose, like the "good, innocent" girl resurrected by Dickens's Jesus, "rose up" from the edge of death.

Given all this, the son-father-mother-and so on portrait in Brownlow's parlor can credibly be understood in trinitarian terms. It introduces the possibility of a doctrine that the daylight Dickens habitually eschewed but that the Dickens who communed with blessed virgins in visions (the episode in Genoa was not unique) could believe was the truth, for him anyway. ("For *you,* it is the best:" to be sure, a curiously individualistic commendation of a "Catholic" faith.) God sends down an emissary, or perhaps son, who by the time of his baptism has proven himself to be worthy; Oliver's father, looking down on his only son through the visage of his true bride, has, literally and legally, willed that this son shall come into his kingdom only if he turns out to be both male and sinless (351). Beholding his boy for the first time, now twelve years old—twelve being the age at which according to *The Life of Our Lord* (following Luke), Jesus first showed himself in the temple and "astonished" the high priests—this father has reason to believe that he, too, will be well pleased, that his son will fulfill the promise of his birth.

For one thing, like Jesus in *The Life of Our Lord,* the Oliver who returns the portrait's gaze is thereby certifying his inheritance of special, psychic powers. Dickens's Jesus is forever reading people's thoughts and seeing into the future; Oliver would not be communing with his father had he had not inherited and kept untainted the innocent eye that made the painting possible, were he not able to reciprocate it and in so doing halfway revive the intercessory woman loved by both. Or, actually, more than inherit and reciprocate: redeem. "Wandering" father, like "erring" (334, 368) mother, was himself a sinner, in the single act that brought Oliver into existence. That is all the more reason why Oliver needs, 1. to be like Christ, and, 2. to be more Christlike than his parents. As Morgentaler says, "the virtue of the child presupposes the essential goodness of the parents from whom he sprang, and so absolves them of sin."[44] A heterodox version of scripture, certainly, but one that follows logically if you believe that Mary was Blessed but no Virgin, that she had as much in common with the fallen, wandering outcast of underground tradition[45] as with any Raphael Madonna,[46] that the begetter of the son who was the world's savior himself required saving, and redeeming in return.

How else is Oliver Christlike? Count the ways. He is born in the dead of winter. For a time he is apprentice to a carpenter—Mr. Sowerberry, maker of coffins. As a child he escapes those who wish him ill by running away. He consorts with prostitutes and other lowlifes without being corrupted by their influence; instead, he helps one of them achieve salvation. Those with eyes to see (Nancy, Rose, Fagin) recognize in him a changelinglike quality setting him apart from the world they know. (Even the dense Blathers asks in jest if he fell "out of the clouds" [197].) His dreams and musings typically bring him into communion with heaven. He forgives his enemies: indeed his last recorded words of the book, spoken in Fagin's cell—"Oh! God forgive this wretched man!" (364) can hardly fail to recall Jesus' own last words on the cross: "Father, forgive them, for they know not what they do."

There are, certainly, divergences, but if anything they tend to make Oliver all the more convenable to the Dickens version. As he was born, not from a sanctified commingling of absolute with immaculate, but rather of the will of man and of the will of the flesh, in an act both sinful and expiable, so he is capable at the start of fibbing and conniving, and, when purified, of resolving not to. His is, in part, an achieved—or at least successfully maintained—purity. As in the Gospels, Dickens's Jesus undergoes his time of testing in a wilderness, but in *The Life of Our Lord* it is in "a wild and lovely country called the Wilderness"[47]—an extremely odd choice of adjectives, certainly, but then "lovely" is also the word bestowed on the rural surrounding of the Maylies' home (210), where Oliver completes his own time of testing and transformation (and confronts Satan—Fagin at his window), and where his greatest pleasure is picking "wild flowers" for Rose (212). Oliver reaches the Maylie threshold in the company of two thieves, one on each side, and is wounded and abandoned while fainting (as it seems) dead away.[48] When he regains consciousness, he overcomes his "agony," heads for the Maylie garden and the Maylie portico, and is after some confusion taken up and succored by two women who see that he is put to bed, where he lies with his "long hair" streaming over the pillow and his wounded arm "crossed upon his breast" (191).

V.

As Oliver comes to incarnate Jesus, Fagin approaches the opposite role, not as defined by the abstractions of theology but as fed by the folklore of child roasters, cannibal kings, and witches. In this company, Fagin is not a Jew but the Jew, the one who as the devil's earthly stand-in must drain and drink the blood of Christ's stand-in, a saintly Christian child, of whom the two most famous in English lore are William of Norwich, aged twelve, and Hugh of Lincoln, aged somewhere between eight and ten. Butchers, including the would-be variety, get butchered in their turn, as surely as the witch of "Hansel and Gretel" must end up in her own oven. *Oliver Twist* is a fairy tale in modern dress, and the tale in question is the blood libel.

How well did Dickens understand what he was doing? G. K. Chesterton is far from the only reader to have felt that the novel's characters "were keeping something back from the author as well as from the reader."[49] John Forster, Dickens's first biographer, had started speculation moving along such lines when he disclosed that Fagin had been named for Bob Fagin,[50] Dickens's workmate in the blacking warehouse. Dickens had been twelve at the time, Oliver's main age, and later remembered that Bob had taught him "the trick of...tying the knot,"[51] an expression that turns black the minute you imagine it in *Oliver Twist*. Pretty much everyone who has written on the subject accepts that the novel draws on this experience; some, such as Mary Anne Andrade, have speculated that the novel's preoccupation with altered consciousness arose as the accumulated stress of writing to deadline, of quarrels with publishers, and, above all, of the death of Mary Hogarth produced "an inspired dreamy sleepwalking state," which among other things brought back the blacking factory days.[52]

Although that is certainly possible, the fact remains that neither the death of Mary Hogarth nor the struggles with publishers (both of which episodes, along with the blacking factory memory, leave their traces in the text) involved Jews.[53] Dickens's creative issues, so far as can be told, had nothing to do with any particular Jew. Bob Fagin had not been a Jew.[54] According to the record, nothing important in the author's life at the time, or up to it, would have conduced to anti-Semitism.

Indeed, outside the pages of *Oliver Twist,* Dickens's feelings toward Jews were much what we would expect. As Robert Newsom says, Dickens was "relatively" though "not entirely" free of "the conventional anti-Semitism prevalent among the early Victorians."[55] There is, to be sure, the occasional snide crack in his correspondence, and he did, in the heat of battle, once call his publisher Richard Bentley an "infernal, rich, plundering, thundering old Jew."[56] But Bentley, as Dickens of course knew, was not Jewish, and the words in question were a direct steal from Bill Sikes, hardly a character whose views Dickens or anyone else would be inclined to second without irony. *Oliver Twist* aside, in Dickens's overall handling of Jews and Jewishness there is little or nothing of the obsessive—and for Dickens, that is saying something.

So when, about twenty-five years after *Oliver Twist,* the Jewish Mrs. Eliza Davis protested that Fagin had harmed her people, Dickens was, in the words of Fred Kaplan, genuinely "surprised and defensive."[57] He went so far as to put an anti-Fagin, Riah, in his next novel, *Our Mutual Friend,* Riah being a kindly old Jew who, rather than using Christian boys as a front for his wicked ways, is instead himself thus used by a conniving Christian. He gave him a one-rotten-apple speech, which might as well have been entitled, "Don't blame Fagin on us." Most impressively, in revising *Oliver Twist* for the 1867 edition, he excised most occurrences of the phrase "the Jew"—no small matter, considering how much of the book's power comes from that phrase's hammering repetition. Evidently, he was sincere when he told Mrs. Davis that he had meant no harm.

And yet, and yet: Riah, to this reader among others, is a weak gesture, because so obviously willed into existence for some pious purpose. He is one of a number of instances of Dickens's, as we would say today, politically correct side, which is not his best side. Riah is a curiosity, a dancing dog; Fagin is a phenomenon. When it came to telling a story about Jews fronting for Christians, there was nothing that mattered in the cultural heritage for Dickens to draw on. Not so the other way around. As Meyer says, "Dickens did not eradicate the antisemitism from *Oliver Twist* in his revision of 1867 because the antisemitism could not be eradicated from the book."[58] Mrs. Davis really did have a point, and Dickens's response to her, in the "surprised and defensive" words described by Kaplan, indicates, I think, that on some level he knew it:

> I must take leave to say, that if there be any general feeling on the part of the intelligent Jewish people, that I have done them what you describe as "a great wrong," they are a far less sensible, a far less just, and a far less good-tempered people than I have always supposed them to be. Fagin, in *Oliver Twist,* is a Jew, because it unfortunately was true of the time to which that story refers, that that class of criminal almost invariably was a Jew. But surely no sensible man or woman of your persuasion can fail to observe—firstly, that all the rest of the wicked *dramatis personae* are Christians; and secondly, that he is called a "Jew," not because of his religion, but because of his race. If I were to write a story, in which I described a Frenchman or a Spaniard as "the Roman Catholic," I should do a very indecent and unjustifiable thing; but I make mention of Fagin as the Jew, because he is one of the Jewish people, and because it conveys

that kind of idea of him which I should give my readers of a Chinaman, by calling him a Chinese.

The enclosed is quite a nominal subscription towards the good object in which you are interested; but I hope it may serve to show you that I have no feeling towards the Jewish people but a friendly one. I always speak well of them, whether in public or in private, and bear my testimony (as I ought to do) to their perfect good faith in such transactions as I have ever had with them; and in my "Child's History of England," I have lost no opportunity of setting forth their cruel persecution in old times.[59]

The subscription enclosed was two guineas for a Jewish charity.[60]

Although in most matters an exceptionally honest man, Dickens had a way of tacking in the other direction whenever he felt his character was called into question. This letter is an example. To begin with, it is not true that all of the other "wicked" characters of *Oliver Twist* are "Christians." Fagin has an accomplice named Barney, "another Jew, younger than Fagin, but nearly as vile and repulsive in appearance" (94), who is ready to murder a "Christian"—if that is the word for Sikes—at a sign from Fagin (94). In fact, in keeping with the venerable convention that although two of something may be a coincidence, three is another matter, there is a third Jew as well: "As Oliver was told that he might do what he liked with the old clothes, he gave them to a servant who had been very kind to him, and asked her to sell them to a Jew, and keep the money for himself" (84). Although a minor figure, this third Jew is the means by which Fagin finds and abducts Oliver—"as if," says Meyer, "all the Jews in London have an almost supernatural connection with one another, forming a sort of cabal."[61] He conveys Oliver's rags to Fagin—and, three being a crowd, in the process helps multiply the Jewish presence into a throng: "At length they turned into a very filthy narrow street, nearly full of old-clothes shops" (99)—that is, full of Jews, as confirmed by Fagin's transaction with the old-clothes man. Sure enough: Fagin is lodged on that street, in one of his hideouts, snug in the neighborhood of his "filthy" brethren.

Nor is it true—though heaven knows why it would have been a consolation—that Fagin is characterized exclusively in terms of race rather than religion. To be sure, he is not observant, but neither are most of the "Christians" on display. He is, however, hostile to Christians as a group—given to jibes at "psalm-singers," at those condemned men who confess to the "old parson" and die "with prayers on their lips," (102, 52, 360), at gentile "gentlemen," at Oliver's "Sunday" suit (100). There may also be a religious innuendo when Fagin tells Noah that the "magic number" is not three (or seven), but "one" (293)—what might be called the major point at issue between Christian and Judaic versions of monotheism. Although in the death cell he spurns the comforts offered by "venerable men of his own persuasion" (361), his "rocking...from side to side" (363) suggests that he may retain some vestige of their rituals. (And besides, hasn't Dickens, vis-à-vis his letter to Mrs. Davis, slipped up, with that word "persuasion"?) Above all, he is the exemplary non-Christian in the one Dickens novel that most decisively equates salvation with Christian salvation.

And: it was obviously disingenuous of Dickens to say that calling Fagin a Jew is comparable to calling someone "Chinese"—unless we are talking about, say, some Yellow Peril novel in which the Chinese are forever emerging from underground opium dens to strangle Occidentals with their pigtails. And, again: Dickens's letters show that he did not in fact "always" speak well of Jews. As for testifying to their "perfect good faith in such transactions as I have had with them," there is just one such transaction on record, the sale of Dickens's property to Mrs. Davis's husband. Dickens did indeed report that he was gratified by Mr. Davis's fair dealing, but also that he was surprised by it, because—well, guess. And, according to what usage did this single transaction become plural "transactions"? Dickens is, at the least, fudging here.

To conclude the arraignment. *A Child's History of England* is indeed sympathetic to Jews. *The Life of Our Lord,* in which the crucifixion is largely a result of Jewish spite, is not.

This Pecksniffian performance is not like Dickens. He was, all in all, an exceptionally humane man[62] who detested cant. Subtract *Oliver Twist,* and even on the vexed issue in question he should probably get about a B or B+. *Oliver Twist* is not something he would have written. The person on show in that letter to Mrs. Davis is, I suggest, an older man who has been found out, twenty-five years after the fact, as if by the Spirit of Meannesses Past. If *Oliver Twist* was an indiscretion of youth, it would follow that the young Dickens had been capable of being a nasty piece of work. It is not as if he had misbehaved after the fashion of other young men, had, for instance, drunk too much claret and dashed off soppy verses to his sweetheart. It as if he had drunk too much claret and kicked a cripple.

VI.

Dickens's response to Mrs. Davis suggests that, later in life, he understood, on some level, what he had done. I think he understood it at the time, too. Just because *Oliver Twist* is preoccupied with altered states, sometimes of induced oblivion, it does not necessarily follow that its author was courting, or achieving, anything comparable, that he was out of touch with what his words were doing. True, *Oliver Twist* is intensely attentive to psychological extremes and can seem written at such a pitch that we cannot help but feel at times that the author's own psychology is part of the action. In a narrative driven to a new level of dramatic expressiveness, it is easy to believe that the narrator is among the emoters. It entwines character psychology with narrative movement and texture to a degree probably unprecedented, for instance in the way chapter endings tend to coincide with someone's, usually Oliver's, loss of consciousness.[63] In a number of ways, it wants to turn over rocks, to bring the submerged, including submerged selves, to the surface, and its excavation into, and intermittent narrative fusion with, dreams and related states is part of that project.

But it is not necessarily blind as to where it is going and what it finds. This is not a text innocent of the shades it calls up. Scenes from *King Lear, Macbeth,* and *Othello* are incorporated with evident self-consciousness. Biblical types and constellations of types come into view in ways sometimes obvious and sometimes borderline. That bloodied arm "crossed" on Oliver's breast, for example.

Or, as a case of consciously orchestrated counterpoint, the name given Noah Claypole, the fellow apprentice who bullies Oliver during his stay at the Sowerberrys and who later follows in his footsteps to London. Thematically, Noah may be said to stand in relation to Oliver as reality check to ideal, reminding us that the author still understands that rural poverty does not necessarily produce saints. Their first names, I suggest, help underscore the distinction—Noah of the Old Covenant, Oliver of the New. (Dickens generally believed that the latter was inspired, the former, not.) "Claypole," conveying something on the order of claywitted clodpated beanpole, follows suit.

Claypole is also, as it happens, the name of a village in Lincolnshire, for Dickens evidently a land of dolts.[64] I bring up this *recherché* item only because I believe that Lincolnshire, specifically, its county seat of Lincoln, is where Noah and Oliver come from—and that if so, this fact, buried like much else in a book of occultations deliberate and otherwise, becomes an important one when brought to light.

The appendix will make, as best it can, the case for Lincoln. My reason for including it is, first, that I believe that the Fagin-versus-Oliver story is a variant on the blood libel, and, second, that the medieval tale of Little Saint Hugh of Lincoln is its main model. The first point does not require the second, but given the testimony about Oliver's origin, the possibility strikes me as worth pursuing.

Lincoln or no Lincoln, Oliver's origin is a child-quelling center, and if the place I'm suggesting, it is one inclined that way by tradition. Oliver's escape from it to Fagin's den is from frying pan to fire, between two places that remain eerily linked thereafter. Thus Noah and Charlotte fall into Fagin's company the minute they complete their trek from Oliver's town to London. Monks, apparently on the same wavelength, travels their course in a reverse direction, even manages to find out the gold mementos, which were surely meant, in Dickens's original plan, to match up with the gold watch and other loot hidden under Fagin's London floorboards. Dickens abandoned that part of his story, but "gold" remains a word that the one murder center has in common with the other, and the scene of the old Jew grubbing for treasure in his secret hole—itself almost a parody of anti-Semitic iconography—is all the more striking because unaccounted for; it is as if Jews and their delegates are drawn to gold by a special kind of magnetism, with or without any other assigned rationale.

It is also striking for being one of the sights that Oliver sees during his two hypnagogic trances, during which we are to understand that he is clairvoyant. In the second, never really explained either,[65] he beholds Fagin again, along with Monks, at his window in the Maylies' cottage. His words on awakening are "The Jew! The Jew!" (229). No one else sees Fagin or any traces of him. Perhaps some sort of psychic inheritance has given Oliver the power of second sight when it comes to avaricious, bloodthirsty Jews, one matching Fagin's own instinctive attachment to him. Perhaps, by the time of the window scene, the current between these two principals can be said to go both ways.

Not to belabor the point, but Lincoln would be eminently qualified to share a part in such transactions. For centuries, its place in folklore has been as the scene of England's most famous blood libel and its aftermath. Part of that aftermath was that a number of its Jews were hanged in London. Among others, the Jewish names cited in accounts of the story include Copin, Agim, Jopin, and Falsim—in the case of the last, anyway, not that far from "Fagin."

We can be reasonably sure that after the Lincoln episode, no large settlement would have contained enough unsupervised Jews to be considered a serious conspiracy. (The Norwich story came earlier.) Metropolitan London, especially after the Jewish influx beginning in the early nineteenth century, makes up for the lack. It is the only place where one can still envisage a localized network of Jews, the only place where, if one believed in the Hugh of Lincoln story, one could imagine it happening again. I have said that *Oliver Twist* is a fairy tale in modern dress, the fairy tale of the blood libel; the combination of these two places would be just what it takes to pull off such a revival, with London supplying the machinery, the personnel, and the critical mass, Lincoln the script.

The story of Little Hugh is quickly told. He disappeared from near his home on July 31, 1255. A month later, his body, marked with what were taken to be signs of crucifixion (in some versions, the five wounds of Christ), was discovered in a well. Under torture, a local Jew testified that Hugh had been killed by other local Jews. He added, in a story corroborating an account obtained under like circumstances in the William of Norwich story, that Jews were required to kill one Christian child every year.[66]

Over time, details accrued. The Jews seized, bled, and killed Christian boys to acquire the blood needed for the matzoh of their Passover feast. They also tortured them in ways parodying the crucifixion of Jesus—spitting on them, mocking them as false messiahs, disemboweling them. (As several have observed, garbled accounts of the Purim custom of insulting an effigy of Haman may have prompted this idea.) Likewise, their consumption of bloody matzoh mocked the Eucharist. Like Hugh, all the martyred boys were, therefore, versions of Christ, as the Jews were versions of Judas and of the Jews who had called for Christ's crucifixion.

These boys were perforce held to have been pure of spirit. In some versions of the tale the Jews, true to their excrementious nature, of which more later, had thrown Hugh's body in a privy, but somehow it kept surfacing again, in one body of water or another, until it was eventually found in a well. Both well and burial site became miracle-working places of pilgrimage.

In outline, the blood libel never died out. (It is all over the Internet.) Chaucer made it one of his Canterbury tales. Shylock wants a pound of Christian flesh, but is out-shylocked by being denied any Christian blood to go with it. The Romantic era's retrieval of ancient tales and songs revived much anti-Semitic material, notably "The Ballad of Little Sir Hugh," of which Francis J. Child, compiling his *Ballads,* found eighteen versions. Contemporary blood libel accounts carried the tradition forward into Dickens's time and place, where a rapid influx of Jews[67] must have made such reports only too welcome in some circles.

Dickens could not have not been familiar with the anti-Semitic tales of his time. In fact, as editor of *Bentley's Miscellany* he published an especially revolting example, loosely based on *The Merchant of Venice*, entitled *The Professor of Toledo*. Of course he didn't believe it. Still, he must have thought it made for a good story.

Then as now, the blood libel was the preeminent anti-Semitic narrative—and it is, I believe, the narrative behind this novel. As Chesterton understood, what works in *Oliver Twist* works more in spite of its often gimcrack plot than because of it. It becomes better, sicker, the more we accept that. Shrugging off the implausibilities, the reader is left, not believing nothing, but instead face to face with what holds up. Fagin and Oliver hold up. The appearance of Fagin at Oliver's window is ridiculous, according to realist standards, but not according to narratives inhabited by undead gold-hoarding grotesques brandishing oven forks at pure Christian lads and sucking the life out of the other Christian lads with whose grease the walls of their lairs are coated. In narratives of that sort, such figures can fly—sometimes with giant forks,[68] although brooms will do—and therefore leave no footprints. They are folklore's witches, whose cauldrons were used to boil down and render the corpses of Christian infants, producing the greasy unguent necessary to their existence, and they are folklore's Jews, butchering Christian boys out of a similar need. One part of Dickens's genius lamentably at work in *Oliver Twist* is that it susses how the word "grease" and its variants, by Dickens's time a staple of anti-Semitic discourse, might apply to the old witch burning tales as well, might help fuse coven and ghetto, those two legendary centers of communally coordinated infanticide, into one, and might in the process help bring the fact of contemporary infanticide, so to speak, down to date.

Modern historians of the European witch craze often observe that in many ways it was a revival of the blood libel. As Lyndal Roper puts it, "Witchcraft beliefs were also connected to much older and more amorphous beliefs about Jews, beliefs which latched on to inchoate fears about magic, blood, and sacrifice."[69] (The witch's sabbath probably takes its name from the Jewish "sabbat."[70]) Not infrequently, the new obsession intersected with the old.[71] Although as historical hypothesis this connection may not have been in circulation at the time, the Dickens of *Oliver Twist* was capable of thinking it on his own. Fagin's oven fork, the sausages he roasts with it (50), the "cleft stick" candleholder in his den (100), the "melting-pot" (94) in which he alchemizes the precious metals filched by his minions, the intimations of supernatural powers—not least the power of flight—are all folklorish signs of witchcraft. So are Fagin's appearance and demeanor. Men could be witches too. Although the novel never puts Fagin and his gang directly in touch with the weird sisters of the workhouse and their associates, its thematics work to make the two groups consonant.

With that link, moving from community to individual, the baby murdering promiscuously on display in the first volume is given a point of focus, a solitary figure dispatchable with the jerk of just one rope. To recognize Mrs. Mann and the Poor Law Board and so on as resembling or even reincarnating figures out of legend is to reciprocally legitimize the legend. Demonizing the bureaucracy, one reifies demons. Especially in the play between its first and third volumes, *Oliver Twist* enacts something like a dialogue with itself along these lines. Fagin is an ogre who creeps out of the shadows to snatch and dispatch little boys, and such figures do not exist: they are, as Mr. Grimwig would say, the matter of "lying story books" (113). But, Mr. Grimwig, see here: the board, the Beadle, Mrs. Mann, Gammidge, and the Sowerberrys exist. They exist to hang, flog, starve, burn up, box up, and bury little boys. This, in the nineteenth century. Does it not seem likely, especially for an author who habitually scorned any sentimentalization of "the good old days," that something equivalent was going on in the thirteenth? That behind the stories was something awful and true? That neither "Hansel and Gretel" nor "The Ballad of Little Sir Hugh" came out of nowhere?

There are places in *Oliver Twist* where the vision is that of Goya's "Saturn Devouring One of His Sons." The body politic has and must ever have had shreds of children's flesh in its teeth. Infanticide is foundational. Maybe it always was; maybe it has to be. More, the family, emphatically including its female members, is a sub-Atrean horror show. Spouses and descendants alike are, transparently, all too consolable at the passings of their ostensible beloveds (35). An old woman seizes on the death of her daughter as an opportunity to cadge food and clothing from the authorities (32–33). (Of course she does: she's hungry and cold, and her daughter is now neither here nor there. Dickens does not seem to condemn her. Would you?) Other old women exult over the dying and gloat over memories of deathbeds past. Boys bully, girls grovel, and the most powerful urge in human nature, whether the target is Oliver, Sikes, or Fagin, is to clump into a mob for the purpose of watching someone else die wretchedly.

If it weren't for Fagin, who would we blame all that on? There are worse things than killing one old Jew. Think of all the others who would have to go to the wall if justice were meted out justly. Fagin's extinction at book's end is classic scapegoating. He doesn't die for Nancy. He dies for little Dick, for the little Dicks in their hundreds of thousands, and he dies that Oliver may not. He dies because everyone knows that when Hansel and Gretel are sent out, the witch at the end of their trail is there to finish the job—that she, not the woodman, is the *genius loci* of that child-immolating forest. The communal fury that breaks out and consumes Fagin in the last few chapters does not arise from reports of someone else's recent murder of an anonymous prostitute. It is the eruption of forces that have been building since page one, when Agnes, the lamb, perished, and her little lamb of a son began the charmed pilgrimage in the course of which he would insouciantly set off the chain reaction to bring Fagin down, and then, all infuriating innocence, show up in Fagin's death cell to forgive him for being thus brought down. In another tale, Fagin might have by that point gone up in blue smoke, comically tearing at his beard and stamping the boards. Not here. The "apparatus of death" being hammered together outside his cell window is real, all right. Too many real bodies, especially little boys' bodies, have been piling up for it to be otherwise, and he is somehow the cause. How? Well, "somehow," as in, "He has been the—the—somehow the cause of all this."

This half-grasped insight also explains why Fagin—a man, after all, about to be hanged, not gutted—asks why they are going to "butcher" him. Because that is what people like him do to people like Oliver in stories like this, is why. Because superstitions about kosher butchers have long played a part in sustaining the blood libel. Because in some versions of the tale, Little St. Hugh is disemboweled. Technically wrong, Fagin still, "somehow," has the right idea.

Other filiations adumbrate this basic, horrible story. Although Dickens never got around to linking Fagin to the workhouse hags and their legacy of little corpses, the stolen gold hoarded by both comes from out of a common matrix.[72] Fagin never hears of either Agnes or Rose, but together they add up to at least a fair facsimile of the Virgin Mary, and in blood libels the Virgin Mary commonly shows up to sanctify the spot where the Jews were killed for having butchered the Christian boy.[73] So: Fagin is left to his fate at the end of the next-to-last chapter, and at the end of the last chapter, with the Jew freshly dead, Rose and Oliver stand together in church, their nimbi triangulating with the beam of light from the plaque reading "Agnes." Blood sacrifice, purification, sanctification. Monks, in a lucid interval, wonders how Oliver can keep "start"ing up out of nowhere, when he should have been finished off long ago (217)—and starting up from well[74] or privy is what the posthumous little Sir Hugh of legend does. Quite against character, Monks also makes a point of refusing to shed Oliver's blood

(171). Since that is exactly what Fagin wants to do ("Saw his head off!" [363]), we have here a defining distinction between Jewish evil and non-Jewish evil, to wit: Jews want to bleed Christians. Monks may be evil, but at least he is no bloodsucking Jew.

Fagin's other disciples likewise serve to set him apart. Even Sikes dies rather than jump in a pond of excrement.[75] It is, at the next-to-lowest level possible, a saving grace. Fagin, by contrast, pretty much *is* excrement.[76] In perhaps the book's most rebarbative sentence, Dickens comes about as close as permissible to saying that excrement is Fagin's food of choice[77]—the "rich offal" he seeks for a "meal"—as well as his natural medium, the "slime" from which he was "engendered" (120–21). The words "slime" and "filth" (the latter, especially, Dickens's standard euphemism) define Fagin and his locales throughout. When Fagin and Monks make their appearance at Oliver's country window, it is the smell, the "close and confined" atmosphere of Fagin's den replacing the "sweet air" of the country, that first alerts the half-awake Oliver to their presence (228)—and, again, we are to understand that in such states he cannot be wrong. The smell of the room thus brought to mind did not come off of Monks, who so far as we know was never inside that room. What we have here is a venerable cliché of anti-Semitic lore, the "*fetor judaicas*," which (within, but certainly not far within, the limits of propriety) *Oliver Twist* labors to identify with the smell of excrement. *Of course* little Saint Hugh's murderers dropped their victim in a privy. It was just a characteristic indecency, a fitting insult added to the nature of the offense. Fagin, the man who picks through his own feces for money,[78] would, uniquely in *Oliver Twist,* have had no problem with that. In Sikes's place, he would have jumped in and swum for life (345).

Other distinguishing features, including some discussed earlier, can be understood as arising from the same source. Consider again the recurring motif, reviewed earlier in section III, of solid core wrapped in layers becoming increasingly penetrable the closer they are to the surface. Applied, as it is, to an island nation, the trope becomes a xenophobe's dream, especially when the enemy in question both comes from beyond the nation's borders and is by reputation a race give to "insinuating" itself. Londoner or no, Fagin is an alien presence, at book's end expelled from its host organism by a mob whose origins trace to the undefiled English countryside exemplified by Chertsey, about which there is absolutely nothing multiculti, and where we first hear the hue and cry for "The Jew! The Jew!" As Meyer notes, Chertsey is presented as a "distinctly English Christian village,"⁷⁹ not just geographically centered but sunk deep in time, like some core sample of ancient English virtues. It is a tree with deep roots, and Jews(Ahaseurus being the prototype) are by convention rootless. Sympathy is memory, and this alien has no memories, personal or ancestral, that have taken root in this soil. Which is why he has to die alone, with no one to sympathize except for the boy who, being a type of Christ, is required to sympathize with absolutely anyone.

Such formulations as this are made tenable by the supernatural potentialities that, I have argued, are in play throughout. Entertaining ideas of occult correspondences across both space (as in Fagin's trackless journey to Oliver's window) and time (the portrait of Oliver's mother), *Oliver Twist* opens up a field in which opposites draw inexorably together and archetypes may double as incarnations. Because of the latter dispensation, Hugh can plausibly be reincarnated in Oliver as a type of the eternal Christ, Fagin as a type of what Goebbels called the Eternal Jew. (Fagin doesn't just *see* Oliver at their first meeting; he *recognizes* him.) One could speculate that Dickens's promotion of these and other uncanny effects, especially those—trances, dreams, premonitions, instances of déja vu, clairvoyance, and telepathy—notably psychic in nature, might be doing double duty as authorial excuse, a possibility that takes us back to that peculiar exchange with Mrs. Davis. In a work where so many are driven by powers beyond their ken, is it that surprising, or culpable, if the author is one of their number? Mr. Brownlow, recounting one of the book's improbable twists, talks of "a stronger hand than chance" being responsible (335). Well, of course that stronger hand was Dickens's writing hand, unless perhaps we are to understand that something stronger still was also at work, Ouijalike, pushing its pen. Dickens himself was often given to describing himself at work as a kind of medium, charged with characters and their stories "bottled up" inside, who "*will* get out,"⁸⁰ and there is much testimony, from John Forster for instance, as to how his characters gave him no rest until he had finished their stories. He *had* to kill Little Nell. So the excuse was ready to hand—and, what is more, quite possibly, at least partly truthful.

He did not resort to it. It would, I think, have involved disowning too much. *Oliver Twist* had served not just his impulses but his interests. It is, as many have remarked, his first novel, *Pickwick Papers* having been a brilliant something-or-other. It is where he found out for sure that he was a born teller of tales. If *David Copperfield,* as he later said, was his favorite child, this was nonetheless his first. On various occasions in its pages one feels—or anyway, I feel—the excitement of someone finding out how powerful ("power" was to become his favorite word for his creative gift[81]), this story-making business can be, how considerable a thing it is to be master of it. (Tellingly, this power is a major theme of the novel: Mr. Brownlow's life-canceling absorption in books, the true-crime tale that spreads and grows to bring down Sikes, the book of wicked tales with which Fagin expects to pervert Oliver, and so on.) But where did that power come from? The common charge was that he pandered to the public, but *Oliver Twist* came as much from the depths as from the street, from something farther back than the reading public, most of it, could guess—simply the darkest, historically most compelling story in Christian tradition, a story at whose heart is a precise inversion of Christian *caritas:* instead of Christ risen and the human race forgiven, Christ cannibalized and the chosen race condemned. *The* black reverse of *the* story.

Dickens had, as everyone knows, his own demons, but none of them were Jewish. Making them Jewish gave him a story, a great story.[82] If he was never much of an anti-Semite himself, his storytelling instincts sensed how anti-Semitism's legacy would add juice. He was right. Pickwick and Weller made him famous; Oliver and Fagin made him unstoppable. From then on he was the ages storyteller-in-chief.

That he was, again, on the verge of understanding what he had done is made fairly clear in the book's ending. One Christ stand-in is enough for any book, and Fagin does not step into Oliver's sandals. Nonetheless David Wilkes has, I think, a point when he says that the Fagin who is conveyed from courtroom to cell suddenly becomes, for a short spell, like the Jesus of Calvary, spat on and shrieked at by a Christian throng exemplifying everything ugly in the word "mob."[83] The author who wrote that scene knew what he was doing, knew how shocking it was, even momentarily, to turn Antichrist into Christ. And as is often the case, the most shocking moment in this transfiguration is presented as unfaceable—a visitation, delivered involuntarily by someone who immediately thereafter covers his ears, shuts his eyes, and paces about "like one distracted:"

> "You should have heard the people groan," said Chitling; "the officers fought like devils, or they'd have torn him away. He was down once, but they made a ring round him, and fought their way along. You should have seen how he looked about him, all muddy and bleeding, and clung to them as if they were his dearest friends. I can see 'em now, not able

to stand upright with the pressing of the mob, and dragging him along amongst 'em; I can see the people jumping up, one behind another, and snarling with their teeth and making at him; I can see the blood upon his hair and beard, and hear the cries with which the women worked themselves into the centre of the crowd at the street corner, and swore they'd tear his heart out!" (341)

"Swore they'd tear his heart out": again, Fagin has a point about "butcher." Little Sir Hugh, in some versions, is butchered.

Although sometimes undecided about capital punishment itself, Dickens never equivocated about his loathing for the passions it brought out in the spectators. One would have to go awfully far to find any more pitiful, pitiless words than these, about the citizenry gathering around Fagin's scaffold:

> From early in the evening until nearly midnight, little groups of two and three presented themselves at the lodgegate, and inquired, with anxious faces, whether any reprieve had been received. These being answered in the negative, communicated the welcome intelligence to the clusters in the street, who pointed out to one another the door from which he must come out, and showed where the scaffold would be built, and, walking with unwilling steps away, turned back to conjure up the scene. (362)

This is written as if it were about a royal wedding. "Two or three" gathered together, scripture tells us, make a church. Pointing out places of interest to one another is something tourists do, or locals in some festivity. And what can one say, on hearing that "anxious" inquiries about someone else's chances for life are met with "welcome intelligence," by those who can only regretfully take their fond eyes from where he should be appearing next? "Irony" may be the word we reach for, but there should really be some other word.

The man writing this knows the import of what he has been writing. In the 1841 edition, a mob, the type of mobs to follow, brings down Oliver, trying to escape from Fagin's minions. This is how it reads:

> Stopped at last. A clever blow that. He's down upon the pavement, round upon the heap of faces that surrounded him.[84]

"A clever blow that": the speaker is us, *hypocrites lecteurs*. To paraphrase another, later writer, the man who wrote that is someone whose eye has seen what his hand did.

Appendix 1.1: Oliver and Lincoln

The question of Oliver's birthplace is a thorny one. No single candidate satisfies all accounts. The first installment of what was to evolve into *Oliver Twist* was set in "Mudfog," Dickens's fictional version of Chatham, and was intended to be the latest in a series of "Papers" based there. The name was soon deleted, and the locale moved north toward the Midlands.

Still, David Paroissien has argued vigorously that the initial setting continues to linger. The town where *Oliver Twist* begins is on a river, and Chatham is on the Medway. According to the probably reliable testimony of Bumble, a body dropped into that river would be "twelve miles downstream" by the morning (255), and Chatham is approximately twelve miles from the Medway's mouth.[85] It is linked by canal to Birmingham, and so was Chatham. There are hills around Oliver's town, as there are around Chatham; Paroissien sees other topographical similarities as well. Ships' captains and coalheavers are evidently within reach, as one would expect in a place near the coast. Finally, Paroissien says, the coach journey recounted in chapter LI, completed between three o'clock and dinner, is realistic in London-to-Chatham terms, but not for any trip between London and the town, more than seventy miles to the north, from which Oliver is supposed to hail.[86]

On the other hand. As I have remarked, there may be a Lincolnshire note being sounded by "Claypole," one that would be consistent with what we see of Oliver's hometown, a singularly provincial place.[87] In this regard, anyway, that town would have more in common with Lincoln than with Chatham. If sea captains and other maritime types really are as thick on the ground as a Chatham locale would require, they have failed to bring with them any trace of either the cosmopolitanism or the rowdiness synonymous with ports. Chatham was sometimes called "the wickedest place in the world,"[88] a bustling center of ships, sailors, and soldiers;[89] Oliver's birthplace could not be more unlike. We meet no foreigners, merchants, or roisterers: in fact, the crowds of "drunken men" and women Oliver encounters in London are to him a new and shocking sight (49). Paroissien's thesis that sea captains inhabit the neighborhood rests on a single episode in which Bumble is "despatched" to locate one (20); Paroissien seems to have him completing the errand in "a morning's work," but as Philip Horne points out, that is a conjecture unsupported by the text,[90] and in any case Bumble never gets beyond "preliminary inquiries" (20).[91]

Like Chatham, Lincoln is on a river, the Witham. It is about thirty miles upstream from the seaport town of Boston, where Bumble presumably could have gone to make those inquiries of his. It is on a (single) hill, and Oliver's memory of his home is of "the hill," not "hills" (43). River and canal link it to Birmingham and other cities. Lincoln was once a major trading center, sending wool down the Witham to Boston for export, but by Dickens's time its mercantile eminence was a memory; the waterside of Oliver's town is a place of empty warehouses, ramshackle settlements of "old worm-eaten ship-timber," and down-and-outs pretending to work at nonexistent river jobs (249, 251). Meanwhile, the Chatham of Dickens's time and Oliver's was booming.

Evidence about relative distances is fuzzy and perhaps inconsistent. Yes, Oliver is introduced "at three o'clock in the afternoon" traveling by carriage from London, and yes, he will reach his old home by dinner (347). This would be pertinent information if we knew when the journey began, but we don't. What we do know is that Bumble's earlier coach trip to London, going the other way, starts at six in the morning and arrives in time for him to take care of his charges, have dinner, and call on Brownlow, who is still up, receiving visitors, and sharing what seems to be some postprandial port with Grimwig (110–11). Twelve hours (if anything, probably more) would be about right, given an average coach speed of twelve miles an hour[92] and allowing for stage stops, and the distance should then be somewhere over a hundred miles.

We are also told, near the end, that Oliver's mother died in Bumble's workhouse after taking ill while "on her way" to her lover's grave in Rome (354), therefore to a ship that would take her to the continent. Her exact origin is unclear, but we do know that she lived most of her life in the vicinity of Chester, a town on the border between England and the northeast edge of Wales, and that shortly before her journey her father had moved the family "into a remote corner of Wales" (351). We do not know just which "corner" this was, but if it was anywhere in the area nearest her old home—that is, somewhere in the north of Wales—the logical port for her to head to, assuming it was still functioning, would have been Boston, almost due east across England at almost its narrowest width, along a route that would have taken her through Lincoln.[93] (Actually, that would have been the closest port coming from any point halfway down the Welsh promontory.) A tramp to Dover (or Chatham), nearly twice as far away, would have been crazy.

Finally, there is the matter of the milestone, giving the distance to London as seventy miles, which Oliver reaches on the first day of his flight from home (44). The description of how he arrives at it has caused some confusion. First, "It was eight now; and though he was nearly five miles away from the town, he ran, and hid behind the hedges by turns, till noon, fearing that he might be pursued and overtaken" (44); only then does he come upon the milestone. Some have added the two numbers together and concluded that Oliver's home is seventy-five miles north of London, but that overlooks the four hours of flight between eight and noon. (The season is winter [45], the place somewhere near the fifty-third parallel, and he has set out at a daybreak [43], which would not, in winter, have occurred before seven a.m.) Given that, twenty or so miles in four hours' time seems, I would say, well within the range of the possible. Alas, that would still put his starting point somewhere around twenty miles south of Lincoln. Although there may be some stretch available there, I cannot honestly claim twenty miles' worth. I can only point out that Dickens makes clear his wish, "for many reasons," to refrain from specifying the town in question (1). If only because you ought to have something in mind before you can start to obfuscate about it, I would suggest that he seems to have a fairly definite idea of what he is keeping from us, along with a fairly elastic idea of what he should tell us about its coordinates. So, to review: it is a town, not a village or a city, on a hill, not hills. It is inland, but to its east probably within reach of a port by way of its river. To the south it is a seven days' walk or one day's long coach ride to London, from the west a spot some pedestrian might pass through on her way to embarking for the continent. Its economy is agricultural, but still shows signs of a time when it was a major trading center. As far as my inquiries have been able to take me, the only town close to meeting these specifications is Lincoln.

CHAPTER 2

"Thankee, Mum," Said Toodle, "Since You *Are* Suppressing"

> But language has a great part in dreams. I think, on waking, the head is usually full of words.
>
> —Charles Dickens[1]

I.

Like *Vanity Fair,* also published in the interesting year of 1848, *Dombey and Son* is a silver-fork novel in reverse, written out of a spirit of contempt for its genre and for the lot that genre celebrates. The young gentlemen of Dr. Blimber's academy—each of whom owns, as it happens, a "massive silver fork" (154[2])—are preparing to assume their estates by learning and forgetting the dead languages of empires past. At dinner, their headmaster edifies them with tales of "the days of the Emperors, . . . when whole provinces were ravaged to supply the splendid means of one Imperial Banquet" (155). The venue for these silver-fork doings is Brighton, late site and center of the time when, as Cousin Feenix remembers, "men lived very freely" (822). This living freely, we are here and there reminded, was mainly a matter of four-bottle men (821), of "bucks" throwing wine glasses over their heads "by the dozens" (284), of the prodigiously corrupt Duke of York, his fat friend the Prince Regent, and the Prince Regent's very own Brighton Royal Pavilion, whose image adorns the workbox of one Brighton resident (102) and whose legacy of wretched excess is still on show in the shaky specimen of Cousin Feenix himself, joined occasionally by such fellow veterans of the age as gouty Major Bagstock, moony Miss Tox, the grotesquely coquettish Mrs. Skewton, and the "superannuated beau" glimpsed giving away his daughter to her superannuated groom (59).

Especially when Mrs. Skewton gets to quoting Byron, there is a distinct note of comeuppance being sounded in Dickens's portraiture of these leftovers from a time even grosser than his own. "Beau," indeed. It is as if some cultural conservative of the present were to make an admonitory show out of the more drug-wasted relics of Woodstock or Studio 54.

Counterpointing this roster, predictably, come exempla of proletariat vigor and virtue. It is not accidental that, when the purse-proud Mr. Dombey, who has always "habitually looked over the vulgar herd, not at them" (273), is knocked unconscious, he should be carried to safety by "certain menders of the road" (576) emerging out of the ranks he "habitually" considers beneath his notice, or that when he goes bankrupt his financial survival should be secured, once again anonymously, by the bottom-level clerk he has patronized and dismissed. Throughout *Dombey and Son,* wealth and health, including social health, do not trickle down. If anything, they percolate up.

As is often the case in Dickens, literal cohabits with figurative: real fountains and springs are much in evidence, almost always as signs of beneficent bounty, whereas precipitations are irksome. The upper classes go to spas to take the waters bubbling up; the lower orders get rained on. The rich need the poor to sustain them from underneath, but whether the poor have any comparable use for the rich remains in question. Mr. Dombey's bankruptcy apparently causes little more than inconvenience to his employees and servants, who, being useful sorts, find places elsewhere; he alone is left at a loss. The prevailing relationship between the two classes looks less two-way symbiotic than top-down parasitic.

That relationship is established, in the second chapter, with a tableau of class-driven exploitation that Engels might have underwritten. Phiz's illustration captures the fundamentals (Illustration 1).

On the right side are two exiguous ladies, "weazen" (687) Miss Tox and brittle Mrs. Chick, both dry as sticks, both upholstered in mourning and ribbons. On the left are one blooming, beaming young man; two blooming, beaming young women (one the wife, the other her sister); and five blooming, "apple-faced" infants ranging in age from six weeks to about five years. Behind the family group on the left stands an open door; behind the two ladies on the right depends—"like a monstrous tear" (24), like a Damoclean sandbag, like a dead baby in a sack, like something lumpish hanged till dead and left to hang some more—a muffled-up "chandelier or lustre" (24): light, sacked up. As for daylight, the two tenebrous ladies have their backs to it; the newcomers are standing in it. They are standing upright, with the woman holding the infant

Illustration 1 "Miss Tox Introduces 'The Party'"

marking the apex of a rough compositional pyramid that slopes downward across the heads of the two ladies in black, one of them weirdly contorted and the other, apparently, sitting at attention.

The latter is in command—but not necessarily for long. For one thing, she and her friend are outnumbered, eight to two, and the picture makes as clear as it can that the ratio will only increase. Husband and wife are obviously delighted with their children, who have been arriving with the near-maximum frequency of one a year, and are not about to let the borderline poverty evidenced by patches on trousers and aprons dissuade them from having more. (They will, in fact, continue reproducing at about the same rate.) After all, on inspection the young wife, in contrast with her desiccated interviewers, appears to be buxom and broad of hip, and shows no signs of duress from her history of annual deliveries. For his part, the young husband has, on closer inspection, the ear of a satyr.[3] A domestic satyr.

The contrast points to why they are here. They are here to be milked, at the behest of the dry sticks under the bagged light, who accordingly want visible proof of rude animal health. Specifically, the mother is here to be milked by the new Dombey heir, having been recruited for that purpose from a lying-in hospital, which "encouraged its poorer clients to gain employment as 'wet-nurses'."[4] The children are here as proof that the milk will be of good quality and that the breed is sound, that the newborn Dombey will suffer "no contamination from the blood of the Toodles" (46); it is therefore a matter of importance that the blister on one child's nose is "not constitutional" (16)—not, for instance, venereal. The husband is here to serve as a guarantor of legitimacy, to authorize his newborn's enforced detachment from what Mrs. Chick, in a different context, calls "its natural nourishment" (83), and to agree to his own protracted detachment from Polly, lest marital relations with her contaminate the milk source.[5]

To keep her commandeered springs in full flow, the new wet nurse will be given all the porter she can drink, along with any food not likely to raise the acidity level of her discharge (21). "Discharge" is, so help me, the term applied to her office by Mr. Dombey (18), whose tin ear in these matters also allows him, in almost the same breath, to forbid her to "become attached" to the child soon to be sucking her nipples (18). Once that business is over, and the woman is—his word, again— "discharged," she is to detach herself permanently from the child she has nursed to health and return to the child she is now, for the duration, forbidden to visit, Dombey not being one to stand for any unauthorized withdrawals from his hired-out milk bank. Money will make all this possible.

Shelley, in a famous poem, likened the Regency regime to leeches, sucking the life out of the commons. *Dombey and Son* is of a later age, but one in which, as the Brighton sojourns recall, some things obviously haven't changed, at least not enough. One point as clear to bourgeois novelist as it was to radical poet is that this state of affairs may not continue indefinitely. Those Lucullan pig-outs admired by Dr. Blimber were, so Dickens's educated readers, reared on Gibbon, would have believed, one reason for Rome's decline and fall. Again: "Whole provinces were ravaged" to supply one banquet—and so, too, in the Dombey age, the dispossessed from England's own provinces are being "swallowed up" by its own capital, are "food for the hospitals, the churchyards, the prisons, the river" (462). In a novel where some people go hungry, there are a lot of meals, especially the expensive ones, left uneaten; the most expensive of all is notable mainly for all the food it lets go to waste (435).

II.

Clearly, the material is at hand here for a tract for the times, one deploring the materialistic and mechanistic expropriation of natural powers, mother's milk turned into money and so on. But *Dombey and Son* is not a simple novel, and although there are times when it tends toward didacticism, it has a way of complicating and undermining what can otherwise seem its own most fervent preachings. Cash nexus or no cash nexus, Polly Toodle will prove a loving nurse to Mr. Dombey's child, whose last request will be to see her, and her own children will continue to thrive despite her absences; the one exception, ironically, will come to grief through Mr. Dombey's well-meant attempt to help him get on. Although certainly attuned to the temper of its time, overall, *Dombey and Son* winds up being less ideologically engagé than, for instance, *Oliver Twist, Nicholas Nickleby, Hard Times,* and perhaps two or three other Dickens novels.

Exhibit A in this regard is the advent of the railroad, certainly one the novel's major subjects and a topic of intense political controversy at the time. On this central subject, *Dombey and Son* is notoriously hard to pin down. The railroad is shown making some things (probably) better and others (perhaps) worse, and there is no clear critical consensus as to how the pluses and minuses balance out. One can easily imagine a classroom discussion based on the question, "Is the railroad of *Dombey and Son* a force for good or evil?" It is not something one would likely ask about, say, *The Octopus.*

The same goes, I would venture, for its handling of capitalism and imperialism, both significant subjects for the book, but neither given any satisfactory ideological spin. About the former, George Orwell was right: you cannot make Dickens out, or at least not, if you have any stake in the issue, in a way you are likely to find gratifying. And when it comes to imperialism, Dickens seems to view what many would call the most significant geopolitical fact of his time, the expansion of the British Empire, as close to being a matter of indifference—good when it is good, bad when it isn't, in any case not the main point. For him, the main point is, always and obviously, the people of England. Those who like the Mrs. Jellyby of *Bleak House* direct their attention to the fates of natives in foreign climes, under British rule or not, to the neglect of the children around them, are just not understanding the eternally valid dictum that charity begins at home. Dr. Blimber is silly to admire the Roman Empire, but the big problem is what he is doing to the children of England.

The same resistance to ideological imperatives applies to what might seem to be the most important issue raised: patriarchy. Dombey is wrong to shut his daughter out of the firm (and family) for being female, but as of the happy ending that firm is still being managed, this time successfully, by men. Feminist issues, although not exactly irrelevant to the action, are marginalized(frustratingly so, it can sometimes seem, given what modern readers, and, I venture, at least some female readers of the time, would have welcomed). If anything, *Dombey and Son* seems written in resistance to such wishes.

Instead, the Midas-and-match-girl discrepancies, though certainly present, tend to accrue from the margins, by increment and indirection—as when an agitated Miss Tox starts snipping away at her house plants "with as little favour as a barber working at so many pauper heads of hair" (399), or when an heiress, Florence, forced to exchange her finery for rags, is startled to find that few people see her, "or if they did, believed that she was tutored to excite compassion, and passed on" (76). Signs of injustices like these, certainly numerous enough and real enough, are typically by-the-way, subordinated to other matters. In *Dombey and Son,* such evidence is not, as a rule, advertised, by author or by any other considerable character. It is something one has to pick up and put together, on one's own, bit by bit.

In fact, that it is not on the surface is a main—I will be arguing, *the* main—point of this novel, which is all about how what matters has been occulted, marginalized, and, especially, pushed under. It is not just that some people have been suppressed. So have their stories, along with the language in which those stories would have been told. The process at work, and the other processes it brings forth, are pervasive, literally part of the landscape. Those springs and fountains watering the retreats of the rich have their cautionary counterparts in the "wells" (143—actually, fireplaces, perpetually unlit) secreting their blighting subterranean chill into every room of Blimber's home. The H. G. Wells who reportedly derived the idea for *The Time Machine*'s sunken cylinders, leading its submerged cannibals up to their overbred prey, from his memory of the ventilating shafts in the underground passageways through which servants, including his mother, carried dainties into the master's mansion,[6] probably would have had a fair idea, when he read *Dombey and Son,* of what to make of them. Money can tame and make accessible the hot springs of Leamington and Baden-Baden, but it can also, when it sets to digging up a working-class neighborhood in order to open a train line, yield something, in these Chartist days, worryingly similar but different: "Hot springs and fiery eruptions, the usual attendants upon earthquakes"(65). Although the real subterranean geography of England is hardly so thermally volatile that one might expect a geyser or volcano to erupt from any random excavation, the reader of *Dombey and Son* learns to expect just that kind of result. Explosions, as much as benisons, work themselves upward. It is fitting that Mrs. Pipchin, for most of its length the book's standard example of ruined fortune, should have lost her money in mines; those mines were the other-side-of-the-medal counterpart to the road menders who rose up from their ground-level trade, invisible beneath his horse's hooves, to rescue Dombey.

III.

Consider, along this line, one extremely strange eruption—a mainly humanoid one, in slow motion. Around the middle of the novel, a triple instance of reversed repression appears to James Carker, who is, not coincidentally, along with his master Dombey, one of the two most (in the modern sense) repressed characters of the book. First, he comes upon Edith Dombey, visibly fuming—head trembling, breast heaving, tears starting out, in language that without much alteration could do duty for earthquake or geyser—the reason being she is about to be sold into marriage (by Carker, among others). Then there appears a crone, one who will eventually help kill Carker, and who here starts up, having "scrambled up from the ground—out of it, it almost appeared" (370). Third in the ensemble is "the trunk of one large tree, on which the obdurate bark was knotted and overlapped like the hide of a rhinoceros or some kindred monster of the ancient days before the flood" (369).

Now, for some reason, this tree is important. It and its setting will be referred to hereafter, typically in tones implying profound significance. Why? I don't really know. As we will see, *Dombey and Son* includes many cases (what the "waves are saying" is certainly one) of unresolved or uncertainly resolved portent. Still, what with language like "monster" and "before the flood," it obviously means *something*.

Perhaps one approach would be to ask why it is introduced when and where it is. Given the players on the scene, I would suggest that, first, the underground force thus evoked is sexual, and, second, that its "obdurate" emergence is of a piece with other uprisings, real and threatened, from beneath, against the novel's interlocking forces of repression.

That first hypothesis would at least help explain what the tree is doing in this place and time. It presides over the spot where Carker, contemplating how he may most expeditiously deliver one woman into the bed of his employer, is recognized by another woman, the one seeming to come out of the ground, as the man who debauched her daughter. A fortune-teller with a long memory, she is showing up at a conjunction of sexual violations, both ghost of bad-sex past and spirit of bad-sex future. Her name is Marwood. If we allow—surely no great stretch—that the Victorians were capable of recognizing a tree, particularly one so "obdurate" and rhinoceronian, as perhaps having something to do with what *Finnegans Wake* calls the "mythiphallic," we may suspect that the name "Marwood" is not without a certain Restoration-Comedy suggestiveness. After all, the man this Marwood is addressing will turn out to be the most sex-obsessed of the book, someone who at the height of his lust will want only to "root" the woman he desires (729). And that woman is Edith, whom he has helped secure for Dombey's bed, who will in that bed be traumatized by her husband's callousness, and who, when she tells that husband she is not going to sleep with him anymore, will give as her reason that "every sentiment that blesses marriage, or justifies it, is rooted out" (545).

"Root" is a word with a checkered history. In the 1749 *Fanny Hill*, the pornographic classic that, as Joss Lutz Marsh has shown,[7] Dickens has incorporated into this novel, it always denotes an erection—that is (and *Fanny Hill* certainly makes this clear), a penis made rigid with congested blood. And either the obdurate tree in question or one near it (I can't make out which) is described, in this same scene, as an "old tree" with a "veinous root" (371). (Not, note, "roots": don't trees, as a rule, have "roots," in the plural?) And there are other veins cited in *Dombey and Son*, particularly those perennially swelling the flushed, turgid, overheated face of Major Bagstock, an old man of much-vaunted barky toughness, who periodically becomes apoplectic and explodes, whose name, Steven Marcus has suggested, "conceals a sexual pun,"[8] and who is, like Carker, Dombey's appendage.

Well. Let it be conceded that the reading offered in the last paragraph is, in one sense at least, far-fetched. (I am, anyway, not at all sure about that Bagstock bit.) It is far-fetched in the sense of relying on material dispersed throughout remote reaches of the book. But, whether or not this convinces, that is how repressed truth, the truth that matters most, is, in *Dombey and Son*. Under the force of repression it gets shattered and scattered about, like the bones of Osiris. When the storm-tossed Walter Gay is thought lost at sea, Sol Gills tracks him down by going from port to far-flung port, picking up a bit of news here and a possible lead there. He understands that seeking out the hidden is a business of hunting and gathering. And that is certainly true, in this self-consciously Victorian production, about sexual reality. It is unquestionably there—critical, in fact, to most if not all of the book's turning points—but underground, like a "root." Indeed it constitutes a kind of textual underground, discernible mainly by way of equivocal surface features whose significance must be assayed through attentive survey, detection, and sometimes a certain amount of speculation.

For instance: I have just made some harsh generalizations about Dombey's bedroom manner—that it is so callous as to leave his wife traumatized. Of course, we never get to see that directly. What we get instead are off-hand reports, typically conveyed as ancillary to something else, for instance about Edith's evening dinings-out, always without her husband's company, and her late returns home. We are allowed to learn that husband and wife have separate bedrooms, and to infer that he is not lately much used to seeing the inside of hers. We hear Carker's taunt when Edith spurns his advances: "Come, Edith. To your husband, poor wretch, this was well enough" (724). Along with that remark about how all connubial feelings have been "rooted out," there is Edith's memory of her wedding night as a "struggle...in which I wish I had died" (628) and her final refusal to "submit myself wholly to your will" (628). (As Shakespeare, for one, made clear, "will" is another word with a shady past; "die," too.) As I have suggested elsewhere, there is also the telling moment, on the return from their honeymoon, when Dombey sights Edith, with Florence, being warmly affectionate in a way "new to him" (485), and, before that, a displaced weather report of the wedding night itself, its double entendres conveying a story of assault and resistance, resentment and estrangement.[9]

Above all, there is one major piece of negative evidence, whose significance, as usual, must be gathered from remote places. Edith never becomes pregnant. Normally, this would be unremarkable in a marriage of a relatively short duration. In *Dombey and Son,* however, it says a great deal. Dombey has purchased Edith as his bride for the purpose of producing an heir to replace the one recently lost. He commences his courtship upon ascertaining from Major Bagstock that Edith is around thirty (of childbearing age), a widow (respectable: neither old maid nor damaged goods), who has had a child (is not infertile) who was male (an heir!) but has lost it (no non-Dombey rival) in an accident (no "constitutional" defect in that line) that was not her fault (not careless in such matters [286]). All that settled, he wants value for money. Has he not secured the services of Doctor Parker Peps, a court physician "of immense reputation for assisting at the increase of great families" (4)? Has he not the right to expect, as with his first wife, that "the hope of giving birth to a new partner in such a house, could not fail to awaken a glorious and stirring ambition in the breast of the least ambitious of her sex" (2)? ("Stirring" is what babies, poetically, do, in wombs.) Does he not, for their honeymoon, take her to Paris, known to be conducive to such transactions? He has obviously, as his sister would put it, made an effort. But it is all no-go. Something is wrong.

That becomes even more evident when Mr. and Mrs. Dombey are put up against the field, one that may perhaps begin with the first of that family-increasing "court physician" Doctor Peps's patients, the queen, who gave birth six times during the eight years between her marriage and this novel's publication. It certainly includes those baby-a-year Toodles, along with the Perches—Mrs. Perch's seriatim pregnancies are a running joke—and Florence herself, who returns with a child about one year after her marriage and has produced another by novel's end. There is also every sign that it will include Mr. Toots and his bride, pregnant at the shortest decent interval after their marriage, like Florence possessed of two children as the book concludes, and, if Mr. Toots has anything to say about it, due for many more (831).

In his prospects for making good on this ambition, Mr. Toots, a kind of anti-Dombey in this regard at least, has exactly the right spirit. In *Dombey and Son,* a man's moral worth can be measured by his regard for women, and Toots is probably the man who adores women most. He first adores Florence, and then, when his clumsy overtures don't pan out, her maid, who in time responds, reciprocates, and, of course, reproduces. And that, it seems, is the key. There is a coy phrase, running through Dickens's letters, to describe wives who seem to be pregnant all the time. He calls them "ladies who love their Lords."[10] He means, most obviously, that they desire to have intercourse with their husbands, and second—a logical enough inference from the first—that they enjoy it. The enjoyment is essential. *Dombey and Son* apparently subscribes to the venerable belief, under critical scrutiny in its day but still widely held, that for conception to occur, orgasm is as necessary for the woman concerned as it is for the man.[11] Intercourse, so the idea went, induces warmth, which if mutual, and only if mutual, will induce ovulation at the right moment.

Certainly those two exemplary breeders already introduced, the rosy-faced Mr. and Mrs. Toodle, would seem to support this thesis. Mr. Toodle, in particular, is the "cindery and swart" (for heaven's sake) "stoker" of engines (one of them, for heaven's sake again, shown repeatedly "plunging" into tunnels (276)), with (maybe) the satyr's ear, the red cheeks, and the fiery interior, a drinker of (hot) tea and smoker of (burning) pipe, forever "tearing through the countryside": "He was always in a whirlwind or a calm, and a peaceable contented easy-going man Mr. Toodle was in either state, who seemed to have made over all his own inheritance of fuming and fretting to the engines with which he was connected, which panted, and gasped, and chafed, and wore themselves out, in a most unsparing manner, while Mr. Toodle led a mild and equable life" (512).[12] Well, of course he does. Mr. Toodle—as contrasted, for instance, with frigid Dombey and blocked Carker—is a picture of powerful drives, regularly released. And why not? He adores his woman; she adores him; both delight in the offspring being produced by their mutual exchanges of warmth. Mr. Perch, for his part, is ludicrously uxorious with Mrs. Perch, who reciprocates. Toots worships his wife, who has come to love him back. Florence really loves her husband, and he really loves her. All the parties in this proliferant catalogue, when they go to bed with their spouses, want to be there. That, in *Dombey and Son,* is how people have babies.

So Dombey, without heir after two marriages, is, by deduction among other things, probably a sexual brute,[13] one no sensitive woman could warm to. The "obdurate" tree is there in part to tell us something about that side—that underside—of him. And all this must be conveyed indirectly, both the nice bits and the naughty ones, of which latter there are quite a few. For instance: Florence, depicted throughout as a fluttering dove, sets sail with her young man on their honeymoon ship, which ship is (772) "spreading its white wings to the favouring wind." Hm. Miss Tox, the book's resident old maid, a scissor-wielding snipper of houseplants with wanly romantic designs on the senior Paul Dombey, at one point (89) takes "the little Paul in her arms...making his cockade perfectly flat and limp with her caresses." Hm, again.

At least in the second instance, Dickens is probably having some fun of the sort that crops up elsewhere in his books—with Master Bates, for instance. But *Dombey and Son* represents a departure, I think, in both the extent of such divagations and in its way of making them integral to its texture and its dynamics, in fact to the whole business of reading it right. The deforming pressures exemplified by that "veinous" tree are at the heart of how things happen in this book. They control the characters, the narrative they propel, and, above (or rather beneath) all, the language in which that narrative is rendered.

The effects include, but go beyond, the familiar repressions of Victorian prudery—the smell of horse manure a "fragrant air" (88), pants called "inexpressibles" (37), pregnancy "an interesting situation" (423), hell "another place" (433), and so on. By themselves played, usually, for laughs, such moments nonetheless have their place in a systemic denial of the real, and can have tragic as well as comic consequences. Paul Dombey dies, in part, because his father cannot acknowledge the facts of life embodied in Polly Toodle.

Such evasions arise out of one of the novel's laws—that the capacity for saying something is inversely proportional to how much it matters. Mrs. Skewton, at the end, cannot abide to hear the word "die"—she could speak it herself easily enough when feeling chipper (379)—precisely because she *is* dying (548). Florence's inability to express her love for her father is a function of its intensity. When Miss Tox refers to Captain Cuttle as "the gentleman with the—Instrument" (135), it is not because she doesn't realize that the instrument is a hook, but because she does. This is not just a condition of the book's hypocrites. In all their varieties of vice or virtue, people are ostriches. Florence, distracted, runs "anywhere, to hide her head" (638); when stationary, she is given to burying her face in her hands. Mrs. Skewton employs her hand-screen to the same end. Absent such accessories, "half-shut eyes" can serve the same screening function (146). Edith's eyelashes are her last line of defense. There is accordingly a good deal of lying, to self and others, among both good and bad. Although not as pervasive as in *Bleak House*, where it is close to being the only game in town, as in that other novel the lying of *Dombey and Son* seems to antithetically generate a character—there Tulkinghorn, here Carker—whose scrupulous honesty is part and parcel of his villainy. Of all the book's characters, Carker has, in this sense, the most interesting relationship with the truth. The smartest person around, he understands instinctively what Conrad's Marlow means by "the convention that lurks in all truth and...the essential sincerity of falsehood."[14] He knows that there is nothing so revealing—so sincere, in its way—as a lie. That is one reason why most people in *Dombey and Son* make a point of not detecting one another's lies, however obvious: it would be like suddenly seeing someone naked. Mrs. Skewton's lies about death show that she knows she is dying, an unfaceable fact that everyone (except the odious Bagstock) avoids recognizing; Florence's lies about her father tell anyone interested (and Carker is interested) where you can wound her.

Carker himself chances no giveaways of that sort; his, rather, is a strategy of at least comparatively full disclosure. Mr. Morfin, looking over the firm's accounts, is surprised to find that, far from cooking the books, Carker left the record of his perfidy "plain and clear" (714). His distinguishing feature is his teeth, always bared in a smile that is always really a snarl. It's not his fault if the others won't see it.

IV.

That kind of naked-is-the-best disguise strategy can work in an environment like this one, where the grounds of communication, like the ground itself, is perennially uncertain, subject to change. That good people tell so many lies and Carker tells so much truth just goes to show how equivocal truth is, how shaky is its purchase on anything solid. That is because there *is* nothing reliably solid. It reflects the undermined, earthquakey terrain as it is. Just leaving things alone will not help: nothing but the passage of time has "perplexed" the untrod carpet patterns in Dombey's house (311), rendered two notes of Miss Tox's harpsichord "dumb from disuse" (210–11), and made the long-stagnant minds of Mrs. Skewton and Cousin Feenix into the bric-a-brac attics they are. Active or passive, static or in motion, everything that matters in *Dombey and Son,* at some time or other, gets twisted and fractured. There are a shipwreck; two bankruptcies; a kidnapping made possible by an access of "wild confusion" (70); any number of calamitous deaths, sudden removals, and reversals of fortune; the "thunderbolt" of Edith's break; and of course the railroad's many disruptions of the physical world, including its temporal dimension: "There was even railway time observed in clocks, as if the sun itself had given in" (218). (Yes, and the great clock in the Blimbers' hall, sanctuary of classical verities, is taken to pieces.) Mrs. Skewton's death comes from a stroke, which leaves her in "pieces" (507). Dombey's house is first a museum, then a mortuary of shrouded forms, then a showcase of conspicuous consumption, then a denuded ruin; it is never any one thing long enough to become a home. Rivers flood parlors; snails stick to front doors. As so often in Dickens, children get knocked about all over the place, but, this time around, minus the expected note of authorial outrage: the child Florence, for instance, is routinely wrenched and jerked, poked and thumped by her maid, the entirely sympathetic Susan Nipper. It is just the way things are. Hearts break, and noses too, and that's life. Mr. Toots's companion the Game Chicken, the boxer whose face sports some new rearrangement at each reappearance, could be this novel's genius loci.

In keeping, the narrative moves from explosion to explosion, like an internal combustion engine—or rather like its forerunners, those steam engines "bubbling and trembling there, making the walls quake, as if they were dilating with the secret knowledge of great powers yet unsuspected in them, and strong purposes not yet achieved" (218). Those engines are the novel's main example of energy in action, which is in turn a matter of barely contained pressure, engendered out of primal elements (water plus heat, in turn the result of solar energy, long hidden underground in deposits of coal, being released by fire[15]), problematically channeled. It as if the hot springs that erupt from Staggs's Gardens when it is made over into a train center were being somehow bottled and compressed in boilers. And we are not allowed to long forget how explosive that energy is, how destruction always threatens and will, sooner or later, have its way (no generation of life, remember, without mutual climax), as when, in its extreme form, Carker is reduced to "mutilated fragments" (743) (like Mrs. Skewton's "pieces") courtesy of one such engine.

The novel's visits to Staggs's Gardens itself, first as neighborhood turned inside out by the earthquake of the new development, then so unrecognizably altered as to seem vanished altogether, testify to one contributing cause of these convulsive transformations. It is modern bourgeois capitalism, the engine behind the engines, the same force being simultaneously described by one other notable 1848 production: "It has accomplished wonders far surpassing Egyptian pyramids, Roman aqueducts, and Gothic cathedrals." That is the relatively good news: Staggs's Gardens is indeed rebuilt, along monumental lines, to general if not universal approval, and "great works and massive bridges" are going up all around the country as part of the same project (276). On the other hand: "All that is solid melts into air, all that is holy is profaned, and man is at last compelled to face with sober senses, his real conditions of life, and his relations with his kind." That is one of the things that Carker, lynx-eyed agent of a man who makes nothing but money, sees with total clarity. He sees this too: "The bourgeoisie has torn away from the family its sentimental veil, and has reduced the family relation to a mere money relation."[16] Polly Toodle and Edith Dombey, breasts for hire and uterus for sale, could tell us a thing or two on that score.

These quotations are, of course, from *The Communist Manifesto.* As a description of the social landscape of *Dombey and Son,* they are, certainly, to the point, but as a theoretical explanation of its causes, the document from which they come is not. Again: except in the debater's-point sense that everything uttered is, *Dombey and Son* is not a particularly ideological production. If anything, it seems to go out of its way to frustrate, at least, the most obvious of the formulaic reflexes that some of its material might otherwise invite. The exemplary Mr. Toodles, content enough already when introduced, will duly rise in his profession—as, of course, he should—without the intercession of any revolution. What is wrong with Mr. Dombey is, to a great extent, what was wrong with the Henry VIII under whose portrait he courts his second wife; the rise of bourgeois capitalism, intervenient between the two, has mainly served to put old wine in a new bottle. The novel's disorienting dislocations are not, on the whole, traceable to class and cash; massed capital accelerates, but does not transform, what was there all along.

And, most strikingly, Dombey is not a railroad man, not even—so far as we can tell—by investment. That is a remarkable fact, surely. The 1840s were boom-and-bust years for the railroads. The obvious course, for someone writing a novel such as this, would have been to make its number-one capitalist and number-one capitalist enterprise part of the same story. (Compare: *The Way We Live Now, Little Dorrit.*) Instead, one falls while the other continues forging ahead. The relation between the two is, if anything, mainly one of contrast. The railroad is a new technology that still has some problems to work out. Dombey *is* a problem, of a perennial kind.

Dombey and Son is no more about mankind's creations despoiling his natural inheritance than it is about the tyranny of capital or any other major human production. Trains and banks alike extend human capacity wonderfully, but there is little sign of their turning on their creators or taking over. Human agency remains intact, in part because humans turn out to be a very tough, determined breed. Major Bagstock's diet alone ought to have killed him several times over, but never does. It takes a train to kill Carker. For all his misadventures in the ring, the Game Chicken is so unfazed by the end that in desperation he resolves to try drinking himself to death. These are not, for the most part, creatures of the operations of machinery or money. For better and worse, they are obdurate organisms driven, like that rooted tree with its knotted grain, by deeper and older impulses. In another novel, the reason Sir Barnet and Lady Skettles put up with having their riverside home regularly flooded would probably be that waterfront property is prestigious and they want to show everyone that they own some. Here, although that may be part of the reason, a bigger part is that the Skettleses are human, and humanity, in *Dombey and Son,* is drawn to water. It is drawn and driven by all kinds of things, all of them entrenched forces that have been around for a long time, moving in vectors of desire and repulsion, to and from and around the landscape, engraving patterns that the railroad replicates but did not initiate. Those patterns are hardwired. When Mr. Toodle describes the movements of his mind in railroad terms—coming to a "branch" here, coupling on a "whole train of ideas" there (512–13)—he takes his metaphors from his trade but the facts from introspection. It is not mainly a case of the dyer's hand, nor yet of chicken and egg. Toodle's brain came first.

In one fantastic episode, in fact, a train has apparently been possessed by a human spirit. The train that kills Carker has the two "red eyes" first encountered, imbedded in the phrase "blea*red eyes*" (466: my italics); in the person of Mrs. Marwood, who has hated him from way back and initiated the sequence of events—the train of events, we might as well call it, in line with the author's practice—that bring man and machine together. It is her agent, her extension. Why else, after all, would Dickens give it those two eyes? (He may have gotten the idea from observation. See Illustration 2.)[17] Phiz, in his synoptic frontispiece, not only makes them eyes and nothing else but gives them pupils, focusing on their prey.

The train is Nemesis, and its eyes are Mrs. Marwood's (Illustration 3).[18]

That is an extreme case, but an instructive one. Trains are creatures of "strong purposes" because made by purposive beings. If, being machines, they move on wheels, well, so, in this book, do a number of characters too (Mrs. Skewton on her "wheeled chair" [280], Paul on his wheeled bed [110], the "little wooden house on wheels" in Dombey's dockyard [76], Cousin Feenix being run ahead "as on castors" [427])—reminding us that, even in this, humans came first. The same goes for the turntables on which engines reverse directions: "when the Doctor put out his right foot, he gravely turned upon his axis, with a semicircular sweep towards the left" (150). Above all, they travel in lines because people do, because people's minds do. There were one-track minds before James Watt came along. There were also "locomotive" sorts, like Walter (80), before there were locomotives, and human boilers, overpressurized types like "Spitfire" Susan Nipper and plethoric

Illustration 2 "The Railway Dragon"

Illustration 3 Detail from *Dombey and Son* frontispiece

pop-eyed Major Bagstock, before there were boilers. (Dickens himself often spoke of himself as a boiler, getting a head of steam up to write.) Twelve of the book's illustrations feature characters arranged in single or double file, or some character following in someone else's footsteps or lurking in someone's wake[19]—a fair representation of how its characters typically travel. They move that way because their minds move that way—as Dombey, "pondering," "tracing figures in the dust with his stick," illustrates (278). So does Diogenes the dog, next to trains the book's simplest index of primal urgings, when, reaching toward an out-of-range object, he stretches out "at the full length of his tether" (253), drawing a straight line from where he is to where he wants to be.

The train is an extension of the way people work, which is in turn a function of the way things work, which is to move from one point to another along lines and in lines, usually consisting of units linked together, either by design (people in this book are forever linking arms to march in double file) or according to built-in billiard-ball principles of causality. Action, typically, is a chain reaction.

The kind of accelerating momentum to which such a principle lends itself is one reason the book contains so many runaways and collisions. Carker's brother John fears that he can see Walter slipping "a little and a little lower" into the "headlong" fall that wrecked his own life (179), and in Dickens's original scheme he would have been proven correct. (Instead, Dickens has Walter surviving a shipwreck and rescuing men at sea, a course that we are to understand was determined by the tales of nautical derring-do in which he was inculcated as a boy (42–43)—an alternate course of sustained momentum.) Polly's boy Rob, packed off to the Charitable Grinders, is early on literally forced into skulking in "narrow passages and back streets" (70), setting in motion a habit of deviousness from which he never, until the very end, emerges. Similarly, life-altering courses can follow from accidental deflections of direction. Delivering the mail, Walter happens to drop a letter written in Florence's (cursive, connective) handwriting, therefore displeasing to Mr. Dombey, who therefore assigns him to the West Indies post just mentioned by his manager as an ideal station for getting rid of displeasing people. Later he thinks better of it, but it's too late: the same manager has set the train-of-thought engendered train of events in action, with consequences almost leading to Walter's death.[20]

The language that people speak enacts both the fact of this tracks-leading-to-tracks world and, at its most developed, their synchronization with it. Edith's final repudiation of Carker, for instance, is an impressively Ciceronian sentence comprising 151 words, including nine dependent clauses and other clauses within clauses, plus appositions and prepositional phrases, the gist of which is that the sight of him reminds her of when he kissed her, which in turn reminds her of when Florence encountered her with the "taint" of that kiss on her and she realized that in seeking to free Florence from one chain of consequences, "the persecution I had caused her by my love," she had initiated another, the "shame and degradation [brought] on her name through mine," in yet another series of links that would last for "all time to come" (728). The syntax and the concatenation of consequences it recounts—link, link; branch, branch—are of a piece. People, especially Edith, Carker, and Dombey himself, habitually think or try to think that way in this book because that is how things are perceived to happen. The world has its grammar, a train grammar of individual units (letters, words) coupling up into molecular composites and propelled, with varying degrees of success, in a fixed path to some definite place. In both cases, it is a worrisome thing when the couplings give way and the units break free. Carker is partly killed by the letter "J," detached from one shred, also detached, of an originally cohesive document. (He writes out "D-I-J-O-N" as part of a note to Edith giving directions for their assignation; she tears the note up; Rob retrieves the scrap with the town name and later spells it out for the vengeance-bent Dombey, one letter at a time. Rob gets through all five letters, but "J" is enough for Dombey to distinguish it from Dieppe, the only plausible alternative.) Walter's shipwreck and apparent death is confirmed by "the words and letters Son and H," found floating in the sea (447).

Such alphabetical fractionings of lexical continuity have their discursive counterpart in the tics and stammering disrupting the monologues and the interruptions (Mr. Dombey being the prime offender) chronically breaking up dialogues. They are the verbal versions of the collisions and fragmentations that take up so much of the book's action and define much of its characters' psychologies. Cornelia Blimber, whose father undertakes to atomize all learning into "names of things...a trifle of orthography, a glance at ancient history, a wink or two of modern ditto" (161), is both following in his footsteps and exhibiting a symptomatic mental map when she shows up with scraps of playbill advertisements erupting here and there from the curlpapers in her hair (195). Another product of the same alphabet soup environment is Mr. Toots, he of the exploded brain and stammering incoherencies, who at one point tries to compose an acrostic poem on the name "Florence" and never gets past "F" (306).

V.

Mr. Toots, does, however, have his moment, and its signature is, significantly, syntactical. Near the novel's end, he is able to summon up the presence of mind to come out with this forceful sentiment, delivered to his wearisome attendant the Game Chicken: "'Chicken,' returned

Mr. Toots, 'after the odious sentiments you have expressed, I shall be glad to part on such terms'" (765). Before, such a sentence would have been beyond his verbal range. But now, having finally gotten over his fixation on Florence and found in its place the love of a good woman who loves him back, he has pulled himself together and achieved something approaching coherence. In this he is the mirror image of Mrs. Skewton, who goes the other way: "smashed" (the Major's word) speechless, her mute attempts at writing a matter of "wrong characters" seeming "to tumble out of the pencil of their own accord" (507). Mrs. Skewton, in pitting her petrified mannerisms against the currents of time, has earned her stroke, and with it the unintelligibility whose early warning signs were a tendency to mix up her syllables ("Granger" and "Dombey" becoming "Domber" and "Grangeby"), to "cut some of her words short" (547), and to wander off the track of her train of thought. By the same token, Toots has earned his access of coherence, by rolling with the punches life throws him (the Game Chicken may have taught him something, after all) and by adapting, over time, gradually.

The key word there is "gradually." The happy ending of Toots's story is made possible by his conversion to the principle of what the scientific debates of the time were calling uniformitarianism (change, especially geologic change, occurring by increments over long stretches of time) as opposed to catastrophism (major change a matter of sudden upheavals). It is a policy that political controversialists of a later age would call "gradualism,"[21] and an exemplary policy it is for *Dombey and Son*. Time and trouble teach Toots to take things one at a time, and that, in this book, is usually a good idea.

Consider his history. As a child he was half-cretinized by an educational system bent on forcing the maximum amount of material into his head as quickly as possible. (Cornelia's curlpapers are an outward and visible sign of the explosive results such a system can provoke.) Then he fell in love with a young woman out of his reach, blurted out his feelings, and had his heart broken. As part of that debacle he made a fool of himself several times, the crowning humiliation coming when he tried to snatch a kiss from Florence's maid Susan—the idea being that this would somehow help out his cause with her mistress—and was beaten back and laughed at.

Clearly, suddenness does not work for Toots. On the other hand, in the second half of his narrative, step-by-step does. He winds up sharing a carriage with the same Susan who had fended off his surprise attack advances, falls into conversation, discovers their common devotion to Florence, invites her to dinner at his place (chaperoned, of course), and so on. Circumstances continue to bring them together, and in time, by degrees, he progresses from loving Florence to sharing Susan's love of Florence to loving Susan, as Susan in turn comes to pity, then admire, then prize him for his own devotion to the same—it turns out—mediating figure.

He has, in other words, been weaned, gradually. By contrast, the "sharp weaning" that blights and kills Paul Dombey (92)—his sudden cutting-off from mother, then nurse (his "Second Deprivation" [64]), then sister—establishes, early on, the novel's main model of how not to go about that sort of thing. Susan understands this: that is why, out of service and about to become a wealthy woman, she nonetheless puts on her old servant uniform in order to minister once more to her former mistress (817)—to mediate the large changes coming over both their lives, to make those changes less abrupt. (Amy Dorrit will do much the same for Arthur Clennam, near the end of *Little Dorrit*.) For her part, Florence will wean her father by degrees from his shattered state by gradually reconciling him to the song with which—in a earlier facilitation of tempered transition—she sang Paul to sleep: "He could not bear it at the time; he held up his trembling hand, imploring her to stop; but next day he asked her to repeat it, and to do so often of an evening; which she did" (819). The difference between Toots's first abortive lips-out lunge at Susan and the way that each later becomes slowly acclimatized to the other is the difference between how things shouldn't go between men and women and how they should, and the lesson applies equally to less comical matches. It applies, for instance, to the difference between the brutish headlong phallicism that "ruined" and "lacerated," respectively, the bed partners of Carker and Dombey, on the one hand (717, 724), and on the other, the drawn-out, near-book-length series of stages by which Walter and Florence pass, very, very slowly, from their chance encounter to that spread-wings consummation inaugurating their voyage around the world. Captain Cuttle may be right that from the first they were made for one another, like (speaking of wings) "two young doves" (448), but it still takes many years, and hundreds of pages, for them to work it out.

As with Toots and Susan—as with all the successful convergences and consummations of the book—that realization is facilitated by a series of mediations and substitutions. Walter gets to know Florence in the first place by way of his inner adoption of the storybook role of knight-errant rescuing a damsel in distress. As her rescuer and protector, he substitutes (for Florence) for the father who has spurned her; as her denominated brother (263); he takes the place of the dead Paul. Then history apparently repeats itself: presumed drowned, he becomes her second lost brother. There then follows a ridiculously drawn-out sequence of maneuvers, the whole point of which is that Florence must learn very gradually that he is alive, must be weaned from the conviction of his death. Chased from home, she returns to the old place where she and Walter were brother and sister. Hark! Diogenes the dog picks up a scent! He barks! It is, we will learn, the first detection of Walter's return, but Florence must not be told that. Instead she is told, repeatedly, by formerly lovable old Captain Cuttle, that her dear Walter is—get this through your head, sweetie—dead, dead, dead. Nothing in this novel, surely, is so discordant, so out of character and all-around off the wall, as the way Cuttle delights in reminding Florence that her Walter is "drownded, an't he?" He says it over and over; at one point he calls it through her keyhole. In any normal transaction between two real-life people, he would have been shot, and would have had it coming, too. But here it is all part of a plan whose culmination comes in his protracted process-of-elimination narrative of how everyone on Walter's ship was lost, except for some, a few, two, one, and that one... All the while, not yet Walter—not just yet—but first his shadow creeps and then looms across the wall... (Illustration 4).

Only then can he appear in the flesh. And it doesn't stop with that. There follows an emollient scene in which, after much dithering, Walter finally gets it that things have changed in other ways: "I left a child. I find a woman" (678). The two melt into one another's arms. Brother morphs into lover. They engage. But it is still not over. There are the marriage banns, three rounds of them. They drive Mr. Toots crazy, but—in the book's characteristic pattern—less so each time. And for the couple, they are occasions for joy. These two are no hot Shakespearean wooers, panting for the sun to set and the wedding night to be upon them. *Dombey and Son* is a novel in which banns are good. For one thing, as regulators of the gradient between celibacy and connubiality—the railroad builders of the time were concerned with gradients, too—they constitute good riddance to the sharp-elbows courtship of the bucks and the beaus. They are also guarantors of prolonged continuity. As with a train, the momentum builds up so slowly because the vehicle is so weighty. The long time it takes to get going forecasts the longer time it will keep moving on its set course.

And then, finally, they are married—in their way. First, they spend their wedding morning visiting (honestly, now) Paul's grave. Well, of course: it confirms the passing of the brotherly torch, and also sets the tone for the proceedings to follow. The church in which the ceremony takes place is a virtual tomb, including a sexton who at one point sets his

The shadow in the little parlor.

Illustration 4 "The Shadow in the Little Parlour"

grave digger's hat in the baptismal font (768)—an alpha-omega conjunction of the sort anticipated by the book's earlier weddings and funerals, every one of which features some reminder of the other. The couple set sail in a shipshape little cabin made as much as possible like Florence's little room in the shipshape shop she has just quitted: another soft transition, gentled through similitude. More transitional logic: shipping was integral to both Florence's father's and Walter's step-father's occupations; Paul's last visionary voyage was on waves; Walter has been hired as a supercargo, and a supercargo is someone who mediates between land business and sea business. Walter and Florence, finally coming together on that ship, have been brought, through prolonged operations of incremental adjustment and regulated displacement, to the point that their conjunction will implicate a blended resolution of many of the book's contraries—between man and woman, land and sea, sexuality and virginity, home and empire (China), generation and generation (she bears a child), life and death (her mother's daughter, Florence almost dies in childbirth), father and daughter (the child is a boy, named for her father), and brother and sister (it is also named for her brother).

The Florence and Walter courtship is the book's most extended case of what I have called its gradualism, but there are many others. In every major new relationship between one person and another, the relative sharpness or softness of their convergence or sundering is a matter of consequence, one enabled or otherwise by intermediaries. Lucretia Tox, with glimmering hopes of winning Mr. Dombey for a suitor, eases her way into his household by way of her acquaintance with his sister, Mrs. Chick. (Mrs. Chick, in turn, has her own hopes that such a match might make Dombey pay more attention to her, by way of her connection to Lucretia.) In time, her attendance on Paul Dombey Jr.—another intermediary—gets the attention of Paul Dombey Sr. and earns the "token" of a gift. This gift, a bracelet, she takes home and treasures, correspondingly withdrawing her attention from her neighbor Major Bagstock (because concentration of pressure in one zone requires dissipation of pressure in another) with whom she had been in the habit of flirting mildly. (This flirtation was, in turn, a substitution for the amours, soon quenched under Mrs. Pipchin's influence, of her own Brighton girlhood [394, 687]: she, too, was sharply weaned, back then, with the "weazen"ing consequences on display in, for instance, the "dead leaves" of her gloves.) His gallantries thus abruptly curtailed, Bagstock is put out enough to contrive revenge. He learns about Paul; he learns about his new rival Dombey; he learns about Paul's school in Brighton; he learns that this same school is being attended by the son, one Master Bitherstone, of an old regimental comrade; he writes to the father in order to gain access to the son in order to gain access to Paul in order to befriend Dombey in order to cut him off from Miss Tox in revenge for her having cut him off. A hundred years later such a sequence might have called for invocations of Rube Goldberg, but here, it goes without a hitch: the link with Dombey is forged. Later on, at the end of yet another sequence of connections and disconnections, that bond will be instrumental in having Miss Tox dropped by the Dombeys—Mrs. Chick, once again, being the intermediary—right before the Major's pop eyes.

It all works because that is how the world works (except when, because of suddenly disproportionate pressure, it suddenly doesn't): trains of connection, chains of substitution, a universal regulatory physics governing tolerable degrees of friction in its subsidiary couplings and decouplings. It is not only between people: it is true of people because it is true of everything. Paul's "sharp weaning" is fatal because in being cut off from mother and nurse he was also being cut off from the life-force founts embodied in womb and breasts—from, in the novel's symbolic scheme of things, the sea. That is why he is forever trying to return to it. His Brighton education only reteaches him this same essential lesson about the order of things. Sadly, beginning with beginnings, he has started educating himself by having his "alphabet and other elementary works of reference" (110) wheeled down with him to the edge of the sea: learning, after all, is also built up, by degrees, from elements. Enter the Blimbers, who, because they don't know that, immediately load him down with a stack of books that he can never hold together: "the middle book slipped out before he reached the door, and then they all tumbled down on the floor" (161): another connective series, this one vertical, buckling under too much strain.

But then, Florence arrives. She understands that things have their order of progression, that you don't just leap from A-B-C to Cicero. In a reversed reenactment of Paul's collapsing stack, she gathers her own copies of his schoolbooks from different venues, sets out to "track" his "footsteps" through the curriculum, by degrees gains on and passes him, and after that pulls him along as an engine does a carriage, freeing him to follow after "where Florence had just toiled before him" (167).

By such experiences, Paul is the book's foremost authority on weaning and all that weaning is made to stand for. It is therefore in keeping that, on the verge of his own melting transition into the next world—compare, at the opposite extreme, Mrs. Skewton's and Carker's percussive exits, "smashed" and smashed up, respectively—he should be the one to convey the novel's definitive exposition of how everything fits or should fit together:

For all that the child observed, and felt, and thought, that night—the present and the absent; what was then and what had been—were blended

> like the colours in the rainbow, or in the plumage of rich birds when the sun is shining on them, or in the softening sky when the same sun is setting. The many things he had had to think of lately, passed before him in the music; not as claiming his attention over again, or as likely ever more to occupy it, but as peacefully disposed of and gone. (200)

An array of blendings, in different registers. Rainbow, iridescent (rainbowlike) plumage, sunset: from the spectrum, an incremental continuum in the visual field. Music: from scales, an incremental continuum in the audible field. This is a seer's vision, conjured in the borderland between sleeping and waking, poised on the brink of the real world Paul is leaving, and blended, like the images it favors, both out of traces of that world and intimations of the celestial one on the horizon.

Such blending is typical of this book's visionary moments. Of its many mergings, the ones that matter most are between worldly and unworldly. All or almost all of its dreams and other borderline states are both 1) implicitly supernatural to some degree and 2) recognizably confected from memories of lived experience. That heavenly "music" of Paul's, for instance, comes from real music, either being played at the very moment or echoing from the moment before. The "rich birds" come from the birds—illumined, like Miss Tox's "glorified sparrows" later, by the sun (395)—that he habitually watches from his seaward-facing window (170). (He was watching them at "twilight" [166], when "the sun is setting.")

In the same vein, the topnote "wild waves" finale, which to a degree continues this sea-birds-at-sunset *ecstasis*, is on the one hand both built out of things and memories of things and on the other an authentic glimpse of the divine. We are, after all, surely not meant to dismiss the poor fellow's conviction that his mother's spirit is hovering before him as he crosses the bar (225), any more than we should doubt the authenticity of the vengeful "stone arm" a delirious Mrs. Skewton sees raised to smite her on her deathbed (560), or the seismic "trembling" (731) forecasting a deranged Carker's death by one of the trains introduced as "bubbling and trembling" (218). In all cases these premonitions of the beyond also plausibly register the actual. That stone arm is probably a troubled recollection of some memorial statuary in the family mausoleum, which Mrs. Skewton would have seen (562) on her many visits to the estate. "Trembling" is a natural feeling for Carker at the moment. Seeing his mother through the veil, Paul is also remembering "her picture in the drawing-room downstairs" (223), just as the aureoled Jesus looming up before his failing sight, though doubtless really Jesus, would likely not be there had not a print (193) of the same been hanging in the stairwell, where Paul could see it, hovering above him, every time he plodded up to his room. Similarly, whatever the waves may be saying, they are clearly, in his mind, compounded out of his memory of his Brighton window on the sea, the sight from that window of his sister "waving" to him (169), and, in the present, with the curtains "waving to and fro" while "his feeble hand wave[s] in the air." "Wave" is one of the book's many multiple signifiers, extending as well, in the present scene, to the ship's sail, which seemed to "beckon" him to the sea (169), and the waves that used to run up to the wheels of his seaside carriage (110). That same wheeled carriage, and the water around it, is probably in his memory as well when he feels the "rolling river" "bearing him away." The river itself is "golden" because it is suffused with the streaming sunlight coming through the windows. He feels as if the waves are "lulling him to rest" because that is what the sister watching over him used to do, with that song of hers. The question of what all this is "saying" is one that has been with him since he moved to Brighton and lodged in a windy house that "sounded like a great shell, which the inhabitants were obliged to hold to their ears," which sound, of course, as he points out later, is believed to be the sound the sea makes, with its waves (169).

Waves: when I was a child, also sometimes in the habit of holding seashells to my ears, my family would take me to Virginia Beach, where I would splash and swim in the tides and be tugged back and forth. Later, when I took a bath to wash off the salt, I remember still feeling the tug of the tides, as if they were there with me in the bathtub. I'm pretty sure I remember them later, pulling and tugging, when I was in bed. Is it out of the question that Paul has had something of the same experience?

Still, however determinable the different tributaries to Paul's death scene, the central question remains vexingly unanswered. He never says what the waves are saying. ("I hear the waves! They always said so!" Said *what* so, pray tell?). These last words, delivered at the utmost pitch of otherworldly vision, stay unresolved, at least for this reader. The waves speak for the sea, and the sea in this novel stands for the noncomputable, what Captain Cuttle calls the "wonders in the deep" (657). The sea is that which is beyond the calculations of the likes of Dombey and Carker, and, usually, us as well.

V.

Beyond, and also beneath. Those upthrusting forces remarked earlier—geysers, springs, rhinoceros-hide "root"—have, along with the daylit phenomena they effect, their psychological analogues. *Dombey and Son* is a book with a subconscious, and that subconscious has an origin (the uncharted forces of nature), a location (underneath), an energetics, and a language. It submergence explains why Paul, the book's otherworld intermediary, should wake up with "his hair hot and wet from the effects of some childish dream" (108). As with Mrs. Skewton's stone arm and the earth tremblings that forecast Carker's fate, Dickens hedges this hint of the uncanny with a plausible cover story: it may just be, after all, that Paul has been feverish in his sleep. But there is another reading being proffered, one undergirt by much of what the novel tells us about the dream region—that Paul, emerging from the psychic underground, is like some kind of geyser, hot and wet because the place he comes from is hot and wet. When people in this novel wake up or fall asleep, the words "up" and "fall" solicit attention. Sleep, above all dreaming, is yet another subsidence into a deeper realm, a realm unreadable by itself (the waves' voice remains unintelligible) but occasionally and problematically interpretable at the crucial, graduated borderland between the two. After all, that mysterious tree—the one that seems to come out of "the ancient days before the flood," that writhes upward from the earth in which it feeds on underground waters, and that obviously Means Something, but what?—appears in the company of a witchy fortune-teller, one whose prophecy will come true. *Dombey and Son* is a book where witches, from whatever source, may have something to say.

In fact Mrs. Marwood, like Paul, is a kind of vatic dragoman, gifted with powers of translation between worldly and otherworldly, paradoxically, as a result of the sharp weaning—her daughter was wrenched away from her, as Paul was suddenly deprived of mother and nurse[22]— that seems to have left an unannealed fissure between present and past. Like Hamlet's father's ghost, cut off when unprepared for his transition from one world to the other and consequently able to migrate between the two, both of these half-human figures, mother-witch and changeling-child, seem possessed by an abreactive urge to return to the source of their breach. Paul's—very pronounced—death wish comes out of a desire to heal the breach opened at his birth and to return to the mother he lost then. Mrs. Marwood pursues and kills Carker from the same motive that makes her hand hover compulsively (75) over a head of hair that reminds her of her daughter's before that daughter was ruined by the same Carker—out of an impulse to return and undo. In both cases probably, and in Paul's case certainly, this backward momentum, in a book where any momentum, whether of men or machinery, is prone to run away with itself, does not always stop at its intended terminus;

it can carry over (or, like the train with its tunnels, inward) into the unknown, the otherworldly, the preexistent, the not-yet-formulated, the subterranean, the subconscious.

In *Dombey and Son,* that can and does happen, frequently. Waking world and visionary world, consciousness and subconsciousness, bleed into one another all the time. Almost everyone, sooner or later, falls into some trancelike state between the two. If, as noted before, dreams are always transmutations of daylight experience, the reverse operation, the upwelling of submerged knowledge into the waking mind, is just as pronounced. People are often given to wondering whether they're dreaming, and the answer is seldom a flat-out yes or no: when Florence awakes "as from a dream" of words spoken to her and seems "to feel the touch of lips on her face," the point is that the "dream" was reality: Edith has visited her, had spoken to her, and kissed her, in her sleep (623).

Dickens may or may not think that these two realms need one another equally; in any case he certainly believes that, just as upper class needs working class more than the other way around, the day depends on the night. The chronic insomnia that overtakes Carker during his final flight is a sentence of insanity, the reason that, being unable to make his nightly visits down into the world of dreams and then return, he winds up being overwhelmed from below. His journey becomes "like a vision," with "nothing quite real," "a vision of things past and present all confounded together" (738). It is as if Dickens were anticipating the next century's rapid eye movement studies, the ones indicating that if people weren't allowed to dream in their sleep they would compensate by hallucinating when awake. For Carker, the psychic uprising from underground (those "red eyes" signaling the woman who seemed to rise up to him from "out of the ground") constitutes a return of the repressed, vengeance from below against this man who always professed to deal in computable "certainties" (616).

Given that the *Dombey* subconscious is often represented in terms of underground waters (e.g., Paul's "hot and wet" dream), it makes perfect sense that this Carker is repeatedly compared to a cat. Cats, proverbially, hate water. Carker, as much as Dombey, has tried to make of his life a breakwater against what the sea, surface and sunken, stands for in a novel where the ideal (Paul at the sea shore, the "gradual change from land to water" that characterizes the setting of Sol Gills's shop [117], crowds moving in "shoals," a house made of an upended boat [66], a church steeple becoming a maritime "beacon" awash in the tide of time [420]), is a swampy merging of the two. Growing into knowledge, Carker's antithesis Paul exemplifies, as usual, this amphibian ideal: "More and more light broke in upon them; distincter and distincter dreams disturbed them; an accumulating crowd of objects and impressions swarmed about his rest" (91). The antecedent to "them" in that last sentence is not "thoughts" or "studies," but "slumbers." Paul learns in his sleep, storing and connecting "dreams" and "impressions" alike, in that middle state of his, the one that will eventually enable his migration from land back to sea.

In keeping, the reality of *Dombey and Son* persistently verges on the phantasmagoric. Dickens's fictions are always fantastical to some degree, but here it is of a new order. Here we are dealing not just with flights of fancy, or with comical or sentimental or gothic commentary on narrative reality. We are dealing with an alternate version of narrative reality, ever imminent, typically figured as lying beneath the surface of events, as sometimes merging with or emerging through those events, as often controlling them in half-divined ways. Mrs. Pipchin really is an ogress in a castle with serpentine growths in the front parlor and a dungeon in back. When "some wandering monster of a ship" is witnessed ""roaming up the street like a stranded leviathan" (117), it is, to be sure, no real leviathan, but it *is* a real ship, in that amphibious neighborhood of Sol Gills's, roaming among the streets—and what walking whale could be stranger than that? Mrs. Marwood may not literally come out of the ground, but she certainly seems to have some weird powers of the kind traditionally associated with spirits from that region, and you ignore her words at your peril. In Dijon, Edith, fending off Carker, holds up her hand "like an enchantress, at whose invocation" the bell announcing her avenging husband's arrival just happens to ring (730). Her mother's daughter, she is admittedly something of a tragedy queen, and it's possible that this is just an act. But it's also possible that the invocation really had something to do with summoning that bell.

Symptomatic of its amphibious way with such questions is the book's handling of names, which are also, typically, immigrants from some otherland of uncertain significations. First, consider the kinds of names Dickens usually coins. Pickwick. Magwitch. Pecksniff. Pumblechook. Uriah Heep. Scrooge. Sairey Gamp. Boffin. In *Dombey and Son* it is different. Elsewhere, most memorable Dickens names are, as someone has remarked, a kind of English version of *Symboliste* poetry—a matter of suggestive overtones, evocative and only semidefinable. The names of *Dombey and Son,* by contrast, are like a foreign language recognizably of the same family as the one in use—a Latin, say, behind the vernacular Italian—often, with some practice, translatable backward. There is parley between the two. Take, as a first instance, Carker. Given that one of his intended victims is the flowerlike Florence, his name perhaps suggests "canker." But it definitely *means* "carker," one who eats away (as with teeth) at something or someone. (So, when the toothy Carker's machinations turn against him, he feels himself "gnawed" [737] by self-recrimination.) A carker, that is, is someone who performs what the text reminds us (143) is commonly called a "carking" operation.

Dombey and Son is one of only two Dickens texts—*The Old Curiosity Shop* is the other—to include "carking," or any other derivative of the word. That is not, I think, accidental, any more than it is accidental that a novel with someone named Dombey in it should also give us "dominion," "domineering," and "dominant," or that most of its words sharing that distinctive o-m-b sequence—"sombre," many instances of "tombs", "tombstones," "hecatombs," and so on, the black "bombazeen" of Mrs. Pipchin's mourning—should also share Dombey's funereal mien.[23]

Dombey and Son contains a robber named Rob (and, sure enough, various references to "robbery," to people being "robbed"); a clerk named Clark (and plenty of other "clerks" about); a broker named Brogley who breaks up the shop of the bankrupt Gills (and lots of "brokens"); a beaming oldster named Sol (and, yes indeed, a passing mention of "solar heats"); and a woman, Lucretia Tox, whose name combines history's most famous poisoner with the root of the Latin for "poison," who tends, with gloves "like dead leaves," a macabre little garden introduced as a kind of Ovidian plot of tortured souls translated into flora (and—what do you know—lurking apart in the text, the word "intoxication"). To an extent that no other Dickens novel equals, language in *Dombey and Son* seconds and extends naming; uppercase formulations slide into lowercase, in which capacity they are turned loose to circulate and propagate in the larger linguistic medium.

Names, that is, constitute another form of the amphibian, of entities situated at some midpoint on a graduated continuum between one element and another. Like Paul at the seashore, they are half in and half out. The Blimbers consort in measured degree with the text's "blinkers" (215) and various "blindings," some of which clearly fall within the Blimber orbit (like the bust of "blind Homer" [150] in the doctor's study) and some of which extend beyond it. Paul is echoed by "pall," "pale," ("my pale child" [197], "appalling," Saint Paul, and Polly, his nurse; Florence blossoms into "flower"ings and "flow"ings; a death's-head woman named Skewton has an attendant who "should have been a skeleton" (381); forever trying to regain the rose-colored complexion of her youth, she has two other servants named "Flowers" and "Withers," in turn occupying a text in which the words "flower" and "withered" (and many variants on "rose") are much in evidence. Mr. Chick is subject to "checking" himself in mid-sentence, to receiving "checks" from a henpecking (therefore chicken) wife (15). A woman of the streets named Alice is called "Ally" (470) by her mother, the same who led Florence "through narrow streets and lanes and alleys" (75). Sol Gills: "a gill of old Jamaica" (232). Mrs. Blockitt: "blocked" (23). Mr. Feeder, B. A., teacher and herder of youth: "the sheep are feeding" (276). (I want to believe that his "B. A." should be pronounced "Baa.") A comfy sort named Morfin: "muffin" (1). Miss Nipper: "nipped" (136). The morbidly superstitious Mrs. Wickham: "witch" (80—the root is "wicca"). The stiff, super-selfish Anthony Bagstock: cf. Mrs. Marwood's "bag [that is purse] of a throat" (473) and Mr. Dombey's "tight stock" (280; "Anthony," of course, pairs him with Mrs. Skewton, a.k.a. Cleopatra.) Biler: "biles" (108). Edith Granger, widow of the late Mr. Granger: Edith, says Mrs. Skewton, has "garnered up her heart" since his death (358). ("Garner" is one letter short of being an anagram of "Granger," and a grange, in its original sense, was a place of garnered grain. Edith vows to spare Florence "one grain of the evil that is in my breast" [419]; Carker, addressing Dombey about her in her presence, in the space of ten lines sounds the words "grain," then "garner," then "stranger" [575]: the story of their marriage, in three slant-rhymed steps.[24]) Walter Gay, son and heir: "Walter" gets translated into "Walters," partway to the "waste of waters" in which he is supposed to have drowned (321); he sails away on a ship named the *Son and Heir* accompanied by—well—sun (shining) and air (blowing), as in a "gale"; he is, of course, congenitally a creature of "gaiety" (136), saved in the end, we are told, because he stayed "cheery" when others lost hope (658).

The word-names of *Dombey and Son* have a grammar of meaning. They participate in the same system of referentiality that connects the noncapitalized words. Richard D. Altick notes that the name "Grinder," as in "Rob the Grinder," is one item of a text in which "all ... contemporary meanings of grind and grinder" come into play.[25] Frank McCombie finds something similar happening with the name "Pipchin."[26] Quite remarkable transactions occur between fish names and fish words: an old salt named Gills, another named Glubb, another named Cuttle (the word "inky" lurks elsewhere [152] to facilitate the connection) who goes through life enveloped in a dense mist, a Mrs. MacStinger who regularly emits her own stinging mist and whose tentacles Cuttle cannot elude (several personages, here and there, are described as being "stung"), a prosing beadle named Mr. Sownds in a text that elsewhere mischievously informs us that a fish's "sounds" are its inflatable bladders (155), a man named Perch who recoils at the sight of a hook (229). These punning equivalencies and near-equivalencies are part of the same verbally aquatic environment in which Bagstock is a hard-shelled, pop-eyed lobster, Mrs. Skewton, stricken mortally, crawls backward toward death like a crab (546), and Carker turns at times into a predatory creature of the deep (385). Indeed, it may be that, along with everything else, we are to take that name of his as a half-homonym ("Mr. Carker grinned at him like a shark" [296]) for "shark."

That, to be sure, would be an odd conjunction of roles for someone usually compared, with his (carking) teeth, to a cat, but the kind of interplay we have been reviewing between names and nouns seems bound to yield odd conjunctions. Florence's name, as one fairly obvious example, connects her both to the faded flower that is Mrs. Skewton and to the flowing river that carries off her brother. But connects her how, exactly? And how both? What does Mrs. Skewton's decrepitude have to do with Paul's apotheosis? And what about the relation of either, if any, to the Major Bagstock whose regimental nickname, he informs us, was "The Flower" (356)? One could, perhaps, after the model of the New Critics, construct a plausibly paradoxical solution to many such questions, but I am not at all sure that *Dombey and Son* wants to let us completely do that, any more than it wants us to know for sure what the waves were saying. Dickens's decision to implicate names so deeply in his network of significations has, I think, an oddly double-edged result. On the one hand, it is a function of the leap in architectonic rigor that distinguishes *Dombey and Son* from its predecessors. As never before, this author wants names to be part of the pattern, because he wants everything to be part of the pattern. On the other hand, there is no getting around the fact that the generation of names follows a different logic from that of words. One is genealogical, and as such a vertical intrusion into the ongoing play of concurrent referents. Names in this capacity exist to signal continuity in time (Anthony Bagstock is the latest in the line of Bagstocks) and singularity in space (he is the only Anthony Bagstock around.) Perhaps nobody understood that better than Dickens, literature's champion creator of memorably *sui-generis* characters with memorably *sui-generis* names. Non-onomastic language, on the other hand, signifies laterally—syntagmatically, as Saussure had it—by the interplay of each word with those next to it and in the vicinity. On the large scale of the novel, it signifies, in part, through the orchestration of filiations across a shared semantic field: the similar-but-different manifestations of "dust" in *Our Mutual Friend,* the permutations of fog, fogginess, mental fogginess, bureaucratic obscurantism, and so on, in *Bleak House.*

Except in the most flat-out of allegories—a genre pretty much closed to a work set in a real city with real streets with real names—it is the nature of names to resist the kind of symbolic and structural concinnity theoretically achievable with words. The logic of genealogy on the one hand and of declensions and conjugations on the other are things apart. That is probably why, for Doctor Blimber's students at the beginnings of their careers, as for Mrs. Skewton at the end of her life, names are the hardest things for them to learn and to keep straight.

VII.

I have said that the names assigned in *Dombey and Son* exemplify its way of merging surface narrative with a submerged reality—what I have called the book's subconscious. "Skewton" plus "skeleton," like "Paul" in conversation with "pall," equals a coded prophecy, in both cases fulfilled, of foreordained death, and thereby puts the reader in contact with an oracular dimension, one in which such prophecies can be decoded and will come true. But, again, they also exemplify a certain resistance—among other things, to being decoded in the first place, to being appropriated by the book's dominant discursive system. (In not telling us what they were saying, the waves were, in a manner of speaking, holding on to their turf.) It is another case of relative degrees of uniformitarianism or catastrophism, of tolerances being sometimes respected and sometimes exceeded in the transition from one state to another. Sometimes blending harmoniously—Paul's rainbow vision is the gold standard here—at other times world and otherworld grind against one another. The *Dombey* otherworld is indeed dense with undertones of myth and fancy, that phantasmagoric element never far from the surface, but often not—not, certainly, when the strain of transition has been too much—of the friendly variety. As with the book's other transitions from state to state, its emergences can be more or less stressful, and the difference between the two matters a lot. Mrs. Marwood, emerging from her subterranean grotto, next to that weird "root" of a tree, is a witch, a harpy, and above all, right out of the *Oresteia,* a Fury, royally miffed at having been displaced by the daylight world embodied in the hyper-Apollonian Carker and determined in return to seek retribution through powers that the novel allows us to think of as magical. That dream from which the "hot and wet" Paul surfaces has, clearly, been a nightmare, one that he had to struggle to escape. Like the long-repressed sexual current that finally erupts, in Dijon, to smash his composure, the dream-state hallucinations that rise up to harass

Carker thereafter are, he feels—and he certainly seems to be right about this—out to get him. Although various fairy tale motifs play more or less constantly around her, it is still not good news for Florence when, left alone in her father's mansion, she seems to be literally turning into the fairy princess of an enchanted castle. It threatens to be a kind of seizure from below, a version of what happens to Carker, and, to be sure in a more benign way, her brother.

So there are rules, as well as rites, of passage, between one kingdom and the one below it. *Dombey*'s underworld is something you can neither smash into nor shut out. Those *Dombey* names that often, and often problematically, accommodate themselves to the narrative's verbal coordinates are also arrivals from a mythy world of primordial forces—the Skeleton, the *Dominus*, the Blocker, the Eater of Everything, the Marrer of Wood come up to a world full of wooden men, Ceres and her Persephone as Grange(r) and Flower(er)—where they may not quite belong either. Indeed, these capitalized entities don't really seem to fit easily in either place. There are pieces of myth—pretty heterogeneous pieces at that—but no Olympian road map. The result can seem like a broken-down allegory: bridges between levels half-finished, a chart of correspondences mostly undeveloped, no consistent rhyme or reason.[27] Maybe Dickens set out to write a prophetic work, but, being in the end a product of his increasingly skeptical time, couldn't muster the conviction to follow through.

Maybe, but there is another possibility. I have remarked how the most important truths of *Dombey and Son* all seem to be "shattered and scattered about." Those truths (sex, death, what the sea says and the heart feels) are, in a metaphoric sense, adopted wholly and deeply by Dickens. They are under the surface, and they are under the surface because they have been forcibly pushed there (like Mrs. Marwood's fury[28]), and in the process they have (like Mrs. Marwood's tree) been squeezed and twisted, and made to contort themselves in forcing their emergence upwards. It is as if all those violent, nongraduated eruptions and earthquakes wound up causing as much destruction below as above. The Ceres and Persephone story, for example, is certainly a component of this novel's undertext, but it is not a master key in the way the Christ story is for *Oliver Twist*. It cannot ride up and make everything cohere. Indeed, given the tectonic tensions between the two levels, it is a good thing that it cannot.

That is because the likes of Dombey, Blimber, Carker, and others of the daylight kingdom, denying it any validity or point of access whatsoever, have "catastrophically" reduced it to the book's field of fragments, the landscape of destructions both above and below. To a degree, *Dombey and Son* is about the forces aligned against its own effort to discover the larger meanings behind its grand scheme, such as it may be. Except for those two doomed seers, Paul and Mrs. Marwood, the truth seeking that occurs is provisional, incipient, perennially coming into being.

It is also topical, as opposed to global. Paul, at the price of his life, may wind up seeing the big picture, but his equally sublime sister is the one who makes it all the way through to the end, and she experiences no such all-encompassing revelation. Instead, she remains busy at "her work," a phrase the book repeatedly assigns to her. That, to begin with, is no bad thing in *Dombey and Son,* with all its case studies of effervescing human energy looking for outlets; the world would be a better place with more potterers and fewer idée-fixers. But it is above all right that this work should be woman's work, such as sewing and knitting. A business of one stitch or one row at a time, such work is therapeutically gradualist in a way that the book favors. It is also as close as any physical activity featured to figuring a way of truth. Paul, who used to "hold skeins of silk for Mrs. Blimber" (194) (even she, at such moments, becomes a woman with something womanly to teach), for whom the Blimbers's scullery maid tied together the loose "strings" of his outfit (160), and for whom as well his Sunday outings with Florence did the "work of strengthening and knitting up a brother's and a sister's love" (162), is probably drawing on such life lessons in his final vision of a universal blending. Certainly Florence herself is, after Paul's death, when, pulling herself, as the saying goes, together, she is again able "to look upon the work with which her fingers had been busy by his side on the sea-shore . . . as if it had been sentient and had known him," and takes to it again (242–43).

These moments are, in the book's terms, characteristically womanly—gentle, ameliorist—in a way counterpointing the more abrupt manifestations of male will (the railroad above all) and, beyond matters male and female, pointing to a comprehensive dialectic of breaking and reknitting. One of the things that makes Sol Gills a sage is that, in a book of many loose ends (for instance poor Miss Tox's chronic inability to make any two ends of anything she wears come together [7]), he is an expert at tying knots; his "knotted" walking stick (215) probably amounts to one of the book's ambient puns. For every one of the manifold destructions noted earlier, it seems, there can be a reverse impulse toward reconstruction. Time and again, we see the dispersed swarm contract and ball back up. Dombey's house is dismantled, the very stair carpets stripped off and the "stair wires" that held them in place removed, but then those wires are bundled back into "fasces" (790). (His other bankrupt "house," the business, is also coming back together at the end.) Walter's ship, all "bedraggled" when he first boards it, emerges as a thing of beauty, of taut sails and gleaming prow, when its furnishings have been put back where they belong and, setting off, it resumes its rightful ship shape (266–67). In *Dombey and Son,* few accolades can compete with "shipshape."

As always, mental activity corresponds to material model. People's minds typically pass from some "cloudy," "foggy," "gauzy," "misty," or "mist-enshrouded" miasma to eventual focus, usually by finding one central saliency around which the rest of the nebular mass then coalesces. For Edith it is "one resented figure," her husband, around whom the "indistinct" "foreshadowings" flickering through her mind, cohere (579); for Paul, doubtless influenced by his roommate from India, it is the "tigers and lions" in the pattern of the Blimbers' wallpaper (168); for Dombey it the one word "Death!" on which the roar and rush of his train ride converge (275–76).

Such achievements of understanding can have a connect-the-dots quality, made out of the dispersed alphabet of signifiers with which the various stammerers, interrupters, jackhammer pedagogues, tearers-up of papers, and so on, litter the field. Here, for instance, is Mr. Dombey, falling into one of the sub- or semiconscious states that typically, in this book, come over people when closest to seeing into the heart of things, picking up pieces that both he and the novel's reader will later want to sort out:

> So thought Mr. Dombey, when he was left alone at the dining-table, and mused upon his past and future fortunes: finding no uncongeniality in an air of scant and gloomy state that pervaded the room, in colour a dark brown, with black hatchments of pictures blotching the walls, and twenty-four black chairs, with almost as many nails in them as so many coffins, waiting like mutes, upon the threshold of the Turkey carpet; and two exhausted negroes holding up two withered branches of candelabra on the side-board, and a musty smell prevailing as if the ashes of ten thousand dinners were entombed in the sarcophagus below it. The owner of the house lived much abroad; the air of England seldom agreed long with a member of the Feenix family; and the room had gradually put itself into deeper and still deeper mourning for him, until it was become so funereal as to want nothing but a body in it to be quite complete.
>
> No bad representation of the body, for the nonce, in his unbending form, if not in his attitude, Mr. Dombey looked down into the cold depths of the dead sea of mahogany on which the fruit dishes and decanters lay

at anchor; as if the subjects of his thoughts were rising towards the surface one by one, and plunging down again. Edith was there in all her majesty of brow and figure; and close to her came Florence, with her timid head turned to him, as it had been, for an instant, when she left the room; and Edith's eyes upon her, and Edith's hand put out protectingly. A little figure in a low arm-chair came springing next into the light, and looked upon him wonderingly, with its bright eyes and its old-young face gleaming as in the flickering of an evening fire. Again came Florence close upon it, and absorbed his whole attention. Whether as a fore-doomed difficulty and disappointment to him; whether as a rival who had crossed him in his way, and might again; whether as his child, of whom, in his successful wooing, he could stoop to think, as claiming, at such a time, to be no more estranged; or whether as a hint to him that the mere appearance of caring for his own blood should be maintained in his new relations; he best knew. Indifferently well, perhaps, at best; for marriage company and marriage altars, and ambitious scenes—still blotted here and there with Florence—always Florence—turned up so fast, and so confusedly, that he rose, and went up stairs to escape them. (414–15)

About this extraordinary passage, I would like to call attention to the following. The fact that it describes Dombey contemplating his upcoming marriage, and that "uncongeniality," in its first sentence, derives from *genialis,* "nuptial." The way the "blotching" in that same first sentence resurfaces as "blotted" in the last—internal picture supplanting external pictures. The fact that a "hatchment," three words before "blotted," designates a kind of escutcheon, as in the Victorian cliché "blot on the escutcheon." The fact that twenty-four is both twice a jury's number and half of forty-eight, Dombey's age at the start and a talismanic number throughout:[29] two rows of twelve, conveniently convertible to coffins, backed by those black hatchments, lined up to pass judgment on the man sitting between them. The way the "almost" twenty-four nails in the same number of chairs suggest a microcosmic mirror effect, later taken up by the reflective table top. The half-echo of "mused" in "mutes," and the subtle synchronization of those mutes with the kind of incapacitated attendants one associates with a court of the sort summoned to consciousness by the Turkey carpet. The way that, in the sexual symbolic terms established earlier, the nature of that incapacitation, castration, seems seconded by "withered branches," visited on this man on the verge—the "threshold"—of discovering that his family tree will have no heir. The near-anagram of that man's name in "entombed," following logically as it does from the intimation just formed. The neat way that the "musty smell" of past dinners first merges with the sarcophagus smell of disinterred corpses and then expands into the "air" of all England. The way that one of those corpses turns into the "body" of the second paragraph, then in turn into the Dombey we have already been primed to think of as a tomb. The way "Feenix," occurring thirty-two words after the first mention of the "ashes" locked up in the sarcophagus, and recalling the decrepit cousin of that name given to gloomily commenting on the "long homes" to which all alive are heading (826), works to dampen rather than encourage any thought of Phoenix-like revival. The way "deeper and still deeper" in the first paragraph sets the stage for the sea soundings of the second. The word "representation" used to begin a representation of Dombey's re-presentation: more mirrored mirroring. "Lay at anchor," occurring about 200 words after "state:" the way the phrase "lying in state" hangs in the background there, helping to keep in play the fact that the sea into which this brooding self-seer peers is a dead sea. How "plunging" (from *plumbum*," lead) reinforces the heaviness implicit in "anchor." The way that, with this nautical theme established, Edith's envisioned "brow and figure" summons prow and figurehead. The way "wonderingly," describing the apparition of Paul, has the effect of making him complicit with the Edith who puts out her hand "protectingly" to Florence. The way that Paul's face, remembered "flickering" in firelight, so matches the flickering effects of candles on mahogany as to make it impossible to tell surface from depth in the sight of this man of whom the narrator has frequently said that he is opaque, that one cannot tell his inside from his outside. The way the cruel pronoun "it," applied only to Paul, isolates Dombey as the solitary male in this procession, and then the way that this pronoun ambiguously shifts to "his" only when Florence, "close upon it... absorbed his whole attention"—ambiguously, because it is also Dombey's attention that is being absorbed, thus extinguishing Paul's first "bright," then "flickering" light. The Dombey-sounding "fore-doomed" yet another variation on the name; the Christ-summoning "crossed" applied to the daughter whom he will later curse and strike "crosswise" (637); the "estranged," which, as already remarked, will later implicate Edith Granger as the "stranger" Dombey is about to marry. The nicely calibrated ambiguity of the words "appearance," "blood," and "relations," and the way "at best" comes along to undercut the "best knew" of the previous line. The way "blotted" picks up on "absorbed" and "turned up so fast" retrieves and accelerates Florence's "turned" head earlier. The pathetic force of "he rose," after the very different kinds of risings just recounted.

Then I would call attention to three words being clustered in one clause: "Mr. Dombey looked down into the cold depths of the *dead sea* of mahogany on which the *fruit* dishes and decanters lay at anchor." (My italics.) First, obviously, this gives us the Dead Sea. The Dead Sea is, of all the world's bodies of water, the one most recessed below sea level—"deeper and still deeper." Situated in the Holy Land (which is to say, in Dickens's time, ruled by the Turks, with their Turkey carpets) and fed by the Jordan in which Jesus was baptized (Paul and the "crossed" Florence looking up from the depths), it has long been a byword for sterility and is by tradition the site of the Cities of the Plain, said to have sunk beneath its waters. It is also famously so thick with salt—dense and opaque, like mahogany—that no body can stay submerged (unless, one presumes, weighted with an "anchor," with the lead weight nested in "plunged") and will always rise "towards the surface."

So that is the mirror in which Dombey seeks his image. It is a magic mirror too, imbued with the power of prophecy, and like all such prophetic agents in this book it calls on divinatory skills. For instance: pluck out the "dead sea" in the previously mentioned clause, capitalize it, splice it to the "fruit" six words ahead, and you have a phrase that, first, ought to have established in the minds of the culturally literate public of the time the legend of the Dead Sea fruit said to turn to ashes in the mouth, and that therefore, many chapters later, might have returned to memory when that public read that Dombey's marriage has become "a road of ashes" (618), or that "every loving blossom he had withered in his innocent daughter's heart was snowing down in ashes on him" (796). The same readership may even, if it knew its Milton, have remembered that in *Paradise Lost,* Book X, the fruit turns to ashes in the mouths of Satan's legions as they themselves are turning into serpents, and that Dombey's evil agent (the grounds of whose home feature "willow and ash" [454]) ends up dying on "a train of ashes" (743) at the climax of a sequence in which he has been figuratively changed from cat to snake, undoing his "coil" (602, 603), "spurned like any reptile" by the foot of the woman he tempted (731).

Again: conscious and subconscious interchange. Surface and depth, opacity and transparency, interchange. The faces looking up through the mahogany veneer variously reconfigure Dombey's face, reflected on it. The lights illuminating what he sees are reflected candles, burning behind him. The exchange between one-dimensional and three-dimensional translates into a temporal equivalent as well, a mirror of Dombey now and a window of past (the dead Paul) and future (the road of ashes). This is what it is like, in *Dombey and Son,* when people are in contact with their subconscious, are picking up intimations but remain unable to disentangle them from the environing thicket of liminal signals and knit them together, making the connection between, for instance, "dead sea" and "fruit." It is akin to the kind of "undifferentiated," "unintellectualised feeling" that J. Hillis Miller finds in the novel's moments of transcendence,[30] but with the difference that these moments are, often or always, implicitly affiliated with other signs, often scattered throughout the text, with which they may, at least incipiently, add up to something quite intricately meaningful, or suggestive of meaning. Thus, the "prismatic" glints refracted through tears in Florence's eyes verge on coalescing into a "rainbow"—a reminder, surely, of Paul's—"faintly shining in the far-off sky" (653). At the other end of the continuum, the dying Mrs. Skewton senses a "glimmering of remorse" that "could neither struggle into light nor get back into total darkness" (508). That is the general condition of the book's would-be seers, and it is one shared by us readers, trying to negotiate the broken-mosaic field of its meanings.

The book wants us to notice such effects, else why would they be there? I can't say how frequent their incidence may be, but once you sense that they're out there it can be like picking blackberries—first you see one, the next moment you see hundreds. (Some of them, most likely, imagined.) That, probably, is part of the idea: to put us in the same boat with the characters, with those halfway "glimmering"s of theirs, sensing connections but almost never getting them all, or always, right. Unsurprisingly, the Bible seems to be the main, though by no means only, quarry. Consider, for instance, chapter LIX ("Retribution"). It would take too long to attempt at piecing together all the Christological notes being sounded within its pages, let alone their ramifications, out to other related elements distributed elsewhere, but the following list, presented in order of appearance, may give an idea of their extent: "garment"; "watch-guard"; "tumbling the Lots about"; "three days following"; "sheets"; "In agony"; "he...saw the face...and heard the one prolonged low cry go upward"; "going on before"; "thrown upon bare boards"; "a kind hand could have been stretched out"; "risen up"; "A spectral, haggard, wasted likeness of himself...lifted up its head"; "if blood were to trickle"; "Papa, don't cast me off"; "parted"; "Gone to heaven"; "Oh my God"; "last cup"; "winding"; "suffered" (786–804).

My most recent addition to this catalogue, made just while writing this draft of this chapter, was "sheets." I was looking the list over, and it occurred to me that if "winding" was in there, "sheets" should be too—and sure enough, on reinspection, it was. Earlier, remembering that in the Gospels the soldiers—the "watch-guard"s—who "cast" (or were "tumbling") "Lots" for Christ's "garment" also "parted" that garment between them, it had occurred to me to look about for "parted"—and voilá. One comes to expect that kind of experience in *Dombey and Son,* and to appreciate as well the semisurreal logic behind it.

A perhaps more manageable case, also allusively biblical, is the "motes and beams" seen hovering over the cradle of the baby, Paul, who will eventually see Jesus (90). Later on in the novel, good people will often "beam" rays of light with their eyes, massive objects speeding by will "fall like a *beam* of *shadow* an inch broad, upon the eye" (276), and Florence will find that the sanctified room she inherited from Paul has "beams and boards raised against it without, baulking the daylight" (390), which daylight, elsewhere, comes in "sunbeams." Meanwhile, the book's arch-hypocrite will be seen fastidiously wiping "motes of dust" off his "white hand" and "glossy linen" (292). Surely, Christ's words about those who can see the mote in another's eye but not the beam in their own have to do with all this. On the other hand, the language of the original does not go with the associative refractions Dickens makes latent in that word "beam," nor does it scatter its significations across a field of 350,000-odd other words, and for obvious reasons: if you want to give people the truth, you do not send them out on some crazy scavenger hunt to find and gather it in. It may be that the phrase "motes and beams" is supposed to be the hint that will alert readers to start tracking and assembling homonyms and synonyms and whatnot, but if so—well, that is asking a lot, and the job is not made easier by the fact that, after all, the whole idea of the original is that "motes" and "beams" are opposites, not the equivalents that the *Dombey* quote makes them.

One might expect this kind of riddling in matters sexual—and, yes, when it comes to sex Dickens, as we have seen, does make his reader go foraging. He can also go in for the kind of artful verbal *bouleversement* just considered. Thus: in one scene, furious from the conviction that his wife is cuckolding him, Dombey strikes his daughter and tells her "what Edith was" (637). And what, exactly, was that? Well: earlier in the chapter, Edith had torn off and discarded the tiara (631) that had shortly before been called "her arch of diamonds" (628). About half a page later, Florence spots the partner in sin, Carker, passing under an "arch" on his way up to Edith's room (Illustration 5) (631), where the two will make final arrangements for their guilty flight together. The Latin for "arch" is "*fornix,*" from which we get the word "fornicate," from the tradition that prostitutes—women of the "streets"—are to be found under arches.[31] So: I would say that now we know at least approximately what Dombey said "Edith was"—a whore—and can, perhaps, remembering that that arch of diamonds was a wedding gift from him to her, reflect that in marrying her he was, in ways the novel has underscored by other means, making her his whore.

Illustration 5   "Abstraction and Recognition"

In cases such as this (the handling of "root" is another instance) we can understand why Dickens goes in for such tricks.—He has to. Still, the majority of his fragmented occultations relate to matters perfectly respectable—sometimes, indeed, to apparent testaments of high piety. So why is he doing this to us?

Because *Dombey and Son,* in a way mirroring the landscape it depicts, is built over the upwelling underground sea of the subconscious, whose strenuous interaction with the world above has wrenched that world into disconformities, into flaws and fissures distributed at unpredictable intervals, through which otherwise unvoiced truths glint, "glimmer," leak, and spout. Its preoccupation with what I have been calling gradualism amounts in part to a kind of hydraulic engineering concern that, through an appropriate chain of mediations and modifications the resulting pressures can be beneficially released and diffused, the geyser becomes gusher becomes spring.

It is just the kind of hydraulic problem those other engineers, the ones building up and releasing pressure from the boilers of their steam engines, are experts at managing. (Chief representative of the process, again, is Toodle, the stoker who, having "made over all his own inheritance of fuming and fretting to the engines," can regularly decompress, in lawful coition with lawful spouse, into his own "easy-going" [512] norm.) Ordinary people, however, keep running into difficulty. If trains are the main example of energy in action, the human editions seem to have a lot of trouble keeping their valves and gauges in order. (The number-one human gauge is the clock; none of the timepieces of *Dombey and Son* are reliably on time except for Doctor Blimber's great clock, and that gets dismantled.) All the characters of consequence, even—in the end, especially—Dombey and Carker (whose own watch, at his fatal hour, turns out to be "unwound" [740])—experience serious spells of interior dislocation. In a book rife with forebodings and forgettings, truths repeatedly loom, emerge, and then glimmer away, and people grope about like absent-minded myopics forever losing, finding, losing, and so on, their glasses. (It is *not* a good sign when Dombey allows Carker to adjust his eyeglass [377].) Reality goes in and out of focus, arriving from and passing back into what is variously experienced as "imperfect shadows of the truth" (487—like the shadow Florence sees, in the second illustration), as "shapes and substances of incompleteness" (65), as "half-intelligible sentiment, diffused around" (200), as thoughts of "indistinct and undefined existence" (262), as a "dim world" of "solemn wonderings and hopes" (314), as visions "all blurred and indistinct" (482), as "confused" (259), "shapeless" (598), "vague and dreamy" (621), "indescribable and terrible" (482), "unintelligible and inexplicable" (731), "nameless" (635) "indistinctly resolved" (739), "filmy" (306), "scarcely shaped" (314), "hazy" (422), "half-formed" intimations (93).

These "hazy" simulacra are seldom simply delusions to be dispelled. "It's a fine thing to understand 'em," says Captain Cuttle about Sol Gills's navigational instruments, "And yet it's a fine thing not to understand 'em." (45). Although understanding is, on the whole, best—Sol's expert seamanship, trained and sharpened by those instruments of his, is what makes it possible for him to track down Walter—on the other hand Cuttle's blissfully ignorant take on how those instruments are making him mysteriously "magnified, electrified, polarized" (45), and so on has its own claims on a novel that at least entertains a belief in what Rob thinks of as kind of cosmological "electric fluency" (701).[32] Cuttle's wondering speculations are, if not the truth itself, often on the way to it.

In fact there is a recurring tendency throughout the book to figure any vital reality as multiply shrouded—enwrapped in layers upon layers, arranged in what is often a roughly concentric pattern. It is, yet again, a prescription of gradualism, of knitting up by degrees, this time as epistemological model. Sol Gills himself, true-hearted as anyone, comes surrounded with a perpetual fog through which others must seek out those sunlike eyes of his. London, in many ways the heart of darkness, is the "mist-enshrouded city" (465), somewhere inside whose "blurred" precincts lies another city—*the* "City,"—at the center of which lie in turn the offices of Dombey and Son, those offices themselves arranged into outer office, middle office, and inner office, housing Dombey himself.

Such bull's-eye arrangements are common. One of the distinguishing oddities of *Dombey and Son* is the way its habitations are forever being laid out as boxes within boxes. I can't be sure, but I seriously doubt whether there is a single important dwelling that does not come with some "little room inside" (187), "little back parlour" (205), a "closet within the drawing-room" (287), "secret chamber" (665), an assortment of "quaint nooks and recesses" (454), or some such. People are forever seeking inner sanctums or hiding in secret closets or back rooms. When Dombey and the Major travel down to Leamington, it is in a carriage in a carriage.[33] Florence and Walter have their honeymoon in a box in a box: their trim little cabin, set in a trim little ship; poor Paul Dombey's final home is a coffin in a vault in a church. The grand interior spaces of Dombey's mansion all converge, one room leading into another, onto the little "glass chamber" (24), where he breakfasts alone. At the beginning of chapter LIV, Dickens spends about 400 words detailing the Dijon apartments occupied by Edith and Carker, especially the rooms-within-rooms arrangement, finally focusing on the "smaller room within the rest," whose lamp, "through the dark perspective of open doors...looked as shining and precious as a gem." And: "In the heart of its radiance sat a beautiful woman—Edith" (720–21). (Carker, approaching this gem at the heart of the room in the rooms, is heard "laying a long train of footsteps through the silence, and shutting all the doors behind him as he came along" [722]: a creepy Hitchcockian effect just right for such multiply nested interiors.)

These are the topographical and architectural equivalents of a human landscape in which real hearts are not, as in *Oliver Twist,* cores, but rather "chords" "touched" (679) by degrees and "thrilled" as if in the original sense of being pierced through, surface to center. When the weeping Florence lets fall a tear onto the dog Diogenes, it is "as if his hairy hide were pervious to the tear that dropped upon it, and his dog's heart melted as it fell" (249)—melted, that is, as the tear imbued it, after seeping down through hair to hide to body to heart. A less benign version occurs when the "chill of Paul's christening" has "struck home" (91), seeping all the way down to a heart unprotected by the layers of warmth with which mother's or nurse's milk would have swaddled it.

In general, there is throughout the book this centripetal impulse to filter down through all intermediary outworks—"this round world of many circles within circles" (477)—but one constantly running up against the fact of how tricky that can, in fact, be, given the overpressurized, faultily gauged, prone-to-explode, out-of-sync cast of characters. Florence's tear may succeed in getting straight through to Di's heart, but at other times he can be a difficult animal to deal with, one capable, when not sure what to think of someone trying to make friends, of simultaneously growling at one end and wagging his tail at the other (641). Conflicted, in a word. As for Florence herself—well, yes: "the woman's heart of Florence, with its undivided treasure, can be yielded only once" (768), but the fact is that Florence, and later Walter, spend most of the book's length working out the divisions impeding the way to that heart, for instance, the problematical difference between love of brother and love of lover. She has her conflicts too.

It is that way with all the major characters: a hidden source somewhere deep underneath and inside, springing out of that underground reservoir of suppressed elements, but hard to get at because of the manifold of mixed and crossed signals interfering with almost any effort, these signals constituting a resistant surround of layerings whose gradual, mediated negotiation is the main business of human relationships.

And they all do have hearts, however long it takes to reach down to them. Mrs. Skewton, forever talking about "heart," doesn't find hers until the moment, near death, when she says to her daughter, "I nursed you" (561). Carker, about to die, looks out on a "garden" emblematic for him of the sister whose love was the last he knew and beholds a heart-stirring sunrise, as if for the first time (743). Dombey's tortuous discovery of his own heart is the main story of the book.

The language of the book, in ways unlike anything Dickens had written before, both beckons us into the Paul-revealed heart of things and sends up flak in our flight path. Its names distill essences, but then they slide off into semicoherent commerce with a language of unprecedented capacity for diversion and deflection. In addition to the name-word permutations and migrations discussed earlier—dead-sea-fruit-ashes, crossed-crosswise, and so on—the very structures of language can lead off on strange paths.

Accordingly, grammar, both in its office of making things cohere and in its tendency either to overdo it or to break down in the effort, is itself a major presence in the proceedings. The issue, for narrator and characters, is not so much high style versus low as tight versus loose. There are Ciceronians, monosyllabists, sputterers, taciturn word-hoarders, never-get-to-the-enders, just-plain-incomprehensibles, incorrigibly unpunctuated runners-on (Susan Nipper being the main exhibit here), blitherers, sentence-fragmenters, dealers in broken-backed syntax (Mrs. Skewton, after her stroke) and, in the poignant case of Cousin Feenix, a character who keeps trying to speak in the periodic sentences current in his heyday but who has lost the mental vigor needed to keep them in proper subordinated order. Dickens foregrounds matters of grammar because he has come to understand it as the essential matrix of character and, ultimately, of the patterns the characters will make together: his book, that is. (A maladroit grammarian like Dr. Blimber is not just a buffoon; he can be a menace to society [ask Toots], not least because of his way of turning epics of the sort *Dombey and Son* may aspire to be into "abstracted" fragments.) The syntactic grooves thus revealed are the inner trackways of his human trains, for instance, running the Susan Nipper who can never mind "her stops" (250) into one collision after another or diverting Cousin Feenix into accidental sidelines.

Abetting such perturbations in the system of meanings is the text's own "doubtful" Folk-Etymologies-Gone-Wild way with scores or—who knows—perhaps hundreds of its key words. They will *not* stay put. If *Dombey*'s names want to become words, its words and phrases can reciprocate with a humanlike inclination to propagate, and they seem to have their own distinctly non-Skeatian ideas of origins and family ties. It isn't just that they are prone to forming unexpected conjunctions across large distances in unpredictable ways ("mote," "beam," etc.): by themselves, in their iterations, they tend to evolve into variants according to semidiscernible linguistic logic.

Take the beginning of the first sentence: "Dombey sat in the corner of the darkened room in the great arm-chair by the bedside, and Son lay tucked up warm in a little basket bedstead, carefully disposed on a low settee immediately in front of the fire and close to it..." That the newborn Paul Dombey is "*disposed* on a low settee," (my italics) in, on consideration, alarming proximity to the word "basket," should ring a bell, or at least prepare for the ringing of later bells. "Basket" may or may not implicate "wastepaper basket" (a term current in Dickens's day), but it certainly has something to do with the grave digger's "shovels and baskets" later seen in the church where Paul is first baptized and then buried (59), and in either capacity puts a mordant spin on that word "disposed," later to return in the sense of "dispose of," for instance, when the Paul's last dying thoughts are "disposed of and gone" (200). Here and elsewhere one senses a pressure toward literalizing the moribundly metaphoric—an outcome, I think, of the centripetal, center-seeking impulse just considered—but one acted on in idiosyncratic ways seldom likely to be recognized at Dr. Blimber's, or any other, academy. The Blimber scholars might, to be sure, appreciate their great anthropomorphized clock's having its "face" removed and its innards explored in an "operation" (192)—but then what would they make of Edith, whose widow's weeds are "seaweed" (563) cast up over her feet, whose "lustrous" eyes (454) presumably have something (but what?) to do with the "lustres" "depending" (24: another word of vagrant modulations) from the ceilings of the house in which those eyes sometimes glisten with tears, whose "pencils are all pointless" (378) in the same chapter where her mother speaks "sharply" (411)? When they heard that the first Mrs. Dombey was subject to "decay" (5), would they take the word quite so literally as to anticipate the "mildewed remains" (24) from that lady's last illness (the "fragments of the straw that had been strewn before the house" (24)) littering her neighborhood after her death, or to pity the way those "remains," "by some invisible attraction," still seek to flee across the street, away from the house where their original was broken, "decay"ed, and died (24)?

Dombey and Son simply cannot resist doing things like that with words like "remains"—making them, or remaking them, unsettling. Similar freewheeling derivations are to be found at play in the deployment of (to give an unsystematic sample) "wheel," "toil," "familiar," "strike," "struck," "stroke," "graced" (becomes "grasped"), "rule," "execution," "dust," "flood," "overwhelmed" (which, via "whelm," links back to "flood"), "custom," various forms of "break," "temporary," "receipt," "carriage," "air," "want," "free," "train," "organ," "quick" (meaning both fast and alive), "shrewd" (sharp, shrewish), "vessel" (people, ships; chimes with "vassalage"), "strain," "grave," "interest," "horse," "hoarse" (the Major enunciates "hoarsely" [350], with a "horse's cough" [270]), "nevy" (a naval nephew), "crown" (of hair, of royalty, of spikes, of thorns), "reflexion" (Dombey commends it to Edith while she is looking in her mirror [546]), "cooing" (both people and pigeons do it), "precipitation," "wagging,"[34] "return," "fluttering" (hearts do it, birds do it), "share," "extinguisher" (literally present in Dombey's offices, figuratively in Mrs. Pipchin's establishment), "sanguine" (the Major is "too sanguine," literally and figuratively [353]), "inspiration" (yawning over and over, Mrs. Skewton is experiencing "inspirations" [93]: in-breathings), "share," "toast" (to celebrate, to burn), "know" (the "biblical" sense sometimes works), "charge," "groom" (Edith regards Dombey no more than "if he had been her groom"—but he *is* her groom), "capital," "blood," "brood," and—the most semantically proliferant of all—"breast."

These and other words, when they occur, are not so much in use as in play. Sometimes the oscillating buzz of lexical valences will yield up a clear-cut pun, as when Carker is made to resemble a "monkish carving, half human [half monk] and half brute [half monkey]" (574), or when seagoing mercantile interests are said to come to grief on "rotten banks" (773), but for the most part such doublings are dispersed and open-ended: something for the reader to notice, assemble, and make the best of. In *Finnegans Wake,* when one character asks another "Why can't you beat time?" the double sense, believe it or not, is simple: anyone who can't keep time with the music will not achieve artistic immortality. But what is one to make of the same expression in *Dombey and Son,* in the scene where "Paul heard Lady Skettles say to Mrs. Blimber, while she *beat time* with her fan, that her *dear boy* was evidently *smitten to death* by that *angel of a child,* Miss Dombey?" (197—my italics) Since Paul is neither the "angel" nor the "smitten" boy being referred to, any more than he is really being beaten by Lady Skettles, one cannot, reasonably, compose out of this sequence a prospect of Paul's having been pummeled into the great beyond by that time-beating fan of hers.

Not reasonably, no. But then, *Dombey and Son* does not always seem to care very much about how reasonable such operations should be. And this same Paul does happen to be the one who was introduced into the world accompanied by the sound of two watches "which seemed in the silence to be running a race" (10)—each, that is, trying to beat the other's time.[35] He will ever be the "old-fashioned" boy not quite able to catch up with the time set by Mrs. Blimber's husband's clock, and to whom the same Mrs. Blimber's daughter will say, in language that itself portends more than she knows, "Don't lose time, Dombey, for you have none to spare" (160). And, when he finally loses that race, "dear boy" will be one of the last things he hears (224), before being rapt up to what the author assures is the realm of "angels of young children" (225). So: all in all, I would say that mere fact of "angel of" coming three words after "death" should have been enough to cue us to something—prophetic, as it turns out—happening below the surface. The same goes for "beat time." The words are there. The syntax is for us to sort out.

Compounding the looseness of this already loose-knit web of significations is a penchant for malapropisms, portmanteau words, and various verbal misprisions either nonsensical or not, and the general ambience of mental uncertainty that goes with them. Mrs. Chick's comical confusion between the kind of scales that fall from one's eyes and the kind used by a grocer (403) go nowhere, perhaps, but I'm not so sure about Captain Cuttle's saying "garden angel" (524) instead of "guardian," given that the book does have one garden angel (unknown, however, to Cuttle), Harriet Carker. And why does Susan Nipper say "some one pray" when she means "come what may" (217)? Is it because she's just come from Paul's death room, a scene suitable for prayer? Does the "daily breath" coming from Carker (455) mock the "daily bread" of the Lord's Prayer? Probably, given that in the same sentence Carker seems to become a perverted Communion host, a "master" who "issues forth some subtle portion of himself" (455) to all around. And what about Mrs. MacStinger's lament that she has been "struck down in the herth" by a "felion?" (532) (In the hearth by a felon? To the earth by a fellow? In the heart by a villain?) When, in answer to the importunate Mrs. Chick's offer of a glass of wine, Polly answers, "Thankee, Mum ... since you *are* suppressing" (21), is it her subconscious or the author's penchant for deflating wordplay that's in charge?

Garrett Stewart has astutely remarked the novel's frequent use of syllepsis, defined as "a word understood in two different ways at once"—for instance "stiff with starch and arrogance" or "borne by Fate and Richards." He also observes that such a device "perfectly suits a novelistic structure whose chief ideological work is to render implicitly mutual, without exploring too closely, the dimly twinned realms of matter and spirit, the worldly and the eternal, the palpable and the unglimpsably distant."[36] Quite right, I would say, but it also suits a novel in which the language in general, and the people who employ it, are both congenitally given to confusing one thing with another—Miss Tox thinking that the "stoker" Toodles is a "choker" (16), Mr. Skettles assuming that Mr. Baps's "figures" refer to high finance rather than the dance floor (198), Dombey uncertain whether the crape on Toodle's hat is for Toodle's dead child or his (275), a chicken roosting on a donkey cart because "persuaded, to all appearances, that it grew there, and was a species of tree" (287), and many more such. It should also be added that some of the distant prospects of which Stewart speaks can come to seem more glimpsable than they were before, and that overall they are not so much dim as disarticulated. To an extent, they can be explored more "closely," made, if not right, more right, by drawing the correct connections. Slippery syllepsis, described nicely by Stewart as a "syntactic glissade," can yield, at least locally, to sturdier zeugma. The question it poses—which other word, exactly, does this word go with?—is one that crops up repeatedly. (A modern copy editor would be filling the margins with "ref?" queries.) Still, such questions can, eventually, be answered, more often than not, either as "this one" or "both." Such resolutions are sometimes achievable because the subconscious medium where their answers lie is presented not as some separate otherworld on an utterly removed vertical plane but as disseminated, often oddly and unexpectedly, throughout the texture of the narrative's here-and-now—thus, at times anyway, retrievable from somewhere. It is underneath, all right, but an underneath that keeps seeping (or spouting) up and through in places, as if by capillary attraction. As a result, the vertical takes on a horizontal range as well, so that looking down into the depths can also mean looking around the pages—not so much reading between the lines as reading around and among them. More precisely, it means expanding one's field of vision into the "unintelligible and inexplicable" penumbra of intimations that everyone except the most hard-core tunnel-vision types (and even most of them, in the end) senses at some point. The ocean has its depths but it also has a horizon, and Paul always wanted to see not just down into the first but beyond the second, to the distant shore, which, after all—a point made literally enough when Walter and Florence circumnavigate the globe—ultimately rounds back into our ambit. That is probably why so many of the book's uncanny suggestions come as shadowy presences just beyond the verge of one's field of vision, as if they were hovering in the wings or looming up behind, out of view but still sensed.

At least one case not only involves both character and reader but requires them to work together. In the formal center of the novel, while returning from the church where the Dombeys have just been married, a strange feeling comes over two members of the procession: "And why does Mr. Carker, passing through the people to the hall-door, think of the old woman who called to him in the grove that morning? Or why does Florence, as she passes, think, with a tremble, of her childhood, when she was lost, and of the visage of good Mrs. Brown?" (431). In this case, the answer to those questions is nowhere in the text. Instead, readers will have to turn and look to the accompanying illustration, which in the standard edition anyway faces the page on which that question is asked (Illustration 6).

There she is, Mrs. Marwood/Brown, the one who first appeared "out of" the ground, here all but swallowed up in the middle distance, a semisubliminal presence halfway detected and denied by both Carker and Florence out of the corner of the eye. The underground apparition has become a borderland one. And we readers, too, have to look, literally, outside the borders of that customary preserve of meaning, the written page. It is yet another example of how the evidence of what matters, especially of the ominous sort, is liable to be displaced, to be something and somewhere not recognizably part of a normal novel's normal syntax of meaning.

VIII.

Dickens, as I've said, finds in the train and its tracks an apt model for the actions of his characters, who score the tabula rasa of the landscape, both inner and outer, with their linear courses. The train has, after all, much in common with the resident obsessives. Its smoke obscures, and its speed blurs, the surroundings it dashes through—as compared, for instance, to the lovingly described expanses of nature afforded on the carriage ride to Warwick (375).

Also blurred, or overlooked altogether, are the spaces between train lines, as well as the tracts, like the once "busy great north road of bygone days" now "silent and almost deserted" (455), rendered obsolete. These are the unregarded waste spaces—blind spots and soft spots in the system—corresponding to the phases of normal, sympathetic human existence left unattended by the locomotive headlong-rushers, from which the book's eccentric underground spirits spring up to trouble the edges

Illustration 6 "Coming Home from Church"

of awareness: indeed, Mrs. Marwood herself lives near that same north road.

Any medium of transaction from that underground will be out of the way. It will be something discarded or overlooked, something, in the eyes of those who most should see it, barely there. One of the ways the novel stresses this theme, of the importance of the unnoticed, is to repeatedly take something apparently negligible, something naturally overlooked or looked away from, and make it pivotal. Florence in rags, like the workmen who save Dombey's life, is invisible. An inconsequential letter, accidentally dropped, sends Walter off to near-certain death. A dog's bark is the first faint note of what will build to the orchestrated crescendo of Walter's homecoming. He had been shattered, lost, shipwrecked, clinging to "a fragment" (661) in the empty sea, as the first Mrs. Dombey, outward bound on her own journey "upon the dark unknown sea," had clung to the "slight spar" of Florence (11), but fragments are not to be overlooked in this book of breakings. Dombey learns the name signaling Carker's destination at the last possible second, from a drunken—possibly drugged—informant on the verge of nodding off. After Edith has stolen into the sleeping Florence's room and whispered "Good Night," "Florence would sometimes awake, as from a dream of those words, softly spoken:" the message has sifted, from waking world to dream world, down through the soft interposition of the in-between "Night," at the liminal moment when each was drifting away from the other (623); six chapters earlier, Edith had likewise asked her dying mother "can you hear me?" and given her forgiveness, and a kiss, at the moment of death (561). After Staggs's Gardens becomes a "vanished land" like one of those mythical kingdoms said to be sunk beneath the waves, Walter and Susan search wildly around and can find only one survivor "who had once resided" (219) in its precincts, their sole intermediary to the submerged country. They were seeking it because Paul, setting out on his own otherworldly journey, had wanted to see his "old nurse," his link to that lost time and place, just as he had earlier been taken to the doctor who had been with his mother when she "drifted out upon the dark and unknown sea" (11).

So it is a recurring pattern. "I only am escaped alone to tell thee." These moments come like a baton between passed from or to a depleted runner—almost literally a baton, indeed, in the case of the "knotted stick" given from Sol to Walter at the outset of the latter's near-fatal voyage out to sea.

Dombey and Son is full of such intermediary remnants, human and otherwise, because it is pervaded by a sense, shared by author and characters, that its events stand poised between two realities, uncertainly reconcilable. The "eastern" guests and "western" guests at the Dombeys' party who fall out by "magnetic" antipathy (491) are in fact, it turns out, not from eastern and western hemispheres but from the globe's far east and the town's West End: they don't even share an idiomatic frame of reference to disagree in. The search for such a point of agreement, a common language between disparate codes the nature of whose dissimilarity is itself in question, lies behind much of the book's brooding anxiety about meaning in general. The characters have a habit of communicating in passwords, codewords, and prearranged signs like whistles and double-knocks, as if such made-up one-on-one signals were the only trustworthy language around. And there is a secret codeword quality as well about the author's way of conveying such information as that Dombey's marriage is like Dead Sea fruit, due to turn to ashes.

Dombey and Son has no shortage of emblems for its achieved points of contact between known and unknown, inner and other. Lips, about which it may be fairly said to have a fetish, often represent the zone between one world and another, as when Edith kisses the sleeping Florence or her dying mother. But the preeminent emblem is surely the breast. (Logically enough, the doubly preeminent emblem is, in turn, the bringing together of both, lips and breasts, in suckling, just as the main example of the opposite is their abrupt separation—Paul's "sharp weaning"). Against heavy competition, "breast" is the most semantically loaded word in the book, one situated at the boundary between every major set of antithetical or incompatible entities. Although it can be male—as in, "Dombey had truly revealed the secret feelings of his breast" (49)—the female edition obviously predominates. It can at times be revealing—can heave or glow with passion or, in Florence's case, blazon the mark where her father struck her—but throughout is mainly the site where secrets, tender or otherwise, are locked away from the world. Tender or otherwise: it is both the seat of human kindness and the place where both Edith and Dombey hide their knives.

Edith's knife is there to threaten, and answer back, the Carker who had promised her to "bury what I know in your breast" (506), a choice of words typically Carker-like in its innuendo of menace and sexual encroachment. As that exchange may remind us, breasts are—another boundary—both sexual and not. Neither here nor, so far as I can find, anywhere else does Dickens ever give one of his females "breasts": it is always "her breast," as if in overdecorous denial of the most obvious thing about them, that they come in twos. (Plenty of English authors, before his time and during it, were comfortable with phrases like "her breasts.") Like "bosom," "breast" in *Dombey and Son* often seems on the verge of subsiding into a quaint, vaguely biblical term indicative of internal sublimity. But counteracting that reading are certain facts obviously at odds. Dombey is hiring Polly Toodle for the milk from her breasts (both of them, presumably), not her inner sweetness. Carker becomes carnally interested in Edith at the moment that a glimpse of her heaving "bosom" (370) reminds him of his former mistress, her cousin. When Dombey hits Florence in her "breast," the word abruptly ceases to mean anything other than, shockingly, her milk-giving, mark-bearing, female-defining flesh. That is why he hits her there, and why, in this book where striking a woman, in that of all places, is pretty much the moral equivalent of spitting on a crucifix, instantly brands him as someone on the verge of perdition.

That it was his daughter's breast, of course, makes the act only worse: sexualizing her in the act of choosing that place to strike, he was also sexually assaulting her. Accordingly, this is the point at which Florence begins her prolonged father-to-brother-to-lover sequence, weaning herself, in stages, from aborted family love to achieved erotic love, in the process repairing the balance between the two kinds, shattered by her father's fist—a balance symbolized, once again, by her breast(s), given to her lover and then to her child. Another such balance will be found when, in an eyebrow-raising sentence, Polly Toodle, the old nurse summoned to the bedside of the dying Paul, takes his hand and "put it to her lips and breast, as one who had some right to fondle it" (224). In a book full of momentous sexual events, that is as close as *Dombey and Son* overtly gets to the language of eros: a dying boy-man exercising his right to "fondle" the breast of the nurse who once substituted for his mother.

In this and in other ways, the *Dombey* breast is the universal regulatory intermediary, the model interface between disassociated zones. Also, between their disproportionate pressures. A nipple is a valve. Poor desiccated Miss Tox: she speaks admiringly of Polly's "fountain" (22)—judging from results, an entirely apt description—while herself coming from a plot of withered houseplants and the "little green watering-pot" (398) from which she "trickled" her "sprinklings" (402) onto them. Unlike her, Polly is indeed a "fountain," one whose breasts both supply and regulate flow. A nipple is a valve, the more necessary the greater the underlying pressure. Even those mighty *Dombey* trains, with the future simmering inside them, need periodically to pause and lap from a "spout" along the way (276). A spout is a valve. When Mr. Chick, perhaps thinking of the James-Watt-and-the-kettle story—hence trains—suggests that a "teapot" might temporarily substitute for Paul's defunct mother's milk, he has, in the in-house logic of this book, a point. As Frank McCombie, commenting on this passage, remarks,

> Later...the advent of Mrs. Pipchin picks up the joke, for her name is a play upon 'pipkin', which is a small earthenware pot without a spout. The fact that the lady is useless as a supplier of nutriment to Paul, of any kind whatsoever, is emphasized by Dickens when, introducing her, he says: 'She was such a bitter old lady, that one was tempted to believe...that all her waters of gladness and milk of human kindness, had been pumped out dry'."[37]

Yes, and this is the same Mrs. Pipchin with the hollow house ("like a great shell" [100]), the semiarid front yard, and the "front parlour, which was never opened," but which does boast a remarkable collection of—honestly, now—cacti (100–1), the same lady as well whose native "acidity" recalls Miss Tox's concern that Polly not upset herself for fear it would make her breast milk "acid" (101, 21).

Breasts are reservoir, conduit, and (courtesy of nipples) regulator to this book's version of the universal life-source, repeatedly identified with the sea: that is why Paul, by way of compensation, gravitates to seaside when deprived of mother's and then nurse's milk. Importantly, each of these capacities can be realized only through interaction with outside forces. It is yet another kind of interface. A man must make a woman pregnant before she can lactate: hence, the display of Polly's newborn before Dombey, shopping for his milk machine. A child must be put at her breast before her flow can be, in Dombey's dreadful word, properly "discharged" and managed, for the benefit of both: when we hear of Florence that her "overcharged and heavy-laden breast must sometimes have...vent" (241), we may rightly, as often, take the words pretty literally. A nursing mother, in this book of mediations, is its ultimate mediator, the fuse through which life courses and life's fitful surges are tempered and smoothed out, not least for the nurser herself. (Whatever the case with human females, it was common knowledge that the distended udders of unmilked cows could be excruciating, that milking them was an act of kindness.) Denying Dombey a child, Edith was also denying herself this healing office, which may be why, mirroring Mrs. Marwood, the aunt and mother-double given to striking herself in the breast, she put that knife where she did, like an apprentice Amazon.

The figure of the nursing woman is the center toward which the concentrically arrayed approximations of *Dombey and Son* gravitate. In that capacity the mediator of life, she is also the mediator of meaning, of the subterranean, fountain-and-geyser kind this book identifies with the overlooked—the harmonizer; the sensitive matcher of end to end and adjuster of surface to surface; the mild, patient, seaside knitter-up of scattered and discordant strains. And although woman, in this arguably proto-feminist work, obviously predominates as exemplar, breasts would not be the universal mediators it proposes were they not occasionally androgynous,[38] and did they not work, so to speak, both ways, at times—two times, to be exact, in each case as verbs.

One of these occurrences describes, of all things, the action of a speeding train: "Breasting the wind and light, the shower and sunshine, away, and still away, it rolls and roars, fierce and rapid." (276). Given the "fierce and rapid" energy there, one may suspect the presence of "braving" in the semantic background, but the main idea, surely, is to give this creature of definitively male energy the female figurehead—typically one of impressive *embonpoint*—of its oceangoing counterpart,[39] breasting the waves.[40] (And isn't the first "away" in that passage doing what is sometimes called a bit of grammatical "squinting" between words before and words following, in its former capacity making for "breasting away"—pushing away—the wind and light," as a ship's prow pushes away water?) Used in this way, the verb "to breast" runs against the usual sense of the noun as signifying a stable reservoir of replenishment. Breasts, in that latter sense, do not "breast," do not (in the *OED*) "apply or oppose...stem, face, meet in full opposition."

The same applies, in a more complicated way, to the other occurrence of this verb: "Oh! could he but have seen, or seen as others did, the slight spare boy above, watching the waves and clouds at twilight, with his earnest eyes, and breasting the window of his solitary cage when birds flew by, as if he would have emulated them, and soared away!" (170). This is, of course, Paul, experiencing a preliminary hint of his visions of the rainbow (the clouds, the refracted twilight) and the waves, while being seen and not seen by his father. But in what earthly sense can he be said to be "breasting" his window? As is so often the case, an apparently unrelated word in the vicinity, "waves," helps give the answer: he is doing, or aspiring to do, what a ship's prow does when it breasts the waves.

Male or female? He is also, in that yearning of his, literally pressing his breast against his window. He gives his breast, as a mother to a child, to this transparent surface on the other side of which lies the sea in prospect, seeking connection that will "emulate" the great thwarted connection of his life. In so doing, in his aspiring imagination, he forges ahead, like the "[b]reasting" train, into the elements of water and wind, of waves and flying birds. He also, with that "slight spare" body of his, "emulate"s the birds as well—those birds who, as everyone has seen, will, when at rest, be "watching" west, like Paul, toward the western "waves" where "twilight" is settling in. The "breast" here is active and passive, male and female, a locus of inward and outward pressures of (because of that window) conformability, usually indeterminable but, in this case, achieved.

As we have also learned to expect from such passages, more or less detectable biblical allusions are playing around the borders of what is said: "Who are these that fly as a cloud, and as the doves to their windows?" (Is 60:8), and, better known: "And I said, Oh that I had wings like a dove! for then would I fly away, and be at rest" (Ps 55:6). Those birds Paul is watching are probably not, in fact, doves, but the associative lineages called into play by Dickens's choice of language nonetheless connect them to the scriptural doves that are types of otherworldly spirit, that hovered over Mary at the Annunciation and over Jesus at his baptism, that "brooded" over the sea at the Creation and flew back over another sea, "the face of the waters," to bring the olive branch to the ark, and then flew away. Through the mediation of such culturally accessible formulae, they connect as well to *Dombey*'s most symbolically pertinent birds, the doves and (courtesy of the "bird-fancier" Rob) pigeons that hover and home, and that in so doing repeatedly signify the heart—or, often, the "breast"—that wishes to do the same. Like her brother at the window, the Florence whose heart's voyagings the novel tracks from first page to last also emulates these birds: she and her destiny-ordained lover were, according to the infallible Cuttle, "as two young doves" from the start (448), and the course of her romantic ups and downs thereafter is a matter of flutterings, broodings, flights (chapter XLVIII is entitled "The Flight of Florence"), and nestings—until, as I have earlier suggested, it is her "white wings" that we are to imagine spread to the "favouring wind" that speeds her wedding ship.

Like Paul, too, she spends most of the book, "as doves to their windows," pressing against some invisible barrier separating her from the connections she senses instinctively. (It is, after all, in part her "waves," seen from the other side of his window that Paul is invoking at the end.) As the book's two main tutelary spirits, both brother and sister are, like the pigeons kept (usually locked in boxes) by Rob, homers[41]— sensing distant, magnetic affinities from which they are, almost always, blocked, prone to "wheel and falter" (318) when set free.

However they may aspire, neither, and especially not Florence, is much of a high-flyer: the point is not to reach as far as possible but to find the right surface on which to settle. Soaring is not the way of truth in *Dombey and Son*—never is, I think, in Dickens's work. The way is rather, like these two, to hover and falter, to test and alight, here and there, in a fluttery flight whose landings are scattered, unmapped points in the field of the language of the book they are in. Then, finally, to brood—to nestle and, well, "brood," ponder deeply, into the medium in which they rest, remembering as well that the book, in one of its many semantic "glissades," encourages us to take the word as a variant of "breed" (356). For readers seeking to divine the book's hidden language, that is also the flight plan to follow.

CHAPTER 3

"In a Thick Crowd of Sounds, But Still Intelligibly Enough to Be Understood"

I

Miss Flite lives on the top floor of a building at or near the center of a "monstrous maze" (482)[1] into which human sacrifices, especially of the young, are fed. Also swallowed up are sheep (parchment, tallow candles) and trees: fiber for paper, oak galls for ink. The oaks and elms of Chesney Wold, a hundred miles away, are right to wring their hands (766) and feel "sullen" (347) at the programmed extinction of their kind, as Lady Dedlock is more right than she knows when the prospect from that estate seems to her "a view in Indian Ink" (11). They are alike sensing from how far afield what Miss Flite describes as the magnetizing "Monster" of Chancery can "draw" its prey (441), how readily Lincolnshire may be made over into raw material for Lincoln's Inn Fields. Miss Flite's own mind has become "crazy" (126; cf. 197) in the preclinical sense of off-kilter—her version of things is more bent than bonkers—as if deflected by proximity to the same force at work on even the most rurally remote: the "sheep...all made into parchment, the goats into wigs, and the pasture into chaff" (514).

Down one story from the crazy lady lodges an opium addict who dies of his addiction early on; down two stories, on the ground floor, is an alcoholic who dies of his addiction later, and his pet, a cat, named after a clueless girl who, maiden sacrifice being nothing new in English or other history, was, for reasons of state, beheaded at sixteen.[2] Perhaps in a spirit of reincarnational revenge, this cat is given to corpse chewing

(129–30), and she certainly lives in the right place for it. Each of the in-house deaths has coated the walls with the splattered residue particular to the room's late inhabitant—gin and grease for Krook, ink for Nemo—and in both cases it as if that inhabitant, before expiring, had distilled within himself, to and past the point of bodily capacity, a distinctive Chancery essence. Gin kills Krook by impregnating and rendering combustible the lifetime's accumulation of the greasy fat that elsewhere pervades Chancery scriptoria and document repositories. Nemo's opium was the necessary accompaniment to his marathon sessions of commissioned ink work. The "rain of ink" left after his death (124) can plausibly be taken as precipitate, further condensed by the heavy admixture of tobacco smoke, of his room's opium-saturated air.

If that last sentence seems a mite fanciful—well, yes, but such fancies are all over the place in *Bleak House*. Jo, the novel's idiot savant, seems to be intuiting this one when he remembers the inquest on Nemo's body as an "Inkwhich" and mangles "nothing" into "nothink" (200). "Nemo," of course, means "Nobody," close cousin to Nothing, and this particular Mr. Nobody obviously wanted to forget his past—that is, he wanted not to think. To that end he employed two compounds: opium and ink. His body is discovered by a man whose manner may serve to remind us that "caustic" derives from the Latin for "ink" and whose name, Tulkinghorn, is an anagram for "inkhorn glut."

So: Miss Flite's fellow inmates, stacked up in this particular bleak house, one of many such residences. Outdoors and nearby, pub-goers sing a hymn to death's coal-black poisoned wine[3] (Tulkinghorn's wine comes out of a cellar), while the children, over and over, are rising and crumbling into the mud as they chant "Ashes! Ashes! All fall down!" (412). Informed opinion today says that it is not likely true after all that this song dates from the London plague years. Still, one wonders what Dickens thought, given that the Lord Chancellor is "the most pestilent" of sinners (6), that this lordship's handiwork is a slum from which diseased corpses are routinely exported (278), and that the other Lord Chancellor, Krook, leaves behind him the "ghostly...traces" of his "chalked writing on the wall" (492). Plague-stricken homes of old were marked with chalk, and we know what kind of future "writing on the wall" portends.[4]

Small wonder Miss Flite chooses to lodge as far above ground zero of this monster-centric maze, and as close to the free air above, as she can. Her name reveals both the wish (flight) and fated outcome (mis-flight). As usual with Dickens, her pets—her birds—are extensions of their owner. They, too, wish to fly away. Caged, they live for the sun above, coming to life and breaking into song only when the cover over their prison is removed and the sun let in (54). Eventually, when Jarndyce and Jarndyce runs out of money, Miss Flite sets them free, free to fly in the sunlight. Free! Of course, they will all be killed.[5]

As is by now perhaps obvious, I think that there is a story behind all this, and that it is the story of Daedalus and Icarus. A labyrinth; an omnivorous monster specializing in consuming the "flush and fire" of youth (471); feathered creatures flying sunwise; their deaths. The requisite Daedalusian materials are not lacking: everybody in the vicinity writes with feathers and seals with wax. There is even an Ariadne—Ada, whose love for Rick enables her to thread through the maze to its center (610–11). As for the moral: "All generous spirits are ambitious, I suppose," says John Jarndyce, late in the book, "but the ambition that calmly trusts itself to such a road, instead of spasmodically trying to fly over it, is of the kind I care for" (717). Nemo—or Captain Hawdon, to give him his proper name—was a Byronic high-flyer who crashed and burned. Contrast that with, for instance, Boythorn's bird, a canary whose excursions never carry it out of sight of the master to whom it always returns. In a novel featuring a number of moralized airborne creatures distinguished by their flight paths, count on the canary to carry the day.

And count on bats to carry the night. When Esther approaches Chesney Wold at dusk, the bats "almost" touch her in their "fitful flight" (453). "Almost": what the science of later days was to designate as ultrasonic "echolocation," the faculty of computing distances by the time it takes their squawks to echo back from whatever those squawks hit, saves them from collision. In contrast to the magnetism Miss Flite senses in the heart of Chancery, the impulse at work here is from the other pole, propelling flights not of larklike aspirings toward transcendent completion (some of Miss Flite's birds are larks), but of a succession of avoidances, of one near-miss after another.

Bats, that is, can be seen as opposites of overreaching Icarus types. In the scene where they "almost" collide with Esther, that makes them tutelary spirits:

> I went out alone, and after walking a little in the park, watching the dark shades falling on the trees and the fitful flight of the bats, which sometimes almost touched me, was attracted to the house for the first time. Perhaps I might not have gone near it if I had been in a stronger frame of mind. As it was, I took the path that led close by it. (453)

Being in a weaker than usual "frame of mind," Esther feels herself impelled toward the building housing her mother and Sir Leicester

Dedlock, the latter still unaware of the secret the two women have just come to share. Housed there as well, and situated at the focal point of the drawing room, is the portrait of Lady Dedlock, which, or so it seems, reminded Mr. Guppy of Esther and started him wondering about what connection the resemblance might signify.

Obviously, going into this place at this time would be a bad idea. Esther knows that, but advances anyway. Her will—her "frame of mind"—is weakened, the prospect is enticing, and she has just learned that her mother lives there. Approaching it, she quickens her pace:

> I was passing quickly on, and in a few moments should have passed the lighted window, when my echoing footsteps brought it suddenly into my mind that there was a dreadful truth in the legend of the Ghost's Walk, that it was I who was to bring calamity upon the stately house and that my warning feet were haunting it even then. Seized with an augmented terror of myself which turned me cold, I ran from myself and everything. (454)

Of course, she is not really running from a ghost, or even from herself. Rather, like the echolocating bats, she is recoiling from the steadily amplifying echo of herself, of her "warning feet." As the daughter drawn toward the single "lighted" square signaling the lost mother she has missed and dreamed of for twenty years, Esther verges on being yet another type of Icarus, hurrying lightward toward ruin. Instead, she winds up checking her flight at the last second.

II.

Two other mythical couples, I believe, interlace significantly with the Daedalus and Icarus story: Perseus and Medusa; Orpheus and Eurydice. Before turning to them, however, it should be noted how many other stories there are, so to speak, echoing about the precincts. *Bleak House* is nothing if not self-conscious, and like other such productions, it is given to viewing its own narrative through the mediation of earlier narratives.

This habit is shared by some of the characters. Esther's own name may be a biblical allusion;[6] her maid, she thinks, is "one of Flora's attendants" (540); that she was raised by a godmother automatically elicits comparisons to the immured princesses of fairy tales, minus, alas, Prince Charming (17). Perhaps she inherited this reflex from her father, who certainly showed some mordant, learned wit when, settling in the lair of Miss Flite's voracious "Monster," he took the name "Nemo"—that is, in the Latin version, the name Odysseus assumed in the Cyclops's cave. Others have displayed a similar mythopoeic bent in naming their offspring. Mr. Turveydrop and Harold Skimpole have both imposed names intended to amberize their children in their fathers' outworn fantasies. The elder Rouncewell brother has named his son Watt in honor of James Watt, patron saint of the new iron age gathering force in the industrial north, but probably as well with some mischief in mind toward the feudal Sir Leicester, who sees all such developments as signaling a return of another "Wat," Wat Tyler (79).[7] Then there are the unforgivable names that Jarndyce gives to Esther—all of pantomime hags and old maids, some of them traditionally played by men in drag.[8]

A similarly allusive cast of thought runs through the discourse of what is usually called the Omniscient Narrator, hereinafter the narrator. In alluding to a passage of his own from *Dombey and Son,* for example,[9] Dickens seems to invite us to consider this novel as a prequel to the other,[10] which of course reminds us that it *is* a novel. The heavy borrowing from Shakespeare among others reminds that it is also a work of literature. "Tom-all-Alone's," for a while Dickens's working title, recalls the blasted heath where another Poor Tom, naked, was a-cold, and indeed every "Tom," including the Tom Jarndyce who blew his brains out, is forlorn; one of them, a destitute orphan, is even named Tom Neckett—naked Tom, a-cold.

In this as in other ways, *Bleak House* can seem like the most urbane, the most *educated* of Dickens's novels. The old chip on the shoulder about not having been to university is seldom in evidence. And it helps for us to be educated too, at least when it comes to picking up on mythical overtones. If nothing else, in a novel where bewilderment haunts not only characters but readers too, such cues can offer at organizing material into recognizable narratives. The Icarus story is one example.

Here is another. Lady Dedlock, guided by Jo, is seeking out the grave of her lover:

> Go before me, and show me all those dreadful places. Stop opposite to each, and don't speak to me unless I speak to you. Don't look back. (201)

Going on before, Jo brings her through a "little tunnel" to the locked gate of the most dreadful locale of the book, a reeking, rat-ridden place of bones in piles and the half-buried dead—not "blessed," as he remarks with his usual sideways acuity, but "t'othered," damned. The lady tells him, "again," to look away from her. He does, stretching out his broom toward the grave that she has paid him to find. "Now," she says, "show me the spot again!" Again, he does—and, "At length, looking aside to see if he has made himself intelligible, he finds that he is alone" (202).

Lady Dedlock has vanished, on the edge of this home for the damned dead, at the moment of fixing her eyes on the site of her lover's body. Myth and folklore could supply any number of analogues to this sequence, but the one that seems to me to ring truest is, again, that of Orpheus leading Eurydice out of Hades. "Don't look back" might be the guiding rubric of Lady Dedlock's life (and of many another character[11]). It is also the injunction given to Orpheus in the underworld, and what makes it especially pertinent to *Bleak House* is that he is forbidden to look back at what he most wants to see. There seems to be some principle of direct proportionality between the force of desire and the obduracy of its prohibition.

Whatever its source in the folklore, this principle governs *Bleak House*. Think of Ada at Esther's locked door, weeping and begging to be let in to join her stricken beloved (388; 432), or of Esther, in response, standing at the window "behind the window-curtain listening and replying, but not so much as looking out" (388) at her, or of Ada and Rick being told they must keep apart, ought not even to look at one another (301), or of Esther's weird allergy to the presence of the man she loves ("I often slipped home at about the hours he was expected" [604]), or of Krook, document-hoarding illiterate (writing, writing everywhere, and not a word to read), being admonished that he may "admire" Ada's shining golden hair so long as he keeps hands off (50), or of Sergeant George turning his back and feigning indifference when the mother he yearns to embrace passes near him (427).

Again, there seems to be some kind of exorbitant impost on desire itself. It's not that you want what you can't have; it's that you can't have what you want and that the more you want it, the more you can't have it. Both Jo and Lady Dedlock get so hungry that they can't eat. Allegory, Cassandra-like, points incessantly to the spot where a murder will occur, on the condition that no one understands him until it's too late. The more Richard needs Jarndyce's aid and counsel, the more he resists them.

Variations on this rule drive the lives of the characters. In chapter I, Miss Flite is seeking justice in the one place in England where she is least likely to find it. In chapter II, "my Lady Dedlock (who is childless)" is introduced "looking out" from her Chesney Wold window at a gamekeeper's family: "a child, chased by a woman, running out into the rain to meet the shining figure of a wrapped-up man coming through the gate" (11). This family's life—the child above all—is what she wants.[12] And that, in *Bleak House,* is just too bad. Lady Dedlock, is, to repeat, "childless," and, in her late forties, too old to become pregnant.

Her unhappiness is not just a matter of the grass being greener. Nothing in the novel suggests that the keeper's wife envies her mistress back. Lady Dedlock is right to feel bereft, because *Bleak House* women are fulfilled through motherhood, and that is that. (Mrs. Jellyby and her colleagues serve as horrible examples to mothers who don't understand this.) Having her one baby, Esther, pronounced dead at birth and taken from her arms left Lady Dedlock hollow, the effigy on display throughout the novel.

Later, that child's restoration brings her back to emotional life, but only with fearsome qualifications, one of them being that Esther will have—must have—gone through a near-death ordeal leaving her disfigured. That is, Lady Dedlock is allowed to address her daughter once, on two conditions, the first being that this daughter has ceased to resemble her. Phiz apparently got the point (Illustration 7).

The other condition is, "Don't look back." Mother and daughter will never again see one another face to face.

That Esther's reconciliation with the one person she has always dreamed of meeting should come about only on the condition of a wasting fever leaving her old self annihilated is simply one more instance of the way things work in *Bleak House.* Mother and child, lover and beloved: whatever the nature of the connection, the rule is that one must not approach/see/touch whatever is closest to oneself. Had Esther still resembled her mother, whose image she presumably once bore to some extent, their meeting could not have happened.

As a logical extension, this rule applies most of all to encounters with, recognitions of, oneself. Hence, Esther's mirror phobia—a counterpart, surely, to the fear that makes her run from her own echo at Chesney Wold. The aversion is most in evidence after her illness—when, through travail and ritual, through the screen of her veil and then the screen of her hair, she by degrees nerves herself to look in her mirror—but seems to have been at least incipiently with her all along. In the first chapter of her narrative, arriving in London and directed to a "little looking-glass," she is content to take "a peep" at her bonnet (29), then to turn her attention to other matters—above all to Ada, she of the "rich golden hair" lit up by the "fire shining upon her" (30). Ada's blond beauty, flashing onto Esther's mind like a sunburst onto film, instantly eclipses any remembrance of her own reflected looks. The impression

Illustration 7 "Lady Dedlock in the Wood"

is magnified by its contrast with the faintness of Esther's self-image, a faintness natural in someone who makes a point of not looking at herself. In her childhood she had had "a little glass," but one placed so high above her head (doubtless one of her godmother's moves to discourage the sin of vanity) that she needed to stand on tiptoe if she wanted to get a glimpse of herself (224). Evidently, she didn't, much.

I have called this instinct a phobia, but from much of the evidence of *Bleak House* it is if anything a benign one—a salutary avoidance mechanism, like fear of heights. It seems to be a sign of good-looking Sergeant George's worthy instincts, for instance, that his own mirror, used only for shaving, is "a looking-glass of minute proportions" (324). Mirrors can petrify. When Esther comments, disapprovingly in spite of herself, that Harold Skimpole looks like an artist's self-portrait, it is pertinent that making such a portrait requires a mirror (65). Skimpole is a serial narcissist whose successive self-portraits have been inscribed and fixed, one at a time, on his three hapless daughters.

Exhibit A is Lady Dedlock herself. One of the first things we hear about her is that although, "seeing herself in her glass," she seems above the reach of "ordinary mortals," in fact the mortals in her retinue look right through her (14). What is a mirror to her has become a window to others. That is probably a matter of cause and effect, and as such an omen of what will become of her and why. Later, we hear that she "knows its influence"—the influence of the "splendour and beauty of her appearance"—"perfectly" (415). It is precisely the quality that makes her both so formidable and so vulnerable. When Tulkinghorn, having gained the upper hand, tells her that she has been behaving "transparently" (580), he is delivering a coup de grace. Reflectivity is the mirror's armor, by means of which it repels incursion, at the price of sealing in place the image entrusted to it. Without that power in force the image becomes denuded, innermost frailties "chalked up on the walls and cried in the streets" (508). Losing that power, becoming transparent but remaining brittle, what remains returns us to the exposed woman, as we first met her and last see her, looking longingly through glass at what she wants instead of what she has, abandoning the seat of her reflecting and reflected glory to seek out, in lost daughter and dead lover, the last remnants of what she was rather than what she is. Esther is on to something when she compares the first sighting of her mother to "a broken glass" (225), the shattering of a mirror. Writing seven years after the event, she may even be mindful of the bad luck it brought.

With her reflective screen down, Lady Dedlock becomes just another reactive element within the novel's play of forces. After an incredible forty-plus-mile trek in terrible weather she succeeds against all odds in retracing the way to Captain Hawdon's cemetery—probably with the intention of expiring, tragedy-queen-like, on his grave—only to be prevented from traversing the last few yards by a locked gate. She is later found with an arm reaching through the bars (713). In this, she performs in earnest a scene earlier gone through in the book's first half, when she still had a name and image to protect. Then as well she was stopped at the same gate, but shrank from it (202). Instead, she had Jo do the reaching for her. Following her directions, he stretched his broom through the bars toward Hawdon's grave "to the utmost powers of elaboration," but could not quite touch it (202).

Both visits are variations on the pervasive theme of thwarted desire, but the second is given an extra turn. The first time around, Lady Dedlock disappears. This time, she dies. Then her daughter finds her. Esther lifts up the body, turns its head toward her own, and, finally, looks straight into her mother's dead face. A categorical statement here: that could not possibly have happened had her mother been alive, any more than the first meeting could have occurred if Esther's face had been intact. In *Bleak House,* falling just short of such desired consummations is the story of Lady Dedlock's life and of Esther's life, because it is the story of life. Consummations are thwarted because their completion equals death. Eurydice merges with Medusa. Esther twice seeks in her mother's face a partial mirror image of herself. She fails the first time because her own face has been drastically changed. The second time she is face to face with a corpse. To look upon what matters most to you, especially if that is yourself or a facsimile of the same, can freeze and then destroy them or you or both. For example, those birds of Miss Flite's, who yearned for the sunlight and will consequently die in the sunlight, or Miss Flite herself, compelled to look upon the Chancery "Monster" and thereby be transformed into a lunatic automaton (440), or those "long-preserved dead bodies sometimes opened in tombs, which, struck by the air like lightning, vanish in a breath" (362).

It is simply of course in this novel that Krook should be one minute away from handing John Jarndyce the key to the whole Chancery puzzle but "cannot resolve" to do it (181), that he should later be on the verge of giving it over to those able to read it but explodes just before the appointed hour, that the document in question should finally surface, and be subjected to literate scrutiny, at the precise moment when its power is spent, that this document was in turn rescued on the verge of being burnt for once and all. It is of course that Esther, the beleaguered orphan who learns almost simultaneously that 1) she is the child of a great lady in a grand house and that 2) this fact makes her a bastard, should have unknowingly received letters handwritten by her father, should have gravitated toward that father's neighborhood and even passed outside his door, but should be allowed to cross the threshold only during her second visit, after his death. It is in keeping with the way things are that the baby that Ada finds in the brick maker's hut should die at the moment she uncovers and touches it (200), and that her own baby's birth should correspond with its father's death (763).

Ada is, according to the terms in place, a natural, uncomplicated woman, therefore one who desires family and children above all else. She wants most to give her husband a child and fears most that "he may not live to see" it (724). So, guess what happens. Caddy Jellyby wants most to give *her* husband a child. She does, but the birth almost kills her, and the baby she presents to the fiddle-playing dancing-teacher father grows up to be deaf and dumb. Before she became dead-locked as Her Ladyship, Honoria Barbary gave birth to a stillborn baby girl, or so she has believed for twenty years; for her part that girl grew up fearing that the delivery had killed her mother. All perfectly reasonable, in this novel—and to a degree, right: as a result of that birth one of them will die in a pest-hole.

The other will grow up courting oblivion, not only reluctant to look at herself but eager to disappear into the woodwork. Esther *likes* it when people call her "little," seems to like it even better when they treat her (her father's daughter) as the "no one" she becomes in a dream (45). For the second half of the book her face is usually veiled, to be exposed only rarely, and then usually as a test of virtue, against Guppy in particular. *Bleak House* is mined with this and many another unfaceable, of things not to be seen or said; the veiled and ambulatory post-disfigurement, bet-you-can't-look Esther is just one among many. You can spot them by the diversionary bat-flights of those in their vicinity—Esther forever biting her tongue and changing the subject, Richard's coy side-glances at the "forbidden ground" of the Chancery suit (207), John Jarndyce disappearing into his Growlery. Even Woodcourt, who has seen more than his share of dreadful sights, "shrinks back" from the innocent Jo "with sudden horror," has to contend "against an avoidance of the boy" (557), when he hears, not quite correctly, that Jo infected Esther.

Such face-to-face moments are accordingly few and fraught. The bats have it right. One progresses, if at all, by dodging and deflecting. A straight path is for romantic (and Romantic: everyone in this book with ties to the Romantic era either comes to a bad end or should) fools. This principle applies, above all, to the language as used by narrators and characters alike. "As the crow flies" is an innocent enough cliché when introduced early to describe a narrative trajectory (10); by novel's end we have been reminded several times that the crow is a scavenger, its flight taking us to the heart of Chancery, to Tulkinghorn and later Grandfather Smallweed (whose voice is a croak), its nearest avian relations the "ravenous" (403), ink-expending, feather-wielding, tree-consuming, sheep-killing scribes who first show up to make money off of a coroner's inquest. The point of its straight line of flight is to most efficiently deliver a kiss (or peck) of death. Denial, avoidance, and sublimation are accordingly the order of the day.

Hence all the lying. Certain other Dickens novels feature one dominant variety of compulsive behavior, something that its characters do more than anything else except for walking and talking: drinking in *Pickwick Papers,* weeping in *Nicholas Nickleby;* blushing in *Dombey and Son.* Here, it is lying. Open a page at random, and odds are you will encounter at least one evasion, prevarication, fib, or fraud. One may perhaps be inclined to discount the Esther pages on the grounds that so many of the lies are to herself.[13] True enough, but look again. This is a woman who likes being "pleasantly cheated" by the lies of others (65), who lies pathologically to us about Woodcourt, the one subject that matters most to her, and who is fully capable of other kinds of lies, for instance, in withholding the true story of her epochal meeting with her mother from Ada (456), or in seconding false reports about the state of Caddy's health (602). As in the Ada case, she is especially given to lying by omission, for example, when, explaining to Mademoiselle Hortense "the impossibility of engaging" a maid—later in the same chapter she will engage a maid—she finds it unnecessary "to say how very little I desired" this particular candidate (286).

Polite fictions of this sort are the lubricant of civility, and indeed many, probably most, of the novel's hundreds and hundreds and hundreds of lies are of the excusable type. Still: quantity, as the man said, has a way of becoming quality. By weight of sheer numbers, mendacity is the medium in which *Bleak House* life is lived. So, of course, the novel begins in a fog, emanating from and sinking back into an urban swamp populated by questionable breeds tending toward the amphibious, the hybrid, and the fanciful, where one cannot know miasma from solid ground. That sort of surface, after all, is proverbially the lair of liars. In *Bleak House,* that includes virtually[14] everyone.

It is true that several characters—the Chadband set, Conversation Kenge, perhaps Skimpole, whose trick is to let people think that he is kidding when he isn't—have become so used to the condition that it might be said of them, as Disraeli said of Gladstone, that their powers of self-deception are so inexhaustible that they are never insincere. The morally serious characters, however, are the ones who have come to terms with the necessary alloy of lies in their lives—who become, consequently, adept in the improvisatory acrobatics necessary to keep some kind of upstanding equilibrium, all the while negotiating a field where every other step is liable to be a false one.

Mr. Bucket, for example, is a fabulous liar. He is also the man who, contemplating Skimpole's brand of self-serving make-believe, passes on to Esther this rule: "Fast and loose in one thing, fast and loose in everything" (682). Amazingly, he means it. Given the opportunity, he could doubtless offer a persuasive rationale for how someone like him could sincerely believe something like that. Probably there would be times when it seemed to come close to crossing some line or other, but in the end, the more you paid attention, the more it would hang together. One thing it would not be is fast and loose.

Bucket is a morally complicated character, and he brings a host of ethics-class, lifeboat questions along with him. Had "triage" in the medical sense been a term around at the time, he could have adopted it as a watchword. He hounds Jo, but he also takes him to a hospital (559), effectively bars him from the plague-lands that have poisoned him from birth (Allan Woodcourt was unable to do as much), and supplies him with what might have been the wherewithal, were Jo's case not hopeless already, to make a go of it in healthier climes. Whether in sum his actions hastened or delayed Jo's death is a nice question, true. But then, so is this: had he succeeded in intercepting Jo earlier, might not Esther have been spared the infection that almost kills her?

Then there are the collaterals. Bucket's actions in regard to Jo are intended to save the life of someone else, Lady Dedlock, who appears to have a much better chance of survival. (Again: triage.) Yes, his motives are also, to some extent, mercenary. And, yes again: that the rich lady is perhaps salvageable but the waif is probably not is a fact due in multiple ways to the gross system of injustice that is one of the book's main themes. Bucket knows all about that, but he also knows that his business is to make the best of things, given what things are. Whatever Engels might have thought, deliberately sacrificing Lady Dedlock would not have evened the score in any unmad way. Everything Bucket does, including the arrests of Gridley and Sergeant George, are according to the same not-contemptible calculus, in which self-interest figures but does not domineer.

Not that such a calculus is infallible. Infallibility does not exist in *Bleak House*. Indeed the death of the person Bucket is most concerned to save, Lady Dedlock, is partly his fault—although ironically it may be said to validate his usual duplicitous approach. He abandons that approach and goes in for the kind of Icarian overreaching that, as he of all people should understand, has brought down many another. He rises too high ("he mounts a high tower in his mind"), to see too far ("and looks out far and wide" [673]), to fly too straight (straight to Lincolnshire) for too long (had he turned back an hour sooner, Lady Dedlock might have been saved). As under normal circumstance he would be the first to point out, that sort of gammon will never do in this world, his world.

It is a forced error. The extreme time pressure puts him off his game. He still remains the best there is when it comes to making it across the spongy consistency of this book's epistemological and moral grounds. So, why is that not good enough?

III.

John Forster reported that on returning from his 1842 visit to America, Dickens gave him a copy of Hawthorne's *Mosses from an Old Manse,* "with reiterated injunctions to read it." Thereby hangs a crux. Although some of the book's stories had appeared in print earlier, as a volume it was first published four years after the American trip. Noting the discrepancy, the editors of Dickens's letters write that the book in question was probably in fact Hawthorne's *Twice-Told Tales.*[15]

Whichever it was, there is no doubt of Dickens's enthusiasm. Several scholars have detected borrowings from Hawthorne in later works, including *Bleak House.*[16] I suggest that one such borrowing—more of an absorption, actually—was from the story in *Mosses from an Old Manse* called "Rappaccini's Daughter." Although the collection was unavailable to him in America, Dickens could have read it sometime soon after its 1846 English publication—some time, that is, before he began blocking out *Bleak House.*

"Rappaccini's Daughter" is a variant of the folk motif of the poisoned kiss. As its narrator tells us, one of the earliest versions is of a beautiful woman sent in tribute to Alexander the Great. Alexander is about to "embrace" her, when Aristotle (in Hawthorne's version, "a certain sage physician") intervenes by revealing "a terrible secret," that the woman "had been nourished with poisons from her birth, until her whole nature" was deadly to the touch.[17] This account echoes that of the Persian king Mithridates, who immunized himself against poisoning by taking increasingly larger doses of every toxic substance known, with results good for him but bad for any woman who shared his bed.

Rappaccini's daughter Beatrice has been raised on a diet of poison flowers, which have made her the most desirable woman in existence, the ultimate femme fatale. Her influence attracts Giovanni, the young lover of the story, and, by gradual infiltration, starts to poison him too. Realizing this, he demands from her what in this story is the ultimate consummation, a kiss, certain to be fatal to them both. Instead, Beatrice swallows an antidote and dies. This is sad, but it could have been sadder: had the two lovers actually exchanged that one kiss, the result would have been not only two deaths instead of one, but probably something cataclysmic, something on the order of what Victor Frankenstein prevented when he refused to let his monster mate with one of its kind.

Thus elaborated, the story of the poisoned kiss may, I suggest, be said to ground the three *Bleak House* narratives traced earlier. Like the Icarus story, it is a parable of overreaching. Like the story of Orpheus and Eurydice, it presents desire, especially erotic desire, as destructive along a sliding scale: the more one wishes to look to and approach the object of desire, the more one must not. Like the story of Medusa, it represents the violation of the injunction as fatal to the beholder and adds Original Sin to the mix: through a deep fault line in yourself, what you most desire to approach, behold, touch, kiss, and so on, is ipso facto too destructive to face.

The most consequential kiss of *Bleak House* is one that never happens. It is the kiss Ada longs to give Esther after the door between them is, mercifully, shut on her, locking Esther in along with Charley and Charley's smallpox.[18] Ada is frailer than her friend. Had she made it across the threshold, the resulting infection would have killed her. Of course, in shutting Ada out and herself in, Esther will bring about her own eventual blinding and scarring. But, again, it could have been worse. At least no one dies. And there is one other consolation: afterward—which is to say, before she begins her *Bleak House* narrative—Esther will be immune to the amorphously malignant influence brooding over the book from its first page. As the summer sun purged of the universal miasma, the person writing Esther's half of *Bleak House* has thereby been made safe against its resident contagions. She has been mithridatized.

Others have not. When Ada bends to kiss the ailing Richard (763), he forthwith dies. The kind of passionate kissing liable to lead to the bedroom is kept out of the picture, of course, but visible consequences of such doings are not encouraging. In fact, up until the last few pages, the whole begetting-and-begotten business is pretty grim: Caddy's deaf and dumb infant; the blasted-from-birth Guster; Charley's mother, dead "just after" the birth of her third child (189); the hordes of unwanted

Jo's dying every day; and so on. *Bleak House* does indeed believe that women are made to be mothers, but it also seems attuned to the old "labour"–"labour" pun of Genesis: because of the fall, men must waste themselves in work,[19] women in bringing forth. It is not a happy lookout, but then this is not a happy book.

Of all such offstage goings-on, the pre–*Bleak House* kisses, and so on, between Captain Hawdon and Honoria Barbary were, being undoubtedly the most passionate, therefore the most poisonous in their consequences. When we hear that Lady Dedlock would go to heaven itself "without any rapture" (13), we are being told not that she is congenitally frigid but that all her fire was consumed, back then, in the blaze of that affair. Today her story could qualify as a prime bodice-ripper, literally a Regency romance. A soldier during the swaggering days following Waterloo, Hawdon was moneyed, handsome, "dark" (134)—her mother's daughter as well as her father's, Esther will herself fall for a "dark" man, Woodcourt (126)—and impetuous. Honoria was his match. Their calamitously consummated desire remains, along with Chancery's dead hand, one of the two strongest forces at work in the novel. In a world where Regency survivors, fish out of water, come or have come to bad ends, these two are no exceptions. Hawdon wound up slowly killing himself after a period of checking the "Coroners' Inquests" (129) to see if his Honoria were still alive. She followed up by reading through the newspaper reports of the inquest on his body and ends up dead because, twice, she cannot keep away from his grave.

Hawdon's death is from "poison" (125)—opium, absorbed in increasing doses until he had enough in his stash to "kill a dozen people" (126). That is one reason that Esther, passing his door at a time when he is still alive (54–55), on the other side, does not go through it and into the opium fumes—indeed could not, any more than Ada can be let into Esther's and Charley's infected room. She would have been knocked out—possibly, given those dozen people her father's intake might once have done in—killed outright. The reason that this does not happen to the first two people who do enter the room, Tulkinghorn and Krook, is probably that they have already had some exposure to opium (Tulkinghorn recognizes the smell at once; Krook has been living downstairs, and the smoke was apparently detectible enough to reach his other boarder, Miss Flite [178]), and certainly that both have been hardened by lifetimes of self-induced oblivion. They are mithridaically immunized.

That is not the kind of immunity won by Esther during her disease. In this way at least, she diverges from her parents, who chose not to feel at all—he with a narcotic, she through marriage to a Dedlock.

Esther, by contrast, in an act of enhanced and prolonged fellow-feeling (the noble side of her sometimes-irritating self-abnegation) chooses to embrace what comes to her.[20] The fever that almost carries her away, then leaves her worthy to be the novel's one non-anonymous narrator and only bearer of unblighted young, is of a piece with the other refining fires of Dickens's fiction, for instance, the fever that brings Pip down to the edge of oblivion and then frees him to float back up to, literally to look up at, the emerging face of Jo, whose high nobility he is at last able to appreciate, or the similar fever that accomplishes much the same for Arthur Clennam in re Amy Dorrit.

Esther makes her choice in what is, to repeat, an utterly typical *Bleak House* act—slamming the door on the one person whose company she most desires. Her ordeal, and the illumination that it advances and confirms, is causally coupled with the habit of denial, in both the ascesis sense of the Greeks and the psychobabble sense of today, which more than anything else determines her batlike dealings with past and present. John Jarndyce shows his characteristic (and somewhat creepy) astuteness when he makes Esther the keeper of the Bleak House keys; who better, after all, to lock everything up? His later remark that "there must be two" of her (604–5) comes from the same understanding. In no small part due to John Jarndyce, there are indeed two Esthers,[21] two opposite-facing selves, as there are of that other door-keeping, border-bestriding, key-keeper Janus,[22] and Esther's main inner job is to keep each one, the diminutive maid-of-all-work who starts her chores before dawn and packs Ada's and Richard's bags while the two are obliviously flirting away next to her, and the gowned ingénue who sits between those same two in a balcony box while attending all the London plays "worth seeing" (154), and feels coarsened by a mere clerk's addresses, locked away from the other. So of course her instinct, when the crisis comes, with Charley the menial on one side and Ada the golden beauty on the other, is to shut and lock the door between them. She is, among other things here, doing what she always did, locking this away from that, one Esther away from the other.

She is also, however deliberately, making a choice between the two. Only after this scene does she start referring to Ada as "my beauty," thinking of her own lost looks as she displaces them onto the friend who, though always understood to be better looking, was not necessarily, in the days before the fever, the only pretty one.[23] Having closed that door, she enters wholly into a chamber contaminated by a girl, Charley, whose urban upbringing and history of indiscriminately traveling from household to household have made her tougher than her mistress. (In fact, Charley contracts the smallpox from a child of the urban gutters sometimes named "Toughy.") Which is why, I think—Mithridates again—Charley comes out unscathed and Esther does not.[24]

But there are rewards, unavailable to the likes of Charley, for undergoing the experience. Although never much of a hand at rural lyricism, Dickens does his best to give his heroine, just after convalescence, that capacity to recognize the sacred in the familiar which his friend Carlyle had named "natural supernaturalism"—especially here, on her first post-smallpox trip outdoors:

> I found every breath of air, and every scent, and every flower and leaf and blade of grass, and every passing cloud, and everything in nature, more beautiful and wonderful to me than I had ever found it yet. This was my first gain from my illness. (443)

The keynote is luminous particularity, and it equips Esther for meaningful transactions on the personal level as well as the pastoral. Shortly after learning that Chesney Wold is in some way her ancestral home, post-fever Esther finds herself marveling at how "all the minute details of every wonderful leaf" of its park are glorified in the sunlight. From this illuminated setting then emerges Lady Dedlock, out of the chiaroscuro cross-hatching of a "perspective" made, thinks Esther, uniquely "intricate to the eye" by the interlacing of light and leaf shadows (448). It takes Esther a while to "discern what figure it was," but by "little and little, it revealed itself to be a woman's—a lady's—Lady Dedlock" (448). By degrees, the field of sharp-edged details, as processed through the newly cleansed, newly opened eyes of the observer, gathers into a more and more identifiable form. The novel's pivotal recognition scene soon follows.

I venture the proposition that it had to happen after—that it could not have happened before—Esther passed through her own spell of blindness and psychic sandblasting. Without that experience, she would not have been sufficiently alive to those leaves, or their shadows, or the twenty-years-waited-for figure those sibylline shadows spelled out. Rather she would have been, like the haphazardly inoculated Charley, off picking flowers in some place lacking her "perspective." Charley is sweet, but the fact that the fire she passed through was not quite as fiery as her mistress's, that she has grown up with ears wide open for every bit of village gossip but can never manage the more refined practice of writing that allows her mistress to articulate her innermost, most nuanced thoughts, and that she winds up, happily, marrying a jolly miller instead of an insomniac healer heroically steeped in denial and self-denial on a scale to match her mistress's—well. In whatever form her dead mother might have chosen to return to her, Charley would not have had a clue.

Not that Charley, *fille moyenne sensuelle* that she is, would be inclined to complain. She is not the sort to envy the change—from the unworldly to the verge of the unearthly—that comes over Esther at midpoint. From then on, Esther's veil is there to screen not only her from the world but, like Perseus's shield, it from her—from those eyes, newly opened and even more "noticing" than before (17). In fact, I suggest that after her illness she becomes partnered with the weird pair of disembodied eyes that has been metempsychotically circulating through the novel at least since the gaslight piercing through two holes in a curtain stared down at Nemo's corpse.[25] These eyes have been as close as we get to a visual signature of the narrator who, himself disembodied, can go everywhere and see everything.[26]

With her transformation, Esther takes on some of his powers. Esther's vision thereafter is a classic case of insight out of blindness, and the moment of its making has a surreal de Quincean quality to it. It comes as a fever dream featuring the "great perplexity of endlessly trying to reconcile" the stages of her past life, a Piranesian vista of unending staircases, and this:

> Dare I hint at that worse time when, strung together somewhere in great black space, there was a flaming necklace, or ring, or starry circle of some kind, of which I was one of the beads! And when my only prayer was to be taken off from the rest and when it was such inexplicable agony and misery to be a part of the dreadful thing? (432)

If only because no one is really sure what it means, this passage has attracted much commentary. Let me, again mindful of de Quincey, hypothesize a palimpsestic reading, beginning at the usual jumping-off place. The "circle" of "beads" certainly seems to signal a version of the endlessly-going-around-in-a-ring figure, which, since Dante at least, has stood for damned souls. (Later, in *Little Dorrit,* Dickens will employ that figure for the Circumlocution Office and the corporate psychology it reflects.) It also seems an apt symbol for the extended filiations—by blood, by contagion, by Chancery and chance—that *Bleak House* is made of. It might also (Dickens had earlier imagined Mr. Humphrey watching his clock tell "the beads of time"[27]) be an emblem of eternity.

But: the problem with this is that hardly any of it really applies to Esther. She has, to begin with, no prospect of becoming a damned soul, bureaucratic or otherwise. To the extent that her dream panoramically envisions either British humanity or humanity at large, she would have to be channeling the other narrator, who owns that theme. And although throughout *Bleak House* there is plenty of circulation in the sense of general movement, in the geometric sense the usual pattern of its characteristic actions is in fact not particularly circular. On the contrary: as in backgammon, the game repeatedly played by Esther and Jarndyce, the characteristic shape of movement is not O but U. Thus, in the last chapters, Esther and Bucket turn back after about forty miles, on realizing that Jenny turned back after about thirty miles, in order to disguise the fact that Lady Dedlock had turned back after about twenty miles: three overlapping horseshoes. These U-turns—and there are many others—are not the same as full circles. Actually, their contrasting incompleteness may be part of the point: remember, again, Lady Dedlock returning to rejoin her lover and never quite completing the circuit.

And, besides, it is a pretty safe rule in reading the dreams of Dickens's characters that the first place to look is not to the state of society but to the life of the dreamer. So let us consider Esther's life at this moment. She has smallpox. Her dream's infinity of blackness comes out of the physical fact of blindness, one of its (temporary, in this case) effects. The corresponding sense of eternity comes out of another effect, the delirium in which, as she tells us, time has lost all its usual divisions (431). The "flaming" sensation is probably due to another symptom, fever. (The stricken Jo felt at times as if he were "burning.") The vision of "beads" may have to do with the fact that Esther knows what she has and that smallpox pustules were often likened to (sometimes, in fact, called) beads.

Still, where does she get that "necklace"? Although she doubtless owns one, it has never been important enough to be mentioned. All other occurrences of the word in *Bleak House* refer to the antique pearl necklace, "a rosary of little bird's eggs" (348), gracing the equally antique neck of Volumnia Dedlock, confirmed old maid and bore-in-chief to the "brilliant and distinguished circle" given to gathering at Chesney Wold when its windows show "like a row of jewels set in a black frame" (144), its inhabitants so many "links upon the Dedlock chain of gold" (347). Esther never meets Volumnia, but Dickens will sometimes confer semi-psychic powers on states such as hers: The dreaming Scrooge, for instance, despite never having seen Tiny Tim, nonetheless recognizes his hearthside chair. And, as we have already seen, Esther and Chesney Wold do seem to be on some kind of special wavelength. It is, after all, where her mother lives.

I think that, more than anything else, the flaming necklace represents the novel's major example of what I have describing as its Medusa theme. It presents what Esther least can bear to face. "Dare I hint": what she can barely dare to hint at is not death, which at her lowest moment she is ready to embrace, nor is it any foreboding of her country's fate. It is the prospect of becoming, precisely because of what she is going through now, like the Volumnia Dedlock who is herself in turn a parody of Esther's mother. It is the prospect of growing old without the love of her life and (this woman thing again) his and her children around them.

Ever since Allan Woodcourt left her the flowers (216), Esther has known that the man she loves as a lover returns her feelings. From almost the same moment, she has known that the man she loves as a father wants to marry her. In a novel where everyone worth considering is, as we would say today, conflicted, this conflict surely takes the prize. The fever brings it to a head. From the moment she falls ill, Esther understands that she will probably be made ugly.[28] She also senses (wrongly) that her ugliness will take Woodcourt out of her future, and (rightly) that it has made her correspondingly eligible to John Jarndyce. Realistically enough, she contemplates being Dame Durden forever.

The two sides of this dilemma occur to her almost simultaneously, as follows. On the night before Woodcourt, with those flowers, makes his intentions known, Esther and Jarndyce have a curious exchange. He has just told her the story of her background. She is illegitimate. He cares nothing for that, because he is large of soul. Also, he has been scrutinizing her since her school days, and been well pleased: "'I saw my ward oftener than she saw me,' he added,... She pays me twenty-thousand fold, and twenty more to that, every hour in the day!' To which Esther replies: "'And oftener still,' said I, 'she blesses the guardian who is Father to her!'"

Then this:

> At the word Father, I saw his former trouble come into his face. He subdued it as before, and it was gone in an instant; but, it had been there, and it had come so swiftly upon my words that I felt as if they had given him a shock. I again inwardly repeated, wondering, "That *I* could readily understand. None that *I* could readily understand." No, it was true. I did not understand it. Not for many and many a day.

"Take a fatherly good-night, my dear," said he, kissing me on the forehead, "and so to rest." (214; italics in original)

Game and set. The word "Father" simultaneously reanimates Esther's old, comforting fantasy that Jarndyce really is her father (76) and dashes, for now, his hopes of becoming her husband. (Compare, in modern courtship, "friend.") His echoed "fatherly" strikes something like the tone of bemused resignation we hear in Cyrano's words to Roxanne.

To understand why, it helps to remember where those remembered words "that I could not readily understand" came from. Spoken by Jarndyce minutes before (212), they arose out of ruminations that began with his worries about Richard and Ada. They are too young! By the time Esther knocked on his door, he was, he said, thinking of her. His train of thought? Something, I suggest, like this. Esther has recently turned twenty-one. She is of age. Ada and Richard constitute evidence that it is not necessarily a wonderful idea for young people to marry other young people. Could such a fate await the other young woman under his protection? Is there a way in which he can save her from it? When Ada goes off with Rick, he will be left alone in Bleak House with his... his housekeeper? Really? He knows little or nothing of Esther's interest in Woodcourt. Besides, how many acceptable young men are likely to fall for this retiring not-glamorous servant with the comical old-lady names and the dubious origins? How many people are as generous as... well, as *he* is, about such things? (Rouncewell, the admirable ironmaster, will later make it clear that his family would not stand for a match with anyone carrying such a stain as hers (353).

It may be that, in part, he brings up the subject of Esther's origins at this point as a way of letting her understand how limited her romantic options are. Perhaps, believing it to be high time she knew the worst, he does so with intentions of the cruel-to-be-kind sort. Still, something else is going on. Jarndyce came to love Esther as she grew into the late-teens-early-twenties period when, as his creator knew only too well, some men his age tend to fall for women her age. And why not? It is, no question, true love. So all's fair.

Except that, disturbingly, he seems to have been at work unleveling the playing field since well before. That Esther has reached her majority in a state of virtual unmarriageability has been in large part his doing. He gave her those horrid names and brought her up to be the social anomaly she is—too high for the likes of Guppy, too low for the likes of Richard, with money enough available for the asking but none of her own (no dowry, no settlement, nothing that might help set up, say, a gifted young doctor with no connections), and to all appearances too old ("old woman") for anyone remotely her own age. Why, after all, would you train a young woman, and before that a girl, to answer to "old woman"? Answer: as part of a strategy, acknowledged or not, of minimizing the difference between her and yourself, an old man.

Something there is in John Jarndyce. It discomposes him that Esther interrupts him as he is pondering her (she, in turn, thinks that he is looking exceptionally "worn": ouch), and visibly depresses him for that split second when she registers his reaction to her word "Father." He is sufficiently self-aware to understand why. Hence, his uneasiness. Esther is uneasy too, from the same cause, despite her claim not to have understood for "many and many a day."

Well, honestly, Miss S.: just how many-a-days did *that* equal? Ten? A thousand? This is a typical Esther halfway lie. Doubtless it begins as a lie to herself, concocted at the same moment Jarndyce reassumes his fatherly mask. He has told her that she cannot "understand" his feelings, and Esther, ever obedient, does her best not to. But she has seen what she has seen. If she did not to some degree comprehend John Jarndyce's drift, she would not answer as she does: "Father." With, no less, a capital F (all other capitalized "Father"s in the book refer to God) and an exclamation mark at the end of the sentence. Both are for emphasis.[29] (In which light, the uncapitalized "fatherly" embedded in his response amounts to a wan demurral.[30]) It is the only time in *Bleak House* that she calls him that to his face. She knows why it makes him flinch.

And she certainly knows the story by the time of her illness and the dream it brings on. Prior to that, Woodcourt had been her firewall. Now that she has become too ugly for the man who left her the flowers, there is nothing between her and her duty to the man who gave her the keys. Jarndyce can be grateful to the disease that, making Esther even homelier than he had raised her to think she was, has put her back in his league.

For a number of reasons (his age, for one), there will probably be no children. Esther adores children. She is wonderful with them. She wants some of her own, with all her womanly heart. Tough. Up until the last chapter, that means that she won't have any.

To deal, briefly, with the other salient features of her dream. The "flaming necklace" is also a "ring." Later, Ada's wedding ring will become a center of focus (614), and not a happy one. The specter of a ring circling a neck may remind us that "necklace" was underworld slang for hangman's noose, as was "bracelets" for handcuffs. That last datum explains why Bucket, scrutinizing the "two beautiful bracelets" on Lady Dedlock's arms at the moment she is most under suspicion, "rattles" the handcuffs in his pocket (634); later, he will snap the same handcuffs on the real murderess while in the process of arranging her date with the hangman.

As for what I and others have described as the dream's "Piranesian" vista of endless staircases: the first thing Esther notices on entering Bleak House is that that "you go up and down steps out of one room into another" (62). No wonder the overall sensation was one of "great perplexity," especially in "endlessly trying to reconcile" the stages of her life, including the "old woman" one: a perfectly natural kind of perplexity, I would think, for any young woman facing the prospect of marrying Father.

Esther being Esther, once out of the sickroom she will do her best to whistle away what she saw there. She will deny, displace, project, and, above all, protest way too much. She repeatedly drowns out bad thoughts with the jingling of her keys, sometimes making herself kiss them, as whipped schoolboys were made to kiss the rod. She gives herself lectures about how grateful she ought to be, lectures obviously based on those she used to give her doll, the love of her girlhood and therefore—of course, in this book—buried. (Who buries a doll? Who *kills* one?)

When, too late, Woodcourt proposes to her and finds that she is committed to Jarndyce, her tears, she insists, are "not tears of regret and sorrow" (733). To which: oh, come off it. When Ada looks unhappy, the reason, Esther decides, must be that—get this—*Ada* is the one who doesn't want her to marry Jarndyce (604). (Ada is actually worrying about Richard's health.) After Woodcourt's proposal she goes to bed and does what she has often done before, repeatedly recites (she has it by heart), like stations on a (flaming) rosary, the Jarndyce letter of proposal (733–34)—an act of devotion perhaps, but also of self-indoctrination.

IV.

The apparition of the necklace does not initially transport Esther to any panoramic or otherwoldy vision. On the contrary: it takes her to the verge of the innermost circle of what is wrong with her life. At the same time, by crystallizing her worst apprehensions at her lowest point, it also turns out to be a liminal experience, signaling the beginning of her emergence out of the blindness whose arrival almost exactly marks the novel's midpoint. Darkest, dawn: against the blackest black, starlight: that necklace is, after all, etched in light, is therefore good news for someone who was expecting never to see light again. Indeed, I am persuaded by Robert Newsom that it was inspired by a solar eclipse of the time, that its fiery rim recalls the corona and its beads the "Bailey's beads" dotting the perimeter.[31]

This conceit actually makes surprising sense, given the multiple calamities afflicting Esther. On the one hand, the smallpox beads eclipse her hopes and consign her to a choice between Volumnia-hood and Mrs. Dame Durden/Jarndyce. On the other, they mark the turning point, after which light, both outer (sun) and inner (eyesight) begin to re-emerge. As a matter of physiological fact in the here and now, they may well derive from the first glimmers of dawn to register on the retinas of a woman who has spent weeks seeing nothing but darkness, and who, two paragraphs later, will say that she "first shrunk from the light as it twinkled on me once more" (432). One does not normally shrink from light on the twinkle scale. But that beaded necklace was also a constellationlike "starry circle," and twinkling is what stars do.

Esther shrinks because twinkling is the brightest kind of illumination that someone in her state can handle. One of the physiological facts to which *Bleak House* attends most is that sensation is interactive, a matter of both perceived and perceiver, always conditioned by the relative receptivity of the latter, in turn conditioned by experience. The Mithridates story is a parable of adaptation. How much gin or opium you can take depends on how much you have been in the habit of taking before. How much light your eyes can take depends on what they are used to. (One common example: bats.) Accordingly, you can never be sure of what portion of what you are perceiving is due to which side of the equation.

In other words: is it hot in here, or is it me? When Lady Dedlock's fainting fit gets his attention, that is the question that occurs to Tulkinghorn: was it the heat from the fire to which she was sitting a bit too close, or was it something in that document to which she paid a bit too much attention? Such questions are consistently pertinent. Grandfather Smallweed, Bucket surmises, acquired his habit of shouting as a result of living with a deaf woman (641). The same Bucket's well-worn "great hand" "can scarcely feel" the soft material of Esther's gloves (671). Across the board, people in *Bleak House* experience externals according to the two intertwined factors, interchangeably physiological and psychological, of what they are like and what they are used to. When Guppy and Jobling/Weevle enter Krook's boarded-up building, they can "at first see nothing save darkness and shadows," but by degrees start making out details (492). That is because their pupils, having gotten used to the light outdoors, need time to dilate. From the same principle working the other way, Krook and his night-seeing cat shun daylight. There are, by my count, at least seven other instances where what is seen depends on how well eyes have adapted. Most of the novel's apparitions, coming into sight seemingly out of nowhere, are at least facilitated by just that process.

These sensory reflexes come with their psychological counterparts. What you are able to recognize, like what you are able to see, also depends on what you are used to. Tulkinghorn's mysterious "Allegory" becomes just a "painted ceiling" (336) when viewed by Sergeant George, a military man with little or no experience of such productions, whose attention is, however, activated soon after when he passes "Hanging-Sword Alley, which would seem to be something in his way" (340). Esther, having spent her first years without love, is chronically unable to imagine that it will ever come to her. That is why she is so frantic to earn it wherever she goes, so eager to report, however disingenuously, every sign of affection she gets, so sincere when she says that she doesn't deserve it. As much as anything, *Bleak House* traces the long learning curve in which Esther, born and raised in a state of emotional deprivation, learns to dilate her heart, as at the midpoint she learns to dilate her pupils.

In other words, vision and "vision" follow the same rules, and one of those rules is that, as Gerard Manley Hopkins was later to put it, "what you look hard at seems to look hard at you." Tulkinghorn knows that Nemo has died when the dead man's open eyes stare up into his, knows that Lady Dedlock is defeated when her eyes, framed and highlighted a la Joan Crawford close-up, look back hard into his. Sir Leicester, driven to distraction by the disappearance of his wife, has to close his eyes against the sleet and snow that have swallowed her up because "they seem, *by being long looked at,* to fall so thick and fast" (692; my italics).

Tony Jobling/Weevle, of all people, could explain why that is. Admonished by Guppy that he ought not to mind living in Nemo's old "suicidal" room because, after all, "there have been dead men in most rooms," Tony answers, "in most rooms you let them alone, and—and they let you alone" (400). There have indeed been dead men and women in most of the rooms of this novel, in which just about everything living leaves its trace: Phil Squod, Mr. Jellyby, and Krook with their marks on the walls (Krook's are "ghostly...traces" (492)); Nemo with his ink and opium, one saturating the walls, the other the atmosphere; Esther with the distinctive touches of interior decoration she seems compelled to add to any place she inhabits for any period; the Dedlocks with their gallery of family portraits. And Tony (and Woodcourt, who also observes that ghosts traditionally speak only when spoken to [609]) is right: like the Dedlock portraits (also mirrors), becoming visible to the degree that they are looked at (693), ghosts and ghostly presences tend to be detectable because detected. Seeing—perceiving in general—is a generative act, always to some extent a function of how much the perceiver is used to, and wants to, perceive. Ghosts tend to appear to those who half-expect them to.

Thus, on her second visit to the "dark door" of her father's room, Esther feels "chilled" "by a strange sensation" (178). She felt nothing of the sort the first time there. Why the change? Well, for one thing, the season is winter and the room has no fire going. It chills. Then, too, Esther has just been told that its latest inhabitant has died there since her last visit. It is now officially one of those rooms with "ghosts in them"—a chilling thought. So Esther looks hard, as she did not before. She enters the room, feeling the cold, scrutinizing its bareness, picking up "a strange sensation of mournfulness and even dread." Due to the poverty of its former occupant it has long been minimally heated. Perhaps such rooms retain a certain kind of deep-down chill that some people can sense; perhaps Esther is one such person. Perhaps as well she is picking up something of how, according to the other narrator, all "empty rooms, bereft of a familiar presence, mournfully whisper what your room and what mine must one day be" (693).

But perhaps something else as well. The departed "presence," though not "familiar," was, after all, family. It was her absent father, the one she almost never thought about but whose empty space she dreamed John Jarndyce might fill. What better than a "vacant room," "sad and desolate," to stand for, and conjure up, such a legacy? Is her radar, her echolocation, picking that up? Does her "strange sensation" come not just from the real chill, the gloomy room, and the fact of a recent death, but also from some cognate but rationally inexplicable awareness of who died there? Does "chilled" carry an echo of "child"?

Such possibilities edge us into the *Bleak House* twilight zone, where dwell less mundane reasons why Esther might feel that chill. Premonition, for one. "Chilled" is a word to pause at in a novel so preoccupied with illnesses, their symptoms and causes. Jo, Esther's father's only friend and the vector by which whatever was wrong in Nemo's neighborhood spread to Esther's neighborhood and then to her, almost freezes to death. Partly as a result, he comes down with the illness whose alternation of chills and fever finishes him off. The result will be Charley's smallpox, then Esther's. Esther recognizes the symptoms of its onset immediately: "Charley, she asks her shivering maid, "are you so cold?" The answer is yes, and in the next sentence Esther shuts the door on Ada. She has recognized the symptoms. Smallpox typically begins its course with chills. That is why, the moment she is "stricken cold" (390) herself, Esther knows what is wrong with her.

So: was the chill she felt on her second visit to her father's door a precognition of the moment when she would close another door, on Ada?

The other narrator, for whom contagion is the most multitasking of symbols, would be inclined to say yes. Esther's perspective on such matters is less promiscuous. It puts us inside a limited flesh-and-blood being whose feelings, be they sensations or intimations, we have to account for. Unlike her partner in narration, she cannot leap tall buildings or see through walls. But she can react to stimuli beyond his ken—beyond the range, in fact, of all the male characters, and at least most of the females: Mrs. Bagnet may come close to her level, and perhaps one or two other women, but none of the men are in the running.

In other words, this is a novel that believes in women's intuition, less as profundity of insight than as expansion of sensory bandwidth. Esther says she can feel Guppy's eyes on her without looking at him (112, 114), and I believe her. She may need to veil herself from bright white light, head on, but she is amazing when it comes to the infrared edges of the barely detectable, and not just in the modality of sight. When she can tell from his voice that a man in another room whom she has not yet met is consulting his watch (220), it is not because a fairy told her. It is an instance of the same capacity that soon after allows her to recognize in that man's—Boythorn's—extravagant gallantries a symptom of disappointed love at a young age. ("How did you find that out?," asks Jarndyce, genuinely impressed [110].) A great deal of *Bleak House* wisdom is corner-of-eyes wisdom—of, to steal from Wallace Stevens, "ghostlier demarcations, keener sounds"—and that is Esther's long suit.

Although Dickens the mesmerist believed that under hypnosis it was possible for some people, himself for instance, to commune with distant others, Esther's gift is not of that sort. Early on, she can have only a door between herself and her still-living father and feel nothing; near the end she is, up to the moment she looks into her mother's dead face, completely wrong about that mother's whereabouts. Unlike Dickens's magnetized subjects, she needs cues. She needs the chill, the palpable emptiness, the something in the air that gives her the "strange sensation" during her second visit to her father's threshold. Those cues given, however, she can do wonders, in ways hyperaesthetic rather than extrasensory, as extensions of the perceivable rather than departures from it.

When at the beginning of her narrative she allows that she has "rather a noticing way" (17), she is being, as usual, absurdly modest.

She can also put together whatever she has noticed. To a degree, this is a talent shared with the novel's detectives, notably Tulkinghorn, Bucket, and even Guppy. Evidence in *Bleak House* comes as pieces of what the noticing ones have remarked and remembered: a handkerchief, a portrait, a scrap of paper. The trick is not just to discern them but to coordinate them. No one gets it right all the time, and there are plenty—the paranoids Krook and Mrs. Snagsby are exemplary—who will always get it all wrong, but Esther, because of that extra range of hers, probably does the best.

Which is to say, of course, that there really is something to get right. Hidden connections, including conspiracies, do exist—all over the place, in fact. Krook and Mrs. Snagsby notwithstanding, other paranoids—Jo and Gridley, for instance—are entirely right to feel that the world, or at least their corner of it, is out to get them. *Bleak House* has no serious truck with solipsism or radical relativism. Lady Dedlock really is Esther's mother and Mademoiselle Hortense really does shoot Tulkinghorn. By book's end, both narrators agree on those and on all other items in which the issue is about what really happened and what really was. They see things differently, but the same things. The Mr. Snagsby whom Esther first meets, near the end—"a scared, sorrowful-looking little man in a grey coat," (707)—is the same man we have gotten to know through the other narrator.

So *Rashomon* will have to wait until the next century. *Bleak House* differences of opinion are not a matter of different worlds, but of different ranges of interest, capacity, and receptivity, interacting with the kaleidoscopic special effects—night and day, fog and sunshine, and so on—of external reality. Accordingly, its altered states are variations of real ones—even Nemo, deep into opium, accurately copied off what was before him—always to some degree the products of what its subjects bring to bear, and especially of how energetically they do so. Hallucination comes from looking too hard for too long, insensibility, whether real (Turveydrop) or feigned (Skimpole) from not looking hard enough, "telescopic" vision (Mrs. Jellyby) from concentrating too hard on one point at the expense of others. Lady Dedlock lives "where the throng is thickest, where the lights are brightest" (572), and that is the problem: she should really arrange to dim down one and thin out the other. It is curious, for instance, that in the early pages Richard is the one always making scornful remarks about Chancery. He is paying too much attention—and attention is quantity, a measurable degree of intensity, in comparison with which its tenor is secondary and far more fickle. What Richard thought he thought about Chancery mattered less than how much time he spent doing it.

Esther's way of "noticing" toward the fringes seems to have saved her from the kind of disproportionate hard focusing that afflicts Richard, as well as Mrs. Jellyby and most of the book's dreadfully wrong characters. In fact, her fallibility, especially in the first half, comes from the other direction, from an unwillingness to see the point, especially when she *is* the point. In one of her pre-smallpox halfway-to-right apprehensions, she gets so far as to contrast her own way with that of Mrs. Pardiggle, who wears spectacles behind "choking" eyes and a hoop skirt of wiry circumference, which can be counted on to knock over anything in the vicinity whenever, spinning around, she makes a "vortex" of herself (100). Commanded to join her on one of her (what else?) "rounds" among the poor, Esther tries to bow out on the grounds that, not having acquired that "delicate knowledge of the heart" needed for dealing with people so unlike herself, "I thought it best to be as useful as I could, ... and to try to let that circle of duty gradually and naturally expand itself" (96). Mrs. Pardiggle's skirt is, as an art critic of her next and our last century might have put it, hard-edged, like the field of focus drilled from out of the surrounding blur by the rounds of her spectacles. That is the quality Esther has in mind in saying that the "demonstrative, loud, hard tone" of her voice "had a sort of spectacles on too" (94). Like her colleague Mrs. Jellyby, Mrs. Pardiggle is a prodigy of concentration by exclusion. One is in the circle(s) or one is not. By exemplary contrast, Esther's consciousness, relatively soft at center for most of the novel, is correspondingly porous, cessible, and sensitive at the edges, less shell than membrane.

And that is a good thing, because most of what is at stake in *Bleak House* is to be found near the edges. It is apt that a decisive piece of evidence should be the "deep fringe" of Lady Dedlock's mantle (624). More than hidden depths, a "deep fringe" is what the mind requires to negotiate the landscape. That landscape, as established in the opening pages, is treacherous, muddy, and so on, but above all foggy. The effect, in both the psychological sense dating from Hume and the art-historical sense soon to arrive with Cezanne, is impressionistic. From the moment when the fog pervading the first chapter seeps indoors and throws a "foggy glory round... [the] head" of the "Lord Chancellor" (6) until the moment that a soft angel-light irradiates John Jarndyce for doing his last great good deed (752), the outlines of *Bleak House* characters and properties tend to come enveloped in auras of variable density—haloes, veils, light-suffused curtains of hair tumbling over glowing faces, tears blurring eyes.

These are the specular correlates of other vaguely attenuated, half-detectable presences, the echoes, ghosts, contagions, and so on. In all cases, the eye of the beholder, the physiological/psychological component of that double-sided "impressionism," is in play. Mrs. Rouncewell sounds the theme when she wonders whether the general mistiness of things comes from the wet weather outside or her fogged-up glasses (77). (Again: is it hot in here, or is it me?) Phil Squod's black clothes become blacker in the narrator's eyes because set against "a glaring white target" (271). Such sensory promotions are the work of the visual cortex, which likes contrasts. So is perspective—for instance: "A watcher stands to see the ship with her spread wings cross the path of light that appears to be presented to only him" (584). The spread wings (also the "her") are a bit of anthropomorphic projection, the path-crossing a matter of position and sightlines, the apparent direction of the path an example of extreme-distance triangulation and its corresponding parallax, as read according to subjectivism's innate self-centeredness.

Attuned to the subjective, the atmospherics naturally incline toward the dramatically mutable, to those kaleidoscopic features mentioned earlier. More than anything else Dickens wrote, *Bleak House* adopts Victorian stage effects:[32] the shifting colors and shades presented to an audience, which is to say to a particular human sensibility in a known place and guessable frame of mind, someone whose reactions can be calculated and thus manipulated. In no other novel does Dickens put his deep knowledge of contemporary stagecraft to fuller use. For example, one favorite of British theater, pantomime in particular, was the transformation scene, which worked as follows. A conventionally realistic set, positioned downstage, was separated by a "scrim"—a curtain made of semi-transparent material—from a glamorous scene of fairy fantasy, hidden by the screen. At the transformation, downstage lights would fade, upstage lights would be turned on, the scrim would accordingly become transparent, and the original set would appear to melt into its glittering replacement. (Approximate cinematic equivalent: The *Wizard of Oz,* at the moment of changing from black-and-white to color.)

Compare Esther at the beginning of chapter VIII. Up before dawn, she looks out of the "black pane" of her new room's window and at the two candles reflecting off of it like "beacons"—because, I suggest, they are the only lights in all the darkness, because a beacon (think of a pillar, with one bright light on top) can plausibly be imagined as a giant candle, and because the reflections of these candles seem to be shining somewhere outdoors, which by a trick of perspective makes them look much larger than they are. (As usual, Esther doesn't seem to see her own reflection; if she did, the beacons would probably dwindle back to candles.) As the day dawns, as window's reflective opacity changes to transparency, as black prospect outdoors becomes "faintly discernible in the mist," then so bright and particularized that each new glance could supply "enough to look at for an hour," the candles are reduced to their proper proportions. Next, when the full daylight floods in, their little paling flames are "the only incongruous part of the morning"—and so there go the "beacons." For one thing, they are no match for the sunlight. For another, Esther, absorbed in the view outside, isn't paying attention to them anymore [85]).

That is an example of lighting effects in the service of fantasy, the kind of show in which Cinderella gets prince and palace in the grand finale. They can work just as well for morbid melodrama. Consider the scene revealing Nemo's death. It is night outside, and any light filtering up from downstairs is faint at best. As Tulkinghorn enters Nemo's room, his candle goes out. Again, it will take his eyes some seconds to adjust. In the meantime, he smells and feels the air (heavy, grease-laden). His first visual sensation, not surprisingly, is of confinement and darkness: the room is "small" and "nearly black." The first true visible details he discerns (fireplace grate, table, chair) cluster around one dim light, now starting to register—the "red coke fire" burning "low" in the chimney corner. By degrees, other furnishings come into view. Then he notices some other, fainter lights—the gas lamp outdoors gleaming through "two gaunt holes" in the shutters. His eyes follow their parallel beams down to the human figure on the bed, fitfully illuminated by a candle, which, burnt down and choked by the "scum and mist" surrounding it, is guttering out. At first glance he believes that this figure is alive, in part because the candlelight turns it the yellow of illness rather than the pallor of death, in part because its eyes, reflecting the candle's flickering light, give off the impression of animation. Then the candle goes out. Darkness. The "gaunt eyes" made by the two holes, brighter now with the candlelight gone, are suddenly "staring." The next chapter opens as, being once again unable to see, he feels Krook's "touch," even—this is how dark it has gotten—smells Krook's "breath" before he knows he's there. (Anyone on the planet, if able to see Krook coming, would have taken steps to keep out of range of that breath.)

That Krook, on the other hand, was easily able to find his way makes sense. He has lived as a recluse in the house for ages and knows its every turn. During those years he has become, like his cat, a creature of night vision. Hence, he is immediately able to see his way to the coke fire's dim glow, where he tries without success to relight Tulkinghorn's candle. Night-seeing, he then runs downstairs to fetch a candle. Its light first appears "upon the wall" above the stairway as he ascends: an authenticating specular effect of the sort I have seen in film noir. Carried into the room, it dims by contrast the lights of the two "gaunt eyes," so that they "seem to close." At the same time, brought to shine on the face of the dead man, it illuminates his eyes more brightly than at any other time in the sequence. Newly alight and lacking the reflected flickerings of before, they stare blankly upward as, we are expected to understand, only a dead man's do. Startled, Krook "spread[s] his hands across the body like a vampire's wings,"[33] after first setting his candle down on the floor.

I hypothesize this last item because Krook first notices the opium (on the floor), because he would not likely spread both hands if he were holding something bulky in one of them, because such hands would be more liable to appear vampirelike if lighted from underneath, casting a shadow upward, and because of all English novels written until Arthur Conan Doyle came along, *Bleak House* is as far as I know the one most determined to make the reader work out questions such as, "What became of the candlestick?", questions to which it disdains to spell out the answer.

The candle next appears in the hand of the "dark young man" who appears out of nowhere, on the other side of the bed. Probably it was at some unremarked point handed to him by Krook—in which case his sudden apparition would be at least partly explicable, coming as a result of his sudden illumination (123–26). This "dark young man" is, it will turn out, Woodcourt. Candle or no, how he made it into the room without being seen is still a question. Perhaps he was attending his patient, Miss Flite, when, on hearing Tulkinghorn summon "the nearest doctor," he ran downstairs and hooked into Nemo's room while she continued downstairs and outdoors. Perhaps Krook didn't notice his entrance because, back turned, he was at the moment examining Nemo's portfolio. Perhaps Tulkinghorn didn't notice because, perched on the landing, he was still preoccupied with Miss Flite and his mission. Perhaps no one saw him until Krook handed him the candle, which lit up his face.

Perhaps, perhaps. I am less than confident about any item in that last paragraph. In any case, *Bleak House* will hereafter feature many such instances, and a lot of them balance between "apparition" in the sense of "sudden appearance" and in the sense of "unaccountable materialization."

One especially puzzling example is the account of the events leading up to Esther's transformative illness, in which stagey lighting also figures. Shortly before visiting Jo in the brickmaker's hovel, Esther experiences an "undeniable impression of being something different from what I then was." Why? It cannot be that she detects some miasmatic influence coming from Jo's direction. She is not nearly close enough yet, and besides, her maid Charley will be the one infected. Still, the turning point of her life will follow from the path she is now starting, and the scene itself has "liminal" written all over it. Esther is poised at a gate at the edge of her garden, between leaving the grounds of her home and beginning the way to the brickmaker's squalor, looking up at a late-evening sky "partly cleared" during a break in the rain, the scene itself poised between "two lights," one "a pale dead light" "where the sun had sunk three hours before" and the other a "lurid glare" coming from the direction of London.

Now, what, pray tell, is *that* all about? The scene is Saint Albans. London is about twenty miles to the south. Is the southern "glare" supposed to come from there? Has its glow traveled that far, on a stormy night in which only "a few stars" can peep through? And what about that other light, from the region of the set sun, in the north? In the *north*?[34] Yes: in "the north and north-west, where the sun had set three hours before." So the sunset's afterglow is still visible, three hours later? And if not from the sun (or moon: same problem), then from what? Is there some major light source up there that we haven't heard about?

Dickens could sometimes be casual about such matters, but seldom in this, his most precisionist work. Anything is possible: maybe I am looking for a degree of consistency not to be found in Dickens's novels, even this one. Maybe this is a rare case of pure uninflected symbolism, although of what, beyond the generically ominous, I haven't the faintest idea. Normally, one would think, there must be ways for an author of Dickens's resources to get his protagonist in between two large lights without turning the cosmos upside-down.

What I propose is that in multiplying improbabilities in this way, Dickens is signaling how exceptionally weird this scene is. The normal rules, for the nonce, are swept away. Esther herself tells us that her narrative here is in the margin of "fancy," for instance summoning up "all the unseen buildings of the city [London, to the south], and...all the faces of its wondering inhabitants," none of which, to state the obvious, she can actually see. Although the seen unseen is not usually Esther territory, this sequence, with its flashbulb moment of glare-smitten faces, clouds looking "like a sea stricken immoveable" in mid-heave, Esther herself "stopped at the garden gate to look up at the sky," and so on, is, I think, just that.

Given that Wordsworth's *The Prelude* had recently introduced the phrase "spots of time" for such experiences, it may be pertinent that Esther says of her "undefinable impression" that she has ever since "connected it with that spot and time, and with everything associated with that spot and time."[35] Our own term today might be déjà vu, except that the glimpse is of future self rather than past. In fact this distinction matters a good deal, given the fact of the novel's double-barreled narrative, with one side consistently retrospective and the other consistently present tense. One of the main protocols of *Bleak House* is that, up to the last chapters, these two narrative strains be kept separated, a rule maintained until chapter LVI, when Bucket finds a handkerchief in Lady Dedlock's drawer engraved with Esther's name. From soon after that moment, these two opposite-complementary figures proceed, in tandem, to become the means by which most issues get cleared up. Coming together, they are, for most of the last twelve chapters, two halves of one great—though of course, in the end, as per usual, not quite great enough—brain.[36] (One can, I think, reasonably hypothesize that much of what has gone before is relatively purblind because of the separation of those two halves, of the (female) intuitive and the (male) deductive.)

But suppose that, at one strange moment, the dilated apprehension of the former were to be secretly influenced by the presence of the latter? At the height of her eerie éclaircissement, Esther detects "the sound of wheels coming down a miry hill" (380). Three pages later, leading Jo back to the house where his infection will wind up turning her life around, she passes "but one man" (383). Almost half the novel later, we will learn that this man was Bucket and that the sound of the wheels came from his carriage (679–80). At this one moment, the novel's two master spirits are for once at the same locale, *almost* touching—the same moment that the one we're listening to comes the closest so far to seeing everything.

Retrospective Esther suspects that this moment was a premonition of her illness. I suspect that it is a premonition of retrospective Esther, the one critically formed by the events about to unfold, wanting to tell her younger self something, probably that in the end it will all be all right.[37] It is a preliminary sounding of what will be a major theme, a fraying of the fabric in anticipation of the definitive tear, when Bucket finds Esther's glove:

> He finds it as he speaks, "Esther Summerson."
> "Oh! Says Mr. Bucket, pausing, with his finger at his ear. "Come. I'll take *you*." (671)

In a novel whose first principle seems to be that no one is allowed to see or say what matters most, the early near-miss between Esther and Bucket may constitute a verboten, half-realized communication of the sort otherwise foreclosed. If so, that would make it a big deal. Having violated the rules of *Bleak House,* after all, why *not* go ahead and violate the laws of the physical universe?

Whether this reading convinces or not, the point I wish to stress is that this scene is self-consciously extraordinary—a moment when the novel might be said to be haunting itself. As with the other hauntings, their true status remains problematic, marking the farthest verge of how far the novel is willing to go beyond the reliably detectable. In this regard *Bleak House* stands apart for its stringency. It is, among other things, a mystery, and mysteries come with a pretty tight set of conventions, one of which is, no *deus ex machina* allowed. Most of the subordinate mysteries of this novel are solvable, and solved.[38] But not all—which among other things means that there is a middle range where readers cannot be sure of their footing. That is especially the case given how many of the book's solutions are to be found on the periphery. Is there, one sometimes wonders, such a thing as being too peripheral? Do the edges have vanishing points? Can we ever feel sure that a cigar is just a cigar, a nonbarking dog just a dog who didn't bark, a stray detail all surface and no significance? No, not really, at least not when the detail seems, on second look, odd.

Take Mrs. Rouncewell's brief appearance in Tulkinghorn's chambers (427). What on earth can she be doing there? She is the soul of benevolence, he of the opposite. The answer, as it happens, is simple: "Now, Mr. Tulkinghorn is, in a manner, part and parcel of the place [Chesney Wold]; and, besides, is supposed to have made Mrs. Rouncewell's will" (81). So: her visit has been to consult about her will, perhaps about leaving something extra for Watt should his marriage to Rosa occur after her death. Well—fine, except that these two passages, the visit itself and the datum about the will, occur twenty-seven chapters, and about 160,000 words, apart, and that one of them, so far as I can tell the only clue in the book, is delivered in the most off-handed of ways. (As was the case in the first serial publication: this is not a matter of Dickens's retroactively tightening up his story line.) That, surely, borders on the authorially fiendish, and I for one would never have figured it out had I not reread the book looking for answers to it and other questions like it that had cropped up on my previous read-through.

Which operation, of course, presented a raft of new questions for the next read-through, ten examples of such will be reviewed in the next chapter. Some of them have answers; some of them may. *Bleak House* rewards the reader for being attentive in dealing with the questions it raises, but by sheer virtue of their numbers and of the number of ways they might be resolved, pretty much guarantees that some will remain at best semi-scrutable.

It is not just that the explanation for matters like Mrs. Rouncewell's visit should be tucked away in some corner: such corners, after all, are features of the eccentric building that gives the novel its name. It may also be the case that the explanation is off the screen altogether. For instance: how, to return to a central, untrivial question, does Esther recognize her mother? This is, again, the question raised with the "broken glass" scene (225), when the two women first see one another during a church service.

Let us review the probabilities. Whether the two earlier encounters with her daughter, in the church and the hunting lodge (both in chapter XVIII), will turn out to have subliminally prepared Lady Dedlock for the eventual recognition scene is, I think, one of the novel's iffy questions, but one segment of their time together in the lodge may argue the affirmative. Esther is "just within the doorway," with a lightning storm outside—much the same atmospherics as will be in play when she experiences that "undeniable impression" of becoming another person. Lady Dedlock approaches from behind, out of the shadows, puts her hand on her chair, and asks, "Is it not dangerous to sit in so exposed a place?" (228). This question and its circumstances are freighted with significance: threshold; lightning (probably with the stroboscopic illuminations common to dramaturgic (or cinematic) spookeries, then and now), yet another almost-but-not-quite approach to physical contact. So perhaps Lady Dedlock senses something of the connection Esther is prone to feeling at such times. After all, she has her own reason to ponder the dangers of being "exposed." Maybe the sight of this young woman poised on the edge of a scene of dangerous dazzle rings a bell with her, tracing from her own course at Esther's age; maybe cautioning her now is mixed up with some had-I-but-known regret about her younger self; maybe behind that regret lies a vague sensation of resemblance. In any case it is not enough; otherwise, she would presumably not go on to treat Esther as brusquely as she does, later in this same scene.

As for how Esther recognizes her mother: that, I think, is more answerable. She is, again, in a class by herself when it comes to picking up signals from the fringes of consciousness, a mental process that typically occurs by degrees. Thus, in an earlier passage, her recognition of Jarndyce as the bundled-up passenger she had met six years before arrives incrementally, as a composite. First, his voice "connected itself with an association in my mind that I could not define." Then, his overall appearance: reassuring, but not enough to make the connection. Then, "something sudden in his manner," added to the rest, does the trick (60). Such chordal conjunctions are what her mind works toward. With the eventual identification of her mother, the process is more elaborate, but essentially the same. "The broken glass" is, just as she says, a matter of "old scraps of old remembrances," to be pieced together, gradual step by gradual step, in her mind.

As with Jarndyce, the recognition occurs in three stages. In the first stage, the one in church, the cue is compound. It is not just that Esther sees her mother for the first time. Equally important, it happens at the moment when the pastor is reading Psalm CXLIII from the *Book of Common Prayer*, beginning with the words, "Enter not into judgment with thy servant O Lord, for in thy sight." This is the reading, in combination with her first look into Lady Dedlock's eyes, that makes Esther feel that "something quickened within me, associated with the lonely days at my godmother's; yes, away even to the days when I stood on tiptoe to dress myself at my little glass, after dressing my doll." Probably one factor in play here is that Lady Dedlock somewhat resembles her late sister (although Boythorn, who may be familiar with both,[39] seems to notice no likeness); probably as well her eyes resemble that sister's eyes,[40] and Esther's too. Be that as it may, all such remembrances must be at best, "old scraps." Esther has always made a habit of not looking at herself, so how could she know who she resembles? Probably her godmother's image is more prominent in her mind's eye here—but then, after all, she was a godmother, not a mother. Nonetheless the experience makes Esther feel "quickened."

"Quickened" is a King James Bible word—one, as it happens ("Quicken me, oh Lord, for thy name's sake") included, although not recorded in the *Bleak House* text, in Psalm CXLIII, the reading now underway. Esther's words "Yes, away even to the days" sound a King James Bible cadence: all you have to do to make it unmistakable is to substitute "yea" for "yes" and "unto" for "to," then read it over again.

The language of the Bible, filling the church, is influencing the tenor of Esther's thoughts—and also, I think, their direction. The last time she saw her godmother alive, Esther was reading to her from the Bible, about Jesus forgiving the woman taken in adultery—a text of which she might plausibly be reminded by another text, the one now being read, beginning, "Enter not into judgment."

If that memory, of that lesson in particular, were now being instantly "quickened" by the sight of the mother whose womb-quickening was the reason Esther the child was raised in shame by the other woman who, unknown to her, was her mother's sister, we would surely have to reach for some psychic explanation if we wanted to explain what is happening. I suggest that, as usual, Dickens offers up an alternative. There is at least one other "scrap" of memory at work. In the *Book of Common Prayer,* the reading from Psalm CXLIII concludes at verse 11 with that appeal for quickening. But, in the Bible, the psalm continues to a verse 12: "And of thy mercy cut off mine enemies, and destroy all them that afflict my soul: for I am thy servant."

Now *that* was her godmother's idea of a proper piece of scripture. (Compare Mrs. Clennam in *Little Dorrit,* whose Bible readings are exclusively of this sort.) Esther knows her Bible. (That is one reason the pastor's words can so easily blend into hers.) She read from it, probably nightly, to her godmother, and attended church, or chapel, regularly. Her own scriptural training has, of course, favored passages of the brimstone sort, that the sins of the parents are visited on the heads of their children "according to what is written" (19), for instance. We can be pretty sure that when the readings came round to the Psalms, no opportunity to include the cutting off and destroying of enemies was neglected. Which is why, I propose, that in trying to force her attention from Lady Dedlock's face, Esther "very strangely" starts to hear the words of the service in "the well-remembered voice of my godmother" (225). The words of Psalm CXLIII first remind Esther of that voice, and something in the resulting range of associations interacts with whatever in the eyes of Lady Dedlock most resembles the memory of her sister's eyes. The edges of two filmy fields of apprehension come together, and their zone of overlap, more distinct than either of them separately, borders on detectability, enough so that Esther can summon up, by mental synthesis, a glimpse of her own eyes as seen long ago in the "small glass" from the days with her godmother. That the scene is a church, a locale Esther would naturally associate with that lady, perhaps facilitates the connection.

With her word "quickening," Esther has adopted the venerable trope of mind-as-womb. The second stage of mental gestation occurs during the scene in the gamekeeper's lodge, when Lady Dedlock asks her question. Ada, her back turned, assumes that it has come from Esther. Deduction: Esther sounds like her mother. "I had never heard the voice as I had never seen the face," she says, but it "affected me in the same strange way" as had the encounter in church (228). Again, "innumerable pictures" of herself flash into her mind—pieces of the "broken glass," each an oblique bit of her reflected self. Just as mirrorphobe Esther has trouble seeing her own face in another's, the Esther who will later run away from the echoed sound of her own footsteps doesn't recognize the voice as being like her own voice. In both cases it is largely because she doesn't want to. Nonetheless, this second encounter connects face (albeit in shadow) to voice, identified by a third party, at least, as Esther's own.

By this point, one would think, there are close to being too many "scraps," with too many glancing resemblances and correspondences between them, for Esther not to acknowledge. But then she gets sick. The effect, I have suggested, is to concentrate her mind (is she or is she not going to have the love she craves, the children she desires?) and then to clear it.

Both changes prepare her for the third and final stage, when, in the scene commented on before, she meets her mother coming out of the alley of leaf shadows. She is exceptionally awake to the "intricate to the eye" sights around her. She has recently looked in the mirror at her new face and abandoned all hopes of marrying Woodcourt. She will marry Jarndyce out of gratitude and play with other people's children, never her own.

Once again, the cue is compound. Viewing Chesney Wold, Esther is, for reasons she doesn't understand, experiencing the same "indefinable feeling" with which Lady Dedlock had impressed" her (448), and at the same time "picturing" to herself the "female shape" of the Ghost's Walk story. The "feeling" is from the aura of accumulated hints and guesses of the previous two encounters; the mental image, of a legendarily unhappy woman who was both married to an older man and childless, begins to frame an outline around it. From the shadows, in another of the novel's eerie apparitions, Lady Dedlock's "figure" emerges like a materialization of that outline. There follows the "intricate" knitting together by degrees noted earlier: female, then lady, then Lady Dedlock, then mother. The final cue for the final identification is Esther's handkerchief, retrieved by her mother, from a mother, because the child of one had laid it over the child of the other. It is, a later age might say, the moment of gestalt. With that, the gestation trope, carried over from the previous two stages, becomes obstetric. To pick, in order of occurrence, through the first two paragraphs of the recognition scene: "The beating of my heart was so violent...my life was breaking from me...breast...my child, my child...mother...agony...burst...mother...child...natural love [Esther is her mother's "natural" child]...my mother's bosom...I held my mother." When all that has cooled down some, Lady Dedlock says of her shame, "I bear it, and I hide it" (449). Which is what, respectively, she and her sister did with Esther.

In matters like this, *Bleak House* repeatedly shows itself to be a psychological puzzle palace, one in which mental mechanics are at issue as much as externals. This mystery's central mystery is the mind. In the next chapter, I will consider ten examples of difficult questions the novel poses, all of them requiring that readers do some thinking about how the characters, including the two narrators, do *their* thinking.

CHAPTER 4

Is Esther Pretty? and Nine Other Questions About *Bleak House*

I.

1. In chapter XXIV, Sergeant George meets Esther for the first time and is disconcerted. The subject of conversation being Richard, he suggests that that young man's failure to concentrate on his military training might be due to a romantic interest in "some young lady," obviously meaning her. When she demurs, he blushes—"He reddened a little through his brown"—and, by way of apology, tells her, "I thought I had seen you somewhere." He soon after passes into a "reverie," then brushes his hand through his hair "as if to sweep the broken thoughts out of his mind," and reattends to the business at hand (305). What is going on here?

George has been given no reason to believe that Richard and Esther are courting. The best explanation I can see is that Esther's face reminds him of her father's. In their military days together, he and Captain Hawdon were good friends. Seeing Esther for the first time—first impressions, in this as in other Dickens novels, are typically the most alert and, more often than not, reliable—he has a confused recollection of Hawdon's features.

This approximate recognition, I suggest, prompts another associative connection. Esther's father was a handsome, undisciplined young man in uniform who went to the dogs. Right now, George's student Richard seems bound to become a later edition of the same. Thus do Richard and Esther come to converge within the same mental frame. Boyfriend-girlfriend is the readiest label for it.

Thought through, those two mnemonic templates don't add up—George is not imagining that Esther would marry her brother—but they don't have to: the thoughts, after all, are "broken" and duly swept away. It is a case, common in *Bleak House,* of half-formed, half-conscious perception not making it across the threshold into established conception.

In *Bleak House* in general, blushes such as George's are often symptomatic of such states and tend to be accompanied (as with Esther's "broken glass" encounter with her mother, when she feels herself transported back to her childhood) by what is here called a "reverie." The experience of half-remembered, uncoordinated percepts not only resembles a dream; it can apparently go partway toward inducing one. That is one of the ways in which, in *Bleak House,* waking and sleeping states can come to cohabit.

2. Shortly after having met Boythorn for the first time and having guessed, correctly, that he lost the love of his life when young, Esther retires to bed with the sound of his "lusty snoring" in her ears and falls asleep trying to imagine him "young again and invested with the graces of youth" (111). Her dream takes her back to the days when she "lived in her godmother's house." She adds, "I am not sufficiently acquainted with such subjects to know whether it is at all remarkable that I almost always dreamed of that period of my life" (111). Where does her dream come from?

Two main possibilities. One, this was an ordinary dream, featuring her godmother because she was a major fixture of "that period" of Esther's life. Dickens reported that his own dreams often went back to a period of about twenty years in his past, which would roughly fit Esther's case here.[1]

Two, the sound of Boythorn's snoring either somehow conveys to Esther that this man was her godmother's old suitor or helps her to that (true) conclusion.

The first possibility needs no support. Let me try to make the case for the second. Esther, with nothing to go by, has already, through powers of intuition bordering on the phenomenal, surmised the main story of Boythorn's past life. When he was young, he was in love with a lady who "died to him" (111). She falls asleep and starts to dream while musing about what that must have been like. The train of thought that began while she was nodding off continues its momentum into the dream. The lingering impression of Boythorn's gallantries to her and Ada—the sign that, somehow, enabled her to guess his secret—perhaps contributes to the theme of young love: if that is what he is like now, what kind of romantic young man must he have been during his courtship days?

I suggest that the sound of snoring supplies a ground bass to her dreamwork, keeping Boythorn present in her mind. Dreams in Dickens do sometimes incorporate sensations from the actual world, for instance, when Paul Dombey's dream of a sunflower "expanded itself into a gong, and began to sound," the cause being that a real gong has started ringing (*D&S* 159–60), blending its sound with Paul's memory of the neighborhood marigolds, the flower, that is to say, which according to Shakespeare's Perdita, "goes to bed wi' the sun." Thus: Boythorn in her ears, her godmother in her dreamed-back memories, the two of them converging in one stream. According to this reading, the volitional retrospection involved in imagining Boythorn's youth coincides with and augments the habitual retrospection taking Esther back to her childhood. Mental energetics of that sort—the mind's movement gaining or losing strength, being deflected or accelerated according to a play of forces like those governing the movement of a barge on the Thames—occur often in Dickens. And if Esther is envisioning Boythorn in his courtship days, she might well have some glimmering image of the lady he was courting, the lady who "died to him." The only lady to have died in Esther's presence is her godmother, Boythorn's lost beloved.

Sergeant George, minded almost simultaneously of two marriageable young people, reflexively conjures up the most conventional way of pairing them together within one set of associative brackets. He is wrong in his conclusion, but Esther's similar subliminal operation—probably because in *Bleak House* females, Esther especially, are more intuitive about such things—comes uncannily close to the mark.

However likely or otherwise this hypothesis may be by itself, the latter-day Esther telling us the story takes it seriously. Hence, in part, her confession of ignorance about the associative logic of dreams in general and of this one in particular. That there might be anything weird going on did not occur to her at the time but has since, now that she has both learned of the old connection between Boythorn and her godmother and been through experiences teaching her to take half-sensed perceptions more seriously than she may have at the time.

And it will turn out that her dream has been essentially true. How did that happen? Overall, she doesn't know for sure. She is a mature woman trying to remember back to and through a younger woman's refracted memory of a moment when an older memory met—matched or collided—with an impression perhaps distorted, perhaps distilled by sleep. She has to bear in mind that although what she found out about the old love affair might be bringing the facts into focus, it might also be distorting them—after, for example, the manner of folk etymology's back-formations: maybe, for instance, her memory of the dream itself has been inflected by what she has learned since. In working through such questions, I think, she resembles an astute reader of the book she is in.

3. How does Hortense learn the truth about Lady Dedlock?

Well, she *is* French. As such she is the only member of the Dedlock party to be "in spirits" during the trip to Paris, with its "dancing, lovemaking, wine-drinking" (139). (Impossible, in this book, to imagine those words applied to an English locale. On the return trip she and Sir Leicester's manservant are even being "affectionate in the rumble" (138).) It follows that she is attuned to certain non-English things about the heart and its ways—about, for instance, the interesting configuration once sometimes called a French triangle. The oblivious Sir Leicester, a rich milord married to an unrich beauty some twenty years his junior, is the pattern of a cuckold. Hortense likely arrived at Chesney Wold complacently predisposed to detect some illicit boudoir doings. She is as furious as any stage *cocu* when the dishonored party, according to form discarded for someone younger and more attractive, turns out to be not Sir Leicester but herself, replaced by the girlish Rosa. That makes it a matter of pride. Before, her lady's infidelity would have been just a part of the old *ronde*. Now, if proven, it will mean that she, Mlle. Hortense, is the butt, the odd maid out, the victim, of what she now perceives to be an infamous woman.

So: the motive. Her self-proclaimed capacity for dislike will now be focused on one point, Lady Dedlock. As she tells Tulkinghorn, her fixed purpose in life is "to dishonour her" (518).

That word "dishonour," not incidentally, is our earliest indication that Lady Dedlock's first name is Honoria (642). With her inside track into her mistress's business, Hortense knows such things before we do. What else does she know, and how much of it might have been kept from us?

Dealing with such questions requires that we attend to *how* she knows—what she learns, how her mind handles it. How, for instance, does she know that Snagsby knows about the night Lady Dedlock went out wearing Hortense's clothes? Considering that she had almost certainly never seen him before, Snagsby's idea that, "being uncommon quick," she "caught up" his name on the later night, when she modeled those clothes for Jo and the gentlemen (516), seems the best bet—except that his name was not actually spoken until after she had left and been shown downstairs (282–84). Ruling out authorial inattention, Hortense's sharpness includes either that she has a superhuman set of ears or that she crept back up and listened at the door. (Such eavesdroppings, some reported and some not, are an important feature of this book of thresholds; see, for example, item 5.) What else she heard there would have confirmed, as she already perhaps half-realized, that Lady Dedlock had worn that dress on some clandestine journey into a disreputable quarter.

Again: it is probable that, given her background, Hortense is as predisposed to detect some affair of a *nostalgie de la boue* stamp as she is to recognize any other French-novel sort of plotline, is ready to conceive that such a lady as her lady, obviously bored with proprieties, has been carrying on a *louche* dalliance. The old story, no? Probably, being so "sharp," she witnessed Lady Dedlock's longing gazes toward the gamekeeper's lodge, surmising that her mistress's fantasies were running rather in the Lady Chatterley line.

In any case, as a matter of determinable fact, she can have no knowledge of what Lady Dedlock's real destination was. After all, she was not there, and no one who knows the true story is likely to have told her. Nonetheless she is certain that Lady Dedlock has fallen, and that the fall has been sexual in nature. She is right. So how does she come to know that?

My answer is that she is the first to sense that Esther is Lady Dedlock's daughter. Like Guppy, she seems from the beginning to feel that great things are in store for Esther. "I will do more for you, than you figure to yourself now," she says, begging to be taken on as her maid, "You don't know how well!" (286). Then she kisses her hand and "take[s] note, with her momentary touch, of every vein in it." "Take note": an odd choice of words, that. In the preceding chapter, Jo has testified that the difference between Lady Dedlock's hand and Hortense's is by itself enough to tell them apart, to distinguish lady from not-lady (282). (During the French tour Lady Dedlock's hand had been similarly singled out for its daintiness; Hortense's—of course—had not.) Who knows that hand better than the maid? Who likelier to notice that difference than Hortense herself, keeper of the gloves, and who likelier to notice when the hand of one young lady, especially when so closely scrutinized, marks her off as akin to the older lady she longs to replace with her?

Hortense apart, about Esther's hands the testimony is suggestive but not conclusive. Phiz certainly makes them look delicate. Bucket finds Esther's handkerchief in her mother's "dainty little chest," among gloves notably "light and soft within" (671). I suggest that, as often, there is a fairy-tale component in play here, in which the fineness of the extremities reveals the gentility amidst the cinders. Hortense's attention to "every vein" of Esther's hand probably has to do with the mythology of bloodlines, blue blood, and so on.

But if so, the recognition it facilitates, like others we have noted, operates in peculiarly *bouleversé* fashion. Fairy-tale narrative, followed through, collides with the bedroom intrigue narrative, followed through: Esther's mother cannot turn out to be both blue-blooded queen and hot-blooded whore. Hortense may suspect that Esther is the daughter of this "lady" of hers, the one she first chose to worship and now chooses to despise as an incorrigible adulteress. That, at least, should put paid to any twinges of hurt pride she may have felt on having been dismissed by such a creature. But it also puts her, like so many others, in a bind, where the only option is to look away from what she doesn't want to know. Mademoiselle Hortense: You despise Lady Dedlock and, consequently, desire to serve, indeed revere, her daughter? Please explain.

As to just what Hortense knows: well, very likely she knows nothing about Captain Hawdon or about the true motives of her lady on "that night," the night that "lady" walked the London streets. In fact the phrase "that night" may be a bluff. Still, it suffices. Until almost the last day of his searchings, Tulkinghorn himself appears to suspect that Captain Hawdon is still alive, and Tulkinghorn dies without having found out the name, or even the gender, of Lady Dedlock's child. It is, yet again, all a matter of bits and pieces, and although the puzzle is never complete, Hortense, by way of her half-way recognition of Esther in Esther's mother—like Sergeant George half-detecting Hawdon in Esther, and like Esther herself half-intuiting Boythorn's story through an amalgam of sharp daylight perceptions and what her dreams make of them—probably has enough pieces at hand to pass as one of those in a position to solve it.

4. Tulkinghorn and his sometime accomplice Smallweed spend much of the novel seeking a copy of Captain Hawdon's early handwriting. Yet Smallweed already possesses many documents with Hawdon's signature. Why won't that do? Why must they have the "letter of instructions" (429) from the military days, which Sergeant George is eventually forced to give over?

The legal logic, if such it is, defeats me. Normally, a signature was and is considered the written mark of personal authenticity. Instead, Tulkinghorn must find something to approximate the hybridized handwriting, "law hand" over "original hand," whose sight caused Lady Dedlock to swoon. How could the "letter of instructions" be of any use in that regard? Written when Hawdon, although much distressed, was still in the military, the letter would presumably show no trace of whatever alterations were effected by opium and law-hand drill. Does Tulkinghorn really believe that by pairing such a document with some standard sample of Hawdon's legal penmanship he can prove to himself, or to anyone else, that Lady Dedlock was reacting to an amalgam of the two? Is the idea that by factoring out the standard markings in Hawdon's legal documents he will somehow derive a residue of the real thing, the echt love-letter-writer script whose traces made milady faint? And who on earth would buy such a story? No jury, probably. Nor, surely, Sir Leicester.

In the event, once he does finally get the document, he never uses it. So why all the bother? "McGuffin" may be part of the answer: his hunt certainly does make things happen, storywise. It suits Dickens's authorial purposes, but still—in *Bleak House,* of all Dickens's novels, there ought to be a plausible way in which it suits Tulkinghorn's as well.

The simplest answer may be that Tulkinghorn is fishing. No one in the book (possibly excepting Bucket, who essentially takes over for Tulkinghorn when he dies) has a keener sense of how odd peripheral bits and pieces can unexpectedly come to add up. He may, for instance, be betting that the sudden presentation of such a letter from the old days, even one not addressed to her, will make Lady Dedlock crack, on the spot. That (as we will see in item 6), is his strategy throughout, as exemplified by this earlier skirmish:

> Lady Dedlock, in dialogue with Tulkinghorn (Sir Leicester being present) on the subject of Hawdon's name: "What did they call the wretched being?"
> Tulkinghorn: "They called him what he had called himself, but no one knew his name."
> Lady Dedlock: "Not even any one who had attended on him?"
> Tulkinghorn: "No one had attended on him." (149–50)

That "wretched being" called himself Nemo. Tulkinghorn knows that. The question for him here is, does Lady Dedlock know it too?

Not on this showing, anyway. She maintains her poise throughout, and, her usual flunky being out of the room, concludes by directing Tulkinghorn to take the flunky's place, to open the door for her departure. The old "No one" trick may have worked for Odysseus, but not here. Still, Tulkinghorn has perhaps gained something from this exchange. Know your enemy. Lady Dedlock, as he will later reflect, is tougher than he realized; good to keep that in mind. As for all that open-the-door business: might that not have been an indiscreet overreaction? Might she not, in choosing to demean him beyond the normal—and for him, minutely calibrated—range, have revealed that she knows that he suspects? In which case, what he suspects is that much likelier to be true. He will have to look into that, won't he?

To repeat: I cannot fathom what Tulkinghorn expects to gain from the document. But it is utterly characteristic of him, and of the other smart ones in this novel, to assume that truth lies in duplicity, in incongruous combinations, in fringes inflected by others' fringes. This can sometimes turn out to be wrong: it is, after all, more or less a bunch of single-minded clods who finally—and, as always, too late—come across the smoking gun, a packet of love letters—and Tulkinghorn's researches wind up getting him murdered. Nonetheless, his sense of truth being a thing divided, a thing estranged from itself and as such at best intermittently recoverable, is woven deeply into the epistemological fabric of *Bleak House*. The fact that Tulkinghorn dies on the verge of working things out just puts him in the company of all the novel's seekers of truth, not least Esther, whose last words—and the book's—are an unanswered speculation in the form of an incomplete sentence.

5. His earlier "No one" gambit having been assayed with questionable success—and by "questionable" I mean literally open to question, uncertain of outcome—Tulkinghorn, in his next maneuver, does something unplanned and not part of his usual modus operandi. He makes things up. Relating his thinly disguised account of Lady Dedlock's secret to Sir Leicester, Lady Dedlock herself, and others in the company, he uncharacteristically goes beyond the facts, adding a bogus story of how the grand lady's disgrace caused her maid, whose family felt tainted by the association, to leave her service.

That is the detail that, it turns out, does the trick. Confronting Tulkinghorn afterwards, Lady Dedlock's first question is, "Is this true concerning the poor girl?" (508). She is thinking of her cherished maid, Rosa. Is it true, she is asking, that she knows of my disgrace and is being taken from me? Tulkinghorn, "not quite understanding the question," is momentarily set back. Being used to manipulating evidence but not to inventing it, he is unpracticed in the arts of sustaining whole-cloth fabrications. Recovering, he answers, "No, Lady Dedlock. That was a hypothetical case, arising out of Sir Leicester's unconsciously carrying the matter with so high a hand" (508). What does he mean?

At least in part, this comes out of yet another overheard conversation,[2] also unreported by the narrator. It occurs in the moments leading up to Tulkinghorn's entrance, on the night when he tells Lady Dedlock's story. "Mr. Tulkinghorn," Sir Leicester has been saying, "is always welcome here," and so on, up to his summation: "He is, of course, handsomely paid, and he associates almost on a footing of equality with the highest society" (503). Then, so help me, a shot rings out. Lady Dedlock, her musings interrupted by the sound at the moment when she was dwelling wishfully on the prospect of Tulkinghorn's sudden death, reacts instinctively: "A rat," says my Lady. "And they have shot him" (503). (If only.) For the first and last time in the novel, Sir Leicester contradicts her: no, he says, no rat has been shot. Then, "enter Mr. Tulkinghorn, followed by Mercuries [servants] with lamps and candles" (503). Sir Leicester is righter than he knows: the rat is still alive.

He then addresses, in order, his lady, his cousin Volumnia, the light-bearing servants, and Tulkinghorn. This implicit ladder of precedence is part of what the last-named means by Sir Leicester's "high...hand," but the main issue is that business about being "almost on a footing" with the others. Tulkinghorn must have overheard those words. "Almost on a footing?" Apart from Lady Dedlock, whom he intends to crush, he is by far the most capable person in the room. The others are all bone-headed antiques.

That is probably why Tulkinghorn proceeds to take "a pinch of snuff." Like the company, pinches of snuff are vestiges of the cartoonish past. The only other characters to take snuff are the Regency-Era Turveydrop and, when he is under Turveydrop's spell, the hapless Mr. Jellyby. Bucket is playing on these *demodé* associations when he gets rid of a vain butler wearing a fancy-dress costume of the previous century by asking him to go fetch him some snuff, which, being a man of his time, he proceeds not to take (629). Tulkinghorn himself later says he wouldn't give "a pinch of snuff" for what someone he considers to be a fool is saying (428). So now, in this company, he makes a show of taking some. It is a way of saying what that company is worth. Then he proceeds to tell Sir Leicester that he and his party were "beaten hollow" in the last election. "Hollow" is a thought-through word. Then he turns the conversation to the subject of the election's winners, which subject leads him, in a mimicry, of course lost on his audience, of Sir Leicester's own sentiments, to the subject of the inexplicable pride of such people, which subject leads to his Lady Dedlock story, the main point of which is his story about the maid. Sir Leicester will continue, "unconsciously," with that high hand of his. Later that night, Lady Dedlock comes to talk, sees him with Tulkinghorn, and tries to excuse herself. "Not at all," he answers, "only Mr. Tulkinghorn" (574). In the next few minutes, Tulkinghorn will, with his "clumsy bow," be the one to bring Lady Dedlock her chair, and, on three separate occasions, to ring for the servants. (The first time is at Sir Leicester's polite command, the next two as if it is expected of him.) All this happens on the night he will tell Lady Dedlock that he is on the whole inclined to ruin her and her house. Among other things, those servant-ringings have reminded him of that time she had him open the door for her in lieu of her usual menial.

Two people have been exposed in the process set in play by that overheard conversation. Tulkinghorn has revealed his secret as surely as he has Lady Dedlock's—that he is obsessed with inherited hierarchies and their markers. Like the snuff-taking, his words to his master come with an ironic edge, which, because assumed (correctly) to be too subtle for the hearer, carries with it an extra charge of contempt. His studiously nondescript ways simultaneously broadcast that he is beneath the consideration of his clients and whisper that he is above their pretenses.

6. If Tulkinghorn is so attentive to everything going around him, how can he be careless enough to get murdered?

Like Bucket later, climbing the "tower in his mind," he forgets his own playbook. He allows another person to get too close to the truth, then lets that person get too close to him. By the time Mademoiselle Hortense confronts him in his office, she has come, as we have seen, quite near to finding out the Dedlock secret. For one thing, she seems to know about "that night," when Lady Dedlock visited Hawdon's graveyard. She knows, too, that the means are at hand to "dishonour" her mistress. She realizes, or soon will, that if Tulkinghorn were to be shot, that mistress would become the natural suspect: two birds with one stone. As Tulkinghorn himself says to her, "You appear to know a good deal" (518). Well, yes. So why doesn't he accede to what he himself calls her "remarkably modest demand" that he find her a place, as, after all, he promised he would (283)? Or at least put her off civilly?

For two related reasons, I think. First is his obsession with tokens of hierarchy. That his clothes are ostentatiously classless just goes to prove the point in this book of looking-glass inversions and reverse psychologies. As a matter of fact he is extremely sensitive to all issues of latter-day feudalism, of who is supposed to obey whose orders. This sensitivity is antisympathetic. He has stored up in his heart the times that he was or felt himself to be treated like someone in service. The upshot is that he has no use for anyone who actually is. His inability to recognize Hortense as a person who might turn out to be of consequence is a function of his own neurotic rejection of the idea that he and anyone of her station could have anything in common, in turn a recoil from the perception that they do: "I think," Hortense tells him, "that you are a miserable wretch," to which he answers, "Probably." His attitude toward her is a function of his attitude toward himself.

This is why, I think, someone whose specialty is the fringes—of evidence, of respectability, of society—should miss the point with Hortense. Tulkinghorn is brilliant at handling someone like Jo, at one extreme, or Sir Leicester, at the other; Hortense, by contrast, is too close to home. He knows all about her "ungovernable" temper, but that someone like her could be cunning enough to work out the calculations according to which killing him is a smart move is the one shot on the board he cannot see. After all, whatever her designs, her approach is nothing if not frontal. Tulkinghorn is a sidewinder, conditioned to discount such behavior. His regard for data is inversely proportional to its centrality; what someone once called "the real French disease," not syphilis but "fear and loathing of the bleeding obvious," is his malady, not hers. When he is wrong, consequently, he is really, really wrong. "Violence will not do for me," he tells Smallweed, who has just grabbed him by the lapel (340). As prophecy, this could not be more off-base. Violence is exactly what does for him.

Tulkinghorn's aversion to the front-and-center reminds us that *Bleak House* is, among other things, a mystery story. (Several, actually.) The great trick of the mystery story, as invented in "The Purloined Letter," is the Skimpolian specialty of hide-in-plain-sight. That is why the butler did it. The butler was so to-be-expected that, when the outrageous happened, you thought of anyone but him. Hortense is a discharged lady's maid pleading to become some other lady's maid, one whose position puts her, for Tulkinghorn above all, maestro of everyone else's blind spots, in his blind spot.

7. What, getting back to number 5, is the story with that mysterious "shot" (503) that sounds just before Tulkinghorn commences his exposure of Lady Dedlock?

Not hunters. (It is too late in the day.) As with a number of other gaps in the narrative, the unrecorded eavesdroppings for example, we readers are left on our own: resign to remaining benighted, or hypothesize as best we can. I, anyway, am opting for the former: the shot belongs in the same category as, to take one of many examples, Bucket's materialization from out of the shadows in which, the observer Snagsby would have sworn, he was not present before (275): is it a ghost summoned, or night vision coming into play, by degrees?

As plot device, the shot may function as a red herring. In foreshadowing the later shot that kills Tulkinghorn, it helps to frame Lady Dedlock as a suspect in the murder. After all, as her remark about the "rat" showed, she was wishing him dead at the very moment. But red herrings ought to be more substantial than that. They should seem to come from and lead to a set of circumstances plausible enough to constitute, for a time, an alternative reality. A misdirection whose coordinates are obscure from the start makes little tactical sense.

Instead, I would suggest that, as one of those *Bleak House* events consigned to the realm of the uncertain, that first shot belongs to a major subset of this category, one that might be called psychic deputizing.

To re-cite an example from the previous chapter: when Esther first meets Turveydrop, she will be overcome by negative sensations, which, at the moment, she is too repressed to voice. Instead, another lady, conveniently present in the room, will do it for her (173–74). I think that there is a lot of such deputizing, conscious and unconscious, going on in *Bleak House,* and that Hortense's murder of Tulkinghorn is the most drastic example.[3] On the night whose aftermath will eventually incriminate and kill Lady Dedlock, she looked so much like her maid that only her hand, with its rings, distinguished one from the other. Among other things, that means that the two have the same figure, probably in part because the maid has patterned herself, diet and all, on the mistress.

In Bennett Miller's movie *Capote,* the soundtrack features two explosive noises. The first is from a shotgun, the sound of a murder being committed. The second is from a hanging, the sound of the murderer's neck being broken. An unsettling effect, I remember thinking, carrying an uncertain import: does the echo imply an eye for an eye, or instead the moral equivalence of murderer and executioner? In *Bleak House,* to what extent does the second shot, fired by Hortense, realize the consummation so devoutly wished for at the time of the first? Of the two women, Lady Dedlock has by far the stronger motive, but, as Tulkinghorn remarks, she is supreme in her powers of self-restraint. Hortense's grievances are slight by comparison, but then she is the "quick" and fiery one. And both women will end up dying wretchedly as a consequence of Tulkinghorn's death.

And why, although according to Tulkinghorn Lady Dedlock dismissed Hortense for being "the most implacable and unmanageable of women" (520), did it take her over five years (143) to do so? What kind of pair did they make? Julian Moynahan has influentially argued that in *Great Expectations* Orlick's attack on Mrs. Joe acts out Pip's resentments against her.[4] Variations on this phenomenon recur in Dickens's later novels, perhaps most brilliantly in *Little Dorrit*'s stair-step trinity of Flora Finching, Mr. F.'s aunt, and Mr. F.'s aunt's "stony reticule"—the first all gush (but with unvoiced reasons for feeling resentful), the second all spite, the third a purse, petrified into a blunt flail. Early in *Bleak House,* Lady Dedlock is sitting before her mirror as her hair is being (intriguing word, this) "undressed" by Hortense. She looks up at the image of her own "brooding face," sees Hortense's eyes "curiously observing her," and snaps, "You can contemplate your beauty at another time." Hortense: "Pardon! It was your Ladyship's beauty." Lady Dedlock: "That...you needn't contemplate at all" (147). But how, now, is the maid to avoid doing that while attending to her lady's hair in that mirror? Hortense has been seduced by the optically deceptive fact that when you look into an angled mirror at someone else it does not naturally occur to you that that person can look right back. Her gaze rebounds and unguarded eye contact occurs, the result being that what she most wants to see confirmed in that mirror, her desire to be as one with her mistress, is what she is most forbidden to acknowledge. Not long after she (knowingly) attempts to undo that mistress through the act of reenacting her; later she attempts to kill her through the act of killing the nemesis of both; in each case she is pretending to be Lady Dedlock, her hated and adored other. In *Bleak House,* to recall a point made in the previous chapter, one is probably better off staying away from mirrors.

One last note about that first shot: some time not long after Hortense's dismissal, Sergeant George remarks that he has had "French women come, before now," to his shooting gallery, "and show themselves dabs at pistol-shooting" (305). This is pretty clearly a clue, one of several that never make its way to anyone who could recognize its significance. The person who kills Tulkinghorn with one shot through the heart—in the dark, no less—is certainly a dab at pistol shooting. And, speaking of what I have called psychic deputizing, it is at least fitting that she should perfect that skill in the establishment of someone who has his own reasons for wanting Tulkinghorn dead.

8. Why is Baby Esther, the only child of Prince and Caddy Jellyby Turveydrop, born puny, sickly, deaf, and dumb?

There are, certainly, thematic reasons. As noted before, until its last chapter, *Bleak House* is pretty down on the whole business of bringing forth. Esther's children, not mentioned until that chapter, are the only ones whose arrival on earth is an unalloyed good thing.

But if Baby Esther reinforces this theme, she also serves to complicate it by blunting what would seem to be its obvious moral point. In *Oliver Twist,* every child's death is England's fault. In *Bleak House,* although the same can be said of the deaths of Jo ("Dead, your Majesty")and others, the case of the Turveydrops' daughter is a messier matter. She is, after all, born in wedlock to two decent, loving parents with enough income to bring her up in comfort. Neither Poor Law nor Chancery, nor anything else shown us about the state of England, is responsible for her misfortune. It just happens, an *acte gratuit* by an author who, against expectation, hardly seems to notice. After all, Dickens's way with the fates of children is famously to pull out all stops, and there is always one villain at least. (With Jo, the villain is us.) But with Baby Esther the fate of a child, for good measure a child named after the novel's sacrosanct heroine, verges on being a nonissue.

If it isn't our fault, whose is it? Perhaps we can dead-reckon to some cause likelier than others. Syphilis has been suggested—some of the baby's symptoms may match the profile—but that seems improbable. Neither parent is likely to have contracted it before marriage (or after, of course). They are just not the types. The same goes for Caddy's parents and for Prince's mother, a patient Griselda who wore herself out in slavish devotion to her husband (173).

That leaves Turveydrop Senior. His origins in the Regency, a period Dickens detested for its licentiousness, might incriminate him if there were other evidence along the same line, but I at least can't find any. Certainly in his *Bleak House* manifestation he is the last person one would suspect. Just imagining him naked seems a wince-worthy violation of the novel's—and not just the novel's—decorums. Besides, sexual activity, especially of the indiscreet variety, requires the expenditure of energy, something Turveydrop lives to avoid. True, he did once rouse himself to beget a son, presumably in order take on any labors not already assumed by his wife; it required some effort but wound up saving him much more—all in all an excellent investment, certainly, but any such action on the side would have been utterly contrary to plan.

If not syphilis—or so, far as I can detect, any other hereditary disease—then that leaves the vexed matter of childbirth, the process. In

Bleak House, giving birth and being born are quite rough enough. (Its year of publication, 1853, saw Queen Victoria, who loathed the whole business, first undergoing labor with the aid of chloroform.) Esther herself was believed to be stillborn; childbearing and childrearing have been anything but kind to either the brickmakers' wives or those of their children to have survived; Jo may well be called "Toughy" because he has managed to live past infancy. Taken all in all, Caddy Turveydrop's travail is probably not that out of the ordinary. It is a first delivery that sends the mother into prolonged convalescence (599), and seems to have been at least as hard on the child.

And then there was the matter of nurture: little Esther comes into a home that, sickly mother and child or no, continues to be devoted to the care and feeding of Mr. Turveydrop: "Then there was old Mr. Turveydrop, who was from morning to night and from night to morning the subject of innumerable precautions. If the baby cried, it was nearly stifled lest the noise should make him uncomfortable" (602). This goes on to itemize various other deprivations, but let us pause at that word "stifled." For one thing, it was at the time a traditional term for the killing of inconvenient newborns. For another, it means, most commonly, to silence by force. Caddy's baby could at least cry for a while after birth. Later, she has gone dumb. I suggest cause and effect. Mr. Turveydrop wore out his wife and ground down his son; now he is at work on the next generation.

As for the baby's loss of hearing, there is perhaps a suggestion that she was deaf from birth: when Prince plays her "a chord or two" on his fiddle (602), she seems not to notice. It's unclear to me whether what she's not noticing is just the music or any sound at all. Be that as it may, an environment in which her own attempt to speak is constantly being stifled is likely to be one in which she is not going to get much practice at hearing, either. The medical science of Dickens's day knew that certain human capacities emerge and shut off during delimited developmental stages ("windows," as they are called today)—that, for instance, people born blind and given sight later in life cannot, in the usual sense of the word, see.[5] Whatever handicaps Little Esther may have inherited, her environment, and her arrival into it, seem tailor-made to worsen.

Still, if her plight is a melancholy instance of adaptation, of someone (like Jo, in another register) losing her faculties because never allowed to develop them, the adaptation to it is a more heartening example. Her father, Prince Jr., goes lame, probably from the overexertion demanded by that fat vampire of a father of his. So much for career, income, and provision for his family. But the tomboyish Caddy, toughened by the kind of parental abuse that broke Prince, has grown up to be a highly competent manager of business. Meanwhile the markedly effeminate Prince (meeting him, Esther remarks his "feminine manner" [170]), "though able to do very little" in the business line, is for all that "an excellent husband" (768), and doubtless an excellent parent to his afflicted daughter. After all, no one in the book has had as much practice in dealing with children.

With that, one would think, momentous adjustment—she makes the money, he takes care of the child—they thrive and prosper. True, we never learn how, never learn just what business Caddy is so good at. Whatever it may be, let us note: Dickens has stage-managed a completely sympathetic story of gender role reversal without a snicker within earshot.

This last-chapter tableau of two good people dedicating their lives to the tending of one weak, misbegotten infant counterpoints and answers the myriad instances of helpless children dying "around us every day." I'm sorry for the cliché, but Prince and Caddy Turveydrop are choosing to light a candle rather than curse the darkness. Of all the abandoned children out there, their author is saying they are saying, this one at least will not be left out in the cold. Dickens's forbearance from trumpeting the gesture may itself be part of the point.

9. What does Guppy know and when does he know it?

By about the halfway point of the novel, both Esther and the supposedly omniscient narrator are asking themselves this question. Esther wonders whether Guppy might have had "vague surmises" when he proposed (534). For the narrator, the occasion is the close of Guppy's first meeting with that mother. "Is this," he asks, "the full purpose of the young man of the name of Guppy?" (364)

Well? Beats me. But one thing is for sure: this question is not rhetorical. Guppy possesses, if not hidden depths, hidden shallows. During his cross-examinations of Rachael Chadband and Lady Dedlock he proves that at least in such matters he is, as he remarks to his friend Jobling, "no fool" (400). Nor is he a cad. Being a young clerk, probably the first in his line to wear a white collar, he naturally lacks the seasoning needed to discern just where that subtlest of all of England's tribal taboos, the one against "self-praise" (664), kicks in, and sometimes makes a bad impression by declaring his acts to be acts of generosity. Nonetheless, that is sometimes what they are. H. G. Wells, fifty years on, would have handled him more gently.

Although it can sometimes seem that *Bleak House* makes a point of bollixing up origin quests, Guppy's background presents no such difficulties. Guppy is either, depending on one's perspective, an admirably ambitious up-and-comer or a vulgar upstart. He drops his aitches and lives in an infra-dig neighborhood near his unpresentable alcoholic mother. In striving to improve his family's standing in the world, to rise above his mother's level while remaining a dutiful son, like others in his position (including the young Dickens himself, according to some contemporary reports), he tends to overdo things. In classic not-top-shelf fashion, he aspires, clumsily.

Above all, he aspires to Esther, whose name, believed at the time to mean "star,"[6] may remind us of the Estella aspired to by that other lowborn longer, Pip. The difference, arguably a point in Guppy's favor, is that Estella is exquisite and Esther is not. In fact, that Guppy should fall for Esther while in the distracting presence of Ada, an established beauty who perennially puts her friend in the shade, at least shows that his infatuation is less superficial than many another's.

Just how he comes to fall for Esther is, I think, a puzzle in a puzzle. There are three stages we know of. As the clerk welcoming her to London, he seems to take special notice of her. Next, shown Lady Dedlock's portrait, he is overcome by the feeling of having seen something like the face before. Then he proposes. He tells Esther that he has loved her from the start, that he haunted her former London dwelling "only to look upon the bricks that once contained" her (114). It really does seem impossible to doubt his word. But what brought that about?

I suggest that he discerned within Esther's form, face, and bearing what Blake calls "the lineaments of gratified desire"—that with his sharpened social climber's eye he was, like Mademoiselle Hortense, able to spot what he pined for: a real lady, however obscured by circumstance. (And a good thing, too: without the obscuring, she would have been completely out of his reach.) If I am right about that, it becomes somewhat clearer why the sight of Lady Dedlock's portrait had such an effect. Combining shades of Esther's features with the trappings of class, it reinforced his inklings that through some hidden linkage, Esther came of higher stock than she knew of, and it may have whispered to him how providential was the coincidence that tracking down hidden linkages was just what he was best at. At some point between picture and proposal the images came together, framed in one of the novel's many subordinate narratives: Esther was the princess in the cinders, a lady hidden in motley; he was the devoted young yeoman who would prove her rights and thus bring them both up in the world, merit and blood justifying one another's rise. So he makes up his mind, learns Esther's address, gets himself sent to Bleak House, and proposes.

"I know nothing, now, certainly," he confesses to Esther, yet his offer to use his skills in "pushing" her "fortunes" indicates some vague idea that somewhere in her background there are fortunes to be found. Nineteen chapters later comes the interview with Lady Dedlock, which makes the narrator, and me, wonder how much he has learned in the interim. We know that he has learned that Jo escorted a certain "lady in a wale" to a certain graveyard (239), and that Mrs. Chadband was once Esther's godmother. Does he somehow put those two together? On what basis? In the next chapter he installs Jobling, renamed Weevle, in Nemo's old room and directs him to find out what he can about Krook. Has something in particular made him think that Krook might be a key to Esther or the veiled lady? Again, there is no indication, and that is the last we hear of his researches.

And yet, by the end of the meeting with Lady Dedlock, he can put together the outline of something sounding much like a summary for the prosecution. He has apparently done some unrecorded pumping of Mrs. Chadband since their first meeting, and, perhaps—although it sure seems like the last thing that she would be inclined to disclose—learned that the names of Esther's mother and father were Barbary and Hawdon. (In which case he would also know that Esther is illegitimate, thus opening a whole new dimension of questions about his motives.) Also, he has learned that Krook possesses a bundle of letters written to Hawdon.

This last bit of information, we will learn, came from Krook himself via Jobling. Although a critical link, it still does not explain what Guppy is doing in Lady Dedlock's parlor. As far as the reader can tell, all he knows at this point is that the man once called Nemo was probably Esther's father. In what way can that implicate her ladyship?[7] Possibly, in some paper chase, he has discovered that Lady Dedlock's maiden name was Barbary. Possibly something else. The only thing clear is that the source of some of the evidence Guppy is working from has been withheld from the reader. How he learned about "Hawdon" and "Barbary," for instance.

At that same meeting with Lady Dedlock, he reveals what seems to me a datum even harder to account for, the vivid memory of "the rings that sparkled" on the fingers of the veiled lady when Jo saw her remove her glove (363; cf. 202). There is no reference to those rings in the account of the story we hear Guppy hear. Maybe they were mentioned in his follow-up cross-examination, summarized by the narrator without any direct quotations; maybe he got it from one of the four people present when Jo's story did include those rings (although it certainly wasn't from Tulkinghorn, Bucket, or Hortense, and the fourth party, Snagsby, promised to keep mum, and seemed to mean it [283]), maybe Jo told someone else who told someone else....[8] *Somehow* Guppy ferreted out that damning detail. "If you was to hear him tell about the rings that sparkled on her fingers when she took her glove off, you'd think it quite romantic," he says to Lady Dedlock, rubbing it in. Notice that this is not quite the same as saying that *he* has heard Jo on the subject of those rings. And then, "If your ladyship would wish to have the boy produced in corroboration of this statement, I can lay my hand upon him at any time." Really? The only one who can plausibly make such a claim is Bucket, and Bucket does not take orders from the likes of Guppy. The next time we meet Jo will be in the cottage of a Saint Albans brickmaker, and it seems unlikely in the extreme that Guppy knows or knew where he is, or how to "lay hands" on him.

Guppy bluffs, weaves, almost certainly (like everyone else) lies, and above all works from a field of information unavailable either to his audience, Lady Dedlock, or us, the readers. Are we being bluffed, and so on, along with her? This reader at least cannot make him out. He delivers that line about the rings sparkling on the veiled figure's hand at the moment Lady Dedlock's rings are "glittering" before his eyes. He tells her that this figure was "a disguised lady, your ladyship." Is that double set of echoes deliberate, or not? Again: this is no fool.

At the end of the interview, the narrator is genuinely uncertain on the issue. So am I. It may, however, be pertinent that his suspicions seem to have grown, if not arisen, during the course of the meeting. At the outset, the figure introduced as "the young man...of the name of Guppy" (358) seems way out of his depth. By the time of his departure, the tables have turned. His summation sounds to me like the triumph of a player whose bluff has worked, whose hunches have paid off. Also, perhaps, like the words of someone who has talked himself into confidence. He asserts, for instance, that Lady Dedlock knows the names "Barbary" and "Hawdon" *"very well"*—quite a jump from the slight familiarity she has just admitted to, and close to calling her a liar. The Guppy introduced at the start of the interview would not have dreamed of such impertinence. Perhaps this is still bluster—perhaps Guppy still has no idea how well she knows those names—but if so, it is bluster that, no fool, he senses, correctly, he can now get away with. Maybe Lady Dedlock's loss of composure on hearing the name "Esther

Hawdon" (362) tipped the balance in his mind. That is my best guess, and it is far from being a confident one.

However much Guppy knows, it is not the whole story, and it is not enough. Even at the moment of apparent victory over Lady Dedlock he still does not know whether the letters to Hawdon were written by a man or a woman (398)—although, to add qualification to qualification, the fact that he raises the question probably means that he suspects the latter. Still, the answer might have been otherwise, in which event his case collapses, as in fact it does when those letters seem to have vanished. Even when they turn up again he remains uncertain as to their import (665).

Tulkinghorn is on a wild goose chase; Guppy—somehow or other—seems to have the right idea along with what turns out to be an unconfirmable supposition needed to bring it home; Bucket, at a critical juncture, goes off headlong in the wrong direction. The secret is finally found by a gaggle of mostly senile blitherers who luck out, mainly because, to take a line from James Joyce, a "starving cat left in disgust," thus giving them leave to check out the cat-box.

The novel itself contains everything necessary to answer the questions Guppy is asking. What it does not contain is enough to determine how he comes up with whatever answers he reaches. We are evidently, at a minimum, dealing with yet another unrecorded conversation, or someone's overhearing of such.

10. Is Esther pretty?

"Pretty" is Esther's favorite word. Not including its adverbial occurrences, she uses it in some form forty-five times, mostly in her assessments of other women; her alternate the narrator, in approximately the same number of pages, employs it less than half as often.

This compliment is not returned. Up until the last page, no one calls her pretty. What may appear to be two exceptions to this statement do not withstand scrutiny. First, Caddy describes Esther and Ada as looking "neat and pretty" (177), but "respectively" can be taken as understood. (Elsewhere, Esther is always the neat one, Ada the beauty.) Second, after her illness, Esther reports overhearing a child asking why she is no longer the "pretty lady" she used to be (447). That—the memory of a little girl, perhaps just comparing Esther's new looks with her old and in any case no expert on what the world considers womanly beauty—is as close as Esther gets to reporting a compliment on her looks, and as always her motive is one of self-deprecation: whether or not she ever was pretty is secondary to her need to let us know that in any case she certainly isn't now. So, again: until the last page, no one ever looks Esther in the face and tells her that she is pretty.

This question matters because it does. In a Victorian novel, a young woman's looks are important. The question certainly matters to Esther, who still remembers the beautiful "complexion" (more beautiful than hers, of course) of her childhood doll, and rarely meets another female without immediately assessing her relative attractiveness.

Phiz, the novel's illustrator, is complicit in the mystification. He never shows Esther in full or three-quarter face. After her disfiguring illness, in fact, he never shows her face at all—she always has her back turned or head bowed—but even before then, in the five plates of the book's first half in which Esther appears, he pictures her as someone a later age might call camera-shy. Typically, she looks down or away, her face in shadow, her posture prim, her figure small and firmly corsetted, her one distinguishing feature a tight bun of dark hair.

Then as now, it is the standard image of an ugly duckling waiting for the right man to turn her into a swan, and for the first half of the book something in that vein looks to be where Esther's story is heading, before she becomes ill and, it seems to follow, ugly forever. This is why it matters so much that at story's end, the man she loves will bestow that precious word in language pointedly reversing what the well-meaning little girl had said—"And don't you know that you are prettier than you ever were?" (770)—withheld from her for the first sixty-seven of the novel's sixty-eight chapters. For Esther, it has to be the happiest of endings.

The problem is, she *isn't* prettier than she ever was. If we know anything for sure about Esther's looks, it is that she lost them at the novel's midpoint.

Unless, that is, she got them back, somehow. There seem to be hints to that effect near the end. On that same last page, right next to her husband's bestowing of the long longed-for "prettier," she will admit to sometimes looking at herself in the mirror. That was how she began to suspect, as she tells us (slantwise, of course, as an afterthought) that she has lately been discerning "little momentary glimpses" of her "own old face" in the glass" (722). (But then "old face" has a double meaning here, does it not, if we remember the "old woman" of her housemaid years?) Bucket, who last saw her before the change in her looks (312), has no trouble recognizing her when he again meets her near novel's end, proceeds to chat confidently about her likely future as a wife and mother (hardly remarkable, of course—but then who else ever says anything like that to her, since her illness?), and passes no remark about the change in her looks. Well, of course he wouldn't—but neither do any of the people they meet during their journey together, including the brickmaker set, who also remember Esther from her early days.

So maybe Esther's scars, the pockmarks typically left by smallpox, have faded, at least in part. Stranger things have happened in Dickens.

On the other hand, once again: everyone in *Bleak House* lies. May there not be some diplomacy in play with that phrase "prettier than you ever were"? Does it not beg the question, "And just how pretty was *that,* pray tell?" The nature of Esther's first-person narrative guarantees that the question will never be answered directly. As with the child's pretty/not-pretty "lady," every indication comes by way of comparison and reflection. Vis-à-vis her brilliantly blonde companion Ada (compare Esther's brown bun), she will always be the toad among the flowers, and there are signs that this contrast is not entirely a function of her besetting morbidity. Skimpole and Jarndyce both call Ada "beautiful" and "pretty" without saying anything comparable to the Esther standing next to them (70, 161). (Isn't that *rude?*) Meeting Ada and Esther, Lady Dedlock herself, who should know better, greets the former as "a beauty," then turns and congratulates the latter on... her guardian (229). Caddy Jellyby does pay Esther a compliment on her "dear good face" (290)—a nice enough thing to say, certainly, to a lady on the matronly side, but not necessarily a picker-upper for an unmarried young woman.

Curiously, however, both before and after her illness, Esther's looks have a way of improving by the mediations of others. The issue is not what she looks like when first seen but what she comes to look like, or (this qualification is necessary) seems to look like when her face blends with other faces. Filtered through Lady Dedlock's portrait her face leaves Guppy smitten. With her veil up, she reminds Jo, too, of Lady Dedlock, that paragon of mature beauty (381). When Hortense tells her that she is "beautiful as an angel" (285), she is no doubt flattering her outrageously (the French go in for flattery in Dickens)—but it is also probably a case of her seeing Esther by way of the resemblance to her former mistress and idol, whose place she wishes Esther to take. As suggested earlier, in item number one, Sergeant George's hopes for Esther's romantic happiness may be conditioned by trace memories of her father—perhaps of her mother as well.

All such flattering assessments come as a result of some sort of sensory-mnemonic synthesis. Although she does not wear spectacles herself (doing so would just complete the ugly-duckling schtick), something about Esther brings out a double-lens vision in others, suggestive of that favorite Victorian binocular gadget, the stereoscope, if not of the composite photographs later introduced by Francis Galton. One can never, simply, see her by herself. The twentieth-century sociologist David Riesman would have called her "other-directed," and her chronic inability to consider herself apart from the additions or subtractions engineered by the presence or perspective of others apparently carries over into their perceptions of her as well. Most of the novel's characters, and almost all of the female ones, can readily be ranked by comeliness. Richard Carstone is handsome; Ada is beautiful; Miss Wisk, the masculine feminist whose name probably hints at "whiskers," is not. Liz, the brickmaker's wife, is "an ugly woman" (101), and that is that: she has a good heart, but she is, was, and always will be an ugly woman. Esther has a good heart too. What about her? "It depends" is probably as close as one can come to an answer. Someone dubbed "Dame Durden" and treated accordingly is not going to be glamorous. On the other hand, the new, last-chapter "Mrs. Woodcourt," pockmarked or not, can still be... well, "prettier" than before—not quite the same as "pretty," to be sure, but still within squinting distance of the coveted encomium.

It probably helps that, in this last chapter, "Mrs. Woodcourt" is in moonlight. In an 1856 letter, Dickens was to remark of a young woman that "she had the smallpox two or three years ago, and bears the traces of it here and there, by daylight"[9]—that is, not, one infers, by moonlight. Moonlight becomes Esther; it goes, one hopes, with her hair, but even more with her face. In an earlier and different moonlit scene, the narrator had written that "the moon has eyed Tom [that is, Tom-All-Alone's] with a dull cold stare, as admitting some puny emulation of herself in his desert region unfit for life and blasted by volcanic fires" (551). "Tom" is where Jo came from, and his face, thus anthropomorphized, may, like the moon's, recall the "blasted" features Jo was indirectly to inflict on Esther. In an 1862 letter Dickens was to refer casually to the "largest exhausted Crater" on the moon,[10] thus showing that he went along with the general belief that the moon's cratered surface came from a history of volcanic activity, as opposed to meteorites. Tom's face, a "puny emulation" of the moon's surface, maps the craters of pustular eruptions of the disease passed on to Esther.

But if Esther has a face like the moon's, it is one that comes alive, becomes prettier than ever, when washed, homeopathically, in the moon's glow. There seems to be a kind of Renaissance idea of sympathy in play here: two blasted faces, microcosm and macrocosm, both made luminous by reflected light. The woman whose image, especially self-image, has always been bound up with the influence of others, whether eclipsed by the glow of Ada's "rich, golden" presence, irradiated by memories of her mother's afterimage, veiled by a repertoire of old-maid charades, or in general either blanked out or gazed into compliance—invisible when unseen, otherwise "a dear good face" or whatever else the noticer choose to notice—is finally brought into its own through reflecting her reflection.

Two reflections, actually. The other comes from the love of the husband who, in yet another binocular exercise, sees in the face not Esther's reflection of the image of the great lady whose portrait or person he has never met, but instead Esther's reflection of Esther—the face before him now, glossed from without by moonlight and lit from within by the proverbial glow occasioned by being the mother of his children, calling back to memory the unscarred face he first saw when their charitable visits to the same crazy old lady brought them together, and later cherished in memory, surely, during the hazardous period when his life-risking, life-saving heroics overseas were, as he would later find out, being matched back home by Esther's self-effacing, self-defacing ministrations to Charley.

It helps that, as we are repeatedly told, his face "sunburnt." He is, that is, the natural power source to consort with—to light up—the moonlit Esther of the last page. I have suggested that the circle of "beads" glimpsed during Esther's darkest passage evokes both the distinguishing marks of her new disfigurement and the corona of a sun in eclipse, blocked by the moon's transit. In fact, given the parallel just suggested between lunar craters and smallpox pustules, I will further hypothesize that there was another kind of sympathetic magic, this time maleficent, in play at that moment: the moon empowered to transmit its extinguishing influence, not to mention the imprint of its craters, at the exact moment its life-giving rival is out of the picture.

In which case, the bright moon of the final page is the opposite story, not two bodies canceling one another out but a reflection and refinement by way of the equilibrium of opposites—like, ideally, man and wife. Like the sun itself in this novel's foggy landscape (Dickens, along with his contemporary Florence Nightingale, believed in fresh air and sunlight as the best medicine for virtually all ailments, emphatically including those of the skin), Woodcourt is a healer, last seen in action soothing, cleansing, dressing, and binding Jenny's "sadly broken" skin (554). In his last appearance, I suggest, in a different but analogous case, he does the same for Esther's broken skin.

Is she pretty? The question is finally on the order of, "What is Nemo's handwriting?" The only answer is that it is some sort of hybrid.

The answer is a tangle of what was and is, perceived and real, worked out separately and mutually, between two consciousnesses, over time. All of that is at work in the moment that Lady Dedlock, red flushing through her pale skin as Sergeant George's had when contemplating Esther's face, recognizes it and the story it has to tell. Tulkinghorn is wrong to think that he can reconstitute it simply by some version of putting one and one together. Some unities are not susceptible to that kind of analysis, because compounded of shifting consciousnesses, reflected and reflecting, including the consciousnesses reading them. Esther earns her "prettier" self and, by virtue of having passed through her spell of ugliness, earns as well her place in Woodcourt's (reflected) sunlight, having passed through its eclipse.

II.

The number of these examples, ten, was decimally derived. It could have been fourteen, thirty-six, whatever. Whatever, they all would have been, among other things, variations on the poisoned kiss theme, as expounded in the previous chapter—the interplay of the desire to see and touch and the need not to, and the compromises the mind works out between those impulses. Sergeant George sweeps the "broken thoughts" that would have made Esther his old friend's bastard child out of his mind. Tulkinghorn, living to denude and destroy the figure at the center of his life's work, wastes his time attending to peripheral issues, ignores Hortense out of a need not to have to include her within the bounds of his sense of self, and, because of that blind spot, winds up dying before his goal is achieved. Mademoiselle Hortense, forbidden to look at her mistress, will die because she cannot help it, and because of what those "sharp eyes" of hers pick up. Mr. and Mrs. Turveydrop won't look at what the senior Turveydrop has done and is doing to their family, even at the expense of their child's health. Guppy's quest for the truth is like Oedipus's: the last thing he would want to learn is that Esther is illegitimate. The reason Esther doesn't want to know whether she is pretty is that that is what she does want to know.

In the story of Bluebeard, thrice alluded to in *Bleak House,* a new bride does not know what is on the other side of a forbidden door until her husband gives her the key. She opens it and discovers the corpses of his former wives. Esther cannot pass through the door leading to her late father's chamber until John Jarndyce hands her the keys to a place, Bleak House, named by its suicidal former owner. Only then, through the agency of her surrogate father and prospective bridegroom, is she able to cross the threshold of a different but cognate bleak house and, "chilled," sense what is most wrong in this novel—not dead wives but absent fathers, then as now literature's prize synecdoche for the something essential that is not there.

I think that the logic at work here is, fundamentally, dream logic, not as understood in today's post-Freudian world,[11] but as understood in Dickens's time. Half of the novel's narrative is conducted by someone who is invisible, can fly[12] (as the crow flies, in an early chapter), see or pass through walls at will, and read people's minds. These are venerable fantasy powers, dream powers. If he doesn't have a cape, that's about all he doesn't have. He has the powers, that is, that Dickens the editor proposed as the guiding spirit for *Household Words,* about two years before he began *Bleak House*: "a certain SHADOW, which may go into any place...and be in all homes and all nooks and corners, and be supposed to be cognisant of everything and go everywhere, without the least difficulty...a kind of semi-omniscient, omnipresent creature"[13] who, as he was to specify a few months later, was always to be described as acting in the present tense.[14]

Besides anticipating the non-Esther, perpetually present-tense narrator of *Bleak House,* these words may recall another "shadow" from several years before. "Shadow," sometimes capitalized, was one of Dickens's names for whatever was haunting Madame de la Rue. It appeared in her dreams (she would stave off sleep until dawn, sleep fitfully, sometimes sense its presence in half-waking moments), embodied some unknown but palpable menace, and could not be thwarted except by the magnetizing powers of Dickens himself. Although sure the spirit was male, she was otherwise unable to describe it, because like all proper phantoms or shadows it could not, must not, be looked at: "There is a man haunting this place—dimly seen, but heard talking sometimes—whom she is afraid of, and 'dare not' look at."[15]

Sensing something awful but not being able to face it, not being able to open the door or lift the veil that would disclose it, is and was one of the top ten stories on everyone's nightmare list. Dickens knew that. Having reviewed the scientific studies on the subject[16] and compared them with memories of his own dreams, he concluded that the experience was generic, its variations from the same limited stock:

> How many dreams are common to us all, from the Queen to the Costermonger! We all fall off that Tower—we all skim above the ground at a great pace and can't keep on it—we all say "this must be dream, because I was in this strange, low-roofed, beam-obstructed place, once

before, and it turned out to be a dream"—we all take unheard-of trouble to go the Theatre and never get in—or to go to a Feast, which can't be eaten or drunk—or to read letters, placards, or books, that no study will render legible... or we all confound the living with the dead, and all frequently have a knowledge or suspicion that we are doing it... we all go to public places in our night dresses, and are horribly disconcerted, lest the company should observe it.[17]

To review these items in light of *Bleak House*: the skimming at great pace forecasts its superhero narrator; the thwarted trips to the theater, Guppy, when he follows Esther to the plays she attends but never approaches the presence that draws him (or, for that matter, since he is ever gazing Esther-ward, sees the play [155]); the illegible readings, Krook and many another; the public near-nakedness, Lady Dedlock, who fears most of all "exposure" on a "gaudy platform" before a gawking crowd (512), her husband, who at his lowest moment sees or seems to see a prospect of "thousands of fingers pointing at him" (653), the ever-shivering ill-clothed Jo, constantly being found out and condemned by the Police in different voices, and many another; the moments of déjà vu ("I was in this... place, once before"), Esther, at several critical junctures; the "Tower" perhaps Bucket, who should never have mounted that "tower in his mind." As for the chronic confusion of living with dead: England, the Dedlocks, and above all Chancery and the fungoid cemeteries it licenses are evidence of how widespread, indeed institutionalized, is that confusion on the national scale; several apparitional apprehensions, noted earlier, demonstrate how it can play out in private lives.

Above all is the thread running through these instances, the feeling of being foredoomed not to see or reach what one absolutely must and absolutely must not see or reach—of not quite keeping the pace, of just missing theater or feast,[18] of not being able to read the written words presented. A cancelled passage from *Bleak House*, describing Esther's dream just after she has been given her housemaid's keys, perhaps comes closest to this central syndrome: "I was in such a flutter about my two bunches of keys that I had been dreaming for an hour before I got up, that the more I tried to open a variety of locks with them, the more determined they were not to fit any."[19] She then adds, in one of her many completely wrong assessments, "No dream could have been less prophetic." On the contrary. Until just before the very end of the novel, nothing could have been more prophetic of her life to come and descriptive of her life so far, and of the lives close to her.

As Warrington Winters has shown,[20] versions of this arch-dream had before surfaced in Dickens's fiction. Barnaby Rudge dreams of some obscure threat "hiding...like a cat in dark corners" (*BR* 48), tracking him but never showing its face; in the same novel, the sleep of another character is haunted by a malevolent "phantom" who gathers strength as he dozes off but disappears the moment he starts awake, leaving him filled with obscure fear (*BR* 621). David Copperfield and the Stephen Blackpool of *Hard Times* both suffer from dreams of what in the latter novel is called "a nameless, horrible dread."[21] Just before Scrooge wakes up, a (this word, again) "Phantom" points him toward a tombstone inscribed with his name" (*CC* 142);[22] his recoil from the grave, into which, despite being repeatedly pointed in its direction, he never quite looks or drops, jolts him awake, determined to be a new man.

Perhaps the most striking case occurs in *Martin Chuzzlewit*: the double dream of the conspirators Jonas Chuzzlewit and Montague Tigg. For sound reasons afraid that he may be murdered in his sleep by Jonas, Tigg dreams of the door on the other side of which his nemesis may be waiting:

> His fears or evil conscience reproduced this door in all his dreams. He dreamed that a dreadful secret was connected with it; a secret which he knew, and yet did not know...Incoherently entwined with this dream was another, which represented it as the hiding place of an enemy, a shadow, a phantom.[23]

This is prophetic. Tigg starts awake to find the door open and his future murderer, Jonas Chuzzlewit, standing beside the bed. Later, having fulfilled the prophecy by murdering Tigg, Jonas inherits his victim's nightmare: asleep or awake, he obsesses about some door, present or remembered, on the other side of which lurks his doom. "Do *you* see the door?" demands his accuser in the climactic encounter—and there, sure enough, "standing in the doorway," is the man whose testimony will condemn him—"Another of the phantom forms of this terrific Truth!" (*MC* 782–83).

That last confrontational revelation has no equivalent in *Bleak House*. "Terrific Truth" never makes way through its thicket of interbranching lies. Doors and similar obstructions, literal and figurative, abound, and characters are often poised at their thresholds, trying to hear what is happening on the other sides, but no barrier gives way to allow, for instance, murderer to confront murder's witness, wronged husband to accuse guilty wife. The closest thing to a recognition scene, between

Esther and her mother, is made possible only because it is also a nonrecognition scene.

A fundamental rule of this book's dream logic is that the dreamer wake up before any such showdown. It is only just before his death—the death into the "other world" that "sets this right"—that Richard realizes he has been, all along, the "dreamer" of "a troubled dream" (763). Again, to quote Dickens on the subject: "We all say 'this must be a dream'." Then we wake up. In *Bleak House* the only such waking is into that "other world," outside the novel.

Which is to say that everybody in the novel is asleep, more or less. Several besides Richard reach the point of suspecting that fact, but to know it fully would be, like Richard, to disappear from the scene. Accordingly the novel features a collection of what a later age would call narcoleptics, of varying degrees. The book begins near the end of November, when England's high-latitude ratio of darkness to daylight is approximately two to one, and throughout the succeeding seasons, that proportion continues, by way of fog, rain, shadow, and the "dim London eye" of day (405), to be about right, bat-time not lark-time. All the major venues are at one point or another described as sleeping; at Chesney Wold even the woods look "massively hushed in sleep" (461), its animals dreaming (461–62). (They are not alone in their kind: Boythorn's bird, Esther fancies, may be dreaming [444]; a rook is "drowsy" [141]; the very air is "drowsy with the hum of insects" [228].) At least three characters—Hawdon, with his opium; Krook, with his gin; and the deaf and demented Mrs. Smallweed—live their lives in semi-hibernation. Even the coffee being perpetually drunk by Mrs. Jellyby somehow works to enhance oblivion, not awareness. Others—Guster, for instance, or Mr. Snagsby—inhabit or, as in Skimpole's case, affect to inhabit dream worlds much of the time.

With the rest, it is a matter of degree. Sleep is a middle state, halfway between Hawdon's death from too much "sleeping-stuff" (712) and the caffeine buzz that likewise seals off Mrs. Jellyby from commerce with most of reality. As it overlaps with death in one direction, its border with wakefulness in the other is permeable and uneven. This is one large reason for the raggedness of the novel's evidentiary testimony. It is not that mirror on mirror mirrored is all the show, or that everything is ultimately a matter of documents in the endless *différance*-determined business of misreading other documents, or even that everyone lies. The raggedness comes not out of some radical indeterminability as to what is and as to what happens, but from the variable capacity of the characters, including the narrator, to see and, above all, face what they see.

The major impediment to solving its many puzzles, the main reason so many characters need to be "cryptographers"[24] and that such calipers-and-jeweler's-loupe exercises as have been assayed in this chapter often become necessary, is that the data received by the reader is delivered though witnesses who in variable degrees wish not to see or know. They all have their own doors behind which they will not look, and which each can approach only to within some allowable range: not so much the fabled blind men with the elephant as a bunch of variably purblind people all of whom, to some degree or other, are afraid of the elephant.

So what are they afraid of? Of nothing, I think, in the sense given that word in *King Lear*—of Nemo, of becoming "no one" (45), of the death of the sun (5), of entropy, of blankness, of no-meaning. *Bleak House* is perennially anxious about the prospect that things, including itself, don't mean anything. Coffee, gin, and opium addicts have all turned or been turned away from that prospect to embrace their own fragmentary facsimiles of order; so has Mrs. Smallweed, the old lady who hears only numbers and always hears them as numbers of pounds. Those facsimiles are, respectively, writing (letters), writing (letters, documents, etc.), writing (legal documents), and writing (legal tender, "bills," etc.). Their creator, who dresses Jo and other paupers in "rags" while occasionally reminding us that rags can wind up being processed into paper, is not unaware that he has written these people into existence.[25] Making his paper world, he shares the general anxiety. A lot of *Bleak House* can be seen as a sophisticated defense mechanism against that anxiety. The kind of mind that produces the scavenger-hunt perplexities surveyed in this chapter is hungry to make meaning, and to coax his reader into joining in with him.

That is because, I think, he recoils from evidence of its absence. On the other side of Esther's father's door there awaits, not an ogre, but nothing. The happy ending is—must be—moonlit, because the light of day is liable to fix its beam on what is lost or was never present. If Esther's dream of the "flaming necklace, or ring, or starry circle" is, as I (following Robert Newsom) have suggested, inspired in part by the image of a solar eclipse, it is notable that she is pained at least as much by bright rim as by darkened center. Next time she is out in daylight the sun would, were it not for her veil, show off the disfigurement that, she believes, has subtracted from her life the man who gives her life meaning. She goes from too much blindness to too much sight. In fact "Blindness and Insight" would have been a great title for the chapter where Esther has her dream. The shape of that "bright" necklace-ring-circle is, after all, the traditional shape of zero.

Dickens believed what the theorists of the day were saying, that dreaming, working through free association combined with memory and whatever else may impinge, unleashes the innate desire to make meaning of everything flying about in the mind at the time, including whatever afterimages may have been precipitated out of day or life past. People asleep in their nightshirts while recalling some public occasion will forge out of that accidental conjunction a dream of being almost naked in public. I have noted Dickens's surmisal that his Genoa dream of Mary Hogarth had been forged out of memory, desire, and certain details of the room and city in which it occurred. After dreaming of her phantom, Madame De la Rue had decided not to go on a planned journey because, "trying to put together what scattered words she heard the figure say, she joined and dovetailed them into some threat, having reference to her venturing to undertake the journey."[26] Making meaning in *Bleak House* is typically a matter of "dovetail"ing its data, and the upshot is often that some journey or other ought not to be completed, perhaps not begun.

Bleak House shows that Dickens also had an idea as to why that was so, why "almost," as in the nightshirt dream's "almost naked," was a part of it, why the final door is not opened. Because it would lead to nothing, to no-meaning, to mere nakedness. Its male lead is someone who must regularly deal with naked bodies, but the narrator never shows him doing that. Its heroine is a woman who learned early on that getting through life is more bat-flight than lark-flight. Both are pathologically averse to saying what they think or, worse, know. In this they are both right, or at least relatively right, under the given conditions.

About *Ulysses,* the critic S. L. Goldberg remarked that its technique "attempts not so much to record the characters' passive registration of external reality or the laws of human psychology, as to render the very process in which meaning is apprehended in life."[27] In that regard, at least, *Bleak House* anticipates Joyce. The novel's project of making meaning of its own material proceeds, mainly, in the way of dreamwork—a field of shreds and patches, problematically integrated by a process of hints and guesses, by a composite consciousness, which, like the Dickens's dreamer telling himself "this all must be a dream," is, in inverse degree to his need to make everything cohere, given to spells of questioning this or that, and sometimes of questioning everything, about the ground of its being. This would not work if all of its puzzles turned out on examination to be equivalent to trick questions, if none of its hundreds of lies could be named as such because there was nothing true to compare them to. In that case, it would soon become apparent that reading on (and, certainly, rereading) was pointless. And the thing about dreams, to Dickens as to many another (not me, if that matters: my dreams are unbelievably boring), is that they cannot be pointless.

In probably the most influential essay on *Bleak House,* J. Hillis Miller argues that Esther's necklace dream emblematizes "the moving ring of substitution, in which each person is not himself but part of a system or the sign for some other thing"—that is, of the endless daisy chain of what he elsewhere calls the "synecdochic transference" governing the novel's epistemology, or antiepistemology.[28] I, on the contrary, think that the dream signifies something important about the facts of Esther's life, something recognized at the critical moment when she sees her life most clearly. I think that the reason that some characters likewise get closer to the truth than do others is that there is something real to get close to. A passage such as this

> The weather for many a day and night has been so wet that the trees seem wet through, and the soft loppings and prunings of the woodman's axe can make no crash or crackle as they fall... The shot of a rifle loses its sharpness in the moist air, and its smoke moves in a tardy little cloud towards the green rise, coppice-topped, that makes a background for the falling rain (11)

can fairly be taken as having gotten things right (yes: soaked wood, being cut, does make a "soft lopping" sound rather than a loud crack) in a way that would be hard to account for in a text compounded of texts forever misreading texts. It is one of the many passages where reality seeps through more than it does in other, more paper-choked, passages. That these trees may someday be turned into Chancery paper is not a neutral datum, a fact among other facts. It is one of many signs of how something living and real may be turned into something dead and false.

Interpretation is not so much the problem as the question. Although reading and writing can certainly, like everything else, become drugs, plenty of characters are seen to perform both in sensible ways.

So, when is reading overreading? I would not fall out of my chair on learning that some readers of this book, now nearing its end, have occasionally felt inclined to respond, "Well, here, for example." But I would also respectfully suggest that, at least in *Bleak House,* such responses are anticipated and at times headed off.

For example, most, perhaps all, of the titles of the narrator's chapters can be read in two ways or more. (For example, chapter XXXII, "The Appointed Time": the time of an arranged meeting; Krook's hour of reckoning; perhaps a reminder that Krook doubles with the Lord Chancellor whose final act, according to Miss Flite, will bring about the End of Days.) By contrast, few if any of Esther's chapter titles can be read any way but one. The title repeatedly used to introduce Esther's narrative is "Esther's Narrative," which is always what it is. Is the former too clever by half? Is the latter expounding the obvious? How naïve can one be, without being a Skimpole? How deep can one go, before becoming a Richard?

Bleak House is built out of moments where the reader must decide on the spot (and then, probably, reconsider, on a later spot) which way to go, which way is realer. The course is not, I suggest, most like that of a reader wondering which text might precede all the others. It is more like the activity of a sleeper trying to make, distinguish, and coordinate what the mind has made of the world when most sealed off from it and what the same mind has made of the world when, to be sure, problematically, awake to it.

Afterword: Having It Both Ways

Michael Slater has remarked Dickens's way of "telling and not telling the readers about his past,"[1] of sharing "his most intimate secrets... but in some coded fashion."[2] A number of the novels featured so much detail about life in real prisons, the Marshalsea in particular, that some readers must have wondered where the author got all that information.[3] He put David Copperfield in a close facsimile of the blacking warehouse and scattered blacking references through the rest of his writings. While carrying on with an attractive young woman named Ellen (of all things) Lawless Ternan, he introduced into his last novel an attractive young woman named Helena Landless. Paying the rent for Miss Ternan's hideaway, he sometimes used his first name "Charles," sometimes went by the last name "Turnan."[4]

He seems to have believed that it was not in the nature of things for secrets to stay hidden, a belief his novels often test against phenomena not only cleverly concealed but, apparently, supernaturally generated: the uncanny, as well as the unspoken, can be inclined to tell on itself. As to the nature of what it reveals, he is, much more often than not, divided. Although Scrooge is wrong to think that Marley's ghost can be explained away as an undigested bit of beef, in other venues Dickens was inclined to take, roughly speaking, materialist explanations seriously, to square them against the supernatural, whether about his own secret passions and powers or their sources, hidden, as he knew, even from himself. I have earlier discussed perhaps the most striking such recorded experience, the dream apparition of Mary Hogarth in a Genoese bedroom. Was it, Dickens wondered, a regular dream, manufactured like most others out of memory, desire, and the influence of the surroundings, or an unearthly "vision?"[5] Or, maybe, the former somehow opening out into the latter? Dickens felt compelled to play hide and seek with his readers about personal matters which ostensibly had nothing to do with the work of fiction in question but which in fact might transform it—put it, as the saying goes, in a new light—if they cracked the code; was something on the margins of his own being playing the same kind of tricks with him? And if so, how to represent this important fact of human nature in the lives of the characters he created?

In *The Old Curiosity Shop* he has Nell and Quilp quite explicitly go to heaven and hell, respectively, and in their cases it seems a matter of indifference whether he or we actually believe in the reality of celestial translations and fiery pits. In the three novels covered in this study, on the other hand, such questions matter a great deal. What happens in the subconscious—at the time sometimes called "unconscious cerebration"—exacts scrutiny, an earnest effort at finding a rational explanation. One of the earliest instances, previously discussed in chapter 1, is the appearance of Fagin and Monks at Oliver's Chertsey cottage window. The narrator offers two explanations, one physiological-psychological, the other an extremely, and perhaps deliberately, improbable twist of plot. Neither separately nor together do they satisfactorily answer all the questions arising from the scene. Why, for example, does nobody else see Fagin and Monks? Why do they leave no footprints? Just how fast is the aged Fagin supposed to be able to run, anyway? Unless, of course, he was, in actuality, flying? Or telepathically transported, Svengali-like, by means of a mesmeric force field in sync with one generated by Oliver's hypnagogic revery? (But then, what about Monks? No Svengali, he.) This time around, the author wants us to be asking ourselves those kinds of questions.

Later, I believe, Dickens comes to poise such scenes more evenly between explanations earthly and otherwise. Unitarians have been said to believe in "one God at most," and Dickens was, as much as he was anything religiously, a Unitarian. In the novels just reviewed, his stance on the uncanny, including the religious variety, seems to settle into that "at most" range, on the borderline between belief and skepticism, mysticism and rational analysis. There is, always or almost always, a real-world explanation made available, although not necessarily endorsed. The reader is given a choice.

An early example is the trajectory of Noah Claypole. New to London, Oliver's main hometown enemy immediately finds his way to the one public house, out of thousands, occupied by Fagin, Oliver's main big-city enemy. The two have never met or communicated before. This seems incredible, a matter of providentiality in reverse, or perhaps of animal magnetism in the most literal sense—in any case something, certainly, beyond rational explanation, even taking into account this author's famous way with coincidence. But there lurks in the margins, I think, at least one real-world solution, encapsulated in the old expression "thick as thieves"—not so much that deep calls to deep as that like seeks out like, a tendency that urban life in particular, with its rutted tracks inclining one bird of a feather to find out and flock with another, works to facilitate. On entering London Noah has, on his own, progressively narrowed down his options according to standards of secretiveness, filth, and manifest lowness; at the end of his journey, about to enter Fagin's pub, he is actually standing in a gutter. Just the course to follow, that is, to find a Fagin.

This book has dealt with a large number of such equivocal cases. I dream that my car breaks down, and the next day it does. Coincidence? Delphic prophecy? Or was it that my car had been making worrisome noises that I chose not to notice, which noises therefore found their way into my dream? Paul Dombey wakes up from a dream with his hair "hot and wet": it may have been a nightmare or he may be coming down with a fever, but then again he is soon to die, and dreams and other altered states in this novel come from underneath, the realm of "hot springs and fiery eruptions," in which realm, vice versa, buried "forms," "burrowing in the earth, ... mouldering in the water," can be "unintelligible as any dream" (*D&S,* 65). His deathbed vision of Jesus, hovering over him, reminds him of the picture of Jesus he used to see, hovering over him, as he walked slowly upstairs: how much does the latter contribute to the former? How much does Esther's unconscious memory of a biblical verse neither spoken in her presence nor recorded in the text explain her feeling "quickened" when she first sees the woman she does not yet know is her mother? What tells her, before her transformative illness, that her life is about to change forever? Precognition? Woman's intuition? A (very) sensitive response to early symptoms of a disease that will be at least several weeks in coming? Some sort of semi-psychic communion with Bucket, her fellow detector of clues undetectable by others, who, unknown to her or us, just happens, just this once, to be nearby? Or something akin to whatever lets some animals know when an earthquake or tsunami is about to strike—and, in *Dombey and Son,* enables Rob's homing pigeons to home? Or that enables Florence and Carker to register Mrs. Marwood's background presence, when the text does not?

I have said that Dickens gives us a choice. This being Dickens, neither choice will be in the direction of the humdrum. To the extent that the world is not enchanted, the mind is. Henri Ellenberger's magisterial history *The Discovery of the Unconscious* begins with Mesmer and animal magnetism, and Dickens was disciple, practitioner, and, in his way, researcher in that school, a participant in the part-scientific, part-mystical, part-mumbo-jumbo current of thought that around century's end would resolve into Janet, Charcot, and Freud on the one hand and the neural anatomists on the other. That was why, for instance, he made it a point, when possible, to position whatever bed he slept in on a north-to-south axis, so that microcosm and macrocosm, mind and the earth's magnetic field, would be in line.[6] It was through the coordination of such powers, mental and elemental, that he communed with the faraway Madame de la Rue and wrestled with her "Phantom," who also might be either mental or elemental.

These convictions, and the second thoughts arising from them, play out in his writings. In an earlier book I have proposed that, in *David Copperfield*, Rosa Dartle's thwarted love for Steerforth, goaded to fury by his affair with another woman, becomes a force powerful enough to engender the storm that "cruelly" batters, dismasts, and sinks his boat, killing him.[7] Somehow, perhaps through some variant of animal magnetism, her mind has become aligned with, among other forces, the earth's convection currents, in a murderous version of the magnetic alignment Dickens sought in his sleep. In this book I have proposed that Mrs. Marwood's eyes, glowing red like those of some cartoon hypnotist, stare out of the engine that transfixes and smashes her mortal enemy, Carker. In these and many other instances the mind has its own physics, coextensive with that of the physical universe, and one of its laws is that concentration—of hatred, for instance, fixed, as with a burning glass, on one individual—can produce consequences proportional to its intensity. (Which law, come to think, may help explain Monks's appearance at Oliver's window, after all. No Svengali, he is nevertheless second to none in the intensity of his hatred for Oliver.)

Terry Castle has suggested that Enlightenment attempts to explain away specters as internal distempers often had the unintended consequence of investing the mind with spirits.[8] To paraphrase an earlier commentary of mine on this thesis, Dickens's work can often demonstrate that such a shift could be anything but reassuring.[9] It could mean that the mind was haunted by powers that earlier ages were right to either fear or revere. Maybe evil spirits appear more human than our ancestors imagined (no horns and whatnot), but *something* still around is out to butcher little boys, especially Christian ones, and sometimes has the power to work its will on the sea. Sitting at dinner one day, Dickens held up a wine glass and said, "What an unfathomable mystery there is in it all!" He was talking about his own mind—how it might, if he chose, "spin and weave" "filmy webs of thought" about the glass, "coming from every direction, we know not whence," even make it "instinct with life."[10] Often he called this capacity, simply, "Power." Like Blake, in this one regard at least, he recognized this power as growing from the "Human brain."[11] But as for "whence" it came to reside there and by what laws it worked its unfathomable mysteries—the imaginative investigation of such questions was, at the least, one of the main activities of his life.

Notes

Chapter 1

1. I take this sentence from John Sutherland, in the chapter of his book *Can Jane Eyre Be Happy? More Puzzles in Classic Fiction,* (New York: Oxford, 1997) entitled "Why Is Fagin Hanged and Why Isn't Pip Prosecuted?", 53–63, p. 55. Sutherland makes a strong case that Fagin is railroaded.
2. See Robert Tracy, "'The Old Story' and Inside Stories: Modish Fiction and Fictional Modes in *Oliver Twist*," *Dickens Studies Annual* 17 (1988), 1–33, p. 8. I agree with Garry Wills and others that Fagin's den should remind us that child prostitution traded in boys as well as girls. See Garry Wills, "Love in the Lower Depths," *The New York Review of Books* 36, 16 (October 26, 1989), 227–49. See also Holly Furneaux, *Queer Dickens: Erotics, Families, Masculinities* (Oxford: Oxford University Press, 2010), 46.
3. Unless otherwise indicated, all parenthetical page references in this chapter refer to Charles Dickens, *Oliver Twist*, ed. Kathleen Tillotson (London: Oxford University Press, 1966). For reasons I am not qualified to judge, this edition is controversial. I have consulted other editions whenever a given passage is in question. The quotation cited in the chapter title is from page 363.
4. Beginning at 102–3. Sikes's dog's lunge at Oliver reminds Nancy of her own brutal upbringing, initiated by Fagin and continued by Sikes and his dog. Fagin notes her response and begins to draw conclusions, conclusions that eventually lead him to urge Sikes to murder her.
5. In *Gulliver's Travels,* chapter 1, Swift introduces a "Master" "James Bates" who eventually becomes "Master Bates."
6. Charles Dickens, *Barnaby Rudge: A Tale of the Riot of 'Eighty* (Oxford: Oxford University Press, 1954), 536; hereinafter *BR*.
7. On this point, see Philip Horne, "Introduction," *Oliver Twist or the Parish Boy's Progress* (London: Penguin Books, 2003), xvi.
8. As noted by Horne, vii–viii.
9. Quoted by Horne, xviii–xix.
10. Catherine Robson points out that, including "Old Sally," lying on her deathbed, there are three "hags" in this scene, recalling the three witches of

Macbeth: Robson, "Down Ditches, on Doorsteps, in Rivers: *Oliver Twist*'s Journey to Respectability," *Dickens Studies Annual* 29 (2000), 61–81, p. 66
11. Bram Stoker, *Dracula,* ed. John Paul Riquelme (New York: Palgrave Macmillan, 2002), 304
12. Although *Oliver Twist* was first published in book form in three volumes, most available editions take no notice of the fact. The divisions are: volume I, chapters I–XIX; volume II, chapters XX–XXXVI; volume III, chapters XXXVII–LIII.
13. Joseph Gold, "Dickens' Exemplary Aliens: Bumble the Beadle and Fagin the Fence," *Mosaic* 2 (1968), 77–89, p. 82
14. For the background of this paragraph, see Louise A. Tilly, Rachel G. Fuchs, David I. Kertzer, and David L. Ransel, "Child Abandonment in European History: A Symposium," *Journal of Family History* 17 (1992), 1–23; and Lloyd deMause, "The Evolution of Childrearing," *The Journal of Psychohistory* 28 (2001), 364–451, especially pp. 378–82, 392–96, and 415–18.
15. Michael Slater suggests that the novel may have been prompted by "a great scandal about child deaths" at a baby farm in 1837 (Michael Slater, *Charles Dickens* [New Haven: Yale University Press, 2010], 94). The topic did not fade away, and Dickens did not let go of it. Ten years after *Oliver Twist,* another scandal arose over a baby farm in Tooting at which 155 infants had died within a short period. Dickens wrote four newspaper pieces on the subject and went on to include Guster, a young woman permanently addled during a childhood spent in the Tooting school, into *Bleak House.* See Margaret Wiley, "Mother's Milk and Dombey's Son," *Dickens Quarterly* 13 (1996), 217–28, p. 221, and A. W. C. Brice and Kenneth J. Fielding, "Dickens and the Tooting Disaster," *Victorian Studies* 12 (1986) 227–44.
16. Rose, 36.
17. Rose, 36.
18. Rose, 37–52. DeMause reports that by the end of the nineteenth century, "The English . . . had over seven million children enrolled in 'burial insurance societies'" (DeMause, 282). See also James C. Whorton, *The Arsenic Century: How Victorian Britain Was Poisoned at Home, Work, and Play* (Oxford: Oxford University Press, 2010), 27–30, p. 38. An 1851 Dickens article on the subject of arsenic poisoning remarks on a recent case of two infants murdered for "Burial-club money." (Dickens, "Household Crime," *Household Words* [1851], 277–81, p. 278.)
19. Robson, 67.
20. Robson points out that the novel keeps the reader waiting for six chapters after Oliver's collapse at the end of volume I until his return and revival; serial readers would have been held in suspense for three months. She continues, "this phantasmal extension of the hero's time in the ditch . . . allows Oliver to die the death of one kind of baby, in order that he may begin the life of quite a different kind of baby"—from ditch-delivered castoff to fortunate foundling.

21. Rosemarie Bodenheimer notes of Oliver's semiconscious moments that "he knows something without bearing the responsibility for knowing it." (Rosemarie Bodenheimer, *Knowing Dickens* (Ithaca: Cornell University Press, 2007), p. 9.
22. J. Hillis Miller, "The Dark World of *Oliver Twist*," Harold Bloom, ed., *Modern Critical Views: Charles Dickens* (New York: Chelsea House, 1987), 29–69, p. 30.
23. Hangmen, in song and story, are often described as "twisting" the rope.
24. Robert Tracy, "'The Old Story' and Inside Stories: Modish Fiction and Fictional Modes in *Oliver Twist*" (*Dickens Studies Annual* 17 [1988], 1–33, p. 2).
25. These words appear only in the 1941 "Third edition." (P. 67, note 5)
26. "Safely tucked into the boring bosom of middle-class respectability, Oliver is insulated from danger and drama" (Robson, 74).
27. Compare Bumble, whose heart is "waterproof" (241).
28. As Bodenheimer points out, this is the moral of Dickens's Christmas story *The Haunted Man and the Ghost's Bargain,* where "failures of memory lead directly to failures of sympathy" (Bodenheimer, 66).
29. See Kerry McSweeney, "*David Copperfield* and the Music of Memory," *Dickens Studies Annual* 23 (1994), 93–119, p. 99.
30. See Joseph Gold, p. 81, and Susan Meyer, "Antisemitism and Social Critique in Dickens' *Oliver Twist*," *Victorian Literature and Culture* 33 (2005), 339–52, p. 249. "Lamb" occurs twice else—once when the same nurse, in her deathbed delirium, again applies the word to Agnes (156). The other occurrence? When Nancy applies it to Oliver himself (132). Although sarcastic, her words forecast how she will come to feel in earnest. In the same passage, incidentally, Dickens nudges us into taking the word literally by having Sikes refer to Oliver as "the kid." Sheep and goats.
31. Charles Dickens, *The Life of Our Lord,* www.dickens.jp/etexts/dickens/others/sonota/lord.pdf p. 32 out of 40. The book twice mentions Jesus' connection with the Mount of Olives.
32. Roland F. Anderson, "Structure, Myth, and Rite in *Oliver Twist*," *Studies in the Novel* 18 (1986), 238–57, pp. 253–54.
33. See 72, footnote 3.
34. McSweeney, 99.
35. Goldie Morgentaler, *Dickens and Heredity: When Like Begets Like* (Basingstoke, England; Macmillan, 1999), 41.
36. Morgentaler, 39.
37. For a review of Dickens's feelings about Catholicism, and especially his fascination for types of the Blessed Virgin Mary, see Michael Schiefelbein, "Little Nell, Catholicism, and Dickens' Investigation of Death," *Dickens Quarterly* 9 (1992), 115–24.
38. Charles Dickens, *The Letters of Charles Dickens* (the Pilgrim Edition), eds. Madeline House, Graham Storey, Kathleen Tillotson (Oxford: Clarendon

Press, 1965); hereafter cited as *Letters.* September 30, 1844, letter to John Forster, vol. IV, 196.
39. February 29, 1848, letter to Emile de la Rue, *Letters,* vol. V, 254
40. Dickens, *The Life of Our Lord,* 9–10.
41. Dickens, The *Life of Our Lord,* 3.
42. Dickens, *The Life of Our Lord,* 5.
43. Dickens, *The Life of Our Lord,* 6.
44. Morgentaler, 86.
45. The source is Origen's *Contra Celsum,* denying Celsus' (otherwise unrecorded) report that Jesus' father was a Roman centurion named Panthera. Various strands of the tradition have Mary being disgraced and sent out to wander the roads.
46. Steven Marcus has compared Agnes to the Blessed Virgin Mary, on the grounds that "the immaculateness of Oliver's character suggests as immaculate as possible conception" (Steven Marcus, *Dickens: From Pickwick to Dombey* [New York: Norton, 1965], 86). Morgentaler agrees. (Morgentaler, 88). Both Peter Ackroyd (*Dickens* [New York: Harper Perennial, 1992], 440) and Bodenheimer (13) note the strain of "Mariolatry."
47. Dickens, *The Life of Our Lord,* 6.
48. Roland F. Anderson sees in this "blood-letting" a "rite of transition." (Roland F. Anderson, "Structure, Myth, and Rite in *Oliver Twist,*" *Studies in the Novel* 8 [1986], 238–57, p. 249).
49. G. K. Chesterton, *Charles Dickens: A Critical Study* (New York: Dodd Mead & Company, 1906), 171.
50. Assuming, that is, that this is the proper spelling. We don't really know. See note 54.
51. From Dickens's "Autobiographical Fragment," quoted in John Forster, *The Life of Charles Dickens* (New York: Hearst, 1875), vol. I, 28.
52. Mary Anne Andrade, "Wake into Dream," *The Dickensian* 86 (199), 17–28, p. 18.
53. Mary Hogarth is behind Rose Maylie. Oliver's mouths-of-babes comment that he would rather sell books than write them (85) is surely a swipe at Dickens's publisher. Like most if not indeed all of the novels, *Oliver Twist* includes seemingly innocuous mentions of boot blacking or its manufacturers.
54. See David L. Gold, "Despite Popular Belief, the Name Fagin in Charles Dickens's *The Adventures of Oliver Twist* Has No Jewish Connection," *Beiträge zur Namenforschung* 40 (2005), 385–423. "Fagin," so spelled, is a plausible Jewish name, one with possible echoes in English blood libel tradition, the Irish "Fagan" or "Phegan" not at all. I wonder whether Dickens, and/or Forster, changed the spelling or got it wrong.
55. Robert Newsom, "Jews," in Paul Schlicke, ed., *Oxford Reader's Companion to Dickens* (New York, Oxford University Press, 1999), 309.
56. Undated (1837) letter to John Forster, *Letters,* vol. V, 292.

57. Fred Kaplan, ed., *Charles Dickens' Oliver Twist* (New York: Norton, 1993), 378.
58. Meyer, 250.
59. Dickens, July 10, 1863, letter to Mrs. Davis, *Letters,* vol. V, 269–67.
60. Efraim Sicher says that in making the contribution, Dickens was "submit[ting] to moral blackmail." (Efraim Sicher, "Imagining the Jew: Dickens' Romantic Heritage," Sheila A. Spector, ed., *British Romanticism and the Jews* (New York: Palgrave Macmillan, 2002), 139–46, p. 140.
61. Meyer, 241.
62. To be sure, a much-debated issue, far too complicated to fully address here. In the case of Dickens's charitable public works, I would say the record is clear and highly creditable. In the case of his attitudes, changing and sometimes inconsistent, toward other races—Africans, African Americans, Native Americans, Indians, and native Jamaicans—I generally go along with Grace Moore in her *Dickens and Empire: Discourses of Class, Race, and Colonialism in the Works of Charles Dickens* (Burlington, VT: Ashgate, 2004), *passim*—but especially pages 63–74 and 91–134. As one example, I agree with Moore that although it would be "facile" to "elide the manifest racism" of his notorious essay "The Noble Savage," Dickens's main target was English *nostalgie de la boue* (Moore, 64, 68). Dickens's private life is a whole different question: certainly his treatment of his wife seems hard to excuse.
63. Andrade, 26.
64. In a letter to Forster he calls the people of the region "addle-headed" for having voted Bulwer Lytton out of Parliament and, paraphrasing a proverb, adds, "I don't wonder the devil flew over Lincoln." (July 5 letter to John Forster, *Letters,* vol. II, 322).
65. A motive for their showing up is belatedly supplied at p. 352, but nothing ever explains how they were able to escape over open field without being spotted, or why they left no footprints.
66. For a summary available in Dickens's time, see The Rev. Abraham Hume, *Sir Hugh of Lincoln: Examination of a Curious Tradition Respecting the Jews, with a Notice of the Popular Poetry Connected With It* (London: John Russell Smith, 1849).
67. Derek Cohen, "Constructing the Contradictions: Anthony Trollope's *The Way We Live Now,*" in Derek Cohen and Deborah Heller, eds., *Jewish Presences in English Literature* (Montreal: McGill-Queens University Press, 1990), 61–75, p. 62.
68. Lyndal Roper, *Witch Craze: Terror and Fantasy in Baroque Germany* (New Haven: Yale University Press, 2004), 215.
69. Roper, 40.
70. Jeffrey Burton Russell, *Witchcraft in the Middle Ages* (Cornell: Cornell University Press, 1972), 168.
71. See, for instance, Roper, 40 on Julius Echter, anti-Semite and witchburner of Würtzburg.

72. The famous witch's chorus of *Macbeth* ("Bubble, bubble," etc.) seems to be behind both Fagin and the women. Perhaps this is obvious in the case of the former; in the latter case Fagin is—according to the language—a "blaspheming Jew" who calls Nancy a "drab" (his confederate Monks follows suit later) and operates, if not quite a cauldron, a "melting pot." For his part, Oliver gets "ditch-delivered" in chapter XXVIII, though not quite in the witches' sense of the phrase. (Close, though: see Robson, *passim*.) The whole chorus, and much else in *Macbeth*, can be a queasy reminder of how prevalent infanticide had been, long before Mr. Bumble.
73. For the connection, see Alan C. Koretsky, "Dangerous Innocence: Chaucer's Prioress and her Tale," in Cohen and Heller, 10–24. Roper reports that "it was common for chapels and churches dedicated to the Virgin to be built on sites that had formerly belonged to Jews" (Roper, 40). See also Robert Worth Frank, Jr., "Miracles of the Virgin, Mediaeval Anti-Semitism, and the 'Prioress's Tale,'" Larry D. Benson and Siegfried Wenzel, eds., *The Wisdom of Poetry: Essays in Early English Literature in Honor of Morton W. Bloomfield* (Kalamazoo, Michigan: Medieval Institute Publications, 1982), 177–88.
74. When Fagin gives Oliver a book to read, one he hopes will corrupt him, yet another eerie opening between the two occurs: "Here, he [Oliver] read of dreadful crimes...of secret murders that had been committed;...of bodies hidden from the eye of man in deep pits and wells: which would not keep them down, deep as they were, but had yielded them up at last, after many years" (130). This passage could without alteration have served as summary of blood libel lore. Given my thesis, I am intrigued by what seems a suggestion of *sortes Virgiliniae* in the way Oliver opens this page at random.
75. Desperate, Sikes nonetheless recoils from lowering himself into the ditch because "The water was out, and the ditch a bed of mud" (345). For contemporary testimony that a great deal of this "mud" was human excrement, see David Paroissien, *The Companion to Oliver Twist* (Edinburgh: Edinburgh University Press, 1992), 25–26, 271–72. The "wooden chambers thrusting themselves out over the mud" (331) are the back-room privies from which inhabitants would relieve themselves into the ditch.
76. The association of Jews with excrement has long been an anti-Semitic canard. Edouard Drumont's anti-Semitic compendium *La France Juive, Essai D'Histoire Contemporaine* (Paris: Marpon & Flammarion, 1885), vol. II, 455), for instance, contains much commentary to the effect that "*En tout ce qui touche á l'ordure, le Juife est passé maître.*"
77. For the "old myth" that "Jews are suckled by sows and eat pig-shit," see Roper, 41.
78. Meyer, 244.
79. Meyer, 248.
80. Quoted in Slater, 237, 381.
81. In an account of one memorable occasion, the word is capitalized. Describing his reading of *The Chimes* to a circle of friends, Dickens writes

of feeling "what a thing it is to have Power." (December 4, 1844, letter to Catherine Dickens, *Letters,* vol. V, 235).
82. Slater dates the novel's transformation from an "episodic series of scenes or 'sketches'" to "a thrilling narrative" from its introduction of Fagin and company: Slater, 99.
83. David Wilkes, 'Dickens, Bakhtin, and the Neopastoral Shepherd in *Oliver Twist,*" *Dickens Studies Annual* 24 (1996), 59–79, p. 72.
84. 59, footnote 3.
85. David Paroissien, *The Companion to Oliver Twist,* Edinburgh: Edinburgh University Press, 1992, 228.
86. Paroissien, 70, 69, 78, 276, and *passim.*
87. Beginning in chapter XLIII, Noah is the butt of a twisty sort of joke— induced to dress himself as a hayseed on the pretext that this will constitute a disguise (297). Needless to say, he performs the role brilliantly. It is probably not the sort of role that would come naturally to a Chatham native.
88. Peter Ackroyd, *Dickens* (New York: Harper Perennial, 1992), 440.
89. Michael Slater, *Charles Dickens* (New Haven: Yale University Press, 2010), 7.
90. Paroissien, 69; Philip Horne, *Oliver Twist or the Parish Boy's Progress* (London: Penguin Books, 2003), 491.
91. The "coalheaver" (30) is problematic: although the word originally applied only to shipworkers, by Dickens's time it could also designate any loader or unloader of coal.
92. I take this estimated speed from Walter E. Houghton's *The Victorian Frame of Mind: 1830–1870,* New Haven: Yale University Press, 1957, 7. The upper limit seems to have been around fifteen miles an hour. In one address Dickens described himself as "galloping through a wild country" in a post chaise "at the then surprising rate" of fifteen miles an hour. (Note to May 1 to 19, 1849, letter to Mark Lemmon, *Letters,* vol. 5, 543).
93. This would be true even if, by Oliver's time, cross-channel passenger transit between Boston and the continent had largely ceased. I have been unable to find whether this was the case, but Ms. Katherine Holmes of the Lincolnshire Local Inquiry Team has determined that Boston at the time did offer connections to London and Hull—both busy ports from which passage could have been booked to Europe. She adds that random travelers might have found a place "on some of the trading vessels that left Boston." (March 26, 2009 e-mail) My thanks to Ms. Holmes for her help.

Chapter 2

1. February 2, 1851, letter to Dr. Thomas Stone, *Letters* vol. VI, 278.
2. Unless otherwise indicated, all parenthetical page citations in this chapter are to *Dombey and Son,* ed. Valerie, Purton (London; J. M. Dent, 1997).
3. Some fellow members of the Dickens-L e-mail list have respectfully disagreed with me on this score, and I respectfully disagree back. What looks

to me like a pointy ear may be the effect of Toodle's shaggy haircut. I invite the reader to judge.
4. Purton, note to chapter II of the Everyman *Dombey and Son,* 846.
5. Citing Lawrence Stone's *The Family, Sex and Marriage in England, 1500–1800,* Robert Clark points out that Polly is being separated from her husband because "it was feared that intercourse poisoned a nursing mother's milk" (Robert Clark, "The Family Firm: The Sexual Economy in *Dombey and Son,*" *ELH* 51, 1 (1984), 69–84, p. 77).
6. Norman and Jeanne MacKenzie, *H. G. Wells: A Biography* (New York: Simon and Schuster, 1973), 36, 123.
7. Josh Lutz Marsh, "Good Mrs. Brown's Connections: Sexuality and Story-Telling in *Dealings with the Firm of Dombey and Son,*" *ELH* 58, 2 (1991), 405–26.
8. Stephen Marcus, *Dickens: From Pickwick to Dombey* (New York: Basic Books, 1965), 345. I've never been clear as to what the pun was. In *Queer Dickens* (New York: Oxford, 2009, 5), Holly Forneaux reports Collette Colligan's argument that Dickens connects Bagstock with a homosexual scandal of the time. Noncommittal, is how I feel about this.
9. See my *Physiology and the Literary Imagination: Romantic to Modern* (Gainesville: University Press of Florida, 2003), 78–79. This has been prepared for with remarks about frigid feelings between Dombey and Edith and about the storm their coming together will engender; significantly, the precipitation predicted to result is not rain but hail (291), reminding us that Dombey is a creature of ice. The weather report trope is anticipated by Carker, taunting Captain Cuttle: "You are not made uneasy by the supposition that young what's-his-name was lost in bad weather that was got up against him in these offices—are you?" (450).
10. For instance, in a April 16, 1842, letter to John Forster: *Letters,* vol. III, 198.
11. See Thomas Laqueur, *Making Sex: Body and Gender from the Greeks to Freud* (Cambridge: Harvard University Press, 1990), *passim,* for a review of the historical background behind this belief. Laqueur calls attention to the influence of John Elliotson's English translation, published in 1828, of Johann Friederich Blumenbach's text on the subject. The edition, with some supporting additions from Elliotson, "affirmed the connection of estrus specifically with sexual excitement" (Laqueur, 219; see also 185–86). Elliotson was Dickens's friend and personal physician.
12. "Engines:" I will not insult the reader's intelligence by explaining what *Fanny Hill* makes of the word "engine." In various forms, the words "tear" (as verb) "fret," "chafe," and "spare"—as in "Good Sir! pray do not spare me!"—also occur throughout the book, meaning what one would expect; so do "pant" and "gasp."
13. We can retroactively assess the course of his first marriage by the evidence of its issue: first, early on, a daughter chronically baffled as to why her "overflowing" store of love is never reciprocated; second, at the end, a wan

son, perpetually cold—the first conceived in the expectation of love, soon due for disillusionment, the second in resignation on that score, on the edge of extinction. Here and elsewhere, *Dombey and Son* at least entertains the long-standing belief that children register the circumstances of their conception. Mr. and Mrs. Toots have girls, clearly, because the female component of their union is stronger than the male. The same, at least as far as motivation goes, is true of the match between Towlinson the butler and Anne the housemaid, which may be why Mrs. Perch, who knows whereof she speaks, predicts that they, too, will have "girls" (787). Walter and Florence, an even match, have a boy and a girl, although the boy's arriving first may suggest that Florence was determined to give her father what he wanted at last. The Toodles, also well matched, multiply too rapidly for an exact count, but seem to have a fairly even mix.

14. Joseph Conrad, *Lord Jim* (Garden City, New York: Doubleday), 93.
15. A fact noted by Charlie Hexham in *Our Mutual Friend* (Dickens, *Our Mutual Friend* (London: Penguin Books, 1997) 37.
16. Quotations are from Karl Marx, *The Communist Manifesto,* translated by Samuel Moore (Henry Regnery: Chicago, 1950), 11–12.
17. The two headlamps would have been unusual but not out of the question. According to Mr. Tim Procter, Access Team Project Leader of the National Railway Museum, York, UK, "in the 1840's there was no standard system as there were several railway companies. One such system was the 'Forsyth's Patent Signalling System.'" An illustration of this system in the museum's possession "depicts half a dozen or so arrangements of up to four lamps mounted on the front of a locomotive, including one arrangement which does look decidedly eye-like." (August 31, 2004, e-mail; my thanks to Mr. Procter). Consider as well the train depicted in Illustration 2, drawn by Dickens's friend and collaborator George Cruikshank.

    As Harry Stone remarks, Dickens was familiar with this engraving, which appeared, in 1845, shortly before he began work on *Dombey and Son.* (Harry Stone, *The Night Side of Dickens: Cannibalism, Passion, Necessity* [Columbus: Ohio State University Press, 1994], 208). There is also an intriguing detail in Eleanor Christian's account of Dickens's wild behavior during an outing at Broadstairs—that his eyes were like "danger lamps" (Peter Ackroyd, *Dickens* [New York: HarperCollins, 1990], 316).
18. To complicate this a bit: before Carker's encounter with the train, Mrs. Marwood is twice described as having "bleared eyes," once as having "red eyes." At the moment of collision, the headlamps bearing down on Carker are "red eyes, bleared and dim."
19. Illustrations on pages 157, 257, 282, 342, 365, 430, 475, 552, 607, 660, 734, and 812.
20. The sequence illustrates the connections typical of this book's associative thinking, with the word "nephew" at the critical crossing point. When, earlier, Dombey addresses Walter as "the Son of Mr. Gills," Walter answers

him, "'Nephew, Sir.'" To which Dombey replies: "'I said nephew, boy'" (40). Dombey is not used to being corrected, and has deep-seated reasons for prizing that golden word "son," therefore for finding disagreeable any deflection into less direct lines of kinship. So, when Walter shows up in his office just a beat after Carker has half-facetiously remarked that the West Indies post should be bestowed on "some orphan nephew of a musical friend" (174), that re-sounding of "nephew" connects in memory with the earlier repetition of the word, in association with the young man who spoke it, and who has since made himself unwelcome by rescuing the unwanted daughter whose letter he now, standing there, holds in his hand. These sequences lead into two converging motives: that Dombey cherishes contemplating his son more than anything and doesn't like thinking about his daughter at all.

21. See Joseph Gerhard, "Dombey, Change, and Changeling," *Dickens Studies Annual* 21 (1989), 179–96. Joseph also finds "counter-images of gradualism" at work in *Dombey and Son,* as against its sequence of catastrophes.
22. Others of this sharply weaned company include Alice herself, uprooted and transported to Australia; Rob, snatched from his family and packed off to the Charitable Grinders Academy; most of Dr. Blimber's students (especially Master Bitherstone of Bengal, forever vowing to run away back to India); and even Carker, for whom his sister's decision to stand by their disgraced brother became a much-resented act of abandonment. Walter, by contrast, is a bona fide orphan, but one whose surrogate father (Sol) and surrogate-surrogate (Cuttle) have made all well. Another is the little girl overseen with the guardian aunt who, Florence learns, has made up her loss by giving her "a parent's love" (337). The right substitutions, in this book, can work wonders.
23. To be sure, there are other, non-Dombeyish instances present: "trombone," "pocket-comb," and many variants on "combine." Still, the repetition of, in particular, "tomb" and its derivatives strikes me as insistent.
24. As for the name "Edith": the capitalized word that keeps preying on Dombey's mind, on his train ride to Leamington, and his first meeting with her, is "Death."
25. Richard D. Altick, *The Presence of the Present: Topics of the Day in the Victorian Novel* (Columbus: Ohio State University Press, 1991), 332.
26. Frank McCombie, "Sexual Repression in *Dombey and Son,*" *The Dickensian* 88, 1 (1992), 25–46, p. 27.
27. A point well made by Roger B. Henkle, "The Crisis of Representation in *Dombey and Son,*" in Robert M. Polhemus, *Critical Reconstructions: The Relationship of Fiction and Life* (Stanford: Stanford University Press, 1994), 90–110, p. 94.
28. Signaled, I think, in a typical name-pun, when she goes into a "blind fury" on the subject of Carker (471).
29. As Michael Greenstein points out, it is also the estimated number of minutes of Paul Dombey's life so far, as well as the number of rails in the

fence around Miss Tox's residence. (Michael Greenstein, "Measuring Time in *Dombey and Son,*" Dickens Quarterly 9 (1992), 151–57, pp. 152–53). Captain Cuttle instructs the petitioning Toots to wait twenty-four hours for his next arrival, then, if he shows up, to "sheer off" for another twenty-four—forty-eight in all. The aim of the picquet game being played by Mrs. Skewton and the Major (290) is to reach forty-eight first. Dickens would probably have anticipated that the complete novel would first appear in 1848.

30. J. Hillis Miller, *Charles Dickens: The World of His Novels* (Cambridge: Harvard University Press, 1959), 146.
31. This is another instance of covert complicity between author and illustrator. It shows Alice and Mrs. Marwood watching from under an arch as Carker—the man who made Alice, in the novel's terms anyway, a whore—passes by. A second half-hidden message, of the in-joke variety, is the poster illustrating and advertising what it calls a "Bottle!", presumably of some alcoholic beverage, under the name of "Cruikshank." Before Phiz, George Cruikshank had been Dickens's illustrator. The friendship between the two was strained in part by Cruikshank's fervent conversion to the temperance cause. In 1847 he published a series of eight plates on the perils of drink entitled "The Bottle."
32. See *Physiology and the Literary Imagination,* 74–75. As noted there, Sol Gills's ship shop points due north, as if guided by its instruments, probably because of Dickens's belief in the advisability of aligning such structures with the earth's magnetic field. (He himself made a habit of sleeping along a north-by-south axis.) It is also the novel's fixed center of virtue, a moral compass needle perhaps not unconnected with the "needle" that Florence plies in that "work" of hers, and that accompanies—directs?—her to the shop. Rob himself, of the "electric fluency" quote, is magnetized by the resident mesmerist, Carker, whose teeth become a "battery of attraction" that "drew . . . out" any concealed secrets (298). (This, by the way, is taking the "magnetism" in "animal magnetism" pretty literally: the ostensible conceit may be that Carker's teeth resemble the ranked cannons of an artillery fortification, but "battery" in something like our current sense had been current for at least fifty years before *Dombey and Son,* and was undoubtedly familiar to the Dickens who, as editor, corresponded with Michael Faraday and solicited his contributions.) Dombey, whose friends find themselves brought together "by magnetic agreement" (491) in antipathy to Edith's, becomes something of a magnet himself when in contact with Captain Cuttle's hook: "At this touch of warm feeling and cold iron, Mr. Dombey shivered all over" (135). And there are an awful lot of instances of people being drawn irresistibly toward or repelled uncontrollably from something or someone. Also playing in and out are various demonstrations of sympathetic vibration (Mr. Morfin's cello, for example)—frequently, in Dickens's time and thereafter, cited as the insentient equivalent of animal magnetism. All in all, then, Cuttle's uninformed musings about Sol's

instruments turn out, like many another instance of the "unintellectualised feeling" that Miller finds throughout, to connect up with other cues in the book's range of meanings.
33. "It is probable that Mr Dombey's own carriage was hoisted on to a railway train carriage and pulled behind the other coaches" (Purton, 863).
34. Urchin talk for skipping school; dog talk for friendliness; at one point (297) the urchin Rob gets called a dog.
35. To understand how this effect arises, get two metronomes, set them to slightly different rates, and run them at the same time.
36. Garrett Stewart, "The Foreign Offices of British Fiction," *Modern Language Quarterly* 61(1) (2000), 181–206, pp. 3–4. See also Garrett Stewart, "Dickens and Language," in John O. Jordan, *The Cambridge Companion to Charles Dickens* (Cambridge: Cambridge University Press, 2001), 136–51. See also McCarthy: "Frequent syllepses achieve surprising verbal collocations and suggest curious interactions... The world is tilted, sliding into unpredictability" (McCarthy, 95–96).
37. McCombie, 27.
38. A point made by Patricia Marks in "Paul Dombey and the Milk of Human Kindness," *Dickens Quarterly* 11 (1994), 14–25, p. 15.
39. See p. 90, earlier, for what I have suggested is the implication of ship's prow and figurehead in Dombey's evocation of Edith's "brow and figure."
40. Compare this curious sentence from one of Dickens's letters, recommending a visit to the seaside: "The tide rushes in, demanding to be breasted." (July 18, 1843, letter to Thomas Beard, *Letters,* vol. III, 523–24).
41. A March 2004 series of exchanges in the "Dickens-L" list took on the question of Rob's pigeons. I believe them to be racing pigeons, pitted against one another in gambling matches. The dating of *Dombey and Son,* however, raises a problem: all chronologies of pigeon racing I have consulted say that the sport began in Europe, especially Belgium, in the first half of the nineteenth century, and didn't really catch on in England until the second half. Against this I would adduce "Winged Telegraphs," an article by W. H. Wills and Thomasina Ross in the August 3, 1850, Household Words (vol., 1, no. 19, 454–56). It is about the "pigeon-fanciers" of Europe, Antwerp in particular, but it also records the fact of channel-crossing pigeons flying between the "stages" of Dover and "Montrieul" (presumably a misspelling for Montreuil), and notes that before the recent arrival of the electric telegraph the use of London-to-Paris carrier pigeons was commonplace. Perhaps, in using the birds for races, Rob and his erstwhile comrades are slightly ahead of their time; perhaps there were early pockets of pigeon fanciers not noticed by historians; perhaps Dickens, who spent considerable time in Europe, saw fit to imagine, or rather foresee, the sport catching on in England. In any case, it's clear that homing pigeons were a familiar fact of life when Dickens was growing up and that their ability to return to their origins from over great distances was a subject of speculation.

Chapter 3

1. Unless otherwise specified, all parenthetical references are to Charles Dickens, *Bleak House,* ed. George Ford and Sylvère Monod (New York: Norton), 1977.
2. See Dickens's *A Child's History of England,* (New York: A. L. Burt, n.d., 279–80) on the execution of Lady Jane Grey.
3. P. 413. See Susan Shatto, *The Companion to Bleak House,* London: Unwin Hyman, 1988, 216), for the words to the song "King Death."
4. Much of the language regarding disease and contagion seems more suited to ancestral memories of the Black Death than to smallpox or other contemporary afflictions. Calling to Ada, the infected Esther hides behind the window curtain and refuses to look out, as if her eyes had the power to infect. Conversations through shut doors and windows are common features of plague narratives.
5. "'When my noble and learned brother gives his Judgment, they're to be let go free,' said Krook, winking at us again. 'And then,' he added, whispering and grinning, 'if that ever was to happen—which it won't—the birds that have never been caged would kill 'em'" (180).
6. Janet L. Larson, "The Battle of Biblical Books in Esther's Narrative," *Nineteenth-Century Fiction* 38 (1983), 131–60.
7. See Eric G. Lorentzen, "'Obligations of Home:' Colonialism, Contamination, and Revolt in *Bleak House,*" *Dickens Studies Annual* 34 (2004), 155–84, p. 175.
8. The most infamous of the names assigned to Esther is probably "Dame Durden." William Axton has found that Dame Durden was "the butt of a comic street song popular in Dickens's time which ridiculed the title character's over-anxious desire for a husband while those about her are busily finding mates and lovers." He notes that Esther is similarly "unloved...among a host of young people...who are falling in love and marrying all around her." (William Axton, "Esther's Nicknames: A Study in Relevance," *Dickensian* 62 (1966), 158–63, p. 160). See also Alex Zwerdling, "Esther Summerson Rehabilitated," Harold Bloom, ed. *Charles Dickens's Bleak House* (Chelsea House: New York: 1987), 37–56, p. 41. Esther is, after all, close to Ada's age—in fact a little older, therefore entitled to first dibs, according to marriage-market protocols. She finds Richard attractive, and, unlike Ada, is neither his cousin nor a party in Jarndyce and Jarndyce. This last point matters, as John Jarndyce of all people should know.
9. In *Dombey and Son* the railroad leitmotif is "a shriek, and a roar, and a rattle" (e.g., *D&S,* 275). At page 654 we are told that railroads will soon arrive "with a rattle and a glare."
10. A suggestion reinforced, I think, when the inventory of iron forms in the elder Rouncewell brother's factory yard includes "rails" (741).

11. For instance Esther, burying her childhood doll, burning, as she thinks, her ex-lover's flowers, forever saying goodbye to the old face and the old ways, having the tracks of the road that first brought her to Bleak House smoothed away (85); or Jarndyce, who begs his new wards to "take the past for granted" (58) and lives his life as a repudiation of the ancient suit that bears his name; or Sergeant George, self-exiled from his place of birth because of some vague juvenile transgression; or Nemo, doping himself in order, as the saying goes, to forget the past... and so on. Skimpole's indifference to debts incurred is a lightsome variant on the theme.
12. Likewise, when she flees to Paris she will be confronted with commoners who are nonetheless "gay... playing with children" (139). So she flees back. Doubtless her attraction to Rosa, the childish "village beauty," is a symptom of this thwarted longing. Matronly Mrs. Rouncewell, always right about such things, observes that her lady would be perfect if only "she had a daughter" (142). Later (764) we will learn that the gaze at the keeper's child was habitual.
13. For example, on her second visit to Mrs. Jellyby's, having by now gotten that lady's number, she records her regrets that she "had not been so fortunate as to find her at home" (164).
14. To defend that "virtually," itself a word often useful to liars: 1. Esther takes to Boythorn because "it seemed so plain that he had nothing to hide" (107). If gross exaggeration counts, almost every sentence of Boythorn's is a lie of the socially acceptable variety. Be that as it may, he definitely has something to hide—the unhappy love affair of his youth. He also, to be sure in a good cause, ends up conning Sir Leicester by pretending to keep up his end of their old right-of-way grudge match (764). 2. Sergeant George may seem as true as true, but he habitually speaks to the Smallweeds, under his breath, in embittered double-entendres, and is eventually prevailed upon to hand his case over to "lawyers," a word synonymous, in this book, with "liars." 3. Ironmaster Rouncewell, I have earlier suggested, was also dealing in double-entendre when he named his son "Watt." 4. Knowing that Jo is about to die, Woodcourt reassures him that his death will be "by and by" (571), a phrase that in its other occurrences means something like "eventually, but not now." 5. John Jarndyce, who lives much of his life according to polite fictions, is the one who tells George that "the mere truth won't do" (620). 6. Sir Leicester, who has surely never told a deliberate lie in his adult life, in the end winds up prevaricating about his lady's travails (697). 7. Mrs. Bagnet, as a rule honest to a fault, admits to having hid her true feelings from George when they met in his cell (624). (Also: I am surely not the first to suspect that George is the man she wishes she had married, a feeling concealed and revealed by her rough treatment of him.) 8. Although, like Mrs. Bagnet, Mrs. Rouncewell is normally the soul of truth, even she, in her confrontation with Lady Dedlock, is driven to

disingenuousness, for instance, in reporting that her son is "charged with a murder, my Lady, of which he is as innocent as—as I am" (662). The hesitation signals her bat-swerve from the more familiar formula "as innocent as you or me," versions of which occur elsewhere throughout, most recently a few pages earlier in the same chapter, where Mrs. Bagnet assures her that George is "as innocent as you or me" (656). That was what Mrs. Rouncewell was about to say. Then, at the last moment, she realized that the issue of her lady's innocence had recently joined the incredibly long list of things in this book that cannot be directly addressed.

15. Editor's note to *Letters,* vol. III, 302. The Forster quotation is given in the same note.
16. Eloise Knapp Hay's "Oberon and Prospero" has been cited in the chapter on *Oliver Twist*. She is one of several to detect Hawthorne's influence at work in *Bleak House*. Especially pertinent is Marilyn Kurata's "*The Chimes*: Dickens's Re-casting of 'Young Goodman Brown'" (*American Notes and Queries* 22 (1983), 10–13. Kurata argues that *The Chimes* was inspired by "Young Goodman Brown."
17. Nathaniel Hawthorne, "Rappaccini's Daughter," *Mosses from an Old Manse* (Boston: Houghton Mifflin, 1900), 161–72.
18. Perhaps to generalize the theme of contagion, perhaps because it does in fact seem to come out of a combination of more or less interchangeable infections, the disease is never named. Jo himself, who gives it to Charley who gives it to Esther, probably winds up dying from multiple conditions, each reinforcing the other. Susan Shatto suggests that he is ultimately killed by pneumonia or tuberculosis, both endemic to the slums (Shatto, 209). The resulting debilitation would have undermined his resistance to the smallpox he eventually carried to Bleak House. Given the argument of this chapter, I find it suggestive that the phrase "kiss of death" was at the time used to describe close physical contact—including, certainly, kissing—with sufferers from tuberculosis.
19. Richard, as he himself says (545), tries out three of the four professions suitable to his station, and in all cases finds the work tedious. This is a comment on his unstable temperament, certainly; still, as far as *Bleak House* is concerned, he is right. John Jarndyce, reliable on such matters, says as much (208), and there is plenty of evidence to support him. Fact of life: work is boring and labor is laborious, but Richard is a man and should suck it up. Among the book's women, Esther is the only one not, as far as we know, to suffer in some serious way from the female version of "labour"—no renegade son, no prolonged convalescence, no disgrace, no childbed death or near-death. A suggestion: could that be because, according to the male sense of "labour," she has already paid her dues?
20. Compare George Eliot, in a well-known passage written about seven years after *Bleak House*: "The highest 'calling and election' is to *do without opium* and live through all out pain with conscious, clear-eyed endurance."

(Quoted in Bert G. Hornback, ed., *Middlemarch: An Authoritative Text, Backgrounds, Reviews and Criticism* [New York: Norton, 1977], 43).

21. And have been since childhood conversations with her imaginary friend, her doll. When Esther addresses herself, it is in the language learned then. Prophetically, the doll is distinguished by its "beautiful complexion" (17)—more beautiful, that is, than that of Esther then (and, of course, much more beautiful than Esther now). Well before Ada or smallpox, it is settled that Esther is the one who, paired with whomever, is less pretty.

22. There's a fair chance that Esther's birthday comes in January. It is certainly in deep winter: when she is "almost fourteen," the weather is freezing (24). Later, at boarding school, her birthday presents make her room "beautiful with them from New Year's to Christmas" (26)—which is not quite the same as saying that it is beautiful from New Year's to New Year's, or Christmas to Christmas, or all the year round. A hint? Being born on New Year's—Eve or Day—would qualify Esther to be the book's Janus, patron(ess) of doorways, of key-keepers, and it wouldn't be the only time Dickens hitched his story to birthday mythology: it matters that David Copperfield is born, with a caul, on the stroke of midnight. Dickens himself, born on a Friday, always thought of it as his lucky day. A Google Books search yields no instance of the phrase "from New Year's to Christmas" before *Bleak House* was published. It was evidently not an idiom for anything other than what it says.

23. On this, see Timothy Peltason, "Esther's Will," in Jeremy Tambling, ed., *New Casebooks: Bleak House* (New York: St. Martin's: 1998, 205–27, and Patricia Ingham, *Invisible Writing and the Victorian Novel: Readings in Language and Ideology* (Manchester, England: Manchester University Press 2000), 104.

24. The principle allows for degrees of susceptibility. Refined drudge Esther is less resistant than case-hardened Charley, more resistant than cosseted Ada. Protecting Ada from contamination is therefore her first and last thought. To this end she chooses as attendant "one worthy woman who was never to see Ada" (389). The idea seems to be either that an older, hardworked person from the lower orders will just naturally be sturdy enough to withstand the kind of atmosphere that would have poisoned someone of Ada's background—or that, if not, her death will be less consequential. The former hypothesis would seem to go along, if rather backhandedly, with the novel's proto-Laurentian contrast between hardy proletariat and overbred gentry—between, for instance, Mr. Rouncewell's "strong Saxon Face" and Sir Leicester's etiolated Norman pedigree (352).

25. Some variations on this theme: at pre-dawn, the candles reflecting from the "black pane" of Esther's window "like two beacons" (85); Krook's wide-ranging cat, whose shining night-vision "green eyes" (253) "might have changed eyes with" her master's (126); the "two conductors" of bull's-eye lanterns, Bucket's and a constable's, in their parallel foray into Tom-All-Alone's (277); the "starting eyes" bulging out of Jo when questioned

(282); "the two eyes" of Tulkinghorn, which Lady Dedlock ought to fear more than she does the "five thousand pairs of fashionable eyes upon her" (358); the "two pairs of eyes" following Richard through Chancery (489), which soon thereafter will roam about for signs in Krook's old haunt; Lady Dedlock's "two eyes," which because of stage properties detailed by the author are the first Tulkinghorn sees of her after he has told her story (507); the light of two carriage lamps, reflected on water, which Esther prophetically takes to be the eyes of her dead mother (678–79). The last instance, I suggest, signals the approaching amalgamation of Esther's vision with that of the narrator.

Subsidiary note to the above: the eyes—Guppy's and Jobling/Weevle's—which sweep over Krook's room are described in the singular—Guppy's "eye," for instance. But then, there *are* two people here. Together, I suggest, they constitute another take on the *Bleak House* motif of eyes, disembodied, working to get in sync with one another. Esther and her narrative counterpart constitute the major example.

26. Dickens called him the "Phantom." Also See next chapter, pages 264-7, 271.
27. Dickens, *Master Humphrey's Clock,* 111, in *Master Humphrey's Clock and A Child's History of England* (Oxford: Oxford University Press, 1998), 111.
28. Shortly before succumbing herself, she is relieved that the recovering Charley is, against the odds—about two to one, according to the medical literature—the same "in outward appearance" (390).
29. Later, whether or not the "w" in "will" is capitalized says (at least in the Norton edition, probably the most reliable) everything about how seriously the antagonists take the "will" in question (737). The Norton editors report that in reviewing proofs Dickens changed "Will" to "will."
30. Still, he hasn't given up hope. The adjective "fatherly" is less pointed than the proper noun "Father," and "housekeeper," the name he gives Esther in response, might after all be applied to a wife. What he doesn't call her is "child." With one exception he will not use that word until the moment of his resignation to Woodcourt, at which point he will call her "child" five times in quick succession, adding, "I am your guardian and your father now" (752). (N.B.: "*now.*")
31. It occurred on July 28, 1851, therefore, as Newsom remarks, with "pun fully intended," as an eclipse of the summer sun. My source here is a November 28, 2008, contribution by Robert Newsom (to whom I give my thanks) to the Dickens-L listserv.
32. See Grahame Smith, "Dickens and the City of Light," *Dickens Quarterly* 16 (1999) 178–90.
33. Vampire-themed plays had been fixtures of English theater since the 1820s, when Polidori's "The Vampyre" was put on the stage. In April 1862 Dickens saw Dion Boucicault's adaptation, "The Phantom," and mistakenly remembered it by the original name. (April 29, 1862, letter to Dion Boucicault, *Letters,* vol. 10, 73)

34. Robert Newsom has pointed out (it was news to me) that in summer, English sunsets can indeed be north of due west, adding that—like the one here, visible after three hours—they are typically "prolonged." (E-mail, November 27, 2008). This opens a new can of worms: does the scene in fact take place in summer? I doubt it. If the sun had set around 9:00 p.m.—about average for summers in the south of England—Esther and Charley would be beginning their visit around midnight, and Jarndyce and Skimpole would be up and about well past it. Also, the season following Esther's recovery—certainly some months after the passage in question—is either spring or summer.
35. In "What Books Did Dickens Buy and Read?" Paul Schlicke points out that Dickens purchased a copy of *The Prelude* shortly before writing his account of David Copperfield's soul-restoring session in the Alps. (*Dickensian* 94 [1998], 85–130, pp. 94–95) He began *Bleak House* about two years later.
36. Albeit with some facetiousness, in his essay "Lying Awake" Dickens winds up endorsing "the theory of the Duality of the Brain." (October 30, 1852, *Household Words,* 45).
37. About this same "multiply liminal moment after the fact," Carolyn Dever proposes that Esther "is struck with the perception of her own difference" and begins an "attempt to master her own...discourse." Not exactly my reading, but we agree that Esther-as-narrator and Esther-as-character seem oddly and exceptionally close here. (Carolyn Dever, *Death and the Mother from Dickens to Freud* (New York: Cambridge University Press, 1998), 99.
38. On this subject, see Emily Heady, "The Polis's Different Voices: Narrating England's Progress in Dickens's *Bleak House,*" *Texas Studies in Literature and Language* 48 (2006), 312–39, especially pp. 333–35.
39. The question is, has he ever been face to face with Lady Dedlock? At pains to distinguish wife from husband, he calls her "the most accomplished lady in the world" (109), but this may just be his habitual gallantry, and being "accomplished" has little or nothing to do with looks. On the other hand, he has apparently been a neighbor of the Dedlocks for a long time. It would be odd if he and Lady Dedlock had not at least met before the dispute began. But then it seems odd that he could have met her without recalling his onetime lover, her sister. Please see next note.
40. Esther describes them as "those handsome proud eyes" (224); Jarndyce will later describe the sisters as "two handsome and proud women" (533). Still, he has apparently seen both women without suspecting the relation.

Chapter 4

1. February 2, 1851, letter to Dr. Thomas Stone, *Letters,* vol. VI, 276. At this juncture, Esther is twenty years from when she was handed over to her godmother.
2. As befits a novel where so much depends on fringes, there are many such eavesdroppings, deliberate and otherwise. At Chesney Wold, where the

"Ghost's Walk" recalls a lady "who was always nearer to the door" than the speakers within realized (83), it is a family tradition.

3. A conclusion earlier reached by Taylor Stoehr in *Dickens: The Dreamer's Stance* (Cornell University Press, Ithaca, 1965), 166–67.
4. Julian Moynahan, "The Hero's Guilt: The Case of *Great Expectations*," Michael Cotsell, ed., *Critical Essays on Charles Dickens's Great Expectations* (Boston: C. K. Hall, 1990), 73–86.
5. See, for instance, Thomas Southwood Smith, *The Philosophy of Health; or, An Exposition of the Physical and Mental Constitution of Man* (London: C. Cox, 1847), vol. I, 63. Smith was Dickens's friend and frequent correspondent.
6. Shatto, 46.
7. Addressing this issue, Ms. Sabrina Zaman, a member of the Victoria e-mail discussion list, has proposed that Guppy already knows of Esther's illegitimacy before he sees Lady Dedlock's portrait and begins to suspect the connection between the two from that moment. If she is right, much of my speculation on this question falls apart. In response, two points. First, it seems unlikely that, however smitten, someone like Guppy would covet the hand of a bastard. Esther's illegitimacy is probably a reason she has been raised on the presumption that she is unmarriageable. That neither her suitor Allan Woodcourt nor his inquisitive mother has previously been aware of her background becomes clear when, near the end, Jarndyce reveals the truth (753). In agreeing with him, mother and son demonstrate their generosity. Guppy by contrast is a climber and not about to marry down. Certainly, we readers are being lobbied to come down on the generous side. For us, the play of light which casts a feudal "bend-sinister" across Lady Dedlock's portrait (138) in its place of honor among the gallery of "seven hundred years" of noble ancestors (82), should remind us that almost 700 years before *Bleak House* the English aristocracy was founded by one William the Bastard. Still, that is not the kind of consideration likely to cut much ice with Guppy.

Second, when, and how does Guppy find out about Esther's illegitimacy? Does he know about it when he first meets her in London? She is, at the time, in the company of two orphans, both legitimate. Does he track down a paper trail through the Kenge and Carboy files? Ask around among the Chancery crowd? These are, I think, possibilities, but none of them strikes me as being likely.

Ms. Zaman, in this connection, suggests that Guppy figures out the connection between mother and daughter when, having already learned that Esther's father was named Hawdon, he hears from Jobling that the man buried in the grave sought out by the "lady in a wale" was also named Hawdon. But how does Jobling know? His only source is illiterate. Anyway, the question of how, working from that, Guppy reached or even approached the true solution without a prior knowledge of Esther's illegitimacy continues unanswered.

8. Immediately after Jo's account of the veiled lady, Guppy "takes him in hand as a witness," "worrying him according to the best models" (240). The

narrator reports that in the end it "elicits nothing." Although Jo may have mentioned the rings while being dragged by the constable to the Snagsbys' home, Guppy was not with him at the time: accidentally present at the arrest, he left the scene and promised to show up later, an odd detail that makes me wonder whether Dickens is rationing Guppy's access to the Jo story. For his part, Bucket evidently hears about the rings from Jo himself while in transit from Tom-All-Alone's: "What about those rings you told me of?" he asks when they get to Tulkinghorn's (282)—not, perhaps, the expression he would have used had he first heard of them from Snagsby, who was present at Guppy's interrogation of Jo.

As for the possibility that Guppy picks up the detail from gossip: that Bucket chases Jo out of London and beyond for "making his tongue more free than welcome" (743) on the subject of the charade in Tulkinghorn's chambers, which charade came out of the encounter with the lady in the veil, might constitute some corroboration. All in all, though, it seems a stretch, especially given that Guppy's word to describe the rings, "sparkling," is Jo's word too.

9. July 5, 1856, letter to Walter Savage Landor, *Letters,* vol. VIII, 152.
10. January 6, 1863, letter to Captain Elisha Ely Morgan, *Letters,* vol. X, 190.
11. This is probably my main divergence from Stoehr. For a review of contemporary conventional wisdom on this issue, and Dickens's agreement with it, see Catherine A. Bernard, *Dickens and Dreams: A Study of the Dream Theories and Dream Fiction of Charles Dickens* (Ann Arbor: Xerox University Microfilms, 1977), 16–18.
12. Dickens on his dreams: "Said an afflicted man to me, when I was last in a [mental] hospital like this, 'Sir, I can frequently fly.' I was half ashamed to reflect that so could I—by night." (Dickens, *The Commercial Traveller,* in *The Commercial Traveller and Other Pieces* (London: Oxford University Press, 1964), 132.
13. October 14, 1849, letter to John Forster, *Letters,* vol. V, 622.
14. July 22, 1851, letter to Charles Knight, *Letters,* vol. VI, 446.
15. January 15, 1845, letter to Emile de la Rue, *Letters,* vol. IV, 248.
16. "I have read something on the subject [of dreams], and have long observed it with the greatest attention and interest."—February 2, 1851, letter to Dr. Thomas Stone, *Letters,* vol V, 276. For a survey of Dickens's readings and speculations in the field, see Catherine A. Bernard, "Dickens and Victorian Dream Theory," in James Paradis and Thomas Postlewait, eds., *Victorian Science and Victorian Values: Literary Perspectives,* (New York Academy of Sciences, 1981), 197–216.
17. February 2, 1851, letter to Doctor Thomas Stone, *Letters,* vol. VI, 278–79.
18. "One striking feature about *Bleak House* is that everything of any consequence seems to happen too late": Richard T. Gaughan, "'Their Places Are a Blank': The Two Narrators in *Bleak House,*" *Dickens Studies Annual* 21

(1992), 79–96, p. 89. Also see Michael Ragussis, "The Ghostly Signs of *Bleak House*," *Nineteenth-Century Fiction* 34 (1979), 253–80, p. 275.
19. Textual notes, p. 825, in Norton Critical Edition of *Bleak House,* ed. George Ford and Silvère Monod (Norton: New York), 1977.
20. Warrington Winter, "Dickens and the Psychology of Dreams," *PMLA* 63 (1948), 984–1006, *passim*.
21. Dickens, *Hard Times,* edited by Kate Flint (London: Penguin Books, 2003), 87.
22. Dickens, *A Christmas Carol* (London; J. M. Dent, 1950), 142.
23. Dickens, *Martin Chuzzlewit,* edited by Margaret Cardwell (New York: Oxford University Press, 1982), 651; hereinafter *MC.*
24. Miller, "Interpretation in *Bleak House.*" Charles Tambling, editor, *New Casebooks: Bleak House* (New York: St. Martin's, 1998), 29–53, p. 36.
25. Miller: "Dickens too spent his time, like Mrs. Jellyby, covering paper with ink, his eye fixed not on his immediate surroundings but on an imaginary world." (Miller, "Interpretation," 46).
26. February 10, 1845, letter to Emile de la Rue, *Letters,* vol. IV, 263.
27. S. L. Goldberg, *The Classical Temper: A Study of James Joyce's Ulysses* (New York: Barnes and Noble, 1961), 92.
28. Miller, "Interpretation," 46, 31.

Afterword

1. Slater, 483.
2. Slater, 424.
3. Slater, 424.
4. Slater, 548.
5. September 30 (?), 1844, letter to John Forster, *Letters,* vol. IV, 196.
6. October 7, 1863, letter to Georgina Hogarth, *Letters,* vol. X, 297; Ackroyd, 222; see also September 27, 1849, letter to F. M. Evans, *Letters,* vol. V, 617.
7. John Gordon, *Physiology and the Literary Imagination: Romantic to Modern* (Gainesville: University Press of Florida, 2003), 87–88.
8. Terry Castle, *The Female Thermometer: Eighteenth Century and the Invention of the Uncanny* (New York: Oxford University Press, 1995), 43–61.
9. Gordon, 101–2.
10. Slater, 579.
11. William Blake, "The Human Abstract," *The Poetical Works of William Blake,* edited by John Sampson (New York, Oxford University Press, 1916), 106.

Index

Note: Page numbers in *italics* refer to illustrations.

Ackroyd, Peter, 198n46
adaptation, 137–38, 169
Alexander the Great, 126
altered states, 34, 38, 141–42
ambition, 115, 171
amphibian, 80–82, 124
Anderson, Roland F., 26, 198n48
Andrade, Mary Anne, 34
angels, 15, 16, 18, 21, 24, 100–101, 142, 176
anti-Semitism, 3, 34–35, 39–41, 44, 46, 199n71, 200nn
Ariadne, 115
Aristotle, 6, 126
ashes, 4, 88–92, 98, 106, 114
associative thinking, 155, 203–204n20
auras, 142–43
Axton, William, 207n8

"Ballad of Little Sir Hugh, The," 40, 42
Barnaby Rudge, 3, 9, 182
Barrett, Edwin, 6
bats, 115–16, 123, 137, 183, 185
beads, 131, 137, 178
Bentley, Richard, 34–35
Bentley's Miscellany, 40–41
Bernard, Catherine A., 214nn
Bible, 4, 22, 25–26, 32, 38, 92–93, 100, 107, 110, 116, 128, 150–51, 191
birds, 23, 77, 100, 109, 110, 114–15, 122, 183, 206n41, 207n5
birthdays, 210n22

Blake, William, 171, 193
Bleak House, 2, 4, 26, 56, 62, 84, 113–87, *120*, 196n15, 207–15nn
  Baby Esther's puniness in, 168–70
  echoing stories and inability to look at truth in, 118–26
  Esther's fever and blindness in, 129–36
  Esther's intuition in, 156–58
  Esther's necklace and emergence from blindness in, 136–53
  Esther's prettiness in, 174–79
  first shot in, 165–67
  George and Esther in, 155–56
  Guppy's knowledge in, 170–74, 213–14nn
  Hawthorne and poisoned kiss in, 126–29
  Hortense's discovery about Lady Dedlock in, 158–60
  maze or labyrinth in, 113–16
  self-consciousness of, 116–17
  Tulkinghorn's confrontations with Lady Dedlock in, 162–64
  Tulkinghorn's murder in, 164–65
  Tulkinghorn's search for handwriting and, 160–62
blindness, blind spots, 4, 5, 82, 103–104, 127, 130–32, 136–37, 165, 169, 179, 184, 204n28
  see also eyes; vision, seeing
blood libel, 3, 34, 38–44, 198n54, 200n74

Bluebeard, 179
Blumenbach, Johann Friederich, 202n11
blushes, 124, 155, 156
Bodenheimer, Rosemarie, 197nn, 198n46
body
    holes and pock-marks on, 19–20
    politic, infanticide and, 42
    see also smallpox
boilers, 64, 67–68, 95
Book of Common Prayer, 150, 151
borders, boundaries, 106–108, 183
    see also doors, doorways
Boucicault, Dion, 211n33
bourgeoisie, 64–65
breaking, fragments, bits and pieces, 63–64, 70, 82, 86–88, 92–96, 98–100, 105, 109, 149–50, 156, 161, 179, 184–85
breasts, 106–10, 206n40
Brownlow, John, 13
Byron, George Gordon, Lord, 52

Canterbury Tales (Chaucer), 40, 200n73
capitalism, 55–56, 64–65
Capote (movie), 166
Carlyle, Thomas, 130
Castle, Terry, 192
centripetal impulses, 6, 97
Ceres, 86–87
chain of events, 69–70, 76
change, sudden (catastrophism), 63–65, 71
    see also gradualism
Charcot, Jean-Martin, 192
Chartists, 57
Chaucer, Geoffrey, 40, 200n73
Chesterton, G.K., 34, 41
Child, Francis J., 40
children
    abuse of, 13, 64
    birth of, 123, 128, 135, 168–70
    Christlike, 25–26
    circumstances of conception, 203n13
    death of, 13, 42–43, 168, 170, 196nn
    prostitution and, 195n2
    yearning for, 118–19
    see also infanticide
Child's History of England, A, 37, 207n2
chill, 139–40
Chimes, The, 200–201n81
"*Chimes, The*: Dickens's Re-casting of 'Young Goodman Brown,'" (Kurata), 209n16
Christian, Eleanor, 203n17
Christianity, 25–27, 29–30, 34, 37, 40, 92–93
    see also Bible; Jesus Christ; Mary, Virgin
Christmas Carol, 182, 189
circles, rings, 5, 97, 131–32, 135–37, 142, 172–73, 178, 184, 186
Clark, Robert, 202n5
claustrophobia, 16–17
clocks, watches, 95, 101, 131
Colligan, Collette, 202n8
collisions, language and, 70
Communist Manifesto, The (Marx), 64–65, 203n16
Companion to Bleak House, The (Shatto), 207n3
Companion to Oliver Twist, The (Paroissien), 200n75
connections, linkages, 29, 69–70, 75–76, 109–10, 141–42, 149–51, 171–72
Conrad, Joseph, 62
Contra Celsum (Origen), 198n45
Coram, Thomas, 13
Cotzin, Michael C., 2
cross, 90–91, 98
crown of thorns, 26
crow's flight, 123–24, 180
Crucifixion, 40
Cruikshank, George, 10, 14, 18, 203n17, 205n31
cuckolds, 98, 158

Daedalus, 115–16
"Dangerous Innocence" (Koretsky), 200n73
David Copperfield, 6, 45–46, 182, 189, 192, 210n22, 212n35
Davis, Eliza, 35, 37, 45
day, daylight, 32, 52, 78–80, 85–86, 93, 138, 144, 160, 177, 183–84
Dead Sea, 5, 90–92
   fruit, 4, 91–92, 98, 106
death
   Bleak House and, 144–45, 183, 184
   Dombey and, 73, 76–79, 86, 88–91, 99–101, 204n24
   of Mary Hogarth, 30, 34, 198n53
   see also children, death of
Death and the Mother from Dickens to Freud (Dever), 212n37
death clubs, 13
déjà vu, 147, 181
De la Rue, Madame, 30, 180, 185, 192
DeMause, Lloyd, 196n18
denial, avoidance, evasion, 1, 11, 62–63, 115, 121, 123–24, 129, 131, 136, 160, 185
   see also lying
de Quincey, Thomas, 131
desire, thwarted, 118–19, 122, 179, 185
detection, 59, 63, 73, 141, 147
Dever, Carolyn, 212n37
devil, 11, 34, 199n64
Dickens, Charles
   anti-Semitism and, 35–38, 45
   biography of, 2–6, 34, 199n62
   on dreams common to all, 180–81
   Mary Hogarth and, 30, 32, 34, 185
   on mind and mystery, 192–93
   on omniscient narrator, 180
   publishers and, 34
   Regency and, 168
   religion and, 25–26, 29–31, 190, 197n37
   secrets of, about own past, 189
   visit to America, 126
   work habits of, 6
   see also specific works
Dickens and Dreams (Bernard), 214n11
Dickens and Empire (Moore), 199n62
"Dickens and Victorian Dream Theory" (Bernard), 214n16
Dickens-L e-mail list, 6, 201n3, 206n41, 211n31
Dickens: The Dreamer's Stance (Stoehr), 213n3
Discovery of the Unconscious, The (Ellenberger), 191–92
dispersion, 4, 59, 87–89
   see also breaking, fragments, bits and pieces
Disraeli, Benjamin, 13
Dombey and Son, 2–4, 51–111, *53, 67, 68, 74, 94, 104*, 117, 124, 157, 191, 201–206nn, 207n9
   Bleak House, as prequel to, 117
   breaking and reknitting in, 87–88
   death and dream in, 76–78
   gradualism vs. catastrophism and, 71–78
   ideology and rich vs. poor in, 52–57, 65
   language and wordplay in, 3, 5, 70, 99–102
   marginalization of what matters in, 56, 59, 62–63, 103–105
   names in, 81–84
   sexuality in, 58–62
   subconscious and, 79–81
   trains and human agency in, 65–70
"Don't look back," 117–19
doors, doorways, 129, 179–80, 182–85, 210n22
double-entendres, 59, 208n14
doves, 61, 72, 110
dovetailing, 185
dreams, 2, 191
   Bleak House and, 5, 131–33, 135–36, 156–58, 180–86
   Dickens and, 30, 32, 214nn

dreams—*Continued*
   Dombey and, 77–81, 85–86, 105, 191
   Oliver Twist and, 29–30, 33, 38, 45
Drumont, Edouard, 200n76
"Durden, Dame," 207n8

eavesdropping, 159, 163, 165–66, 174, 212–13n2
Echter, Julius, 199n71
edge, fringe, periphery, 103, 140, 142, 148–51, 161, 162, 165, 179, 212n2
Eliot, George, 209–10n20
Ellenberger, Henri, 191–92
Elliotson, John, 202n11
Emerson, Ralph Waldo, 1
empire, imperialism, 51, 55–56, 75, 199n62
enchantment, 81, 86, 191–92
energy, 64, 79, 87, 95, 109, 168
engines, 61, 64, 66–69, 76, 95, 192, 202n12
eruptions, explosions, 4, 43, 57–58, 64, 70, 85–86, 177, 191
"Esther's Nicknames" (Axton), 207n8
"Esther Summerson Rehabilitated" (Zwerdling), 207n8
Eurydice, 116, 118, 122, 127
evil spirits, 192
excrement, 2–3, 40, 44, 200nn
exploitation, 52–55
eyeglasses, 95
eyes
   Bleak House and, 5, 118, 130–31, 137–38, 140, 142–45, 150–52, 167, 171–72, 179, 207n4, 210–11n25
   Dombey and, 62, 66, *67*, *68*, 76, 80, 89, 92, 93, 96, 99, 101, 103, 105, 192, 203nn
   Oliver Twist and, 18, 27, 28, 30, 33, 46, 47
   see also blindness, blind spots; visions, visionary

fairy tales, 2, 26, 34, 40, 86, 116, 143, 160
Family, Sex and Marriage in England, The (Stone), 202n5
Fanny Hill, 58, 202n12
Faraday, Michael, 205n32
father, 27–28, 32–33, 133–35, 180, 211n30
feminist issues, 56, 109, 177
fevers, 5, 20, 22, 79, 119, 129–33, 139, 191
Fields, Annie, 1–2
Finnegans Wake (Joyce), 58, 100
fires, 64, 115, 128–30, 177
   flickering of, 89, 90
   unlit, 56
   see also fevers
fish, 83–84
flight, flying, 41, 110–11, 114–16, 123–24, 180, 185, 190, 214n12
   see also bats; birds
fog, mist, 21, 83, 84, 88, 96, 124, 141–44, 178, 183
folk-etymologies, 4, 98–99, 158
food, waste of, 55
foreboding, 95, 133
Forneaux, Holly, 202n8
Forster, John, 1, 34, 45, 126, 199n64, 209n15
Forsyth's Patent Signalling System, 203n17
fountains, geysers, springs, 2, 4, 52, 54, 56–57, 64, 78–79, 95, 97, 103, 107–109, 191
France Juive, La (Drumont), 200n76
French, 158–59, 165, 167, 176
Freudian issues, 1, 2, 180, 192
funerals, 73–74, 82

Galton, Francis, 177
Gaughan, Richard T., 214n18
gender role reversal, 170
genealogy, 84, 85
Gerhard, Joseph, 204n21

ghosts, apparitions, phantoms, 30, 58, 79, 90, 103, 114, 116, 136, 138–40, 143, 145–46, 152, 166, 180–82, 185, 189, 192–93, 211n26
 see also haunting; shadowy presences
Gibbon, Edward, 55
Goebbels, Joseph, 45
Goldberg, S.L., 185
Goya, Francisco
 "Saturn Devouring One of His Sons," 42
gradualism, 71–77, *74*, 87, 96, 204n21
grammar, 70, 98
Great Expectations, 11, 129, 167, 171
Greenstein, Michael, 204n29
Grey, Lady Jane, 207n2
Gulliver's Travels (Swift), 195n5

Hamlet (Shakespeare), 79
hands, 159–60, 166, 172–73
handwriting, 160–61
hanging, 3, 9–10, 17, 20, 26, 43, 47, 135, 136, 166, 197n22
Hansel and Gretel, 34, 42, 43
Hard Times, 55, 182
Haunted Man and the Ghost's Bargain, The (Dickens), 197n28
haunting, 116–17, 148, 171, 180, 182, 192
 see also ghosts, apparitions, phantoms
Hawthorne, Nathaniel, 126, 209n16
Hay, Eloise Knapp, 209n16
heart or core, 20–23, 25, 86, 88, 97–99, 138
Henkle, Roger B., 204n27
Henry VIII, King of England, 65
hidden truths, secrets, 182, 189, 208n14
 Bleak House and, 116, 126, 141, 147, 156–57, 162–65, 171–72, 174
 Dombey and, 59, 64, 96–97, 106, 205n32
 Oliver Twist, 28–29, 39, 200n74
hierarchy, 164

Hogarth, Mary, 30, 34, 185, 189, 198n53
Holmes, Katherine, 201n93
honesty, 15, 36, 62, 208n14
Hopkins, Gerard Manley, 138
Horne, Philip, 48, 195n7
Houghton, Walter E., 201n92
Household Words, 180, 206n41, 212n36
Hugh of Lincoln, 34, 38–40, 43–45, 47–49
human agency, 65–69
human nature, 19–20
hunger, 55, 118
hypnagogic trances, hypnosis, 39, 140, 190

Icarus, 115–17, 125–27
illegitimacy, 26–27, 133–34, 172, 179, 213n7
inability to look upon what matters, 63, 122, 148, 165, 179
 see also blindness, blind spots; denial, avoidance, evasion; "Don't look back;" overlooked, unnoticed
infanticide, 11–14, 41–43, 200n72
innocence, purity, 15–16, 18, 27, 33, 40
insomnia, 80
"Interpretation in *Bleak House*" (Miller), 215n25
intuition, 22–23, 156–57, 160, 191
invisibility, 105, 180

Janet, Pierre, 192
Janus, 129, 210n22
Jesus Christ, 25–26, 30–33, 45, 77–78, 86, 90, 91, 93, 110, 191, 197n31, 198n45
Jews, 2–3, 11, 34–37, 39–40, 45, 198n54, 200nn
John the Baptist, 25
Joyce, James, 5–6, 174, 185

Kaplan, Fred, 2, 35, 199
Kenner, Hugh, 6

key-keeper, 129, 136, 179, 181, 210n22
King Lear (Shakespeare), 38, 117, 184
kiss, 106
  "of death," 209n18
  poisoned, 126–29, 179
Koretsky, Alan C., 200n73
Kurata, Marilyn, 209n16

"labour," male vs. female, 128, 209n19
"lamb," *Agnus Dei*, 25, 43, 197n30
language, wordplay
  Bleak House and, 5
  Dombey and, 62, 69–71, 79, 82, 84–86, 89, 98–101, 106, 111
Laqueur, Thomas, 202n11
larks, 115, 183, 185
letters and documents, 160–62, 174, 184
Levin, Harry, 2, 6
Life of Our Lord, The, 26, 30–33, 37
Little Dorrit, 3, 65, 72, 129, 131, 151, 167
London Foundling Hospital, 13
lying
  Bleak House and, 62, 124–26, 173, 176, 182–83, 185, 208–209n14
  Dombey and, 62–63
  Oliver Twist and, 7
"Lying Awake" (Dickens), 212n36

Macbeth (Shakespeare), 38, 196n10, 200n72
magnetism, 10, 39, 106, 110, 113, 115, 140, 190, 192, 205–206n32
Making Sex (Laqueur), 202n11
Marcus, Steven, 58, 198n56
Marks, Patricia, 206n38
marriage, 73–75, 89
Marsh, Joss Lutz, 58
Martin Chuzzlewit, 182
Marx, Karl, 203n16
Mary, Virgin
  Dombey and, 110
  Oliver Twist and, 29–33, 43, 197n37, 198nn, 200n73
Mary Magdalen, 26–27

maze, labyrinth, 17, 96–97, 113–15
McCarthy, Patrick, 206n36
McCombie, Frank, 108
McSweeney, Kerry, 27
meaning
  Bleak House and, 184–86
  Dombey and, 87, 103, 106, 108–109
meaninglessness, fear of, 184–86
Medusa, 116, 122, 127, 133
memory
  Bleak House and, 151, 157–58, 185, 189
  Dombey and, 77
  Oliver Twist and, 24, 27–29, 45
  sympathy and, 197n2
Merchant of Venice, The (Shakespeare), 3, 40, 41
Mesmer, Franz, 192
Meyer, Susan, 25, 35, 36, 44–45
Miller, Bennett, 166
Miller, J. Hillis, 16, 92, 186, 206n32, 215n25
Milton, John, 91
mind, 88, 153, 180, 191–93
  duality of, 212n36
  focus of, 88–91, 95–96
mines, 57
miraculous healings, 30–32
mirror, reflections
  Bleak House and, 119–22, 139, 152, 167, 175–76, 178, 183
  Dombey and, 3–4, 89–92, 95
Mithridates, 126, 127, 130, 137
"Modest Proposal, A" (Swift), 12
momentum
  accelerating, 69
  backward, 79–80
monster, 113–15, 117, 122, 127
moonlight, 177–78, 184
Moore, Grace, 199n62
Morgentaler, Goldie, 29, 32
Mosses from an Old Manse (Hawthorne), 126
mother
  Bleak House and, 119, 128

Dombey and, 77–79, 108
Oliver Twist and, 26–30, 32–33, 43, 45, 49
Moynahan, Julian, 167
mystery, mystification, 2, 29, 96, 138, 148, 153, 165, 175, 193
mysticism, 30–31, 192
myth, 58, 85, 86, 105, 116–18
"mythiphallic," 58

nakedness, 5, 63–64, 117, 181, 185
names
  Bleak House and, 113–17, 207n8, 208n14
  Dombey and, 58, 59, 81–86, 90, 98, 99, 204nn
  Oliver Twist and, 26–27, 38, 48, 198n54
"natural supernaturalism," 130
nature, 21, 79, 130
necklace, 5–6, 131–33, 135–37, 184, 186
Nemesis, 8, 66, 167, 182
Nemo, as "nobody," 114, 117, 161–62, 184
Newsom, Robert, 34, 137, 184, 211n31, 212n34
Nicholas Nickleby, 55, 124
"Noble Savage, The" (Dickens), 199n62

"Oberon and Prospero" (Hay), 209n16
Odysseus, 117, 161–62
Oedipus, 179
Old Curiosity Shop, The, 3, 26, 45, 82, 190
Oliver Twist, 2–5, 7–50, 55, 86, 97, 168, 190, 192, 195–201nn
  anti-Semitism in, 2–4, 33–44, 46–47
  claustrophobia and secret openings, 16–17
  death of Mary Hogarth and, 30–32
  Fagin at Oliver's window and, 23, 41, 44, 45, 190, 192
  hanging in, 9–11
  ideology and, 55
  infanticide in, 11–15
  Oliver as Christ in, 26, 32–33, 45
  Oliver's birthplace in, 48–49
  Oliver's hairsbreadth escapes in, 14–16, 43–44
  outer signifying inner in, 18–20
  tale-telling power of, 45–46
Omniscient Narrator, 117, 131, 170, 180–81, 186–87
Oresteia, 85
Origen, 198n45
Orpheus, 116, 118
Orwell, George, 55
Othello (Shakespeare), 38
otherworldly
  Bleak House and, 183
  Dombey and, 77–80, 85–86, 102, 105, 110
  Oliver Twist and, 29–32
  see also supernatural
Our Mutual Friend, 3, 35, 84, 203n15
outer vs. inner, 18–21, 44–45
overlooked, unnoticed, 103–105, 131, 141–42, 165
  see also blindness, blind spots; eyes; inability to look upon what matters; vision, seeing

Paradise Lost (Milton), 91
Paroissien, David, 48, 200n75
past
  Bleak House and, 208n11
  Dombey and, 79
  Oliver Twist and, 24
  see also memory
patriarchy, 56
"Paul Dombey and the Milk of human Kindness" (Marks), 206n38
pedophilia, 2, 8–9
penetrability of surfaces, 19, 20, 44–45
Persephone, 86–87
Perseus, 116, 131
phantasmagoric, 81, 85

"Phantom, The" (Boucicault), 211n33
Philosophy of Health, The (Smith), 213n5
Phiz, 52, 66, 119, 159, 175, 205n31
physiology and psychology, 137, 143, 190
Physiology and the Literary Imagination (Gordon*)*, 202n9, 205n32
Pickwick Papers, The, 1, 45, 124
pigeons, 5, 206n41
plague, 114, 207n4
pockets and pick-pockets, 19
Polidori, John, 211n33
Poor Law, 11, 13
portrait
   Bleak House and, 116, 138–39, 141, 171–72, 176, 178, 213n7
   Dombey and, 65
   Oliver Twist, 26–30, 32, 45
   self-, 121
Portrait of the Artist as a Young Man, A (Joyce), 6
precipitation, rain, 52, 100, 114, 118–19, 183, 186, 202n9
pregnancy, 59–61, 108
Prelude, The (Wordsworth), 147, 212n35
prettiness, 8, 174–79
prison, 1, 7–8
"procreative symbolism," 29
Procter, Tim, 203n17
Professor of Toledo, The, 41
prophecy, premonition, precognition, 191
   Bleak House and, 139, 147, 165, 181–82, 210n21, 211n25
   Dombey and, 77, 79, 85, 86, 91, 101
   Oliver Twist and, 10, 22–23, 25, 26, 45
prostitution, whores, 2, 7, 33, 43, 93–94, 195n2, 205n31
Psalm CXLIII, 150, 151
psychic deputizing, 166–67
psychic powers, 32–33
Purim, 40

"Purloined Letter, The" (Poe), 165
puzzles, 122, 153, 160, 171, 184, 185

Queer Dickens (Forneaux), 202n8
"quickening," 150–52, 191

railroad, trains, 55, 57, 63, 65–70, *67, 68*, 73, 76–77, 80, 87, 103–104, 107–109, 203nn, 206n33, 207n9
rainbow, prism, 77, 85, 92, 109
"Rappaccini's Daughter" (Hawthorne), 126–27
Rash, Nancy, 6
rats, 17, 19–20, 163, 166
recognition
   Bleak House and, 149–53, 155, 160, 179, 182–83
   Oliver Twist and, 32–33
Regency, 54, 168
religion, 30–31, 36–37
   see also Bible; Christianity
Restoration Comedy, 58
resurrections, 24, 31–32
reversals, sudden, 63–64
reverse psychology, 164–65
Riesman, David, 177
Robson, Catherine, 13–14, 195n10, 196n20
Roman Catholicism, 30, 197n37
"root," 45, 58, 59, 78, 85, 95
Roper, Lyndal, 41, 200n73
Rose, Lionel, 13
Ross, Thomasina, 206n41
runaways and collisions, 69–70, 79–80

Saussure, Ferdinande de, 84
scapegoating, 42–43
Schlicke, Paul, 212n35
sea, 76, 78, 80, 82–84, 86, 90–91, 102–103, 105, 108
   see also ships; waves
sensory experience
   Bleak House and, 137–40
   Oliver Twist and, 23

sex
   Bleak House and, 159
   Dombey and, 58–62, 72–73, 85–86, 89–90, 93–94, 106–108, 202–3nn
   Oliver Twist and, 9
   see also pedophilia; prostitution, whores
shadowy presences, 4, 42, 73, *74*, 102–103, 130, 145, 149, 152, 166, 180, 182, 183
   see also ghosts, apparitions, phantoms
Shakespeare, William, 19, 28, 38, 59, 79, 117, 157, 184, 196n10, 200n72
Shatto, Susan, 207n3, 209n18
Shelley, Percy Bysshe, 6, 54
ships, 49, 61, 73, 75, 78, 81, 83, 88, 96, 109, 110, 143, 205n32, 206n39
shipshape, 74, 88
Sicher, Efraim, 199n60
Slater, Michael, 189, 196n15, 201n82
sleep, 79–81, 183
   see also dreams
smallpox, 4–5, 127, 130, 132, 137, 139–40, 146, 176–78, 207n4, 209n18, 210n21
Smith, Thomas Southwood, 213n5
snuff, 163
social class
   hardiness and, 210n24
   relations of rich and poor, 52–55
   social climbing, 213n7
solar eclipse, 5, 137, 178, 184, 211n31
stage lighting, 143–47
stars, starlight, twinkling, 137, 146, 171
Stevens, Wallace, 140
Stewart, Garrett, 5, 101–102
Stoehr, Taylor, 213n3, 214n11
Stone, Harry, 2, 203n17
Stone, Lawrence, 202n5
Stone, Dr. Thomas, 214n16
subconscious, submerged, repressed, suppressed, 1–2, 5
   Dombey and, 56–59, 62–63, 78–81, 85–92, 95, 97–98, 101, 102, 105

   Oliver Twist and, 8
   prophecy and, 190–93
   see also hidden truths, secrets
sun, 83, 93, 95, 114–15, 127, 137, 157, 178, 184
sunset, 77, 146, 212n34
supernatural, 77, 189–91
Sutherland, John, 195n1
Swift, Jonathan, 9, 12, 195n5
syllepsis, 5, 101–102, 111, 206n36
sympathy, 23–25, 45
synecdochic transference, 186
syphilis, 165, 168

tears, 21, 97
Ternan, Ellen Lawless, 189
"'Their Places Are a Blank': The Two Narrators in *Bleak House*" (Gaughan), 214n18
time
   Bleak House and, 147, 186–87
   Dombey and, 63, 95, 100–101
   see also clocks, watches
Time Machine, The (Wells), 57
tomb, 89–90, 204n23
tree
   Bleak House and, 186
   Dombey and, 57–58, 61–62, 66, 79, 85
truth, 208–209n14
   Bleak House and, 162, 179, 186
   Dombey and, 62–63, 86–90, 93–96
   see also hidden truths, secrets; honesty; lying
tuberculosis, 209n18
Twice-told Tales (Hawthorne), 126
"Two Scrooges, The" (Wilson), 1

Ulysses-for-Experts e-mail list, 6
Ulysses (Joyce), 185
uncanny, 22, 23, 45, 79, 102–103, 189–90
uniformitarianism, 71
Unitarians, 29, 31, 190

upthrustings, upwellings, 58, 78–80, 86, 95
  see also eruptions, explosions; fountains, geysers, springs
U-turns, 132

"Vampyre, The" (Polidori), 211n33
Vanity Fair (Thackeray), 51
veiling, 123, 131
Victoria, Queen, 60, 169
Victoria e-mail list, 6
Victorian Frame of Mind, The (Houghton), 201n92
vision, seeing, 95–96, 131, 137–38, 141–42, 176–77
  through walls, 180
  "what one must not see," 181, 183–84
  see also blindness, blind spots; eyes; overlooked, unnoticed
visions, visionary, 32, 78, 80, 189–90

water, 66, 79–81, 83
  see also fountains, geysers, springs; sea
Watt, James, 66, 107, 117, 208n14
waves, 57–58, 77–79, 85, 109–10
Way We Live Now, The (Trollope), 65
weaning, 72, 75–76, 106, 204n22
weddings, 73–75

wells, 56–57
Wells, H.G., 56–57, 170
wet-nurse, 54–55, 107, 108
"What Books Did Dickens Buy and Read?" (Schlicke), 212n35
wheels, 66, 78
Wilkes, David, 46
will, 59, 87, 211n29
William of Norwich, 34, 39, 40
William the Bastard, 213n7
Wills, Gary, 195n2
Wills, W.H., 206n41
Wilson, Edmund, 1
"Winged Telegraphs" (Wills and Ross), 206n41
Winters, Warrington, 182
witches, 199n71
  Dombey and, 79, 81, 85
  Oliver Twist and, 34, 41–43, 195n10, 200n72
women
  intuition and, 140–41, 147, 157–58, 191
  regard for, 60–61
  work or labour and, 87, 128, 209n19
Wordsworth, 25, 147
writing, ink, 114, 184

Zaman, Sabrina, 213n7
Zwerdling, Alex, 207n8